Sins of the past could destroy all of their futures . . .

For generations, Quentin Marsh's family has seen its share of tragedy, though he remains skeptical that their misfortunes are tied to a centuries-old curse. But to placate his pregnant sister, Quentin makes the pilgrimage to Point Pleasant, West Virginia, hoping to learn more about the brutal murder of a Shawnee chief in the 1700s. Did one of the Marsh ancestors have a hand in killing the chief—the man who cursed the town with his dying breath?

While historian Sarah Sherman doesn't believe in curses either, she's compelled to use her knowledge of Point Pleasant to uncover the long-buried truth. The river town has had its own share of catastrophes, many tied to the legendary Mothman, the winged creature said to haunt the woods. But Quentin's arrival soon reveals that she may have more of a stake than she realized. It seems that she and Quentin possess eerily similar family heirlooms. And the deeper the two of them dig into the past, the more their search enrages the ancient mystical forces surrounding Point Pleasant. As chaos and destruction start to befall residents, can they beat the clock to break the curse before the Mothman takes his ultimate revenge? . . .

I0665218

Books by Mae Clair

Weathering Rock
Twelfth Sun
Myth and Magic

Point Pleasant Series
A Thousand Yesteryears
A Cold Tomorrow
A Desolate Hour

Published by Kensington Publishing Corporation

A Desolate Hour

A Point Pleasant Novel

Mae Clair

LYRICAL PRESS
Kensington Publishing Corp.
www.kensingtonbooks.com

Lyrical Press books are published by
Kensington Publishing Corp. 119 West 40th Street New York, NY 10018

All Kensington titles, imprints, and distributed lines are available at special quantity discounts for bulk purchases for sales promotion, premiums, fundraising, and educational or institutional use.

To the extent that the image or images on the cover of this book depict a person or persons, such person or persons are merely models, and are not intended to portray any character or characters featured in the book.

Special book excerpts or customized printings can also be created to fit specific needs. For details, write or phone the office of the Kensington Special Sales Manager:
Kensington Publishing Corp.
119 West 40th Street
New York, NY 10018
Attn. Special Sales Department. Phone: 1-800-221-2647.

Kensington and the K logo Reg. U.S. Pat. & TM Off.
LYRICAL PRESS Reg. U.S. Pat. & TM Off.
Lyrical Press and the L logo are trademarks of Kensington Publishing Corp.

First Electronic Edition: July 2017
eISBN-13: 978-1-60183-779-0
eISBN-10: 1-60183-779-8

First Print Edition: July 2017
ISBN-13: 978-1-60183-782-0
ISBN-10: 1-60183-782-8

Printed in the United States of America

For Cindy Garberich

Who cheers my accomplishments every bit as enthusiastically as Mom

did,

and who couldn't wait to meet the Mothman

Thanks, Sis

Acknowledgements

To my editor, Paige Christian, thank you for your hard work in making my version of Point Pleasant shine.

To Lyrical Underground and Kensington Publishing, I'm delighted to be part of such a professional organization.

Finally, to my husband, who has been by my side through every step of my writing journey, and who listened patiently to my endless chatter about the Mothman, Cornstalk and UFOs. Thank you for undertaking two trips with me to Point Pleasant and the TNT. There is nothing like firsthand research when penning a novel!

Prologue

October 10, 1777
Point Pleasant area

Dusk.

It came early with autumn, the high grass browning sluggishly, the woods ripe with the odor of decay. Pockets of mist coiled awake prelude to the coming night. In the distance, the last ruddy rays of the sun were swallowed by the horizon.

Leaves and twigs crunched beneath Obadiah Preech's boots as he threaded his way through the trees oblivious to the bats flitting overhead. Fort Randolph fell away a good mile behind him. He'd waved a greeting to the sentries when he'd passed through the gates, ignoring their warnings about how quickly night fell. After carrying a musket in Lord Dunmore's War, he had no fear of the physical realm. Only of what lurked within the woods.

His heartbeat quickened and his palms grew damp with sweat.

He would kill the demon, but not tonight. Tonight was for weaving incantations to empower the dagger, a blade destined to spill the blood of the Indian chief, Cornstalk. The redskins had summoned the creature through the use of foul magic, thus by black witchery would the abomination die. Willa's death would be avenged.

Locating a clear patch of ground, Obadiah used a branch to sketch a crude pentagram on the forest floor. The soil was soft, moist from recent rains, and turned easily beneath the crooked stick. Two earthworms wriggled through the upturned sod, dark as coffin loam.

A favorable sign when the forest blessed his work.

He plucked them free, then hunkered to gather leaves and twigs for kindling. When he had enough, he lit a small blaze in the center of the pentagram. A kettle went over the flames. Old and pitted, it had seen better days but would suffice for the task at hand.

Casting a hasty glance over his shoulder, Obadiah strained to listen. An owl hooted in the distance and a small animal scurried through the underbrush. Safe from prying eyes, he breathed easier.

It wasn't discovery he feared so much as failure. Practitioners of the dark arts were shunned, but he would risk that and more to slaughter the demon responsible for his wife's death.

Turning back to the cauldron, he dragged a hand across his forehead. The air was sticky and close, unusual for fall. Squatting, he added a handful of herbs to the bubbling kettle. Most of the plants were used in healing, but moldy mushrooms and rotting seeds altered the properties of the brew from light to dark. Grimacing, he dug a bloody mass from the rucksack at his waist. The heart was still warm; the carcass of the stray dog he'd lured with a piece of boiled pork attracting flies and scavengers half a mile behind.

He chanted as the old woman had taught him, spitting sounds that made his skin crawl. Flushed and dripping with sweat, he lowered the heart into the pot.

A twig snapped.

Obadiah spun.

Jonathan Marsh stood frozen behind him. A young man, barely twenty-two, he'd been gone several days, scouting for signs of Indian unrest to the north. With a single glance, he took in the crudely etched pentagram and the witch's pot. Blood drained from his face and his eyes widened with horror.

"Obadiah. What have you done?"

He'd heard. Surely he'd heard the incantation.

Obadiah's heart skipped a beat.

Jonathan took a faltering step forward. "For the love of Heaven, what evil have you summoned?"

Obadiah gripped the knife clipped to his belt. He would kill tonight after all.

Chapter 1

July 1982
Point Pleasant, West Virginia

Do you believe in curses?

Quentin Marsh dropped his forehead against the steering wheel, his hands clasped at two and ten o'clock. Why the hell had he said yes? If he'd written Penelope's ramblings off as crazy, he'd be home in Rhode Island instead of sitting in the parking lot of the Parrish Hotel. His sister had a way of wheedling him into doing almost anything and her pregnancy-induced emotions hadn't helped.

Twins in the Marsh family had rarely fared well through the generations. He was proof of that jinx, right down to the ugly scars on his hand. No matter how much physical therapy he did, he'd never regain the dexterity to play concert halls.

The Marsh curse in action.

Leaning back in the seat, he listened to the soft patter of rain against the windshield of his Monte Carlo. Twilight had preceded him into Point Pleasant, the bulk of the old hotel standing out starkly against a cloud-swollen sky. Three stories high with a sprawling covered porch and ornate double-door entry, the solid brick building dominated the square of Main Street. Bright blue awnings shaded the windows of the two upper stories, an addition that would look cheerful on a sunny afternoon, but now carried a dismal air with rain dripping from the corners. At least it wasn't pouring—yet.

Quentin popped the door, then headed to the trunk for his luggage. Overhead a flash of lightning warned of a coming storm.

Do you believe in curses?
Hell, yes.
The problem was breaking them.

* * * *

A distant flash of lightning made Sarah Sherman pause as she packed a stack of papers into the large plastic carton on her desk. Rain drummed on the roof of her rented trailer. Already the wind kicked up, an eerie moan that made her bite down on her bottom lip. Instinctively, she clutched the opaque blue stone suspended from a silver chain around her neck.

Run from the thunder,
Run from the rain,
Lightning can't hurt you,
The wind is in vain.

The rhyme had been her mantra since childhood, a verse she'd clung to ever since the night her parents' car careened off a slippery road in the TNT. Neither her mother nor father lived to see the sunrise, but her mother's necklace and the singsong stanza acted as a safety net whenever her fear of storms churned to the surface.

Shuffling her anxiety aside, she moved the carton to the floor. Most of the contents amounted to old documents and photos, but there were a few random items tucked among the hodgepodge of history that belonged to Shawn Preech. Sarah had found a small Bible with a faded list of family milestones—births, deaths, weddings—and a 1920s hymnal that had once belonged to Gertrude Preech, Shawn's mother. There was also an oblong wooden case etched with strange symbols. She loathed touching it, but still had to pack it away.

She'd be glad to get rid of everything, especially the case.

Suzanne Preech had given her the entire kit-and-caboodle months ago, hiring her to delve into Shawn's ancestral tree. She'd made a fair amount of headway, her passion for genealogy fueling her research before Suzanne's marriage recently imploded. Afterward, Suzanne had told her to dispose of the documents as she saw fit. She had no intention of ever speaking to Shawn again unless it was through her lawyer.

For his part, Shawn was clueless Suzanne had even found the carton in their attic. He'd often bragged his family roots could be traced back to the time of Fort Randolph, but Sarah doubted he had any true knowledge of, or even interest in, his lineage. More likely, the claim was something repeated in his family through generations, a boast that had become gospel.

The intrusion of the phone startled Sarah from her thoughts. She wasn't certain if it was the storm or the box with the odd markings that had her on edge.

Snatching up the receiver, she dropped into a seat behind her desk. "Hello."

"Hi, Sarah. It's Eve."

Her oldest friend. "Hello, Mrs. Flynn." She smiled, glad to focus on something pleasant as the name rolled off her tongue. "Are you still floating on the joy of being a newlywed?"

A soft chuckle. "Sheer bliss, but Caden's on patrol tonight."

"One of the downsides of being married to a sheriff's sergeant." Eve had snagged a wonderful husband in Caden Flynn.

"Fortunately, I can arrange my shifts at the hotel to match Caden's for the most part," Eve said into her ear. "That way we're off together."

"Hmm. A perk of being the owner." The Parrish Hotel had been in Eve's family for as long as Sarah could remember. Her friend had returned to Point Pleasant last summer after a fifteen-year absence, taking over the running of the establishment. She'd become a newlywed only last month.

"Another perk is getting to see the guest registry." Eve sounded amused.

Sarah's brows drew together. She stole a look out the window as the wind kicked higher. No lightning, and she'd yet to hear any thunder. "Why should that matter?"

"I thought you might be interested in the name of someone scheduled to check in today." Eve paused, allowing Sarah to absorb the thought before continuing. "A man by the name of Quentin Marsh."

"Um…" Sarah tried to think. "Why?"

Eve laughed. "You don't remember? Last fall, the sleepover I had. You, me, Katie, wine, and a Ouija board?"

"Oh." The light dawned. Katie Lynch was the manager of Eve's hotel and a good friend. Together, the three of them formed a tight-knit group. "That was such a silly thing. As if a game could really tell me the initials of someone I'd become involved with. Q.M." She scoffed at the idea.

"And no one in Point Pleasant we know has those initials."

Sarah shook her head. "Eve, it was a Ouija board."

"Which you insisted on bringing. Plus, the predictions it made about Katie and Indrid Cold all came true."

Sarah fidgeted, not certain she wanted to think about Cold or the strange events that had taken place last fall. She'd only been on the fringe; Katie and Caden's brother, Ryan Flynn, at the center. And Caden, of course. In her opinion, he was the one around whom everything revolved. "So did the mysterious Q.M. show up?"

"Not yet. I'm hoping he gets here before the storm kicks in."

A distant rumble of thunder.

"Speaking of storms…" Her grandmother had insisted lightning could travel through phone lines during an electrical storm. The thought only added to her already heightened anxiety.

"I know. I won't keep you. I just had to tell you about Quentin. Nice name, huh?"

"Odd name. Hey, would you mind if I dropped something off at the hotel for safekeeping tomorrow?" She eyed the plastic tub on the floor. "I told Shawn Preech about the stuff Suzanne gave me. He sounded like he couldn't care less, but I don't want to hang onto anything that belongs to him. He said he was going to be at the River, so I thought I could leave it for him to pick up." The River Café was part of the hotel, a regular hangout for locals, and a casual pub/eatery to accommodate the hotel's guests.

"Sure, no problem."

"Great. It'll save me a trip driving out to his place. I want to wash my hands of it." Her gaze strayed to the flat oblong case perched on the end of her desk. She wondered if Suzanne even knew it had been buried in the carton.

"I thought you liked snooping around old documents and building genealogy charts?" Eve's voice brought Sarah back to the present.

"I do." She glanced at the case again. The wood was dark and weathered, infused with the lingering scent of oak. An elaborate faceplate with an old-fashioned lock held the lid secure, but she'd been unable to locate a key in the carton. Part of her was grateful to never know what the box contained, the other part curious. Squiggles and lines resembling hieroglyphs had been carved along the top, offset with the crude etching of a spider. Sometimes when she looked at the case her stomach turned over, a feeling that grew worse when she touched it.

"I just don't want Shawn coming back and saying I have his property." She tried to explain her reluctance. Thunder grumbled, closer this time.

"Is it because of Obadiah? You told me you'd discovered something disturbing about him."

"Not him." Obadiah Preech was the first of Shawn's line to settle in Point Pleasant. Sarah had confirmed he'd taken part in Lord Dunmore's War of 1774 and had been present at Fort Randolph when Chief Cornstalk was killed. But that wasn't what bothered her.

"It wasn't so much about Obadiah, as others. There are references about him in a letter I found. I made a copy to show you. I'll bring it tomorrow, but right now I want to get off the phone." A trickle of sweat broke out on the back of her neck. The rain had stopped but an oppressive weight hung in the air, warning of a brewing squall.

"Okay." Eve understood her fear. "I'll talk to you tomorrow."

Sarah breathed a sigh of relief when she returned the phone to its cradle. Lightning severed the sky in a white flash and zigzagged to the ground. She counted the seconds until thunder rattled the windows. Storms always seemed worse in a mobile home, but the rent was reasonable and the timing had been right when she'd taken it over.

Her attention shifted to a framed photo on her desk. Her grandparents, arms around each other, smiling back at her. They'd raised her after the death of her parents, but each had suffered fatal illnesses within the last five years, leaving her on her own. A bittersweet smile curved her lips as she touched her fingertips to her mouth, then the photograph. "Miss you guys."

Time to finish packing the items for Shawn. She put the remaining documents in the carton, most newspapers and items that had been saved from the 1920s and '30s. There were a few tin-type photographs dating back to the Civil War era, letters exchanged between family members during World War II, and the snippet of the letter she'd told Eve about.

A letter that mentioned Obadiah and something that still induced a chill when she thought of it—a towering winged demon with glowing red eyes.

* * * *

Quentin stepped into the lobby of the hotel and shook rain from his hair. The place was open and inviting, with thick braided rugs over a hardwood floor. A large fireplace dominated the far right wall, the left taken up by a row of towering windows with deep sills and built-in seats. Woodwork, floorboards, even the turned staircase with its thick landing newels and deep risers reflected the construction of a bygone era.

A woman with shoulder-length brown hair stood behind the reception counter. She looked to be close to his age, somewhere in her mid- to late twenties.

"Hi." She smiled a friendly greeting.

"Hi." Quentin approached the desk and set his duffel bag on the floor. Despite booking his stay open-ended, he'd packed fairly light, hoping to wrap his business within a week. "Checking in. I'm Quentin Marsh."

The woman gave him a quick once-over while trying to be unobtrusive. He knew he looked bedraggled, his wavy brown hair plastered to his neck with rain, his jeans faded and worn at the knees. He'd grabbed his most comfortable pair for the drive, knowing he'd be stuck in the car for hours.

"I see you beat the storm. At least the worst of it." The woman's smile stayed in place as she flipped a ledger around for him to sign. "It looks like you're planning on being with us for a while, Mr. Marsh."

"Quentin." He scribbled his signature where she indicated.

"Oh my." Her breath hitched at the sight of deep purple scars road-mapped across the back of his hand.

He should have been prepared. The accident was over two years old, but the reaction of others still caught him off guard. "It's all right." His mouth stretched in a jaded grin. "It's a normal response."

"I'm sorry." She flushed, clearly embarrassed. "I didn't mean…"

"No problem." He came to her rescue by shoving the offending hand into the pocket of his jeans. "Unfortunate accident. Looks worse than it is." There was nothing like ending your career with a single careless blunder.

She fumbled to locate his room key, spots of color bright on her cheeks. "I'm glad you chose the Parrish Hotel for your stay, Mr. Marsh—uh, Quentin."

"No problem." If he'd wanted lodging in Point Pleasant, there wasn't a choice. The only other hotels were located across the river in Gallipolis, Ohio. "Any thoughts on where I can grab something to eat?" He sought to deflect the awkwardness they were both currently feeling.

"That's an easy one." The question seemed to help her relax. She pointed across the lobby to a hallway tucked beneath the staircase. "If you follow that hall it connects to the River Café here in the hotel."

Quentin nodded, following her direction. Wide and imposing, the staircase sheltered a short hallway beneath it. "Looks like this place has been here for a while."

"Since the early 1900s."

"Amazing. Did you by chance grow up here?" She might know something about the curse of Cornstalk.

The woman hedged. "I left Point Pleasant after the Silver Bridge fell and only returned last year."

He'd been a kid at the time of the catastrophe, but it had made national news—forty-six lives lost when the bridge connecting Point Pleasant and Gallipolis plunged into the Ohio River a few weeks before Christmas in 1967. "Bad memories?" He had more than a few of his own.

Her gaze dropped to the registration book where he'd scrawled his name with a flourish on the Q. "My father died in the bridge collapse."

"I'm sorry." Idiot. Now it was his turn to feel stupid. "That was thoughtless of me. Of course, I've heard of the tragedy."

She managed a wan smile. "I guess we both bungled a few things."

"Maybe we should start over." He held out his hand. "I'm Quentin Marsh."

She grinned and accepted. "Eve Flynn. And I believe I owe you a key. You're in room twenty-eight. Second floor, facing front at the end of the hall."

Quentin looked at the ornate skeleton key she passed him. "This *is* an old place."

"Part of the charm."

He hoisted his duffel bag. "I'm sure I'll find that's the case. Right now, I just want to unpack, then grab something to eat." The drive had been long, and even with a few stops interspersed along the way, he was overly tired and hungry.

"My cook does a great beer-battered fish sandwich."

"So you own the place?" He should have realized. Small town, family-owned hotel.

She nodded. "It was built by my great-grandfather Clarence in 1922. Flynn is my married name."

She'd be a good source of local information with her family history, but right now he couldn't wrap his head around the curse, or the promise he'd made to his sister. When he wasn't coming off an eleven-hour drive, he'd think better.

"Thanks, Eve." He gave her a parting smile and headed for the stairs. His family had been cursed for centuries. Waiting another day to get to the bottom of that plague wouldn't matter. And it certainly wouldn't change his misfortune.

Chapter 2

It was dark, pitch black with heavy cloud cover by the time Caden's shift ended and he made it home. He parked his Capri along the street and killed the ignition. Lights glowed through the front windows of the large house on Pine Creek Avenue. Eve was still up, probably waiting for him. He would have been home earlier if not for a detour to the TNT. Over the last few months she'd gotten used to his forays into the place. Once an ammunitions site during World War II, the area had been reduced to a labyrinth of abandoned weapons igloos, ponds, wetlands, and the crumbling shells of a few old buildings scattered over 3,600 acres of woodlands.

Or as most people in the area had come to think of it—the home of the Mothman.

Caden stepped from the car to the smell of wet asphalt and damp grass. They needed the rain. It had been a dry summer, unusual for a town that sat on the confluence of the Ohio and Kanawha Rivers, and had sustained horrible floods through the decades. Old-timers said those floods had been the curse of Cornstalk in play. Maybe the unusual summer was too.

"Hey." He smiled as he stepped through the door, catching sight of Eve on the sofa. She sat with her legs tucked to the side, sipping from a cup he guessed held hot tea. Chamomile by the scent. Her face lit up when she saw him. Within seconds she was across the room, arms wrapped around him to bestow a kiss.

"Missed you."

"Missed you, too." He kissed her back. Their marriage was just over a month old, both still flush with the glow. "Sorry I'm late." It was hard being away from her, but she understood the pledge that kept drawing him back to the TNT. Thankful to be home, he set his hat aside and unholstered his gun. All part of the uniform. The bullets came out before he put the weapon in the drawer of an end table by the door. "I took a drive through the TNT."

Eve's eyes grew wide. "Did you see anything?"

He shook his head. The creature was lying low. Mothman sightings historically played out in spurts, the most recent last fall. There'd been few reports in between. He'd personally encountered the creature once or twice, but for the most part the thing had gone into hiding. Despite the promise he'd made to Indrid Cold, he hoped it stayed that way. Far better the Mothman keep off the radar.

"Have a seat and I'll get you a beer." Eve motioned to the couch.

Nodding his thanks, Caden sank into the cushions while she disappeared into the kitchen. He heard the refrigerator snick open and closed. It had to be somewhere after eleven, but he was still wired from work. He'd be rotating off shift soon and could enjoy two days of downtime before going on daylight.

"We got a new guest at the hotel." Eve returned with a can of Miller.

Caden popped the top and took a drink as she settled in beside him. "That Quentin guy you were waiting on?"

Eve nodded. "Quentin Marsh. He's not what I expected." She wrapped her hands around her teacup and leaned against him.

Hooking an arm around her shoulder, he made room for her to nestle closer. The radio played in the background, something soothing and melodic, likely tuned to the station for her plants. She pampered them as if they were pets.

"I hope he didn't show up dressed in black." Caden wasn't entirely joking. He took another swig of beer.

Eve laughed. "No. He's nothing like the Men in Black from last fall."

Point Pleasant had been inundated with mysterious men in black suits who arrived with little explanation, their sole intent to warn anyone who'd claimed to have seen a UFO to be silent. Given the town had experienced a UFO Flap in October, that was close to half the population.

"But he is odd," Eve continued. "Oh, nothing like Lach or those other men," she added when he sent her a sharp glance.

Lach Evening was someone he wasn't sure he'd ever see again. Caden waited a beat but she didn't say anything further. "What's so odd about him?"

"I'm not sure." Eve pressed her lips together, considering. "When I asked what brought him to Point Pleasant, he evaded the question."

"Why is that so strange? It's no one's business but his."

Eve made a *pffing* sound. "Most guests chitchat, Caden." The concentrated look on her face indicated Marsh's reluctance to talk was only half of what was troubling her. "I told him about my great-grandfather building the hotel, and it got me thinking about him and my grandparents." She swiveled to face him, her eyes wide and probing. "Did I ever tell you what happened to them?"

Something told him he should already know.

A buried memory stirred awake in the back of his mind. His father shaking his head, talking in hushed tones to Caden's mother. A tragedy.

"There was a fire at the hotel," Eve continued before he could answer. "I was four when it happened, so I only know what I've been told." She rubbed a thumb over the diamond ring on her left hand. "The fire broke out on the third floor. No one knows what started it, but they were all up there together—my grandfather and grandmother with my great-grandfather, Clarence."

"Yeah." Caden's voice dropped. "I remember now. I was ten. I remember walking down Main Street the night after it happened. The brick on the third floor was black in the front where the flames shot through the windows. My parents went to the funerals."

"That's when my parents took over running the hotel, along with Aunt Rosie."

Caden tensed. Rosalind Parrish had died over a year ago, taking a secret to her grave that still made him bitter. He lived in the house she'd bequeathed to Eve but wasn't certain he'd forgiven her. "This is old history, Eve." His voice sharpened, a knee-jerk reaction to Rosie being mentioned. "Why bring it up now? Because some guy asks about how long you've lived here?"

"Yes." Eve gripped his hand. "Quentin has me thinking. I grew up hearing about that tragedy and about grandparents I don't remember. Daddy said they never did find the cause of the fire."

Caden drained the last of his beer. "Old wiring. That's what I heard."

"That was speculation, but my father would have *known*. Do you know what my mother said?" Eve's gaze held challenge, but she hurried ahead before he could answer. "She blamed it on the curse of Chief Cornstalk."

Shaking his head, he stood. "Everything that happens around here gets blamed on Cornstalk's curse. Wayne Rosling's dog got hit by a car yesterday and he blamed it on Cornstalk."

"Oh, no." Eve looked stricken. "Is Brisket all right?"

"He's fine." Caden headed for the kitchen and another beer. "Broke his leg, but otherwise he's going to be okay." Rosling, a senior deputy with the sheriff's department, had told Caden about the incident while they caught up on reports. Wayne's frisky Labrador had slipped its leash and bolted into the road just as a Vega rounded the bend.

"Let ancient history be ancient history," Caden called from the kitchen. He paused with his hand on the refrigerator door. The tip of the scars he carried from the Mothman poked from beneath his sleeve. Three branded marks he'd had since 1967 when the Silver Bridge fell, the welts had never changed in appearance or texture.

Until today.

His gaze narrowed.

Normally vibrant red, they were now jet black.

* * * *

Quentin pulled into a parking space at the Parrish Hotel as a small red Volkswagen Rabbit slid in beside him. He'd slept decently last night for being in a hotel and had spent the morning visiting Tu Ende Wei State Park, the site where Cornstalk was buried. Given Penelope's preoccupation with curses, it seemed the best place to start. He'd learned a good deal of historical fact, studied numerous monuments and wandered the grounds, but came away no wiser about breaking spells. Rain departed with the dawn, but the threat of severe weather huddled on the horizon.

A petite redhead exited the Rabbit and hurried to the back where she raised the hatch. She hitched the strap of a leather purse onto her shoulder, then struggled to lift a plastic tub from the rear of the car.

"Need some help?" Quentin walked closer in time to catch her startled glance.

"Oh." She balked slightly then fumbled a smile. "It's not heavy, just awkward."

"Going in the hotel?"

She nodded.

"I'll carry it for you. I'm going there myself." Before she could protest he took the carton and waited while she closed the hatch.

Her smile blossomed into something genuine. "Thank you. That's kind of you." She led the way. As they walked up the steps to the covered porch, she cast a glance over her shoulder. "I haven't seen you around before. Are you a guest here?"

"Yeah." It was the reaction he'd been getting most of the morning no matter where he went. Apparently, strangers in Point Pleasant stood out like sore thumbs. "Visiting for a while." Once inside, he waited for her to tell him where she wanted the carton. The lobby was empty, even the check-in desk vacant.

"On the registration counter is fine." The girl pointed to the empty desk. "I'm sure Eve or Katie are around somewhere."

Quentin set the carton down. It was light as she'd said, just awkward in handling, especially for someone petite like her. "Katie Lynch was here when I left earlier." He shrugged when the girl glanced at him in surprise. "She introduced herself."

"Oh. Well…" Flustered again, she held out her hand. "I'm Sarah Sherman. Thank you for your help."

He grasped her slim fingers, noting the flick of her gaze to the scars that crisscrossed his skin. At least she didn't recoil as if he were diseased. "Quentin Marsh."

Her eyes widened. "Q.M."

"Pardon?"

She appeared to backpedal mentally. "Um…nothing. I just…" Quickly, she withdrew her hand. "Thank you."

He nodded, started to turn away, then hesitated. Light from the windows on the east wall reflected off her necklace, a flat blue stone in a silver setting. He hitched in a breath.

Noticing his reaction, she looked at him curiously. "Is something wrong?" Her hand rose to her throat.

"Your necklace…" Opaque cobalt blue with veins of black. A flawless twin for the amulet tucked in his pocket. An heirloom that had been passed down through generations in his family. "It's…" He guarded his words, unwilling to share the connection without understanding how it was possible. "Unusual."

"Thank you." Her smile reflected melancholy. "It belonged to my mother and has been in my family for generations."

He debated telling her about his grandfather's amulet, but something held him back. The similarity between the two could have been a coincidence. For all he knew the odd stone had once been popular and there were hundreds in existence. Fortunately, Eve Flynn chose that moment to breeze in, allowing him to bow out gracefully.

"Nice meeting you, Sarah." Quickly, he headed for the door with a passing nod to Eve. The necklace bothered him more than he wanted to admit, but he wasn't ready to call Penelope. She'd blow the similarity out of proportion, insisting the sun and moon had aligned and it was some type of sign. Originally, he'd intended to grab something for lunch at the café, but now all he wanted to do was keep looking for a connection to his family's curse. Tu Ende Wei State Park had been a bust but he still had Fort Randolph to investigate. With any luck he'd find something or be able to assure Penelope her fears were unfounded. It all came down to Madam Olga and Pen's theory about twins.

His gaze dropped to the back of his ruined hand. The odor of blood and metal engulfed him. The sooner he could put this damn town behind him, the better. Point Pleasant was doing a bang-up job of resurrecting phantoms he'd thought he'd buried.

* * * *

"Hi." Eve circled behind the registration desk and peeked into the carton. "Is this the stuff for Shawn?"

Sarah nodded, sensing her friend's mind already diverting elsewhere. "Yes. And before you ask, I met Quentin Marsh. He carried that in for me." She tipped her chin in the direction of the box.

Eve plastered a passably innocent look on her face. "What makes you think—"

"Don't be coy. We grew up together, remember?"

Eve chuckled. "Ok, so kick me for being curious. What did you think of him?"

"We didn't talk that much. He liked my necklace." She plopped her purse on the registration counter and tried to steer the conversation back on track. She only had a short interlude of time, and the storm fermenting outside had her edgy. The sky had been overcast and threatening since the moment she crawled out of bed. "I'm on my lunch break, so I can't stay long, but I wanted to make sure Shawn knows his stuff is here. If he doesn't show up tonight, will you let me know?"

Eve regarded her steadily. "You could always come by the café. Quentin will probably grab dinner there. He did last night."

Sarah rolled her eyes, mentally kicking herself for ever taking a Ouija board to Eve's sleepover last fall. "I'm babysitting Sam for Katie tonight. Ryan's taking her to Gallipolis for dinner." Katie's eight-year-old son was a delight, but she would have steered away from Eve's suggestion regardless. It wasn't that she didn't enjoy the River Café as a spot to grab dinner, but she saw no reason to rub elbows with Quentin. Worse, she didn't want to encounter Shawn. He'd likely badmouth Suzanne for giving her the stuff in the first place.

Eve heaved a sigh and nodded. "Another time maybe." She dropped her hand on top of the carton. "So, what is all this stuff anyway, and when are you going to tell me what you found out about Obadiah?"

"It's just papers and photos. Some old books and a few newspaper clippings." She thought of the oblong box and her fingers strayed to her necklace, a reflex action that made her wet her lips. "I found this odd wooden case, too."

Eve appeared intrigued. "What's odd about it?"

She'd sound silly explaining how strange it made her feel when she touched it, so she went for something more concrete. "It's locked, but I couldn't find a key. Not that I'm sure I'd want to look inside. There's an etching of a spider on top, and the whole thing is kind of creepy."

"Wow." Eve appeared poised to dig into the carton. "Maybe I should check it out."

Sarah stayed her with a hand on her arm. "I packed it tight." She'd taken extra care to bury the case on the bottom, as far away from her as possible. "Besides, I thought you wanted to hear about Obadiah."

That did the trick. Eve quickly dismissed the box and refocused. "Shawn's always bragging about him being at Fort Randolph. What did you find out?"

"It looks like he was telling the truth, but I didn't get very far." There was only so much digging you could do before you encountered a blank wall. "I found a lot of records you'd probably find boring. Deeded property, militia ranking, that sort of thing. The one interesting tidbit I discovered had to do with Obadiah's wife. I came across a passage that I think someone must have transcribed from an older letter. Most of the original was missing." She shot a quick glance at her watch, gauging the time when she had to be back at the courthouse. What she wouldn't give for a longer lunch break. She hated to rush, but now that Eve had asked about Obadiah, she was determined to share her findings.

Rifling through her purse, she searched for a folded sheet of paper. "I made a photocopy. I think the passage must have been hand-copied in the mid-1800s, but the original letter would have predated the Revolution. It references Virginia as a colony."

"Wow."

Sarah smoothed the creases from the paper and passed it to Eve. "Take a look." The writing was spidery and faint but legible. "I'm sure it was part of a longer letter, but this was all I found in the carton."

Eve's gaze dropped to the missive. Holding the paper with both hands, she read the words aloud.

"I would be grateful for your visit, Mama. Charlotte and Alton have been most kind to me, but I cannot impose upon my dear sister and her husband forever. I am undone since losing my beloved. Even this rugged colony of Virginia, with its towering mountains and majestic trees leaves me feeling empty without my intended.

"Mama, despite all I have said, I beg you not to worry about me and Charlotte. We are well protected by the soldiers of Fort Randolph. Charlotte's brave husband, Alton, is a highly capable and respected Captain, and all the settlers are well guarded. Without Jonathan, I suffer bouts of homesickness, but I feel I must stay. For my beloved and the life we would have led together.

"Sometimes, I am taken aback by the strangeness of this new land.

"The other day I strolled by the river and saw a most unusual thing. I was a good distance away, so I question my vision, but it appeared to be a man with wings crouched upon the bank. I encountered Mr. Preech shortly thereafter. When I told him about what I saw, he grew very pale and said I must never speak of it again. He was so stricken by my tale, I continued to prod him until he confessed that he too had seen the winged man in the past. He said it was a fiend with glowing red eyes, an abomination conceived of the devil—forgive me, Mama—and that it had claimed the soul of his wife."

Eve paused, clearly shocked. "Do you know what this means?"

"Finish reading it," Sarah said.

Eve's attention returned to the letter.

"I shudder to imagine such a thing. Can demons walk in flesh upon the land? Am I marked too, as Mr. Preech's late wife, for having seen the creature? Oh, Mama, come quickly. Despite all the beauty of this place, I fear there is evil here."

Eve's voice dropped into silence. She wet her lips, her fingers white where they clutched the paper. "I'd like to share this with Caden."

"Keep that copy." Sarah nodded to the note in Eve's hand. "I made several."

"Are you going to tell Shawn about this?"

Sarah shook her head. "If he doesn't know what's in that box, it's up to him to find out." She thought of the wooden case and the uneasy feeling it gave her. Hopefully, some things would never be brought to light. "I have to get back to the courthouse, but let me know what Caden says about the letter. And thanks for getting that stuff to Shawn." Another nod for the box. She could almost relax knowing the strange case was out of her possession.

Almost.

* * * *

Caden used a flashlight to pick his way deeper into the woods. He'd ended his final shift of the week and decided to do one more sweep of the

TNT before heading to the hotel. He'd agreed to meet Eve for a late dinner and a drink. Twilight was still settling over the woodland, but within the tightly congested tangle of trees, night had already fallen. There were few people brazen enough to venture into these woods at night, but he had little to fear. He'd stood in a deserted weapons igloo, conversed with a disembodied voice, then been violently battered by the being's fury. He'd already encountered an alien named Lach Evening and Evening's frigidly distant father, Indrid Cold.

Absently, he rubbed the scars hidden beneath the sleeve of his uniform, marks he had carried since his eighteenth year. He'd been driving home from Gallipolis, stuck in traffic on the Silver Bridge when the whole structure abruptly collapsed into the frigid waters of the Ohio River. Trapped in the wreckage, lungs ready to burst, he'd hovered on the brink of unconsciousness. He would have breathed his last had the Mothman not dragged him from the prison of crushed metal. He owed his life to the creature.

Caden paused. Around him, the woods pulsed with the chattering of night insects and the burbling croak of tree frogs. Fireflies flashed between the leafy branches of oaks and elms, nothing to indicate a seven-foot winged creature lurked nearby.

Walking slowly, he swept the beam of his flashlight through the undergrowth. Clusters of toadstools, moss-covered rocks, and pockets of ferns sprang to life in the cone of illumination. Decades ago, the army had cut dozens of footpaths through the woods. He followed a barely discernable trail overgrown with weeds and brambles. The ragged path corkscrewed through the trees, ending at the weapons igloo where he'd encountered Indrid Cold.

The black bulk of the bunker loomed before him, the heavy metal doors at the entrance weathered and seasoned by time. Battered and streaked by rust, they stood slightly ajar. Tall grasses and trees crowned the top of the structure, making it invisible from the air. Had an enemy plane broached U.S. airspace during World War II, the munitions storage shell would have appeared as a natural part of the woodland.

Pausing by the doors, Caden twisted to pan the torch behind him. Shadows fled from the light, leaping into the trees. Crickets and other night insects continued their noisy chatter, a symphony that would have ceased had the Mothman been nearby. Last fall, Caden had promised Cold he'd look out for the creature, ensuring its safety as best he could. He closed his eyes and waited a beat, reaching out mentally. But if there'd been a channel between them, that channel no longer existed. Before, he'd been able to sense the creature's presence like a whisper on the fringe of his consciousness. Now there was nothing. Could that be why the welts on his arm had changed color?

Stepping into the bunker, he inhaled the heavy odor of must. A denser cloak of blackness settled around him. The dome was windowless, suffocating in some respects. Caden played the beam of his flashlight over the walls. Bits of graffiti jumped out at him. A few stray beer cans and candy wrappers littered the corner. Teenagers often came here to hang out and party. He'd done the same before the Silver Bridge fell. After that life changed. Or maybe, he did.

"Cold." His voice bounced in the empty shell of the igloo. The sounds of the night didn't intrude here. Caden turned in a circle. "I've tried to do what you asked, but the creature has vanished." Was it possible the Mothman was gone for good?

No answer, not even the sensation of frost that preceded Cold's presence. Maybe the best thing to do was forget the commitment he'd made. It was impossible to fulfill a pledge if the object of that pledge eluded him. For all he knew, the Mothman could have crawled away somewhere and died. Every time he'd encountered the creature he'd been blasted by sensations of desolation and melancholy. In some warped way, the thing *wanted* to die. Maybe death had finally claimed it.

Around him, the silence stretched and grew. He counted off several minutes, but there was nothing to indicate another presence in the igloo. Giving up, Caden returned outside and was immediately bombarded by a sensation of rage. A din grew in his head and the wind turned savage with the whistling bite of a switch. The thunder of wings buffeted him. The clatter in his head swelled until it splintered behind his eyes.

He craned his neck and squinted up at the sky. The creature's enormous wings blocked stars and clouds from sight. Ducking his head, he staggered backward as the Mothman swept to the ground. The creature towered above him, its flesh the dark gray of wet ash. It had no discernible face, the glowing orbs of its eyes the only indication of where its head should be. Large and bloodred, those hypnotic eyes were nearly impossible to look away from. A being of char and chaos, the Mothman projected and fed on emotion, using the element of fear as a weapon and defense.

Unlike others who encountered it, Caden had never been subject to terror. What the creature routinely broadcast to him was a sense of bleakness and deeply rooted misery, a longing for something it couldn't attain. But it was fury that pummeled him now. A primal thirst for vengeance. Hatred so deep it left him gasping.

"Stop."

It wanted death. Craved it. Not for him, but something centuries old and foul. An enemy that stirred listlessly awake, slithering to consciousness after a long, dark sleep.

The sensations and images bulleted rapid-fire through Caden's head. Bending double, he pressed his palm to his temple. "You have to…stop."

The brutal punishment ceased as abruptly as it began, the sudden void leaving him dizzy after a flurry of physic bombardment. He sucked down a breath, straightening slowly.

The creature stood before him, unmoving, wings arched high above its back. Then in a burst of motion it shot into the sky, the roar of its wings rolling over him like thunder.

* * * *

Will Hanley settled into his easy chair with an appreciative sigh. After a long day riding his tractor he was grateful to relax for a few hours before calling it a night. He still had ten acres to plow in the lower forty, but for now he was content to unwind with the latest episode of *Mama's Family* and a cold Coors. Tomorrow was Sunday, which meant he could grab a few extra hours sleep. He'd enjoy the luxury then head for ten o'clock service at the Good Fellowship Bible Church. Pastor Fred had promised a picnic afterward, putting Will in charge of making sure the long tables in the rectory were moved outside. June Sweeting had promised to make her famous Dutch apple pie and he looked forward to complimenting her baking. It had been three years since Grace passed away and he was starting to get lonely.

The thought of his late wife induced an unexpected wave of melancholy. Pastor Fred had been lecturing him to find a hobby. Something besides haunting the dirt track to cheer on sprints, or camping out in front of the TV. In his younger days he'd enjoyed fishing, but Grace had always tagged along. From their silly Saturday afternoon dates to weekend trips after they were married, it had been their special way of relaxing. Once Grace passed, he couldn't bring himself to go alone. Too many memories.

His thoughts tumbled away, scattered by a shrill whine from the TV.

What the hell?

The banter between Vicki Lawrence and Ken Berry was muffled by a loud clicking noise. Will was halfway from his chair, grumbling about the faulty reception, when the set suddenly went black. On the back porch, his dog, Misty, launched into a wild frenzy of barking.

"Misty!" Beer can in hand, he stomped through the kitchen. It wasn't like her to put up a racket. "Misty, what's going on?" He yanked open the rear door to find the collie at the top of the steps leading to the yard. Trapped in the square of light from the open door, the hair on her back stood bristled to attention.

"Quiet now." Despite the command, her baying grew more aggressive. Frowning, he reached for her collar. "Is something out there, girl?"

She wouldn't carry on over a rabbit or a cat, but a raccoon or skunk might have wandered in from the fields. Maybe a fox. That would set her off for sure.

Switching on the porch light, he blinked against the white blast of illumination. The clothesline where Grace had hung his dungarees every Saturday stood empty several feet from the porch. Tipped on its side, the wheelbarrow he used to haul seed rested abandoned by the footpath to the barn.

Misty gave a strangled yap and backed up until her hindquarters butted against his legs. The night fell quiet. No crickets, no locust. The dog uttered a small ruff. He kept his hand hooked through her collar, but her strange behavior worked on his nerves. She'd bullet after a raccoon or a skunk, not stay hunkered against him.

Will set his beer can on an overturned flowerpot. "Come on, Misty." Releasing her, he trotted down the steps. Immediately, she bolted ahead and disappeared into the darkness. He was still thirty feet from the barn when she snarled. Cold fear crawled up his back. "Misty, come here."

A low drone rolled from the sky. Growing in volume, the throbbing pulse set his teeth on edge. It reminded him of an angry swarm of bees, a scratchy vibration that made his skin crawl. Misty's growl morphed into a whine nearly as loud as the screech from the TV.

Something moved in the shadows. Will's mouth went dry.

"Who's there?" Dread jackknifed through his gut and into his throat. Fighting panic, he took a faltering step backward. A patch of fluid shadow loomed in front of the barn. Something large and monstrous towered over him, blocking his view of the structure. Two crimson spots bled through the soot of night, rooting him in place. Paralyzed by fear, he gazed up into a pair of malignant red eyes.

It took a second for the fear to slacken its chokehold enough for him to scream.

Will spun and bolted for the house.

Chapter 3

Quentin glanced at the clock in his room. It was late, going on ten, but not too late to hit the River Café. The place kept longer hours on Saturday nights, and he hadn't eaten since noon. He'd spent most of the day doing a fruitless tour of the town that had netted little usable information. He also owed his sister a call with an update on his progress. A night owl, she'd be up until midnight at least.

Without bothering to turn on the lights, Quentin walked to the window and pushed the curtain aside. His room faced Main Street, an eerily deserted stretch that had little to no traffic this time of night. The hum of passing cars and the flash of headlights could be seen a block over heading for the Bartow Jones Bridge. All that traffic had once run through Main Street, but the flow had changed with the fall of the Silver Bridge. No wonder many of the businesses on Main Street saw so little trade.

He was about to turn away when a glint of movement caught his eye. A sleek black Cadillac rolled down the street, a Fleetwood if he knew anything about luxury sedans. A few of his father's clients liked the prestige that came with the pricey vehicle, but it was an oddity in a town of midsized cars and pickups. Even more unusual, the Cadillac's headlights were off.

The car stopped shy of the hotel and sat with its engine idling. Quentin counted off twenty-three seconds until it resumed a slow glide down the road, streetlamps reflecting off its glossy black paint. When he could no longer see it, he switched on a lamp. Whatever the driver's reasons for prowling in the dark, it was none of his business. He had enough worries juggling Penelope and his family curse.

The thought of his sister made him move to the bedside table and the phone. While he waited for the call to go through, he glanced around the room. It wasn't bad, all things considered, though too old-fashioned for his taste. A standing wardrobe, walnut sleigh bed, and writing desk dominated one side; a small medallion-backed sofa and oval coffee table the other. A full-length mirror with clawed wooden feet stood in the corner and a tasseled lamp occupied the edge of the desk. The décor was strictly Victorian right down to the paisley rug over the hardwood floor and the green damask wallpaper.

"Hello?" Penelope's voice traveled over the line, tinged with a note of worry.

"Hi, Pen. It's Quentin."

A rush of breath echoed in his ear. "Thank God you called. I was getting so worried. Do you know what time it is?"

Time for a rum and Coke, maybe a burger, and then a crash into bed. He tempered the thought and spoke softly. For all her wacky ideas, his sister had a way of whittling under his skin. Twins did that. "Sorry. I probably should have called yesterday."

"That would have been nice. Did you get checked in?" The reprimand left her voice as quickly as it came.

"Yeah. How's Dad doing?"

"Grumbling that I'm spending too much time fussing over him." Her voice deepened, mimicking their father's gruff tone. "It was a heart attack not a death sentence. Give me some breathing room, girl."

Quentin grinned. Their father was not one to sit idle, but he'd taken the doctor's warnings seriously as far as Quentin could tell. It was time for lifestyle changes, and that included stepping back from the business. Quentin and his sister were more than capable of running the firm, but Prentice Marsh was reluctant to let go of the small empire he'd built. Maybe because Quentin's heart had never been in the venture. He hadn't gone to Juilliard to earn a living in the business world.

"Give Dad a token or two," Quentin suggested. "Ask for his advice on the Lawford account. He needs to ease into retirement."

"I'm already ahead of you. I shared the portfolio with him this afternoon. He grumbled about the numbers being off, but signed it anyway."

"Did Lawford like it?"

"Sold." There was a smile in Penelope's voice. She was more than capable of running the whole enterprise herself. Would be, if not for the accident that left him crippled with a maimed hand. "That's all that matters. Who would have thought advertising could be so cutthroat?"

"Our competitors." Best not to go down that route. It would make him edgy, worrying he should get back to calling shots as vice president of

Marsh Media instead of chasing moldy history and curses in a flood-prone river town. "Look, it's getting late and I still haven't eaten. I need to grab something before this town shuts down. I'll check in with you again, okay?"

"Are you going to Tu Ende Wei tomorrow?"

"I did that earlier. There's nothing to be gained there."

"What about the courthouse? Check for records."

"Yeah, I know. But I've got to wait until Monday."

"Talk to some of the locals, too."

"Pen." He pinched the bridge of his nose. "I know you believe in this stuff. Maybe I do too after everything that's happened, but if I come up blank—"

"You have to try." Her voice hitched. "When I have my twins, I don't want them afflicted by the same curse that's plagued our family for generations."

"Maybe it's just coincidence like Dad tried to tell us."

She huffed a breath into the phone. "If you weren't my brother—"

"If I weren't your brother—your *twin* brother—I wouldn't be doing this for you." A smile crept into his voice. "Good-night, Pen."

"Good-night." Her tone softened. "Stay safe."

Quentin walked back to the window and flicked the curtains aside. There was no sign of the Cadillac, but the image of it niggled the back of his mind.

* * * *

The café was mostly deserted, which suited Quentin fine. A blond-haired guy sat hunched over a beer at the bar, looking like he'd been there for a while. Two others who bore a facial resemblance and might have been brothers sat adjacent to him.

Quentin got a table in the back, ordered a rum and Coke, then chose a burger from the menu. The waitress was young and perky with a name tag that read: Nancy. She asked a few questions in a chatty manner—Where was he from? How long was he staying?—but he kept his answers short and vague. Despite what Penelope said, he had no intention of becoming too chummy with the locals.

Nancy left him to savor his drink, promising to return when his food was ready. Eve Flynn came in and spoke to the bartender briefly. She was closing the lobby for the night but was expecting her husband at the café. From the deserted look of the place, Quentin wondered if he was the only guest of the hotel. The three guys at the bar all had the look of locals, people long comfortable with the setting. Outside, night blanketed the street, visible through the front windows and the cutaway in a door that exited to the sidewalk. The rum helped ease the stiffness from his muscles, especially his mangled hand. When his burger came, he asked for another drink.

He was halfway through his meal when the blond at the bar swiveled around on his stool to survey the room. He'd seen Quentin come in, but focused on him as if spying him for the first time. Drink clutched in hand, he wobbled from the stool and meandered closer.

"You gotta be staying at the hotel." Uninvited, he plopped down in a seat across from Quentin. The glazed look in his eyes said he was already a good way to being drunk.

Perfect. Just what he didn't need.

"Yeah." Quentin kept eating, hoping the guy would take the hint and leave.

"Nice place, don'tcha think?"

Quentin nodded and put two fries in his mouth.

The man was quiet for a moment, a scowl tugging his lips. He seemed young, maybe twenty-five, with a scruffy look as if he hadn't seen a razor in days. "Let me tell you about Point Pleasant." He plunked his drink on the table and rocked his chair back on the hind legs. It was surprising he could balance. "Do you know who I am?"

Quentin wiped his mouth with a napkin, then took his time setting it on the table. "You're the guy who's interrupting my dinner."

The blond guffawed. "Hey, that's good! But I'm Shawn Preech." He said it like Quentin should recognize the name. "You know...king of the dirt track around here." He spread his hands wide when Quentin continued to stare at him. "Sprint cars?"

Quentin picked up his drink. "Sorry, I don't follow racing."

Shawn's chair thunked to the ground. "Then what the hell are you here for?" No mistaking the belligerent edge. The last thing Quentin wanted was an argument or worse, but it looked like his drunken companion was egging for trouble.

"Hey, Shawn. Get back here," the bartender called. "You don't want Eve to ban you from the place again, do you?"

Shawn snorted. Draining his drink, he staggered toward the bar. "That woman can't do nothing to me."

"Caden's on his way in," the bartender warned.

"Like I give a fuck." Shawn waved his empty glass in the air. "I'm not afraid of some sheriff's sergeant. I'm a celebrity."

"You mean you were," one of the guys at the bar said.

"Huh?" Shawn rounded on the copper-haired man who'd made the observation. "What are you yapping on about, Duncan?"

"It's true," his companion said. Definitely brothers. They had the same inflection to their voices. "You haven't won a race in months. Ever since Suz—"

"Don't say that bitch's name." Shawn slammed his empty glass on the bar. "I'll be glad when this shitty divorce is over."

"Then sign the papers." Duncan pointed out the obvious solution.

"And give her what she wants? Hell, no." Shawn climbed unsteadily onto the nearest stool. "Give me another one, Tucker."

"You're flagged." The bartender barely spared him a glance. "Get out of here. Go home and sleep it off."

Shawn's face grew splotchy and red. "Don't give me shit."

Quentin tensed, sensing a nose-dive toward ugliness. All he wanted to do was finish his dinner and go to bed, but somehow he'd gotten ensnared in small-town drama. The door to the street swung open, distracting Shawn, who looked like he was winding up for verbal tirade.

"Hey." A dark-haired man in a brown uniform stepped inside. A badge gleamed on his chest and a radio and a gun were holstered at his hip. The hat on his head identified him as belonging to the Mason County Sheriff's Department. "I thought Eve and I would be the only ones here this late."

Caden Flynn. Had to be.

"Shawn was just leaving." Tucker inclined his head in what seemed to be a private signal. The corners of Flynn's mouth tightened perceptibly, then quickly relaxed. "Need a ride, Shawn?"

"I'm not going anywhere." Shawn hunched over his glass.

"We'll take him." Duncan stood up, his brother rising beside him. "Time we got out of here, too. I promised Mom I'd give her a lift to church tomorrow."

The other brother walked around the bar and hooked Shawn under the arm. "Come on, buddy. We'll give you a lift home."

Shawn muttered something Quentin couldn't hear, but he wobbled off the stool and let himself be led to the door.

"Thanks, Donnie," Flynn addressed the shorter of the two.

"No problem." The man clapped Flynn on the shoulder. With a parting wave for Tucker, he followed his brother and Shawn Preech outside.

Flynn seemed to realize there was someone else in the café. Catching sight of Quentin, he rubbed his chin and approached slowly.

"Sorry you had to witness that. I hope Shawn didn't give you any trouble."

"No problem." Up close, Flynn looked a few years older than Quentin, his eyes light gray. He had a strong chin and wore his black hair cropped close to the back of his neck. "I heard that guy Shawn say you were a sergeant."

"Yeah. Caden Flynn." The man held out his hand. "My wife, Eve, owns the hotel."

"Quentin Marsh." Quentin shook, surprised Flynn gave no reaction to the roadmap of scars crisscrossing his hand. "Since you're with the sheriff's department, any chance you can tell me where I might find records on early settlers? I've already been to Fort Randolph."

It had been a bust, the same as Tu Ende Wei. While both were rich in town history, providing a wealth of information related to Point Pleasant's founding, neither could supply the details he needed.

"The courthouse would probably be your best bet, but they're closed until Monday." Flynn took off his hat and ran a hand through his dark hair. "My wife's friend, Sarah Sherman, could probably help you. She works there."

"Sarah?" Surprise slipped into Quentin's voice. "I met her earlier today."

"Well, outside the staff at Fort Randolph and Tu Ende Wei, Sarah knows just about everything there is to tell about Point Pleasant history. If you're tracing a family tree or something—"

"I am." Quentin jumped on the idea. He wanted to settle the mess and get back home. It wasn't that he was eager to return to the world of advertising, but he wanted the curse put to rest. For Penelope and her unborn twins. Maybe even for him.

Flynn shrugged. "I'm not sure how well you'll do on ancestry, but check with Sarah. Some of the early records are sketchy from what I understand. In any event," Flynn held out his hand, "welcome to Point Pleasant."

Quentin shook again then watched the sergeant walk away. Interesting how everyone seemed to know everyone else in the small community. Strangers stood out, but were readily welcomed.

That thought led him back to the Cadillac, a car that had crawled down the street as if engaging in surveillance.

What would a vehicle like that be doing in a sleepy town like Point Pleasant?

* * * *

Shawn was ticked. "I can make it inside myself. Just leave the damn thing there." He waved angrily at the front stoop. It was bad enough Donnie had taken his keys and driven him home while Duncan followed in their vehicle, but he wasn't about to let the brothers tuck him in like some pathetic loser. Besides, he needed fresh air to clear the buzz he had going.

"Let me set it inside the door." Donnie looked at him over the plastic tub in his arms. Sarah Sherman had left it at the hotel and Shawn had stashed it on the passenger's seat in his car before he'd started drinking at the River. Since Donnie had to move it for Shawn to crawl into the Charger for the ride home, he must have felt obligated to do something with it.

"I'll get it in the morning." Shawn was tired of arguing, and the exhaust from Duncan's idling car was starting to make him sick. If the two brothers didn't leave soon he'd spew all over the yard. Pressing a palm to his throbbing forehead, he ground his teeth. "Just leave it the fuck on the stoop. Don't make me say it again."

"Okay. Don't have a cow." Donnie's tone indicated his patience had reached an end. He dropped the thing with a thunk, and it teetered off the edge, spilling its contents onto the ground. "Shit! Now look what you made me do."

"Just get the hell out of here. I'll take care of it." Shawn bent over, picking up a few papers.

Donnie moved to help then seemed to think better of it. "You know what, Shawn? You make a hell of a lousy drunk. Do yourself a favor and lay off the booze."

"Get the hell off my property!"

"Gladly." Donnie flipped up his middle finger in a parting salute.

"Bastard." Shawn waited until he heard the car door slam, followed by the squeal of rubber against asphalt. The old Ford LTD rattled down the street spewing exhaust.

With a groan, Shawn clutched his stomach and dropped to a seat on the front porch. Not that long ago he'd shared the home with Suzanne. They'd argued a lot, but she was a hell of a looker. They'd made a great pair—the dirt track king and a former Miss Point Pleasant. He'd still be flaunting her around town if she hadn't found out about Belinda. Two weeks after she'd kicked him out, the thing with Belinda had gone belly up. By then Suzanne had rented a new place and stuck him with the lease on Barnwood Street.

She pissed him off something fierce, but damn if he didn't still want her.

That was the hell of it. All they'd done was fight when they were married. But now that the divorce was pending, he couldn't get her out of his head. It didn't look good for his image that she'd kicked him out. If anyone was going to get dumped, it should have been the other way around.

Muttering, he kicked the upturned tub, disgorging more of its contents over the lawn. Damn Suzanne for dragging the thing over to Sarah's place to begin with. He collected a handful of papers and stuffed them back inside. In his inebriated state, he couldn't see shit.

Let the stuff blow away. Who the hell cared about old documents and photos anyway?

God, his head hurt. If only the damn pounding would stop. At least his stomach wasn't churning anymore. Maybe he should go inside and lie down. Sleep it off.

He staggered to his feet, bumped against the tub, and nearly fell. There was something heavy among all those loose papers. Curious, Shawn bent and weeded through the mess. A few stray sheets blew down the driveway. Another caught on a rosebush Suzanne had planted under the front window.

Spying a wooden case, he grabbed the thing and teetered to the side. A bark of laughter escaped him when he recognized the etchings on the top. His dad had tried to give him the case a few days before his wedding, one of the few times the old man had treated him well. He said it was some kind of family heirloom that needed safekeeping. Then his mom came along and freaked out. She'd babbled about devil magic and witchcraft, ranting like a lunatic, until he finally returned the case just to shut her up. He hadn't needed the headache any more than her incessant Bible-thumping.

Chewing on his bottom lip, he studied the lock. His old man had told him there was a release mechanism, but no one in the family had been able to manipulate it. Generation after generation, male descendants passed the case to the next in line. Sometimes his dad could act as loony as his mom. No wonder he never bothered visiting their graves.

Turning the box over, he looked for a weakness in the wood. He could always get a hammer and smash the top, but he liked the look of the carvings and hated to ruin the case. Probably why no one else had ever bashed it to pieces. The spider was bizarre, kind of grotesque. It would make a great tattoo.

A drunken giggle burst from his throat. On a whim, he angled his fingers over the lock and pressed. Something clicked into place. The lid sprang loose in his hand.

Like freaking magic.

"No shit." Shawn sucked down a breath, abruptly sober. Moonlight glimmered off metal, drawing his gaze to the object nestled in the box. The knife appeared to be close to eight inches long, half of that blade. It reminded him of something his dad might have used to skin a deer, only this knife was ancient looking. The blade was slightly curved, and the handle bore the same strange spider marking as the case.

Shawn licked his lips, his breath shallow. Closing his fingers over the grip, he stood and pulled the knife from the box. A tingle raced up his arm.

The blade was coal black.

* * * *

Caden read the letter through and set the paper Eve had given him on the table. Other than Tucker, who wiped down the bar, and Nancy, who'd disappeared into the kitchen, they were the only two in the café. It was too late to down a regular meal but he nursed a piece of cherry pie along with his coffee. Eve did the same with a slice of lemon meringue. "You say Sarah found this in Shawn's stuff?" He motioned to the slip of paper lying between them.

Eve nodded. "Remember Suzanne asked Sarah to dig into Shawn's family tree? It was in with a bunch of stuff Suzanne gave her." She leaned forward, eyes wide. "You know what this means, don't you? It means the Mothman had to be around as far back as the days of Fort Randolph."

Caden didn't mirror her surprise. "We've known that for a while. Lach told us his people visited Earth before the time of the dinosaurs, and Maggie—" He hesitated. It was still hard imagining his dead sister communicating with Eve and his mother, but her ghost had relayed as much to Eve last summer, telling Eve the Mothman had lived for "a thousand yesteryears."

Eve reached across the table and touched his hand, seeming to hone in on his hesitation. Even now it was hard to talk about his sister. He'd once considered her death his fault.

"But, Caden—" Eve plowed ahead, letting the ghost of Maggie rest. "Don't you think it's odd the creature has been here all this time yet it wasn't until the late sixties that people became aware of its existence?"

"We don't know that. According to this"—he tapped the paper with a forefinger—"Preech must have seen it, and so did the author of this letter."

Leaning back in her seat, Eve fiddled with her fork. She poked the rich meringue layer on her pie. "It's vanished again, hasn't it?"

She didn't have to identify the "it" for Caden to know she referred to the Mothman. He considered telling her how the creature had reacted during their last encounter—agitated, hostile—but saw no reason in making her worry. Better she think the cryptid had simply vanished into the wooded domain of the TNT. For something so large and grotesque in appearance, the creature had an uncanny ability to disappear when desired. He wondered if it had powers he didn't realize. Lach Evening was certainly an untapped source of supernatural abilities, and he was descended from the same alien race as the Mothman.

Caden swallowed a mouthful of coffee. "I didn't see it." He regretted the lie, but until he better understood why the creature had reacted the way it did, he wanted to keep everything low key. Even from his wife. The fewer people who knew, the better. Some of the townspeople had a habit of taking matters into their own hands when they thought the Mothman was on the prowl. "How about this letter?" He motioned to the paper again. "Does Shawn know about it?"

Eve shrugged. "According to Sarah, he was pretty clueless Suzanne had given her anything. Sarah dropped off a box of stuff earlier, and Shawn loaded it in his car before he started drinking." She frowned, obviously thinking of the story she'd heard from Tucker and Caden about how Shawn had to be driven home by the Bradley brothers. "I wish he'd get his act together. He seems to be drinking more now that Suzanne left him. I really hate the fact he started to get huffy with a guest."

"Marsh seemed okay. I wouldn't worry about it."

"Hmm." Eve looked down at her plate. Another poke at the pie.

Caden laughed. "Are you going to eat that thing or not?"

Eve's gaze flashed to his face and she smiled tightly. "I was imagining it as Shawn. That jerk could use a poke or two."

He didn't disagree, but Shawn was young, not quite twenty-five. Preech could be a class-A douchebag, but he still had time to pull it together and learn from his mistakes. Hopefully, he'd pass out when Duncan and Donnie got him home, and wake up tomorrow with a different outlook on life.

Assuming he didn't have one hell of a hangover.

* * * *

Shawn clutched the knife tightly in both hands. He wandered from the porch and the plastic tub that lay open on the grass. From the papers and photographs strewn across his lawn. His sneakers scuffed against macadam as he blundered into the driveway. He licked his lips, suddenly dry, his throat tight with emotion he couldn't explain. His thoughts had been jumbled before, muddled and fogged by alcohol, but now they were sharp, brittle like glass. He could almost taste them in the back of his throat, an acrid smoke that lodged there, whispering of a time long ago.

Of a thing that had taunted him. A creature of evil.

Hate.

Oh, yes, how he hated the demon. From that first moment he'd seen it blot the sun from the sky. His heart had faltered, his innards coiling up inside him. Unable to move, he'd gazed up at the monster, terrified beyond reason. It had bewitched Willa, brought the fever on her. His bladder had released and the warm stream of his shame trickled down his leg. He, a man who had stood before the savages in Lord Dunmore's War, who'd faced the heathen and survived. How could a thing born of sorcery and chaos turn him into a whimpering craven?

Shawn blinked, confused by the memory. It didn't belong to him, yet it did.

Anger warred with shame.

You are my descendant, a voice whispered in his head. *Do what I could not. Kill the demon.*

The spirit that possessed him, awakened by the knife, had no name for the demon it sought. But Shawn did.

Mothman.

He wrenched open the car door and dropped inside.

Chapter 4

His head was pounding. God, it hurt.

Shawn dragged his tongue across his lips, tasting sour alcohol and last night's cigarettes. He cracked his eyes, willing the incessant drubbing silent. His body was stiff, corkscrewed behind the wheel of his car. Someone beat on the driver's door, the relentless hammering magnified by a shrill female voice.

"Shawn! Shawn! What the hell are you doing in my driveway?"

He came awake with a jerk, sitting upright so quickly pain splintered down the back of his neck. Blinking a gray morning into focus, he scrubbed sleep from his eyes. Suzanne's angry face was plastered against the driver's side window, her fist raised to knock again. Behind her, the sky was the color of used dishwater.

"Did you hear me, Shawn? What the *hell* are you doing in my driveway?"

Yeah, he'd heard the bitch the first time.

He hitched the door open and stumbled outside. His stomach seesawed, and for a moment he thought he would hurl on her pink bedroom slippers. With her hair done up in curlers and her face bare of makeup, she wasn't the beauty queen people envied. Hands fisted against her hips and her too-tiny mouth twisted into an ugly sneer, she looked more like a priggish troll. Hell, what had he ever seen in her?

"I want you out of here, Shawn Preech. Get back in that bucket of bolts and get off my property!"

Do not let her talk to you like that.

"Bucket of bolts?" Bracing a hand against the Charger, he used the car to steady himself. He had to squint to see her. His vision was fuzzy from the excess of alcohol he'd downed last night. "I'll park wherever I damn well please." Why the hell had he driven here anyway? Suzanne had walked out on him, was in the process of divorcing him. She'd made him into a laughingstock. Even those twits the Bradley brothers had turned against him, saying he'd lost his moxie on the dirt track because of her.

Show her she cannot push you around. The voice was in his head. The "other" voice of his ancestor. *You did it once before.*

Yeah.

He sucked on his bottom lip. Realized it was cracked and split.

He'd been lit when Suzanne had shown up at the River last fall, intent on dragging him home. Like any woman was going to tell him what to do or where he had to be. He'd given her a hard shove, sending her sprawling to the floor. She'd banged into a table on the way down. So what if she'd been pregnant? It probably hadn't been his kid anyway. She'd just been trying to get her hooks into him because he'd been stepping out with Belinda on the side. Hell, he was only twenty-four. He needed his fun.

"Shawn, if you don't get out of here, I'm going to call the cops." Suzanne leaned forward, one fist clinging to her hip. It was her battle stance, an attitude she'd often flaunted during their short-lived marriage. Why the hell had he ever put up with it?

Not happening today, bitch.

"And tell them what? Maybe I just wanted to go for a drive last night."

She'd been the one to bail out of the house, sticking him with the rent. He should have tried to collect, but he'd never put her name on the lease, too proud to have a woman contributing to the roof over his head. "I never saw your new place before." He nodded to the small ranch behind her. It was cute in a *woman-y* way, just the kind of thing Suzanne would like, with flower boxes trimmed out at the windows and a birdbath in the side yard. A few plastic sunflowers were clumped around the base of the birdbath and a wooden cardinal with revolving wings perched on a stake near a red maple. "Invite me in."

Suzanne's mouth dropped. "Haven't you heard a word I've said, you moron?"

So disrespectful.

"You shouldn't talk to me like that."

"Really?" Her lips curled in an ugly grin. "I'll talk to you any way I want, you worthless son-of-a-bitch. Especially when you're on my property uninvited."

His head was throbbing again. Why *had* he come?

A test. Prove you are worthy of the task I demand.

"Do you hear me, Shawn?"

She pushed into his face, glaring up at him the way she'd done when they'd had screaming-decibel blow-out fights. She was hideous. A hag in a pink bathrobe and slippers.

"Did you get drunk again? Is that it? If you think you're going to show up here for entertainment, you can go pork one of your sluts."

His hand cracked across her face. He blinked stupidly, as if the appendage had a will of its own. Dumbfounded, he flicked his gaze to hers. The blatant fear in her eyes sent wild exhilaration streaking through him. His fingerprints stood out livid against her white skin.

Backing away, Suzanne held a trembling hand to her mouth, her eyes wide with shock. Choking on a cry, she pivoted and bolted for the house.

Do not leave without teaching her a lesson.

Shawn's mouth pressed into a hard line. "My pleasure."

He caught up with her just as she reached the front door.

* * * *

There wasn't much Quentin could do on a Sunday. Point Pleasant mostly shut down, with the exception of its churches and a few restaurants that catered to hungry families. He ended up visiting Pioneer Cemetery, an old graveyard off Viand Street, in the hopes of stumbling over the burial plot of Jonathan Marsh. According to Penelope, Jonathan was an ancestor, though Pen's details were sketchy. Probably because she'd gotten the information from a friend who also happened to be a psychic. Madam Olga had insisted Quentin could break the Marsh family curse by visiting Point Pleasant and unearthing his family's connection to the town.

At the entrance to the cemetery, he discovered historical markers for some of the earliest graves. Two Revolutionary War soldiers and that of a Dr. Jesse Bennett, a colonel in the Virginia Militia. A commemorative marker for John Roseberry read he was with Washington at Valley Forge. The grounds were well maintained, the setting peaceful, but a few of the older tombstones had toppled or broken, pitted with the earmarks of time.

He spent close to two hours studying names and dates but found no connection to anyone named Marsh. Readying to leave, he was halfway back to his car when he spied a black Cadillac across the street. In the gray wash of daylight, the vehicle was spotless, looking like it had been driven off a showroom floor.

"A restful place, is it not?"

Quentin turned abruptly, drawn by the man's voice behind him. Tall and slender, the man who faced him stood with his hands clasped behind his back. His expression was unreadable, but the glint in his coal-black eyes was intelligent and sharp.

"Uh, yeah." There'd been a few visitors to the cemetery while Quentin studied the graves, but he hadn't noticed the man. With his light blond hair, black eyes, and dark clothing, he would have been hard to miss. Who wore black trousers and a long-sleeved shirt in July?

"Do you have a relative buried here?" the stranger asked.

"No." Quentin might have pegged him as a caretaker if not for the cut of his clothing. He wasn't dressed for grounds work, so perhaps some kind of administrator. Someone like that might be able to help. "Actually, I'm not sure. I'm looking for a tombstone."

"An ancestor?"

"Yes."

"I thought so." The man tugged at his chin, drawing attention to his fingers. Slender, but fatter at the tip, the unusual shape made his hands appear graceful and clunky at the same time. Quentin was reminded of the suckers on the tentacles of an octopus.

"Does this ancestor have a first name?"

"Jonathan." Explaining his sister's attachment to all things mystical didn't seem like the wisest track to take, so he avoided mentioning how he'd come by the name. "Do you work here?"

The sliver of what might have been a grin touched the man's lips. "No. But I do not think you will find Mr. Jonathan Marsh buried here."

"Why?" A horn blared on Viand followed by the screech of tires on asphalt. Quentin pivoted, catching the near collision between an S-10 pickup and an older model Monarch. The drivers exchanged a few heated words through open windows then moved on.

Shaking his head, Quentin turned back to address the blond-haired stranger. Only then did he realize he hadn't mentioned the last name of the ancestor he'd been seeking. And yet the man had known it.

Small wonder he'd vanished without a trace.

* * * *

Shawn cranked the radio, blaring "Centerfold" by the J. Geils Band through the open windows of the Charger. The whistling rush of air pumped his adrenalin, propelling him to a glittery high. His gaze dropped to his right hand where it gripped the steering wheel. Dried blood coated his knuckles, thicker in the creases.

Her blood. She deserved what she got.

His soon-to-be ex-wife would think twice before talking trash to him again. She'd had the beating coming. If she knew what was good for her, she'd keep her trap shut about what had gone down in her tiny living room.

He'd left the place in shambles—her too. He'd made it clear the next time would be worse if she blabbed to the cops.

Shawn licked his lips. The idea of a next time jacked his adrenaline higher. Rage was a new and dangerous beast with an edge like lightning when it poured out. How could he go back to his boring life? Working on the docks, drinking at the River. Even running the sprint track. Nothing compared to the giddy elation coursing through his veins.

A gruff snort escaped him. He dragged the back of his hand across his mouth, tasting salt and copper. Suzanne had sunk her nails into him, even drew blood a few times. She'd put up a fight, leaving him the scrapes to prove it.

A glance in the mirror revealed a nearly unrecognizable face. His hair stuck up on either side, his eyes overly bright like shaved glass in sunlight. For a second he imagined another visage superimposed over his features—dark-eyed and hooded with a sharp nose and sunken cheeks. A fat worm burrowed into his gut.

You should release your rage again. The voice was seductive. Not his voice but the words of the "other."

How? It wasn't like he had another wife he could slap around. Steering the Charger around a bend, he sobered as his adrenalin ebbed. The odd knife he'd found rested in the passenger's seat, the blade gleaming with the cold appeal of onyx. Would it severe muscle and sinew? Leathery flesh?

You are not ready to face the demon.

Another bend in the road with houses falling away behind him. Fields sprawled on either side, postcard squares of green and gold.

"When?"

A mailbox jutted at the foot of a dirt lane. Will Hanley's place. A house and barn stood in the distance, set back on a gradual slope.

When you prove you can kill.

He slowed at the lane. Hanley was a righteous SOB, always talking church then dissing him at the track when he didn't make the winner's circle. They were all like that. All the badasses that came out to see him risk his life. Not a single one with the balls to get behind the wheel and drive.

Before Shawn knew what he was doing, he'd turned off the road and headed up the dirt lane to Hanley's house. Will's wife used to teach him spelling in grade school, but she'd died three winters past. He'd liked her. She'd smelled of lilacs and rosewater and sometimes brought home-baked cookies for her class.

Put those memories aside. She is not why you are here.

Course not. But why *was* he?

Shawn stopped at the top of the driveway and killed the ignition. Hunched behind the wheel, he stared through the open window toward the house and the red barn looming in the background. Despite the dingy gray haze of the sky, the setting resembled an artist's rendition.

He and Suzanne might have had a place like that. If his father hadn't been a drunk and his mother had ditched her church meetings long enough to do something about it. They should have provided better for him instead of leaving him to fend on his own. Was it any wonder he'd started filching his dad's Jack Daniels when he was twelve?

You have been cheated too long. Now is the time to take what you desire.

A flicker of his earlier adrenalin returned. He remembered battering his fist across Suzanne's face; her screams and tears fueling his anger. The sight of curlers tumbling from her hair, a ripped bathrobe, and one lone slipper clinging to her foot had made him feel powerful.

We have never been afraid.

We. When had he become two identities?

Even with the extra thoughts crowding his head, he knew bullshit when he heard it. There had been a time when the entity inside him had been afraid. A time of pulse-pounding terror that had sent a stream of shame trickling down his leg.

Never think of that vile moment again!

Rage filled him, pulsing with the blood-thump of his heart. Breathing heavily, he slipped the knife through his belt, careful of the sharp blade. It bore a deadly belly, a detail he covered with his T-shirt.

Shawn trotted for the house.

This one will be easy. This one is already terrified.

"Where?"

The back. The door is open.

He followed the path of a curving walkway around the side. Pink peonies and black-eyed Susans paved the way to the rear yard. A clothesline stood sentry between the barn and the house. Various tools were stacked on the porch, along with a twenty-pound bag of birdseed and a stainless steel water dish.

"Hanley has a dog."

Do not concern yourself. She is elsewhere.

Licking his lips, Shawn slipped the knife free. He passed it from hand to hand, patiently gauging its weight. When he had the measure of the weapon, he concealed it behind his back and crept toward the porch. Rickety boards creaked under his sneakers as he clambered up the steps. An old wind chime suspended above the kitchen window tinkled in the breeze.

"Will?"

Shawn opened the screen, then tried the knob on the main door. It gave easily, opening without protest. He moved slowly, slipping into the house with a careful glance for his surroundings. The kitchen was tidy, the countertops bare except for a Mr. Coffee, and three brown canisters marked Sugar, Flour, and Tea respectively. A square drop-leaf table was pushed against the far wall and a braided oval rug covered the maple floorboards. The place smelled of lemon furniture polish and pipe tobacco.

Shawn's knife hand tingled. Like the flesh was stretched tightly over his bones and a spider scampered across his knuckles. He crept from the kitchen, inching down the hall toward the living room.

"Will." Sweat dripped into his eyes. His heartbeat accelerated, blood pulsing at his temples. "Will, it's Shawn Preech."

Hanley was close by. The man's fear permeated the air, a honeyed drug lingering a finger's breadth out of reach.

The craven cowers from the demon. Spineless and weak-kneed. We do not suffer the gutless to live.

"Shawn?" Hanley's voice was a feeble croak, half its normal volume.

Shawn followed the sound to its source and found Will crouched behind a brown easy chair. He sat with his arms wrapped around his legs, his knees drawn to his chest. Rocking back and forth, he raised his head, his eyes wide and bloodshot. "Is it gone?"

Pacify the fool.

"Gone." He plastered on a smile. "I scared it away."

Hanley's gaze darted to the side, then ping-ponged back in a hopeful expression. "I'm safe?"

"Safe." Shawn extended his left hand.

Like leading a lamb to the slaughter.

Hanley's legs were unsteady when he stood. He gripped the back of the chair and looked about the room as if to ensure there was nothing lurking in the corners. "Where's Misty?"

"Haven't seen her." He smiled encouragingly, hoping to place the old man at ease. "Maybe we should go into the kitchen."

Good boy. Near the door. Set the stage.

"I could make you coffee and you can tell me what happened."

"Yeah. Okay." Hanley dragged shaking fingers down his face. He moved from his hiding place—tentatively at first, like someone who ventured from night into day after years of isolation. "Maybe I should call someone...tell them what I saw." Wobbling, he braced a hand against the wall for support. Another nervous glance about the room, his eyes wide and bloodshot. "I'm worried about Misty."

"There's a phone in the kitchen, isn't there?"

Hanley bobbed a yo-yo nod. Shawn had never noticed before how skinny his neck was. It would be easy to snap, break like the balsa wood planes he used to fly as a kid. He'd saved up his allowances for a nice custom one when he was eleven, then his dad had trashed the thing in a drunken rage. Too bad it wasn't his dad's neck he was snapping.

You will use the knife. You will follow my plan.

He trailed Hanley into the kitchen. The guy seemed to be recovering a little with each passing second. Probably didn't like the idea of dirt-track Shawn finding him cowering behind his La-Z-Boy like a chickenhearted weakling. In a few more minutes he'd have his head together and that would make him a hell of a lot harder to take down. At the very least, he'd put up a fight, which was sure to get messy.

His back turned, Hanley moved to the phone.

Shawn tightened his hand on the knife. He had a clear target now, no resistance, but he wanted to see Hanley's face when the danger registered.

"Will."

Hanley picked up the receiver.

"Will, turn around."

Still slightly dazed, Hanley glanced over his shoulder.

Shawn grinned, but there was nothing friendly in the wolfish stretch of his lips. By the time Hanley saw the knife, all he could do was throw up an arm in defense. The receiver clattered to the floor, bouncing on a springy mustard-yellow spiral of cord. Hanley grunted when the knife sank into his chest, his eyes bulging to the size of marbles.

"Wh—" He clutched at Shawn's hands—both locked on the knife now—but his life was already slipping, leaking away in each ribbon of blood that oozed over his checkered shirt.

"Why?" Shawn ripped the knife free. "Is that what you want to know?"

Hanley slumped against the wall, a wet splutter of breath rattling from his lips. Blood dribbled down his chin.

Slash. Like claws. Like the demon.

Oh, yes. He could do that, and could do it without explanation. Something slipped inside. A hold on reality—his identity—but he no longer cared. The power was electrifying. Let Hanley go to his grave wondering what sin he'd committed to warrant a brutal end.

Shawn hacked at the man's cheek. Blood exploded from the jagged tear, a sight which enflamed his rage. How dare this man live! A pathetic coward who cringed behind a chair, too terrified to face the creature the heathen had summoned.

Another slash, the blade flaying open Hanley's chest. The old man's legs folded and his eyes rolled back in his head. Shawn followed him to the ground, slashing and slashing again. It was only when Hanley's body pitched to the side and lay unmoving that Shawn realized he was dead.

His breath heaved from his lungs; great gasps that made him hunch over and bend double at the waist. He waited for the giddy adrenalin rush that had followed beating Suzanne into submission, but nothing came. Instead he felt sick and dizzy. His head throbbed and his grip on the knife was slick with sweat, prickling with fire.

Finish it.

Shawn tried to pull himself together. He looked around and found a towel in the cupboard under the sink. He was making a mess of things, leaving bloody shoe and fingerprints everywhere. Red teardrops splattered his clothes.

There will be time to clean up later.

He looked over his shoulder at Hanley, disturbed he couldn't reclaim the rush he'd felt earlier. It had all seemed so simple, made so much sense at the time. Now he felt misdirected and confused.

He cleaned the blade off in the sink, washed his hands, then dug through the cupboards for food. Hunger pummeled his gut. He'd drank most of his meal at the River last night and was suddenly ravenous. Finding a large cardboard box under the sink, he loaded it with staples—crackers, bread, peanut butter. He needed food. As much food as he could find. In the cupboard by the refrigerator he stumbled over a pack of Oreos and scarfed half down while he worked. He guzzled a cola, but five minutes later threw the soda and cookies up in the sink.

Shit.

You have enough.

It was time to leave, to get out before someone spied his Charger in the driveway. He cleaned up the sink, wiped up his bloody prints, and looked around for a piece of paper.

There was one more thing he had to do to make the scene complete.

* * * *

Monday mornings were never the highlight of the week and Sarah was glad to have another mostly behind her. She had forty more minutes until her lunch break when Quentin Marsh walked into the Vital Records division of the courthouse. Sarah was at her desk behind the counter, her coworker, Patty Noone, across from her, finishing up a phone call. Sarah waved an aside to Patty, alerting her she would take care of whatever was needed, then plastered a smile on her face and approached the counter. There was something that made her feel slightly on edge when around Quentin Marsh and it had nothing to do with a Ouija board.

"Hi." Sarah greeted him across the counter. He wore faded jeans and a T-shirt today, the shirt nearly the same chestnut brown as his hair. "Looks like we meet again. What can I help you with?"

She wondered if he found the surroundings stuffy and outdated. The whole room had a weathered, yellowed look that reminded her of old newspapers. Half was taken up by an L-shaped counter, her desk and the desks of two other clerks behind the foot of the L. The larger section was composed of parallel rows of wooden shelves, each laden with fat black binders stacked end to end. Two large tables with four chairs occupied the open section of the room, reserved for visitors or anyone who might want to spend countless hours poring over archives.

Quentin cleared his throat. "I hear you're kind of an expert on local history."

"I don't know that I'd go that far." A blush of modesty warmed Sarah's cheeks. "I'm involved in the Historical Society and I've done a lot of research on the area." Behind her, Patty finished her phone call, gathered a stack of papers, and headed for the copy machine. Her smart black pumps click-clacked across the vinyl floor. "Is there something in particular you're interested in?"

"More like someone."

"An ancestor?" Sarah couldn't recall ever doing research on the name Marsh, but that didn't mean a forebear of Quentin's family didn't exist in Point Pleasant's history. The copy machine rumbled behind her.

"Does the name Jonathan Marsh mean anything to you?" Quentin asked.

Sarah puzzled it over. "I'm afraid not. But if you know what type of record you'd like to access, I can help you find the correct references. Many of our earlier records are transcribed, but birth and death certificates date back to 1853."

Quentin scowled. "I have a feeling it would be earlier."

"You're not sure?"

"Afraid not."

"Was Jonathan ever married?"

"Zero idea, again. Why would you ask?"

"Well, certificates of marriage were some of the earliest records for most areas. Our county marriage certificates date back to 1781 and we have some overlap from Virginia, which started recording marriages in

1706. Normally, if someone is researching family ancestry they'll have a time frame they want to reference." She raised her hand, touched the blue stone dangling at her throat. Lately, she'd taken to wearing the necklace more frequently. Perhaps it was merely a reminder that the anniversary of her parents' death lingered around the corner. Eighteen years and her memories of the night always boiled down to lightning and the pendant.

Quentin's gaze was drawn to the stone. He studied it briefly before glancing back to her. "Is there a way to research based on last name?"

"Of course." He had his work cut out for him. "I can set you up with some books at one of the tables." She nodded to the two tables behind him, both presently unoccupied. "It's the long way of doing things but we can go that route. Just give me the decade you'd like to start with. I'd suggest going through marriage licenses first since they'll be the earliest records."

"Sounds like a plan."

Fifteen minutes later Sarah left him at the table, a stack of black binders at his elbow. She'd decided to brown-bag it today and hit the lunch room with Mary Horner from Criminal Records during her half-hour break. Quentin was still immersed in his work, silently flipping pages, occasionally scribbling a note on a yellow legal pad when she returned. Throughout the afternoon, she provided him with more record books, including birth and death certificates.

"Any luck?" she asked at one point when she had a break. Public inquiries had been slow, giving her a chance to catch up on her backlog. She paused at the table on her way to the prothonotary's office, several folders in her arms.

"Nothing on Jonathan, but I've found some other names. Two marriages in the late eighteen hundreds but I don't think it's the same Marsh family. Penelope is going to be disappointed."

"Penelope?

"My sister. She did some preliminary work and was able to trace our family back to the early eighteen hundreds before the line disappears. They weren't from this area."

"Oh." Puzzled, Sarah drew her brows together. "Then why are you looking in Point Pleasant?"

"That's kind of a convoluted story." Quentin flipped shut the binder he'd been studying. "I'm not even sure I believe it, but I'm inclined to be open-minded since arriving in town." He plopped the book on top of another one. "I've been meaning to ask you about your necklace."

He'd mentioned something about her necklace the other day. The unusual stone often drew comments, but as his gaze narrowed on hers, she realized his interest might be more than casual. "It's a family heirloom."

"Interesting."

"Why is that?"

"Because so is this." Quentin dug into his pocket, then plunked an amulet on the table—a black-veined blue stone in a silver setting.

The mirror image of her own.

* * * *

Quentin watched Sarah's face for reaction. Her eyes widened, her lips parting in surprise. The similarity between her necklace and the amulet was too striking to be coincidental. She set the folders on the table then brushed her fingertips over the stone.

"I've never seen another like mine." Her glance was uncertain.

"Neither have I."

"What do you think it means?"

He shrugged, mentally ticking off possibilities. He vaguely remembered the amulet as a kid. Something his great-grandfather took out occasionally and held like a worry stone, rubbing his thumb over the blue gem in the center. When he passed away it was willed to Quentin with no explanation, just something his great-grandfather wanted him to have. Quentin's father said it was probably because he was a twin, as Great-Grandpa Al had been.

Then Penelope found out she was pregnant with twins and had gone to see her friend the psychic for an extra measure of comfort—as she called it—to ensure there wouldn't be complications with the birth. Never mind she had a highly skilled obstetrician at her disposal. Pen had developed a New Age mentality that made her double-check everything against planet alignments and spiritual energy. Not long after her visit to Madam Olga, Quentin found himself chasing down curses and the legend of Chief Cornstalk. Right now all he wanted to do was wrap his visit, head home, and pacify his sister. He wasn't getting anywhere through tourist channels or record books, so he might as well step out on a limb. For all her strange philosophies and soothsayer beliefs, there wasn't anything he wouldn't do for Pen—including looking like an idiot if that's what it took to get answers.

"Seems to me since your family is from this area and mine may have roots here, they must have crossed paths at some time." He picked up the amulet. "I think this has been kicking around in my family for centuries, but the only speculation I have for thinking that will probably sound crazy."

Sarah watched him intently. So intently that when a phone rang in the background, she jerked in surprise. Nervously, she fiddled with the chain of her necklace.

"Can I take you to dinner?" He hadn't planned on blurting the suggestion, but she was his best shot at getting to the bottom of the Marsh family curse. "I'm not trying to be forward." Hopefully, he wasn't coming off like a jerk. "These books aren't getting me anywhere." He waved a hand over the binders. "And they're not really the source of what I need."

She tilted her head. "What do you need?"

"To understand what happened in 1777." He might as well go for it. "October 10, 1777, to be precise."

She was a historian and would know the significance of the date.

"The day Chief Cornstalk died."

"Or was murdered, depending on how you look at it. So, how about it? Would you like to talk moldy history over dinner?"

"Sure." Her composure returned. She picked up her folders and smoothed a hand over the top. "I get off at four-thirty, but somehow I think it's more than history you want to talk about."

Of course she was right. But how did you tell someone you wanted to talk about curses without them thinking you were crazy?

* * * *

Rather than go to the River for dinner, Sarah suggested they grab something to eat at the North Dock, further down Main. Point Pleasant was relatively small and the River was a local hangout where tongues were sure to wag if she had dinner with the hotel's most recent guest. She couldn't avoid being seen, but at least at the North Dock she wouldn't be under the scrutiny of Eve and Katie, who seemed determined to connect her to Quentin thanks to the prediction of a Ouija board.

Inside, the waitress seated them by the front window with a view of the street, gave them menus to look over, and then disappeared to fill their drink order. The atmosphere was casual with booths and tables offset by potted plants and black-and-white photos of riverboats. Her grandfather was in one of those photos, a man who'd made his living on the barges from the time he was barely fourteen.

Sarah ordered a pasta dinner while Quentin chose a steak and potato combo with a side of green beans. They made small talk about the area until their food arrived.

"How long have you worked at the courthouse?" Quentin cut into his steak, the thick scars on the back of his hand plainly visible.

"About five years. I took a job in Cleveland after college, but I missed Point Pleasant." He probably thought her too rural for the city but that hadn't been the case at all. "Small towns have a habit of getting under your skin." She thought about explaining how she couldn't bring herself to leave the area where her parents and grandparents were buried, but feared she would come off sounding maudlin. "What about you?" Time to find out more about the man with the unusual amulet. "What kind of work do you do?"

"Before or now?" His tone carried a trace of bitterness; the edge seemed to surprise him. "Sorry. I guess I'm still adjusting to a career change." He paused and set his knife down to flex his right hand. The gesture looked absent, an automatic reflex he performed without thought. "My family owns an ad agency in Rhode Island. It's well-established and has a strong client base. I accepted the position of vice president two years ago."

She saw no reason for his bitterness. "That sounds great."

"Maybe." He plopped a pat of butter onto the potato. "It's not what I set out to do, but it's tolerable as an alternative."

"To?" She raised her brows and curled a few strands of angel hair pasta onto her fork.

"Music. I entered Juilliard at fifteen."

Shock coursed through her. "Oh, wow. That's amazing."

He shrugged, his mouth tightening slightly. "For a time. I started on the piano when I was two and by the time I was twenty, I was playing concert halls."

She couldn't help noticing the past tense or the rigid shift to his posture. "Was?"

His gaze flashed to her face. He waited a beat before lifting his scarred right hand. "You haven't asked about this."

She could have balked at his bluntness but chose to overlook the sting in his words. "It's none of my business."

"That's where you're wrong." He set his fork down. "You see, Sarah, according to my sister, my family is cursed. And this"—he raised his hand again—"is the result of that curse."

Uncertain how to respond, she grew abruptly conscious of their surroundings. It was early so the restaurant wasn't overly crowded, but many of the tables and booths were occupied. Families with children at the end of the workday, or friends gathering to discuss the upcoming week. Point Pleasant was known as an area where activities bordering on the supernatural took place, but how many people made family curses the topic of dinner conversation?

A comment he'd made earlier abruptly made sense. "That's why you want to know about Chief Cornstalk."

He nodded. "All I know is that he was murdered while he was a prisoner at Fort Randolph."

That much was true. "He didn't originally start out as a prisoner." In Point Pleasant, most everyone knew the tale. "Cornstalk was friendly with the settlers and a proponent of peace."

"I thought the Shawnee fought a battle here."

"They did, but that was earlier in 1774. We refer to it as Lord Dunmore's War. After that, Cornstalk signed a treaty and did everything in his power to uphold the peace. A few days before he was killed, he arrived at Fort Randolph to warn the soldiers the Indians were massing in preparation of a strike. He was supposed to be a guest of the fort, but they put him in the guardhouse, thinking if they had Cornstalk, they held leverage over his People."

"So the settlers actually broke the treaty by taking him hostage?"

"Yes, but they didn't see it that way. In their defense, they probably treated him well while he was detained, but there was no question he was a prisoner." She broke apart a piece of bread as she talked, flaky crumbs falling onto her plate. She whisked them aside with her fingertips. "After a few days when Cornstalk didn't return to his People, his son and another member of his tribe arrived at the fort. They were concerned for his welfare, but like Cornstalk, they were taken into custody and placed in the guardhouse."

"The Indians didn't attack?"

"No, but what happens next is where things get a little crazy." Sarah set the bread down. The meal was good but she was much more interested in sharing her knowledge. Talking about history, especially the history of the town where she'd grown up, had always been a favored subject from the time she was in junior high. Maybe it went back to that stormy night outside the TNT when she'd been found wandering with her mother's pendant in her hand. There were so many unexplained circumstances that had taken place in the small river town through the years. She couldn't help wondering if Cornstalk's death was the catalyst for everything that had befallen Point Pleasant since his passing.

"One of the soldiers was killed outside of the fort. The details are sketchy." She paused as the waitress arrived to ask if they needed anything else. They both declined, and Sarah took another bite of pasta. "No one knows what happened or who was killed, but somehow the man's death was blamed on the Indians."

Quentin finished the last of his steak. "Which probably didn't bode well for Cornstalk."

"Exactly. There was a riot in the fort and the soldiers rushed the guardhouse. Cornstalk, his son, and the other Indian were killed."

Quentin wiped his mouth with his napkin then set it aside. "And according to legend, as Cornstalk was dying, he cursed the town."

Sarah nodded. "Some people believe in the curse. We've had terrible floods through the years. Devastating catastrophes that claimed lives, and destroyed homes and businesses. There've been multiple times when the whole area was underwater. In 1913, the river crested over sixty-two feet. Most homes were only one story at the time, so it gives you an idea of the kind of devastation that took place."

"Yeah, I've heard the area was prone to flooding."

"That's just one occurrence. There were countless others, including a flood in 1937 that was predicted to be minor. Turns out it was one of our most historically damaging. Thankfully, the last major flood was in forty-eight." Her parents and grandparents had talked about those floods as though they occurred only yesterday. Sarah had listened wide-eyed to stories of townspeople maneuvering through the streets by boat, others climbing out on rooftops and ledges. Still others, fortunate enough to live in a home with an upper story, hauled furniture up to the second floor and watched the flood waters rise precariously close to their perch.

"The Army Corps of Engineers finally added flood walls around the city after countless appeals from Point Pleasant to the federal government for aid." She'd been an infant at the time, but couldn't imagine the relief the townspeople must have felt. "Now we have a lock and dam system to regulate the Ohio River."

Quentin nodded thoughtfully. He took a swig of the beer he'd ordered. "You haven't mentioned the Silver Bridge."

Sarah's gaze dropped to her plate. "Our greatest tragedy." The memory still stung sixteen years later. She hadn't lost anyone in the bridge collapse, but she'd witnessed the scars it left on others. Families and loved ones torn apart, the town battered like something that had been ripped open, then stitched haphazardly back together. It was never whole again, never the shining gem of river glory it had been before that cold December night in 1967. "I saw it go down."

Quentin jerked. "What?"

"My friend, Eve Parrish, and I were walking to the theater." It seemed an eternity ago, yet everything about that moment had been seared in her memory. From the brightly colored Christmas decorations on Main Street to the bite of cold evening air across her cheeks, and the pungent tang of exhaust from the string of cars waiting to cross the bridge. "We noticed the cars were backed up, none of them moving even when the light changed to green. I remember there were birds everywhere…a great flock of starlings in the sky, like they couldn't find a place to rest. We heard a loud boom and then the rocker panels on the bridge started to sway. It was terrible. People screaming. Crying. Running from cars. The whole bridge went down in less than sixty seconds."

"Did you…" Quentin cleared his throat, obviously uncomfortable.

"Lose anyone?" Sarah guessed where he was headed. "No. My parents died in a car accident a few years before the bridge fell."

He balked. "I'm sorry."

"It was a long time ago." She gave a halfhearted shrug, uncomfortable bringing it up. "My grandparents raised me, but they're gone now, too."

He stared at her as though unable to comprehend what she was saying. "You don't have other family? Brothers? Sisters? Aunts or uncles?"

She shook her head. It sounded pathetic when she looked at it like that. "I'm thinking about getting a cat." Her mouth twitched. A bit of humor to break the tension. Pasta never settled well with a depressing view of life.

Quentin grinned. "A black one would help ward off curses."

She chuckled. "I guess the whole concept sounds stupid. A dead Indian chief responsible for flooding and a bridge catastrophe." She hooked a strand of hair behind her ear. "But there were other things, too. After the Silver Bridge fell, Bruce Mechanical closed up and left town. They were the primary employer for the area, producing river boats and parts since the early nineteen hundreds. When they left, it put a lot of people out of work. In some ways, Point Pleasant never recovered from that damage. Pile economic ruin on top of a major calamity and there's limited room to bounce back."

"I noticed Main Street is pretty quiet." Quentin tilted his beer glass to glance inside. He swirled the amber liquid before downing the final swallow.

"The Silver Bridge funneled traffic through Main Street across Sixth to Gallipolis on the Ohio side of the river. Every business on Main benefited from that visibility. With the construction of the new memorial bridge outside of town, a lot of those same businesses have closed their doors and left."

"It does sound like a bleak picture."

Sarah nodded. She pushed her plate away then folded her arms on the top of the table. "You haven't asked about the Mothman."

"I figured you'd get around to telling me." He massaged the back of his right hand as if to ease a stitch of pain. "I've read up on it. How some people think it caused the collapse of the Silver Bridge, and others think it tried to warn the town of disaster. It haunts the TNT area and some believe it's here because of Cornstalk's curse."

"Hmm. You have done some reading. Did you know some people believe the TNT is the site of an old Indian burial ground?"

He cocked his head. "I've never heard that one before."

"It's supposed to be crisscrossed by ley lines. George Washington surveyed the area in 1770, and supposedly reported a number of odd findings. He wrote about strange lights hovering over the trees, bizarre sounds that echoed through the woods, and even reports of a creature he couldn't identify."

Quentin raised a brow. "The Mothman?"

Sarah wet her lips, conscious of how focused she'd grown on the conversation. The din of the restaurant faded into the background. Casual chatter from people discussing work or family, kids babbling about school projects, a waitress relaying the nightly specials to a group of newly seated patrons. All of it had become white noise. "The creature might have been here that long. I found a letter recently." She told him about the letter she'd discovered in Shawn Preech's belongings.

He honed in on that immediately. "Interesting that the letter mentions someone named Jonathan."

"I thought of that too, but it was a common name for the time. The odds of the Jonathan in the letter being the Jonathan you're looking for are pretty slim."

"But it's possible. I met Shawn Preech." From the tone of Quentin's voice, the meeting hadn't left him with a glowing impression of Point Pleasant's local celebrity. "I didn't realize his family went back that far."

"To the time of Fort Randolph, according to Shawn."

"So his ancestor might have been there when Cornstalk was killed."

Sarah admitted it was a possibility. "Obadiah Preech was definitely living at Fort Randolph at that time."

Quentin tugged his bottom lip between his thumb and forefinger. "You've shared a lot of information but haven't asked many questions."

She hadn't wanted to pry, giving him the space to volunteer what he wanted to share. "You mean about curses?"

He exhaled through his teeth. "Yeah. Something like that."

The waitress arrived and cleared their plates, giving Sarah a moment to collect her thoughts. A Ouija board had *maybe* predicted his arrival, he was interested in curses and Cornstalk, and he had an amulet with a stone that matched her own. Racking those quirks up to coincidence put too fine a stretch on things.

They both ordered coffee, with Quentin requesting a slice of chocolate cake on the side.

"Are you going to tell me why you're interested in Cornstalk's death?" Sarah asked after the waitress had left.

"Fair enough." He looked uncomfortable, but blundered ahead regardless. "I told you I have a sister."

She nodded. "Penelope."

"Right. She's pregnant and recently found out she's having twins." Sarah hedged. "That's a good thing, isn't it?"

"Yes. She and her husband are excited about becoming parents, but Pen can be, uh...flighty. She consulted a fortune-teller who told her one of the twins will carry a curse that's plagued my family for generations."

Sarah stared. She was used to hearing people in Point Pleasant discuss things like the Mothman, UFOs, and other oddities, but somehow having this articulate stranger—a man who'd studied at Juilliard—talk about twins and curses came across as hard to digest. "Um..."

The waitress reappeared with their coffees and Quentin's cake. Sarah smiled a thank you, then busied herself adding cream to the steaming mug. "What curse are you talking about?"

Quentin swallowed a forkful of the gooey dessert. He slid the plate toward her, motioning her to help herself, but she shook her head. "According to Madam Olga"—he made air quotes with his fingers—"an ancestor in the Marsh line was responsible for Cornstalk's murder. As a result, any twins born in the family are marked by Cornstalk's curse."

"Why twins?"

"I don't know. Madam Olga couldn't explain that."

Sarah swirled a spoon in her coffee. "Do you believe what she said? Do you believe in the curse?"

"I don't know." Quentin rubbed his temple. "I'm tempted to write Madam Olga off as a charlatan, but I can't deny there have been accidents though the years involving twins in the Marsh line. My great-grandfather died in a car crash. I have a cousin who lost an arm in Vietnam. And according to Pen, there were several early deaths back in the line."

"But some of those could be..." Sarah hesitated to use the word coincidence.

"Bad luck?" Quentin took a swig of coffee. "I didn't buy it myself at first, but then I thought about this." He raised his scarred right hand. "The proficiency I had as a pianist is shot. It doesn't matter how much physical therapy I do or how many hand exercises I employ, I'll never get that fluidity back."

Sarah bit her lip. "What about seeing a specialist?"

"I've been down that road. More than once." Quentin swallowed another forkful of cake. "My family tends to the affluent side, so I've paid for the best. A few tell me what they think I want to hear…years of PT and finger-work and maybe I'll regain a measure of the dexterity I had, but I'm pragmatic enough to recognize garbage when I hear it."

The bitterness in his voice was hard to mistake.

"It's my own stupid fault." He sat back, leaving the cake unfinished as if talking about his hand had killed his appetite. "A friend and I went lake fishing. We were loading his boat on the trailer when it slipped. I wasn't paying attention and my hand got caught, crushed under the hull.

"I'm not normally that careless." He shifted, ill at ease. "If not for what Pen unearthed, I'd be less likely to believe in curses."

As unfortunate as the tragedy was, it seemed a typical accident. "But your grandfather and cousin—"

"I know. It could all be coincidental, except Pen started poking around after her visit to Madam Olga. She was able to trace our genealogy back to the early nineteenth century and found several ancestors who died at young ages. All men, all twins. Freak stuff. One was struck and killed by lightning. Another died in an accident at a saw mill. Still another lived to be 101 but was born without feet. And then there's this." He set the amulet on the table. "I don't know much about it, only that my great-grandfather always had it with him. When he died, it was willed to me without explanation. I thought it was some useless trinket, then I show up here and you've got another like it."

Sarah fisted her hand around the pendent at her throat, squeezing briefly before letting go. "Did you ever have anyone examine the stone?"

"Not long after it was willed to me. I wanted to know more about it, so I took it to a jeweler. He couldn't identify the gem and told me it was probably costume jewelry."

"Did you believe him?"

"No. Especially not when he asked if I was interested in selling the amulet. He tried to act like he'd be doing me a favor, offering a few dollars, but I could see in his eyes it was worth a lot more." He leaned forward, elbows on the table. "Your turn. Where did you get your necklace?"

Sarah lowered her gaze. "It belonged to my mother. She was wearing it the night of the accident." The memory lingered in her mind, vivid as yesterday. "I was ten years old. We were coming back from visiting family who lived out of town. My dad took a shortcut through the TNT. The weather was bad, but he'd driven that way countless times. I was in the back seat, and didn't see what happened, but something made him jerk the wheel and swerve off the road. I don't know if it was a deer, or..." An unvoiced thought hung in her head. The same tremulous speculation that had lived there since the first sighting of a giant winged creature. She swallowed hard. "The Mothman. This would have been several years before he was sighted, but I know from the letter I found in Shawn Preech's stuff, the creature had to be around then."

"But you didn't see it?"

"No. I don't even remember what happened after my dad swerved off the road. All I remember is walking in the storm. A couple of teens were driving through the area and found me over a mile from where my parents' car went off the road. They said I was drenched and clutching my mother's pendant. I know it's silly, but I think of it as her way of watching over me. Sort of like a measure of protection."

"It's not silly. Did you ever have the necklace examined?"

"You mean by a jeweler?"

He nodded.

"No. The value didn't matter to me. I wanted it because of the connection to that night. To my parents. I can't explain it—"

"You don't have to." He reached across the table and covered her hand with his. "It seems we're both kind of at a dead end with this."

"Maybe. Maybe not." She drew a deep breath, uncertain if she was bold enough to venture the idea squirming awake in her mind. She'd never been to the oracle igloo in the TNT. In the past, she'd been too frightened, normally avoiding the entire area altogether. The old ammunitions site carried too many ugly memories of that night when she was ten. "I know a place we can go for information." She nodded, trying to convince herself she wasn't making a mistake. "I have to work tomorrow, but I'm free in the evening."

Quentin raised a brow. "To do what?"

"How would you like to visit the home of the Mothman?"

Chapter 5

"You understand my concern."

They were the first words Caden heard when he stepped into the Mason County Sheriff's office Tuesday afternoon. His brother, Ryan, had beat him to work and was camped out at his desk across from Caden's. The observation had been made by Reverend Frederick Clifford of the Good Fellowship Bible Church. Seated in a stiff wooden chair, Clifford was a folksy-looking man in his late sixties who most everyone knew simply as Pastor Fred. This morning, his face was etched with worry around the eyes and mouth.

"We'll check it out, Pastor," Ryan promised, scribbling a note on a piece of paper.

"It isn't just Will." Fred shook his head, his expression a cross of bloodhound-sad and doom-saying grim. "There's been a lot of tongue-wagging lately. I'm hearing rumors of bad tidings all around."

"Morning, Pastor Fred. Ryan." Caden nodded to each in turn, then tossed his hat onto his desk. Across the room, Wayne Rosling was busy on a phone call. Further back, a closed door indicated Sheriff Pete Weston was sequestered inside and didn't wish to be disturbed.

Caden scraped a hand through his hair, taming it in place. "What's going on?"

"Pastor Fred's worried about Will Hanley. Said he's been trying to raise him on the phone for two days and he hasn't answered."

Fred turned concerned brown eyes on Caden. "He was supposed to set up for a church picnic after services on Sunday, but never showed. I thought maybe he wasn't feeling well, so I took a drive by his place last night. Even knocked on the front door, but no one answered."

It wasn't like Will to duck a commitment, especially one that involved his church. Last October, the man had dragged himself out of bed with a 101-degree fever to oversee a charity race on the church's behalf. His wife had been the organist there for decades, right up until she passed away three years ago.

Caden frowned. "Was Will's truck there?"

"In the drive, plain as day." As he talked, Pastor Fred walked a wooden nickel between the fingers of his right hand. An absent habit, he often did it when delivering a sermon. As a kid listening to him preach, Caden had grown up wondering how many nickels the old man had.

"I didn't see Misty," Pastor Fred continued. "Not even a bark when I knocked, and she's always been an A1 watchdog."

Ryan glanced at Caden. "I said I'd take a drive out."

"I'll go with you."

Caden offered the reverend a reassuring grin. "It's probably nothing. Will might have left town unexpectedly and taken Misty with him. He could have gotten a lift from someone to the airport."

"I'd sure like to believe that, but I've never known him to shirk his church duties." Slipping the nickel into his pocket, Pastor Fred spoke gravely, "Too many bad things going on right now. Bertha Quiggly lost her best egg-layer to a fox the night before last, and something crept out of the woods near Nana's old place. Scared the daylights out of Sally Gander."

Mild alarm pinged through Caden. "Something?" He'd been waiting for mention of the Mothman ever since the creature had taken off from the woods.

Pastor Fred chewed the inside of his cheek. "Don't know exactly what it was. According to Sally, she only saw it from the side. Could have been the Mothman, but it was too dark to tell for certain."

"Could have been a person, too," Ryan commented quietly.

Pastor Fred continued like he hadn't heard. "Then there's poor Billy Sayer."

"What happened to Billy?" Caden wasn't sure he wanted to know.

"Heart attack while he was out mowing the grass. Fifty-one years old and now they've got to put a balloon in his chest to open up his arteries. I don't know." Pastor Fred shook his head. "I'm not one to hold truck with superstition, but it seems things have been brewing ever since that winged monster swooped out of the woods. I've got a bad feeling in my bones."

Caden hadn't heard about Billy. He didn't know everyone in Point Pleasant, but word had a way of getting around when something happened—just like it would get around that the Mothman was somehow at fault for

Billy's health problems and the ravenous fox that had taken out Bertha Quiggly's chicken. "We haven't seen the Mothman in months."

"That's not exactly true." Ryan looked almost guilty for having to correct him. "We had four reports this morning. Most of them off Windmill Road."

"Windmill?" Pastor Fred looked alarmed. "That's not far from where Will lives."

"Mothman sightings are typical around here, Pastor Fred. You know that." Caden tried to defuse the situation. "On any given day, we can have several."

"Doesn't matter. Seen or unseen, that monster's a plague on this town." Pastor Fred put a final epitaph to his opinions and stood. "I'd appreciate it if one of you would let me know about Will after you've had a chance to check things out."

Ryan stood too. "Will do." He extended his hand for Pastor Fred to shake. Caden did the same.

"Do you think the Mothman was on the prowl last night?" Ryan asked after the reverend left.

Caden's mouth tightened reflexively. His brother knew about his connection to the cryptid. Ryan had seen the thing himself, even had it probe his mind. "I don't know. But I sure hope Will Hanley dropping off the radar has nothing to do with the 'bird.'" The local name for the creature rolled off his tongue. Every time Mothman sightings exploded, hysteria followed. Anyone could see that cycle was headed for disaster.

* * * *

The Hanley farm was still when Caden and Ryan arrived. No movement of any kind. No cows in the field or sounds of distant machinery. A hush seemed to have settled over the place, the pop and crunch of gravel beneath Caden's shoes as he walked from the drive overly loud in the stillness. Morning sunlight beat down on the old farmhouse, illuminating the white siding and adding a cheerful touch to the Wedgewood blue shutters. Will's wife, Grace, might be gone, but her handiwork could still be seen in the colorful beds of phlox and Shasta daisies bordering the porch. A high-backed rocker moved slightly in the breeze and a crow cackled in the distance.

Ryan knocked on the screen door, waited a few seconds, then pulled it open and pounded on the interior door. Caden cupped his hands against the front window to peer inside, but could spy little other than an umbrella stand and small side table in the entryway.

Ryan shook his head. "Doesn't feel right to me."

Caden had the same feeling. "Let's check around back."

The rear yard was empty, the barn in the distance sealed tight. A persistent prick of warning alerted Caden something was wrong. For a working farm the place was too still.

"I'll check the house." Ryan sprinted toward the porch.

Caden nodded and headed for the barn. A ring of paw prints made by a large dog flattened the grass and dirt in front of the entrance. He hadn't seen Hanley's collie, Misty, but Pastor Fred said she hadn't barked when he'd knocked. The queer pattern of the prints formed a continual loop as if he dog had run in a circle, chasing her tail.

He tugged on the barn door.

"Caden." Ryan hailed him suddenly from the back porch. The screen door yawned open behind him.

"What is it?"

"You better get up here." His brother's face was grim. "Hanley's dead, and it's not pretty."

* * * *

Caden watched Milt Redmond, Mason County's coroner, zip a black body bag on the gurney. A tall, elegant-looking man with silver hair and a quiet manner of speaking, Redmond was a consummate professional. With a nod for the ambulance attendant to wheel the remains from the kitchen, he bowed his head to confer with Sheriff Weston.

In the background, Roy Baxter dusted for prints and combed for fibers. The clicking whir of a camera drifted through the back door as the county photographer worked outside, adding to his catalog of shots. He'd already finished with the interior. Lined up on the table, a series of evidence bags had been sorted and tagged, each containing some parcel of material evidence collected from the scene—including a bloodstained piece of paper.

Ryan had pointed the scrap out to Caden after he'd entered to find Hanley slumped on the floor. Flattened beneath Will's bloody fingers, the paper contained a single word: *Mothman.*

Redmond disappeared outside.

"I want a tight lid on this." Weston joined Caden. "No leaks to the press of any kind until we've got something concrete."

Ryan looked up from the pad he'd been scribbling on. "You mean other than the note from the victim?"

Caden grimaced. All they needed was for the local paper to proclaim Will had scrawled the name of Point Pleasant's notorious cryptid before drawing his final breath. "The Mothman didn't have anything to do with this." He sent his brother a sharp glance. Pete didn't know about Caden's bond to the creature but Ryan did. "If Hanley was attacked by the Mothman that would have happened outside. There'd be a blood trail from the yard."

"Yeah, I get that." Ryan clicked his pen. "What I don't get is why the note."

"We're not even sure Will wrote it." The paper seemed more likely a plant in Caden's opinion. "The killer could have done it."

"Why?"

"I don't know, but if Hanley wrote it, where's the pen he used?" Nothing added up. The crime scene itself was an enigma. Back door open, blood splatter on the wall but no bloody footprints, not even the cusp of a shoe. "It should have been with the note, especially if he was dying when he wrote the thing. I guarantee it was a knife that hacked Will up, not claws."

Weston tugged on his chin. "Could be a ritual killing." A big man with a burly frame, his presence filled the room with no-nonsense authority. "Hanley had money in his wallet, more tucked away in a dresser drawer, but it doesn't appear anything was taken. Robbery seems an unlikely motive, but the Mothman legend attracts plenty of fanatics and cultists. We can't dismiss the out-of-state element that comes to the TNT and flies under the radar."

"Yeah, but no sign of forced entry." Ryan slipped his notepad into his shirt pocket. "Will either knew his killer or invited them inside."

"Why from the back?" Caden glanced to the tape on the floor, outlining where they'd found Hanley's body. "The front door was locked, the back open. Pastor Fred said Hanley missed church and wasn't answering his phone or his front door."

Weston grunted acknowledgement. "It'll be a while until we have time of death. Let the crime scene boys finish and get some luminol in here. I agree the Mothman had nothing to do with Hanley's death. Otherwise, this place would look like the inside of a slaughterhouse." Hands on his hips, he swiveled his head, letting his gaze track across the room. "Someone cleaned up after themselves, but the luminol should bring up a footprint or two. Townsfolk are going to go apeshit when they hear about this. Start with the neighbors and see if they noticed anyone strange around the area…unknown vehicles, that sort of thing. And let's try to get a match on Hanley's handwriting."

Caden nodded. "I'll chat up a few of Will's friends, too. See if he was having problems with anyone. Pastor Fred might be able to shine some light on that."

"Yeah." Weston's expression was sober. "Damn shame, this. Will was a decent man. He didn't deserve to go this way."

"Sheriff! Sheriff Weston!"

The loud cry, followed by two rapid gunshots had all three men racing for the yard. Caden barreled past the crime scene photographer who was doing his best to squeeze into a corner of the porch. Camera clutched like a shield, he speared a finger in the direction of the barn. His face bore the blanched-white look of terror.

"There."

Caden's gaze swept past the photographer to Deputy Gardner. The young man was crouched in a firing stance, ten feet off the porch. Face upturned, his gaze was locked on a giant winged creature perched on the roof of the barn. Without pausing to consider his actions, Caden bolted down the steps and knocked Gardner's arm down as he pulled the trigger.

"What the hell are you doing?" Hyped on nerves and terror, Gardner gulped audibly when he realized who he as addressing. "Sergeant." Swallowing again, he rotated his head, seeming to realize as Caden did that the creature was gone. "I could have killed it."

"You would have only made it angry. More dangerous." The residual fear the Mothman hurled at the men in the yard needled like an abrasive edge. Caden had learned early horror was its chosen weapon. He saw the terror reflected in the eyes of the photographer and a crime scene tech who'd been searching for tire tracks. Mostly, he saw it etched in the tight lines of Gardner's face, the unsteady trembling of his hands.

"Shit." Weston appeared at his side. "The last thing I need is that freaking monster on a rampage. We're going to have to track it down."

"I'll do that. Ryan can handle questioning Will's neighbors." Caden cast a glance at his brother, who approached more slowly. "I can call in a couple more patrols if needed to scout the TNT."

Weston nodded grimly. "We're stretched thin. Do what you can." He looked around the yard at the men who shuffled uncertainly, coming down off a wave of red-veined fear. "Anyone see which direction it went?"

Some murmuring. Mostly shamed gazes darting the other way. Now that the danger had passed, the men were beginning to realize how timidly they'd behaved. Coming out of his crouch, the photographer tugged gruffly on his shirt and distanced himself from the corner he'd used as shelter. He quickly busied himself with lenses, filters, and settings. The techs went back to their various duties, none wanting to look at the others.

Gardner holstered his gun. "I'm sorry, Pete." He approached Weston with a forlorn shake of his head. "I should have had it with the first shot. I don't know why I didn't."

Caden decided not to mention the man's terror or that his hands had been shaking like a leaf in a windstorm. "I don't think a bullet would have killed it anyway." The Mothman had been shot at before. Rather than hurting the creature, the resulting injury had only served to enrage it. The Bradley brothers could attest to that debacle.

"Yeah." Pete offered up a somber nod for the somber setting. "Stay in touch and keep me posted. I'll make a call to Pastor Fred. Will's going to need clergy as well as a friend to handle things for him."

That was the sad, sick truth of the morning. Will Hanley was dead and a killer was loose in Point Pleasant.

* * * *

Quentin picked Sarah up after work. They grabbed a quick sandwich at the River Café then drove roughly six miles out of town to the area the locals dubbed the TNT.

"Tell me why we're going to this igloo again." As Quentin drove down the narrow road, dense thickets of trees sealing him in on either side, it was easy to see why the cryptid called the place home. A living thing could easily disappear in the rugged habitat and never be found. The remote area was the perfect dumping ground for a serial killer—or a creature that shunned human contact. "I get that the bunkers were used to store weapons during World War II, but what does that have to do with the Mothman?"

Sarah was silent for a moment. Fidgeting, she tucked a coppery curl behind her ear. "I don't want you to think I'm crazy."

The idea was laughable. "After I told you about Madam Olga and why I'm here, I'm hardly one to toss stones."

"Okay, but curses aside, this is a stretch." Craning her neck, she pointed to the right. "There…that opening. Pull in and we can walk the rest of the way."

Quentin did as directed, parking his Monte Carlo in a grassy area marked by a rusted swing arm post. Someone had spray-painted Beware the Mothman on the metal barrier in dripping white letters. "Fun sense of humor."

Snugged low to the ground, the barricade marked a path that jigsawed between the trees. Twelve feet back, the narrow trail became congested with weeds. He killed the ignition. "Good thing we wore jeans."

"It's not too far." Sarah opened the door and stepped outside.

It was a little after six in the evening, but a heavy cloud cover made it appear closer to twilight. A dry wind rocked the trees, twirling fat leaves belly upright. The air smelled of loam and wild honeysuckle.

Quentin scowled at the sky, catching a faint flicker of lightning in the distance.

Slipping his keys into his pocket, he rounded the car to join Sarah. "Weird weather since I've gotten in town, but I don't think it's going to storm."

"No." The quick glance she lobbed skyward was edgy. "I wouldn't be here if I thought that." She stepped over the post, then ducked to avoid a low-hanging branch.

Quentin followed. "I know you said the igloo was one of the places the Mothman was seen in sixty-six, but what does the Mothman have to do with Cornstalk?"

"Some people think the two are connected." Sarah waited while he caught up. "But we're not concerned about the Mothman right now."

"We're not?" That was good to know. There were far too many oddities in Point Pleasant—and apparently his family tree—to keep track. He swatted aside a buzzing insect and kept walking. Sarah seemed to know her way, zigzagging a path that avoided prickly sticker plants and a clump of something that may have been poison. It had been a while since he'd seen either.

"Something else lives in the igloo. Or at least it did." Sarah cast a hesitant glance in his direction as if knowing how odd the observation sounded. "People say if you go inside and ask a question, you might get an answer."

Quentin asked the obvious. "From what?"

"That's just it." Sarah ducked beneath another branch. "No one knows. A lot of people used to say it was the Mothman, but there were some strange things that went on here last fall that changed that. Now people believe it's an alien presence. My friends, Eve and Katie, even have a name for it. Um…" She favored him with another uncertain look. "I mean, him. He's an alien by the name of Indrid Cold."

Quentin absorbed the crazy declaration in silence, chewing the thought around in his head. He had driven through several states because of a family curse that may or may not exist, a strange amulet, and a dead Indian chief. Did he have the right to scoff at aliens and UFOs?

"You think I'm crazy." Sarah frowned when his silence continued. "That we're a town full of crazies."

"No. It's not that." He came to an abrupt halt, pushing Sarah to the side as something massive winged past. A low drone exploded in his head and the cold sweat of fear prickled his skin.

Sarah stifled a gasp and pulled him deeper into the trees. "Mothman," she choked.

Quentin chanced a glance at the sky, catching a glimpse of large leathery wings. A rush of air buffeted him. The droning grew louder, drilling painfully against his temples. He couldn't move, rooted to the spot as his mind reeled in chaos. A flash of images and emotions bombarded him.

Leaves matted on the ground, wet with rain and blood...the harsh rasp of breath in his ears...footsteps pounding against soft, wet soil...a scream, feral and alien, unlike anything he'd ever heard...the stench of death... unbearable agony as if something inside of him had been ripped away. Emptiness, desolation...

Quentin choked, reaching to steady himself against a tree. The thing was still there, somewhere above him. His sight was filled with the glow of red eyes. Luminous, large, and insectoid, they blotted everything else from his field of vision. Somewhere over the punishing drone in his head, he heard Sarah screaming. She tugged on his arm, but he was immobile, mesmerized by that malevolent stare.

The eyes wormed into his skull, the thunder of wings battering his ears. The drone rattled his teeth and sent splinters of pain into his neck. Still he couldn't move, those malignant eyes holding him in place. The tug on his arm became forceful.

"Quentin!" Sarah's scream was filled with terror. She choked on a sob. "Quentin, please!"

But there was no need to move. The thing had touched his mind, communicating in a whirl of chaotic thought and pulsing emotion. A combination that was both terrifying and exhilarating as he danced on the edge of an alien consciousness. He tilted his head back, opening his mind to the turbulent rush, knowing that somewhere in that frenetic muddle, there had to be order. A message.

The Mothman stretched a bony arm in his direction, claws extended. Sarah screamed.

* * * *

Caden took the cruiser from Will Hanley's place, Ryan saying he'd catch a ride with Weston when he was ready. There was still a lot of area canvasing to do and phone calls to make to Will's friends and associates, a job Caden had intentionally pushed off on Ryan. His brother was more than capable to handle the tasks without him. Radioing for two patrols, he directed one through town, the other into the TNT via Fairground Road. He took Potters Creek Road at the opposite end and was soon surrounded by trees.

Evening air carried the odors of lichen-covered bark and soft moss through the open windows of his car. Birds chattered from leafy branches and insects kept up a steady buzz in the background. Several miles into the old ammunitions site, he spied a maroon Monte Carlo off the shoulder. The plate on the back read Rhode Island.

Pulling in behind it, he came to a stop then killed the ignition.

Eve had told him Marsh was from Providence. Whether Quentin was a Mothman fanatic or simply out for a hike, Caden wanted him out of the TNT. At least for now. Between sightings of the cryptid, and the worry of having a murderer on the loose, the last thing he needed was a tourist who might get turned around in in an unfamiliar area and end up lost. Or worse yet, become another victim. He radioed the tag for an ID to be sure, and wasn't surprised when it came back registered to Marsh.

Leaving his cruiser parked behind the Chevy, Caden jogged into the woods. Within minutes, the busy jabbering of birds and insects fell silent, muffled by the trees. He slowed his pace, a trickle of sweat dripping down his neck in the dead air. Even the breeze had stopped, the humidity seeming to ratchet higher with each step he took. A few speckles of rain pattered the leaves overheard, but the clouds that had massed over Point Pleasant since yesterday remained swollen and full.

Caden threaded deeper into the woodland, the crunch of leaves and twigs beneath his shoes unnaturally loud. Somewhere in the distance, thunder rolled over the horizon. An inner sense of foreboding slithered awake, warning of danger. The air was too stagnant, the sluggish hush of the forest unnatural. Pausing, he stilled his breath to listen. Seconds passed, one quicksilver tick of time slipping into the next. Still nothing moved. Perspiration beaded in his bangs and gummed his shirt to his back.

Quentin had to be out here somewhere.

"Marsh." His voice traveled a short distance and was quickly swallowed by the lassitude of the trees. His hand strayed to the holstered revolver at his hip.

Something moved up ahead and the brand on his forearm flared with heat, all the signal he needed to break into a run. Like a claxon warning of imminent danger, a woman's shrill scream pierced the air. Gun in hand, he vaulted a fungus-riddled log and bolted in the direction of the sound. The sudden thunder of wings crashed over him.

A second later, he thrust through a tangle of red oak and beech and came to a wrenching halt. Twenty feet away, the Mothman hovered shy of the ground, wings spread wide. Caden barely registered Sarah Sherman's stricken face when she whirled in his direction. All he saw was a lethally clawed hand reaching for Quentin's throat.

There was no time to yell.

He pulled the trigger on the revolver and pumped two shots into the Mothman.

* * * *

Shawn sat in the driveway staring at his house. It was stupid to run. He'd taken food from Hanley's place, thinking he'd have to disappear, but no one knew what he'd done. He was a good old boy, the town's favorite sprint car driver. No one would believe him capable of murder. He could hang out as always, go to work, visit the River, maybe even pick up news on what they were saying about Hanley, poor bastard. Someone had to be a test sacrifice, and Will had made an easy mark.

You cannot stay here.

The voice in his head was starting to irritate him. He needed a shower and a change of clothes. And he needed to pick up all that shit littering the porch and lawn, papers from the box Suzanne had given to Sarah.

Thinking of his ex made his heartbeat quicken. He'd gotten off on slapping her around, but killing Hanley had left him with a queasy feeling when it was done.

You will get used to it.

He wasn't sure he wanted to. Part of him wished he could go back to the old Shawn. The one that spent his days racing and drinking, that didn't know the first thing about killing anyone.

It is too late for that.

Yeah, that was the hell of it. At the very least he was going to get cleaned up, wash the stink of blood off him, and track down the word in town. Maybe not today, maybe tomorrow. He'd call work and tell his boss he'd been sick, coming off a bad hangover. For a supervisor, Newt Brady was okay. He'd let him slide with that excuse before, probably because Brady had firsthand experience with the bottle. No sense in the pot calling the kettle black.

Dragging himself from the car, Shawn plodded for the house. Killing took a lot out of a guy. He was tired, his head hurt, and his stomach rumbled. After a shower, he'd throw a frozen pizza in the oven and guzzle a six-pack of beer. That might make him feel human again.

All that should concern you is finding the demon and completing the task.

The demon could wait. Shawn picked up the scattered papers and photos from his lawn, plopped them in the carton on the porch, then dragged the box inside. He thought about adding his knife to the collection but slipped it through his belt instead. It was part of him now, just like the voice in his head. The spirit had led him to Suzanne and Will Hanley, but the next killing would be one of his choosing.

You are the descendant of Obadiah Preech. You will do as I direct.

So it was Obadiah rattling around in his head. The old man he'd often bragged about, standing true at Fort Randolph against the Indians. Shit. He really did have a line that went back that far.

Shawn wound his way from the living room to the kitchen, then rooted through the refrigerator for a can of Budweiser. Popping the tab, he looked around the small room. Dishes crusted with food were stacked in the sink, and an ashtray overflowing with cigarette butts sat atop a week's worth of newspapers on the counter. Crumbs covered the breakfast table and the trash can in the corner hadn't been emptied in days.

He scratched his stomach. The place was starting to look shoddy now that he didn't have Suzanne to clean up after him, but what the hell. There were perks to living alone.

He guzzled most of the beer, then carried the can into the bedroom where he stripped off his soiled clothes. He grabbed the transistor radio from his dresser and carried it into the bathroom where he cranked the shower. Standing with a hand braced against the cool tile, he let the water wash the stink of blood down the drain. The moist heat bordered on orgasmic as it soaked into his abused muscles. Maybe it wasn't beating Suzanne or killing Hanley that had sucked the energy from him. His exhaustion could be the result of Obadiah hitching a ride in his head.

You will not think such things. I have waited a long time for my heir.

Heir.

He snorted. Like he was some kind of royal prince or something. Hell, why not? On the radio, Rick Springfield finished belting out "Jesse's Girl," giving way to news at the half hour. Shawn reached for the soap, then lathered it between his hands. He couldn't get many stations on the transistor, just a small local one that broadcast from an abandoned factory. Two volunteer DJs who were good at spinning hits and providing gossip with a bit of color. They did a fair job at keeping up with his sprint victories, but lately they'd taken to dissing his performances.

He dumped shampoo into his hair. Everyone was a fucking critic.

"Point Pleasant was rocked this afternoon by the murder of local resident, Will Hanley."

Shawn froze as the announcement crackled from the radio. He wiped soap from his eyes, thrust open the curtain, and stepped onto the floor, dripping wet. Leaning over the sink, he cranked the volume on the radio.

"Police aren't releasing details, other than to say homicide is suspected. Sixty-two, Hanley was a widower and local farmer who lived peacefully in his home off Butterman Road. More details will be released as they become available."

Shawn released a pent-up breath. Something akin to elation streaked through him. They'd found the body. That meant they'd start looking for evidence—fingerprints, signs of forced entry, blood splatter. He'd been careful to cover his tracks, and the fingerprints he'd left behind wouldn't matter. Obadiah had assured him they couldn't be traced.

A crazed giggle bubbled up from his throat. He was going to get away with it. There was nothing to tie him back to the crime.

Why did they not mention the demon?

The Mothman didn't matter.

It is all that matters!

Shawn lifted his head and looked in the mirror. The glass had fogged with steam from the shower. He used a palm to wipe it clear, catching a glimpse of his face. Eyes he didn't recognize stared back at him, but the reflection was his own—Shawn Preech, murderer. By tomorrow the town would be buzzing about Will's death.

He'd done it. Knifed the old man and given the town something to chatter about. Tomorrow, he'd stroll into the River and listen to what they were saying. Idiots like Duncan and Donnie Bradley discussing *his* handiwork without even knowing it. Hell, maybe he'd get up close and personal with one of them, show them what the point of a knife felt like. It might be fun to test the blade out again.

The Mothman wasn't the only one who needed killing.

* * * *

An inhuman knife-like cry ripped from the throat of the Mothman the second the bullets exploded from Caden's gun. The creature blasted him with outrage so intense that the emotional feedback forced him to one knee. The branded marks on his arm erupted in agony, set aflame by the cryptid's shock and fury.

He dropped the revolver and locked a hand over his forearm. With a final shriek, the Mothman exploded into the sky. Caden ducked his head against the tumultuous battering of its wings and grit his teeth. Within seconds, the cryptid became a distant speck swallowed by a heavy layer of clouds. If it had been angry before, it was incensed now. He'd kept Gardner from shooting it then turned around and pumped two bullets into its wing.

Idiot.

He pulled himself to his feet.

But the thing had been unpredictable lately, and he couldn't risk it harming Marsh. He hoped to hell none of the other patrols looking for the creature stumbled across it. As furious as it was, the Mothman would be out for blood.

"Caden, thank God you arrived when you did." Sarah's face was the color of bone. She appeared unharmed, her fingers wrapped around Quentin's arm in a trembling grip.

Retrieving his gun, Caden holstered the pistol and stepped closer. "You two okay?"

"Yeah." Clearly rattled, Quentin exhaled a ragged breath. "If I hadn't seen it...I've heard of the Mothman before, but never really believed...."

"I've grown up here and never seen it." Judging by her expression, Sarah still wasn't convinced of what she'd witnessed. She cast a glance over her shoulder as if expecting the thing to swoop down on them at any moment.

"Anyone hurt?" Caden looked between the two of them.

Both shook their heads. Marsh glanced toward the western horizon where the creature had disappeared. "I still don't understand what happened. I heard a buzzing sound. When it stopped, I was bombarded with thoughts and images I didn't recognize. Like something had crowded into my head."

"It projects emotion, normally fear." Caden's eyes narrowed. Images were new, contact he'd never experienced. Why would the creature broadcast random thoughts to Marsh? "What kind of images?"

"Glimpses of the past." The new voice made Caden pivot. He should have recognized the lilt immediately, the accent impossible to identify. The man who faced him was tall and slender with white-blond hair and coal-black eyes. For once, he wasn't dressed in his customary black, but wore crisp jeans and a white button-down shirt. Despite the casual clothing, he projected a refined air better suited to an earlier century.

Caden found his voice. "Lach."

"Who?" Quentin's tone indicated this wasn't the first time he'd encountered the blond-haired man.

"I'm afraid I did not properly introduce myself at the cemetery." Lach inclined his head toward Marsh. "My name is Lach Evening. You are Quentin Marsh." No handshakes were exchanged.

"How do you know that?" Still looking shaken, Sarah focused on Evening.

"Miss Sherman." Lach favored her with a glance. "It is a pleasure to see you again."

She flushed and dropped her gaze. "Thank you."

A typical feminine reaction where Lach was concerned. Old-world charm and neoclassical features had even made Eve stammer when she'd first met their alien friend. It had been nine months since Lach visited Point Pleasant, following the trail of Katie's ex, Lyle Mason. Caden had butted heads with the mysterious Man in Black, but given time, they'd developed a tenuous friendship.

"I assume you're here for a reason." Caden kept his voice neutral.

"Pleasantly to the point as always, Sergeant." Evening's lips curled slightly. "It is prudent I speak with you."

Given he had a murder on his hands and a patrol that might encounter a rampaging cryptid at any moment, Caden was tempted to brush off the request. But Evening was Indrid Cold's son. If anyone had an inside track on the Mothman or events in Point Pleasant, it was the centuries-old alien standing before him. What a rush it must be to have lived eons and not look older than thirty.

"What about the Mothman?" Sarah glanced between the two of them.

"It is best you do not speak of the encounter." Warning underscored Lach's precisely modulated words. "Reports of the cryptid will only serve to escalate trouble that could otherwise be avoided."

"People have a right to know it's out here," Quentin said.

Sarah nodded her agreement. "If Caden hadn't shot it, it would have hurt Quentin."

"You don't know that." Caden shifted. Lightning flickered in the distance, inciting a blast of dry wind. A low murmur of thunder chased the gust through the grass. "Lach is right." He hoped Sarah would see where he was coming from even if Quentin didn't. "We've already had some earlier upset today that's taxing our resources. The last thing I need is a panic. For the good of Point Pleasant, I'm asking you to keep this encounter to yourselves."

Sarah fidgeted, casting an anxious glance skyward. Caden recalled her dislike of storms.

"What kind of upset?" She honed in on what he hadn't said.

"You'll hear about it soon enough." He narrowed his eyes. "What were you two doing out here anyway?"

Sarah shot Quentin a tense look.

He spoke before she could answer. A little too quickly for truth. "I asked Sarah to show me the TNT."

If they wanted to keep secrets, fine, as long as they maintained the same level of secrecy when it came to the Mothman.

"We should head back now." Sarah appeared eager to be on her way. She sent another nervous glance to the sky as lightning flickered behind the clouds.

If there was a storm it lingered somewhere far off in the distance.

"That's a good idea." Caden didn't expect the Mothman to return, but if the creature had abruptly turned rogue hunter, he wanted Sarah and Quentin out of the fallout zone. He waited until they'd disappeared between the trees, headed in the direction of their car, before shifting his attention to Evening.

"All right, Lach. Why are you here?"

"Not the warmest greeting I have received."

"And likely not the worst either."

"Fair enough." Evening accepted the repartee. "Are you going to radio your sheriff about the creature?"

"You know better than that." Caden turned, taking a hard look around the area. The path Quentin and Sarah had been following led to the igloo Evening's father frequented. Given what he knew from Eve, Sarah tended to avoid the TNT. Her parents had been killed on Potters Creek Road when she was a child and she'd grown to hate the place. So why had she been taking Marsh to the igloo?

Caden's gaze skewed back to Evening. "I promised your father I'd try to communicate with the creature. Protect it."

Evening said nothing.

A rush of breath burst from Caden's lips. "I shot it. I put two bullets into its wing."

A promise broken. To Cold and to the creature. It had saved his life three times in the past. Was it any wonder it had shrieked in betrayal when he pulled the trigger? Grimacing, he rubbed the welts branded on his arm, the skin raised and rough beneath his fingertips. "I thought it was going to kill Marsh."

"Not kill, but there is no question he is part of the situation." Evening played the oddly shaped fingers of one hand over the back of the other.

"Part of what situation?"

"I have yet to assemble all the pieces. Something...dark...has awakened in Point Pleasant."

"Dark?" A sliver of impatience prodded Caden's nerves. Evening often spoke in an antiquated manner, but in this case, his word choice was too ambiguous for Caden. "What does 'dark' mean?"

"A collision of old forces is gathering." Evening stepped closer, his light tread barely disturbing the twigs beneath his shoes. "I recommend you keep an eye on Mr. Marsh. For your own safety and the safety of your town."

Caden disliked riddles. "What does Marsh have to do with Point Pleasant?"

"Time will tell." Evening kept his opinions to himself. "I also strongly suggest you monitor anyone descended from a settler named Obadiah Preech."

"Preech?" Caden balked, his mind spinning to Shawn. How many times had he heard the dirt track driver boast about his ancestor Obadiah, defender of Fort Randolph? If he were to believe Shawn, Obadiah had almost single-handedly won Lord Dunmore's War.

Evening studied him closely. "Do you know such a man?"

"Sure. Shawn Preech. He's a minor celebrity around here."

Unimpressed, Evening waved the comment aside. "Has Mr. Preech behaved differently recently?"

Caden frowned. Preech was a drinker, more likely to fly off the handle since he was going through a divorce, but he'd never been particularly stable to begin with. Caden had responded to more than one shouting match between Shawn and Suzanne, including an ugly fiasco where Suzanne had taken a baseball bat to Shawn's car. "He's a drinker with a short fuse."

"That is not what I mean, Sergeant."

"I'll keep it in mind." Deciding he wasn't going to get anywhere with Evening, Caden switched subjects. "How'd you find me out here anyway?"

A slender brow arched into Evening's hair. "I thought you understood I am not without skills."

"Yeah." Flicker phenomena, mental manipulation, even a strange restorative healing power were all part of Evening's cache of hidden abilities. Caden doubted those talents even tapped the surface, but the less he knew, the better. "Fair enough. Just tell me this—should I be concerned about the Mothman?"

Something unreadable flashed across Lach's face. "Most definitely."

* * * *

Quentin eased his car into a parking spot at the Parrish Hotel, noting how the towering structure loomed over the street. Easy to spot from a distance, it was a dinosaur of monolithic proportions dwarfing smaller buildings within its shadow. He'd felt a similar insignificance when trapped by the crimson eyes of the Mothman. As if the creature swallowed every paltry speck of life around it, devouring anything in its vicinity.

He'd said little on the drive back to town, the same with Sarah. Each had remained hunkered in their thoughts, neither wanting to express the turbulence of disbelief twined with fear. They'd gone in search of an alien but clashed with a monster instead.

Leaves matted on the ground, wet with rain and blood...footsteps pounding against soft, wet soil...unbearable agony...emptiness, desolation...

He didn't understand what any of it meant. A part of him still struggled to believe the encounter had taken place and wasn't a warped hallucination dredged from his subconscious.

Deflating in his seat, he switched off the ignition. He'd come to Point Pleasant to solve the riddle of a curse but found himself confronted by greater puzzles.

Sarah shifted beside him, angling her back to the passenger's door. "Why didn't you tell Caden we were headed to the igloo?" Her voice was measured and quiet, as if she'd been toying with the question for some time.

"I don't know." Outside, a sliver of dying light speared between storm-gray clouds as the sun slipped low on the horizon. Sticky heat spooled into the cooler shroud of dusk. A bronze sheen flared from the hotel's westward facing windows. "I had the feeling your friend wasn't being one hundred percent honest, so I didn't see any reason to be honest in return." Or maybe he was used to keeping his business to himself. If the town of Point Pleasant didn't need to know he was chasing down the origins of a curse for his pregnant sister, then neither did a Mason County sheriff's sergeant. Exhaling, he rubbed his eyes. "I'm still grappling with the whole concept of coming face to face with the Mothman."

Sarah shivered, wrapping her arms around her body. "It could have killed you."

He wasn't so sure. It wasn't fear he'd felt when he'd looked up into those glowing eyes. The creature had no head, just an unnerving nothingness where its face should be. That was the strangest aspect of all. He'd latched onto the thing's enormous insectoid eyes and all else had been blotted from his field of vision.

"It didn't feel like I was in danger—more like it was trying to show me something."

Emptiness. Desolation. The awakening of an old and vengeful evil.

The communication had been muddled, framed by an alien mind, but there'd been a heightened sense of urgency in that bombardment of images and emotion.

"Caden was right to shoot it." Sarah's response was rigid, tainted by fear. She seemed to shrink in on herself, her eyes overly large. The play of shadows under her lashes blotted her skin with smudges of ash.

It was inconsiderate of him to overlook how the encounter had affected her. Taking her hand, he rubbed his thumb across the back of her knuckles. "I'm sorry I got you involved in this."

She startled slightly at his touch, blooms of color appearing on either cheek. "It was my idea to go to the TNT. It's just a lot to absorb. I've heard about the Mothman my entire life, but part of me always believed it was a myth. Around here we take it for granted, but I think most people consider the creature a campfire tale to scare kids."

"Let's forget about it for now." In a few hours or even tomorrow, he'd be better equipped to examine what had taken place.

Turning his attention to the sky, Quentin focused on a string of dark clouds huddled to the east. The weather had been unstable from the moment he'd arrived. If it wasn't raining, then thunder, wind, and lightning played havoc with the air, spawning one dry squall after another. He'd never seen such a freaky climate.

"Looks like another storm is coming." At least the hotel had a great vantage point to watch the show. It would be even better with a beer, or maybe Sarah would like to split a bottle of wine. He was getting used to her company and hated to see her drive off when she was unsettled. "Want to sit on the front porch and watch it roll in?"

"No!" Sarah pulled back sharply, wrenching her hand from his. "I mean, I..." Hastily, she pushed the hair from her face in a movement designed to cover embarrassment. "I'm sorry. I don't like storms."

He sobered, recalling something she'd said about her past. "That was stupid of me. I just remembered your parents died during a bad storm." No wonder she didn't like them.

Expression softening, she nodded. With a glance through the window at the bruised sky, she spoke quietly. "Run from the thunder, run from the rain. Lightning can't hurt you, the wind is in vain." Her hand strayed to the pendant at her throat and her mouth relaxed in a smile. "I've always had a fear of storms, even before my parents died. My mother used to whisper that verse to me whenever I was afraid. I guess it's silly."

"No, it's not." He brushed the hair from her shoulder. "You just saw something terrifying, an encounter that would naturally compound your fear of storms. Why don't you come inside for a while? You can visit with Katie or Eve until the weather blows through."

She exhaled what appeared to be a grateful breath. "Thanks, but no. I should go home before it gets much later."

"I could follow you." He didn't like the idea of her driving alone after everything that had happened. "Make sure you get home safely."

She reached for the door handle. "I'll be fine." Hesitating, she turned back to him. "I'm not going to tell anyone what happened today...about the Mothman. And I don't think I'm brave enough to go back to the igloo. Not now. I want you to find the information you came for, but not at the cost of your life."

He might have joked about her concern if she hadn't looked so serious.

He settled for a slight smile. "Don't worry about me. There's nothing in Point Pleasant or the TNT that's going to hurt me."

Discounting the curse.

Chapter 6

Caden was summoned to Weston's office first thing Wednesday morning. He had time to grab a cup of coffee and mutter hello to Ryan before the two of them trooped inside and shut the door. Caden took a seat in front of the sheriff's desk while Ryan hovered by the side window, a shoulder braced against the wall.

Weston grunted a greeting then immediately got down to business. Leaning back in his chair, he plucked a folder from his desk and scanned the contents. "Baxter lifted a number of latent fingerprints from Hanley's kitchen. He's running them for matches now."

"What about bloody prints?" Settling in for a debriefing, Caden hooked his ankle over his knee. An experienced tech, Roy would be thorough.

"Several fingerprints, plenty of footprints."

"So, someone tried to clean up after themselves?"

"Sloppily. Luminol picked up places that had been swabbed." Weston scratched his chin, reading from a folder in his left hand. "Redmond lists the cause of death as massive organ and soft tissue damage due to multiple stab wounds of the upper and lower thorax. From the size and angle of the wounds, he's estimating a four- to five-inch blade."

"Half the county carries a hunting knife that size," Caden said.

"Noted, but it gets interesting after that. Redmond said the guy used a trailing point knife." Weston tossed a drawing on his desk. Redmond had sketched it on a plain white sheet of paper, a rough illustration of a knife with a slightly curved belly and longer tip. "The point of the blade trails higher than the spine." Pete ran his finger over the tip to indicate what he meant. "There's also a swage, a false edge at the tip that can be sharpened. Put together, those elements make the high point structurally weaker."

"Is there a reason for the lesson in knife construction?" Ryan asked.

Weston flecked him a sour glance. "Somewhere, at some point, the tip was notched."

"You mean like a piece broke off?"

"Could be. Or it could be a defect. Either way, Redmond doesn't think it's enough to be noticeable. It impacted the edge of the cuts, but there's no indication to suggest the blade fractured during the assault."

"So we're looking for a four- to five-inch blade with a notched trailing tip."

"More or less." Weston tossed the folder on his desk. "Heinous butchery. The whole thing makes me sick."

Caden cupped his coffee mug in his hands. "What about defensive wounds?"

"Minor. It looks like Will must have been caught by surprise and didn't have a chance to fight back."

"Another indication he probably knew his attacker." Caden scrubbed a hand over his jaw. The idea that someone in Point Pleasant was a murderer was harder to swallow than imagining a stranger guilty of the crime. If that was the case, someone in town had to know something. "What did Pastor Fred have to say?"

"The poor guy's broken up. I guess he and Will had gotten pretty tight since Grace died." Weston chewed his bottom lip. He looked every one of his sixty-three years. "Said he can't imagine anyone holding a grudge against Will."

"That's pretty much what I got from the neighbors, too." Ryan shifted, turning his back to the window. "By the way, Misty turned up at Ed Shumer's place, not a mark on her. According to Ed she was scared shitless. Said he found her hiding under his porch yesterday morning and had to coax her out. He was headed over to check on Will when I showed up."

"Did he see anything?" Caden asked. "Hear anything?"

Ryan shook his head. "Nothing that stands out. No odd vehicles or strangers. He remembers seeing Shawn Preech's Charger out that way Sunday morning, but no other traffic that he can recount."

"Preech." Caden narrowed his eyes. "What was he doing?"

"Shumer didn't say. He only remembers Shawn driving by because he walked out to get his paper. Said he waved, but Shawn didn't wave back. Shumer said he seemed focused on heading somewhere."

Dropping his foot to the floor, Caden sat forward in his chair. "Maybe we should have a talk with him."

"Preech?" Ryan rolled his eyes. "Caden, get real. The guy's a prick but he's no killer."

"But he might have seen someone who is. Especially if he was out that way Sunday morning."

"Good point." Weston liked the idea. "Look into it and let me know what you turn up."

"What about the press?" Ryan asked.

Weston gave a snort of derision. "Word leaked yesterday. It's no longer a matter of keeping it under wraps, but keeping it calm. Thank hell and high water no one knows about the Mothman note. I don't need people worrying about a killer and the bloody bird." He pivoted in his chair to face Caden directly. "Did you see it yesterday?"

Caden shook his head, quickly covering the lie by downing a mouthful of coffee. If Weston knew the thing had been within inches of attacking a tourist, he'd go ballistic. Even more if he knew Caden had shot it and let it get away.

Ryan watched him with narrow eyes, but Caden ignored the scrutiny. There'd be time for dissection later.

"If that's all, Pete, Ryan and I will head to Shawn's place."

"Do that." Weston picked up the phone, dismissing them as he punched out a number on the keypad. "I want this wrapped by the end of the week. Got that?"

"Yeah." Caden looked at Ryan. They both knew the odds of that happening were thin.

* * * *

"You did see the creature, didn't you?" Ryan lobbed the accusation as soon as they were in the parking lot. "Why didn't you tell Weston?"

Caden never slowed his pace toward the cruiser. "I never said I saw it."

"Yeah, and you forget I grew up with you, brother. I can read you like a book." He paused with his fingers wrapped around the door handle. "Are you going to tell me what happened?"

In the long run, Caden didn't see that he had much of a choice. Ryan was almost as deeply involved as he was when it came down to Point Pleasant's notorious cryptid. He relayed the tale on the drive to Shawn's place, covering everything from discovering Quentin and Sarah in the woods, to shooting the creature, and the sketchy details Evening had shared.

"What a mess," Ryan commented when he was through. "Did you tell Eve you shot the thing?"

Caden nodded. Palming the wheel, he veered toward Shawn's place. "I don't want secrets in our marriage, and she's bound to find out eventually. Especially with Evening in town."

"Is he staying at the hotel?"

"He wasn't as of last night, but the guy isn't exactly normal."

"Yeah." Ryan flipped the sun visor down. "I better warn Katie, too. I know Lyle's out of the picture, but if she bumps into Evening, it's liable to resurrect all that garbage from last fall."

"How's the adoption process going?" Caden decided to change the subject.

"On schedule." Ryan broke into a sloppy grin. "It's weird to think I'm going to be a dad before you are."

"Sam's a good kid."

"I can't believe how lucky I am to have him and Katie both."

"Three more months and you'll be married." Caden was looking forward to taking his turn as best man, as Ryan had done for him when he married Eve. His brother and Katie had picked October tenth for their wedding date, planning a small ceremony with a similar-sized reception at the hotel. Dwelling on something pleasant was a welcome relief after listening to Weston recite the grisly details of Will's death.

Ten minutes later Caden pulled into Shawn's driveway, parking behind Preech's Charger. Finding the car there on a weekday likely meant he was home from work and just as likely hung over from another night of drinking.

"Let's hope we catch him in a decent mood," Ryan commented as they headed up the front walk.

Caden knocked on the door then took a moment to glance around. Had Suzanne still been living there, the porch would have been decorated with glazed pottery and baskets of flowers. Now the only accessory was a lounge chair, folded up and shoved to the side. The sight reminded Caden of Shawn's life, a string of highs that had steadily nose-dived. If the guy laid off the booze, he could still regain the celebrity recognition he seemed to crave.

He knocked again, patiently counting seconds until the door was wrenched open. Shawn hovered on the threshold, his expression snagged somewhere between shock and terror. It wasn't every day two sergeants in full uniform appeared on the doorstep.

"Caden. Ryan." His expression settled into one of curiosity. "What are you doing here?"

"Can we come in?" Ryan spoke for both of them.

"Um...sure thing." Rifling a hand through his hair, Shawn stepped back to allow them inside.

Caden did a quick visual sweep of the room. The place smelled of pizza, beer, and cigarettes. A crumpled bag of chips along with a bag of Doritos and a can of peanuts sat on the coffee table. The TV broadcast *The Price is Right*, but the volume was muted. Newspapers were strewn on the floor by the couch, and an old transistor radio sat propped on an end table. "We weren't sure if we'd catch you here. Thought maybe you'd be at work."

He measured Shawn's reaction, noting a tremor in his hands that might have been caused by a hangover or something worse. There were scratches on his face that looked to be a few days old.

"I haven't been in for a few days." Shawn traipsed to the couch and sprawled in the corner. "Stomach bug or something."

Now that he thought about it, Shawn had been missing from his regular spot at the River. At least Eve hadn't mentioned that he'd been there. "Sorry to hear that." He took a leisurely stroll around the room, soaking up the surroundings, conscious that Shawn's gaze tracked his every movement. "I guess it didn't last long."

Shawn blinked stupidly. "Huh?"

"The stomach bug." Caden pointed to the junk food on the table. "Interesting cure you've got there."

"Oh." More blinking. "Yeah…well…I got to feeling better."

"How were you feeling on Sunday?" Ryan asked.

Shawn swiveled his head around like a turtle. "Sunday?"

"We came by to ask you about Will Hanley." Ryan hooked his thumbs over the top of his belt. "Not sure if you heard, but Will's dead."

Shawn licked his lips but didn't say anything.

Caden dropped into a seat across from him. "Looks like someone knifed him."

"Bad way to go." Shawn's eyes were bloodshot. He wiped his hands on his jeans. "Poor Will."

Caden let him digest the idea for a few minutes. "We heard you were out that way on Sunday morning and thought you might have seen something. From what we can tell, Hanley was killed somewhere between eight and noon."

"Yeah." Shawn tugged at his chin. "I was out that way, I guess."

"Any specific reason?"

"Mostly blowin' off steam. I was ticked about Saturday night."

"Saturday night?"

"You remember—Duncan and Donnie dragging me out of the River like I needed babysitting. I woke up miffed and took a drive to clear my head." Shawn bounced a knee up and down, the heel of his sneaker pitter-pattering against the floor. "Is there a reason you're asking me all this stuff?"

"We hoped you might have seen someone around Hanley's place." Ryan moved in front of the TV, blocking the view of contestants eagerly debating the price of a Hoover vacuum. "Maybe you passed a strange car on the road."

"Sorry."

"Well, if you think of anything, give us a call." Caden stood.

"I'll do that." Shawn stood too, managing to look helpful and remorseful at the same time. "Damn shame about Will."

"Sure is." Ryan stepped closer. "By the way, what happened to your face?"

"My face?"

"Yeah." Ryan pointed. "Those scratches."

"Oh, uh…" Shawn fingered the gashes. "I, uh, took a tumble in the bushes after Duncan and Donnie dropped me off. Guess I was messed up more than I thought." He offered a sheepish grin.

"Guess so." Caden opened the door. "Take it easy, Shawn."

Once in the car, he started the ignition and backed out of the driveway. After a few seconds of silence, he cast his brother a sideways glance. "What do you think?"

Ryan shrugged. "I think if he did see something, he wouldn't have remembered anyway."

"Do you believe him about the scratches?"

"Why not? You're the one who said he was drunk that night."

"Yeah, but he seemed nervous. Did you notice how he was sweating?"

"He could be drying out from another binge." Ryan frowned. "Although I'm not sure I buy the stomach bug story."

"He hasn't been at the River. At least not that I've heard."

"Doesn't mean he couldn't tie one on at home."

Caden considered as a string of trees and houses funneled past. The morning was gray, the sky overcast and threatening rain again. He wished the damn storm would break, a cleansing cloudburst to wash away the ugly dirt of the last few days. "He didn't have much of a reaction when we told him Will was dead."

"I noticed that too," Ryan agreed. "But he probably already knew. He had a newspaper and a radio. The guy looked plain hung over to me."

Shawn had the classic signs. Jittery, bloodshot eyes, yet Caden wasn't convinced. Maybe he wouldn't have thought twice if not for Lach Evening and the mention of Obadiah Preech. His alien friend had his mind spinning in several directions, most of which he didn't want to contemplate.

And damn, if his gut didn't back up that intuition.

* * * *

Shawn waited until he heard the car back out of the drive before moving to the window to peer outside. Sweat soaked the back of his neck and his heart triple-timed with each jagged inhale of breath. Someone had seen him driving near Will's place. His own stupid fault for not being more attentive. Now he had to deal with the Flynn brothers sniffing around, asking questions that made him nervous.

He gnawed on a thumbnail. Did they suspect him or had they really hoped he could help finger Will's killer? Maybe they'd questioned other people too.

Yeah, that was it. Had to be. Murder in a small town shook people to the bones. The mayor, town council, especially the sheriff—they were all probably shitting their pants, rushing to assure the populace they didn't have a sick, sadistic killer on the loose.

But the Flynn boys hadn't mentioned the Mothman.

They do not believe the creature killed him. You should have done better.

Bullshit to that. He was the one who'd been in Hanley's kitchen, hacking away with a black knife. Just because Caden and Ryan didn't mention the damn bird didn't mean other people weren't talking about it.

Turning from the window, Shawn let the curtain fall shut. Time to pull his act together. He'd go to the River tonight. Poke around and see what people were saying, maybe even toss around the word Mothman if no one else did. It was amazing the thoughts you could plant with a little effort.

But first he needed to eat again. Hosting a dead ancestor in his body had given him the appetite from hell.

* * * *

It was shortly after noon when Eve hurried from the café into the hotel lobby, drawn by the sound of the front door. Katie had the afternoon off and Eve's part-time clerk, Sharon, wouldn't arrive until two. The River was exceptionally busy with friends gathering over lunch to mourn Will Hanley and share hushed fears about a killer stalking their streets. She'd popped in to make sure everything was running smoothly, fully aware the nighttime crowd would probably be twice as large.

Rounding the corner into the lobby, Eve drew up short. A breath of surprise whistled between her teeth at the sight of the man who waited by the check-in counter.

"Mr. Evening." Caden had told her he was in town, but he looked so different from the last time she'd seen him, dressed casually rather than wearing his customary tailored black suit.

He offered her a smile. "It is good to see you, Mrs. Flynn."

"Eve," she corrected.

"Then you must call me Lach." A single suitcase rested at his feet.

She loved listening to him speak, his words flavored with a strange and unidentifiable accent. "Gladly." She stepped behind the registration desk. "Are you in need of a room?"

"Yes." He folded his hands on the wooden counter. "Although I am uncertain how long I will be staying."

"I'm sure we can accommodate you." Registrations were down, leaving several openings.

"If possible, I prefer a room that faces the street."

"Of course." Probably so he could monitor the activity outside. Talking to Lach, it was easy to forget he was an extraterrestrial being.

At least until he signed the guest register, displaying his fan-topped fingers.

"I suppose your husband told you why I am here." Setting the pen down, he measured her with onyx black eyes.

Nodding, Eve passed him a key. She hadn't wanted to think about the collision of forces Evening said was brewing in Point Pleasant. The ominous warning made her think of curses and long-ago tragedies. Uneasy, she wet her lips. "Do you really think our town is cursed?"

"Curses are often what we make of them." Lach tucked the key into his pocket. "When you believe in something, it is far easier for that force to become powerful." His gaze traveled across the lobby, up the broad staircase to the second floor. "This hotel has withstood the testament of time. Even curses."

"Not without tragedy."

"You're referring to the death of your great-grandparents and your grandparents?"

She nodded, no longer questioning how he knew matters of the past. Experience had taught her he was just as versed in events of the future.

"Would it bring any measure of comfort if I told you their deaths were not the result of a curse? The fire was caused by a hidden short within the walls of a third-floor room. The wiring was old."

"How do you know that?" He was the son of Indrid Cold, the oracle-like being in the TNT that had led her and Katie to the remains of Katie's missing sister. If Cold could do that, then his son would surely have the same capacity to see past events. "Never mind." She shook her head, realizing the folly of asking. "It's not important that you know, only that you do. Thank you for telling me. Many people are focused on curses right now, especially after what happened to Will Hanley."

"I was sorry to hear about Mr. Hanley's demise." Lach picked up his suitcase. "I fear your husband and his brother will have their hands full

in the coming days. Curses are often found where we least expect them."
He nodded to her politely. "Good afternoon, Eve."

She frowned as she walked up the steps. The last time he'd visited Point
Pleasant the town had been plagued by multiple troubles, the same as now.
Coincidence?

Who was to say he wasn't part of the curse? If unknown forces were
destined to collide, Lach Evening would surely be at the center of that
supernatural clash.

* * * *

The River was packed when Shawn walked through the front door.
He'd lost track of time but guessed it was somewhere after eight in the
evening. Outside, wind chased thunder from the sky. The weather had
been weird as shit lately but tonight's spectacle took the cake. Lightning
trailed him into town, thunder rolling over the rooftops with a sound like
hollow bones. Not a single speck of rain had landed on his windshield, the
street dirt-covered and drought dry. Inside the café, a group of old-timers
reminisced about storms and flooding.

Ignoring them, Shawn elbowed into a corner at the bar. He flagged
Tucker down, then rattled off an order for a Budweiser, bacon cheeseburger,
cheddar fries, and a basket of wings. Just thinking about the feast made his
stomach growl. Tucker slid him the draft, then left to fill the food order.

Shawn sucked the head off the beer, turning to eye the crowd. The place
was packed tonight, every table filled. People spoke in hushed groups, a
few others gossiping chatty and loud. He spied several familiar faces and
debated about wandering over. Beside him, a heavyset guy sat with his
back turned. Shawn had seen him around a few times, and thought his
name was Mitch or Mike. Fidgeting, he gulped a draft of beer. Someone
had to be talking about Hanley.

Do not appear eager.

The only thing he was eager for was food. Hunger dug a hole in his gut.
He polished off his draft and signaled Tucker for another.

The bartender frowned as he set the fresh ale in front of him. "No
problems tonight. Huh, Shawn?"

The bastard. Like he was going to have to flag him or something. Another
candidate for the pointy end of his knife. He forced a grin. "No problems,
Tucker." He'd strapped the knife to his right leg underneath his jeans.
The weight of the weapon bolstered his confidence. Now that Hanley's
death was several days behind him, he'd started to look at it differently.
Small details came back at the oddest moments—the wet sucking sound
the blade made when he'd ripped it from Hanley's flesh; the way the old

man's mouth had twisted, elongating his chin like that freaky painting *The Scream*. Daisy-yellow wallpaper dripping with blood, the bounce and clatter of the phone when Will dropped the handset, the cuckoo clock above the table chirping the hour.

"Crowded tonight," Shawn said to Tucker. He got a nod for his troubles.

"Guess you heard about Will Hanley." Tucker wiped a rag across the bar.

"Yeah. Bad doings." Shawn kept his voice suitably low key. "I heard someone say the Mothman did it."

"What?" The heavyset guy swiveled on his stool and eyed Shawn from beneath stodgy black brows. "Hanley was killed in his house. That's what I heard."

Mitch. Shawn was pretty sure the guy's name was Mitch. Bracing his elbows on the bar, he shrugged. "Could of ran in from outside. I don't know. It just don't sit right otherwise. Who'd kill a decent guy like Will?"

"Couldn't be robbery. Nothing taken." The guy on Mitch's left slid off his stool and joined them. He kept his hand clutched around a bottle of Bud. Shawn had seen him around too. A skinny guy with a shock of red hair who went by the name of Painter.

"If the Mothman wasn't at fault, I bet the guy who did it was some kind of cultist. The damn bird probably made him do it." Painter looked like he'd had a few and was pliable for talking. Undoubtedly pliable for spreading rumors too.

Shawn sucked beer, then wiped his mouth with the back of his hand. "Know what I think? That damn creature is part of Cornstalk's curse and as long as it's here, the curse isn't going anywhere. How much you wanna bet Hanley's just the first?"

"Shawn, what the hell are you talking about?" Scowling, Tucker toweled out the inside of a beer glass. His mouth crimped into a frown, but Shawn ignored the grimace. The bartender had always been a thorn in his side.

"I was here last Saturday when someone said they saw the bird near Windmill Road."

Painter slurped beer. "So?"

"So, Windmill isn't far from Will's place on Butterman. And he was killed the next day. Sunday morning, right?" He let them digest the connection, the link all but visible in Mitch's wide-set eyes. "The Mothman shows up, and in less than twenty-four hours Hanley's dead."

"Yeah." Mitch scratched a stubby finger over his jaw. "I see what you mean. Can't be coincidental."

"Damn right."

Over in the corner, a woman with teased blond hair and drippy gold jewelry keyed "I Love a Rainy Night" into the jukebox. Doreen Sue Lynch, Katie's mom. If she weren't hanging off the arm of Martin Ward he'd stroll over and proposition her. Fifty-something years old, and she was still a fox. The rush he got from the knife stoked his confidence. If he wasn't careful that same barrage of power would lead him to distraction. Learning to control the heightened edge the weapon gave him was like riding the crest of a monster wave, reckless and exhilarating. Chomping down on the inside of his mouth, he refocused.

"Last fall we had all those weird lights in the sky."

Mitch nodded. "I remember."

"And those freak guys in black roaming through town." The words came easier as he paved the way from point A to point B. "Then crazy Parker Kline breaks out of the nuthouse and disappears. We had Mothman sightings then, too."

"And don't forget the Silver Bridge," Painter chimed in.

The wheels appeared to be spinning in Mitch's head. "They never did find that Kline kid and he killed before. Put a bullet point blank in Hank Jeffries' skull."

"Shawn, your food's up." Tucker plopped a plate containing a burger and fries onto the bar. A basket of wings swimming in hot sauce, a few sticks of celery, and a paper cup of blue cheese dressing followed.

Shawn was practically salivating. The combined odor of pepper and grease from the deep fryer hit him in the face, making his stomach contract. Hunching over on his stool, he greedily tucked into the burger.

"Maybe the Kline kid came back." Painter was focused on where the conversation had lagged. "Maybe he's the one who slashed up poor Will."

"Kline's messed up in the head because of the Mothman." Shawn slopped ketchup onto his fries. He clumped four together, and shoved them into his mouth. The gooey mass went down easy with a swig of beer. "Remember, Jeffries killed Parker's twin brother because he thought Tim was the Mothman."

"Damn shame about that." Tucker moved away when someone hailed him for another beer.

Shawn licked cheese from his fingers. The burger dripped mayo and tomato onto his plate when he bit into it. "Fucking starving." He dragged the back of his hand across his mouth.

Mitch snorted and helped himself to a fry. "Imagine the kind of roast you'd get from the bird."

Shawn tensed, irked that someone would pilfer his food. Another time he might gut the guy for the infraction, but there was no sense making a scene when he had his two new buddies playing along so well. "You'd have to kill it first. Hunt it down."

"Should have done that long ago." Painter polished off the last of his beer and set the bottle on the bar.

"Hey, Tucker." Shawn flagged for service. "I'll take another. Give a round to my friends here, too."

"That's generous of you." Mitch clapped him on the shoulder. "Thanks."

"Yeah, from me too." Painter's smile was all teeth. "I used to think you were a jerk when I saw you on the sprint circuit, but you ain't so bad."

Shawn forced a smile, biting back another wave of anger. He shoved the wings toward the two guys. "Help yourselves. I can order more."

"Next round's on me. Wings and beer." Mitch pulled a wing from the basket and took a healthy bite. He licked hot sauce from his fingers. "Talking about the Mothman, I've gone looking for it before."

Shawn grabbed one of the wings. "Who hasn't?"

"Never had any luck though." Mitch dragged a napkin across his mouth then crumbled it into a ball. "The TNT is a fucking maze. Too many places for the thing to hide."

"That's always been the problem." Painter nibbled a wing like he wasn't sure the taste agreed with him.

"You'd have to get enough guys to flush it out." Shawn swept his gaze over the group at the bar. A few appeared to be listening to their conversation. "The sheriff's department sucks at the job. If you ask me I don't think they're interested in finding it."

Tucker returned with three beers and set them on the bar. "Why not?"

"Think about it." Shawn snagged another handful of fries. More people were listening, a group at the nearest table openly staring. "It gives them a reason to feel important. Like they're doing their job. Protecting the town."

Tucker shook his head. "They are protecting the town. You want to talk crap about the Flynn brothers, Sheriff Weston, or anyone else in that department, don't do it in here."

You have pushed too far.

No shit. He could see he'd crossed a line. He didn't need the fucking voice telling him the obvious. Shawn held up a hand signaling retreat. "I'm just saying maybe they're a bit overtaxed."

"It didn't sound like that." Tucker wasn't ready to back down.

"It came out wrong." He couldn't afford to lose his audience. "With Hanley's murder, Pete, Caden, Ryan, and the others have their hands full.

They shouldn't have to focus on some flying freak when one of our own has been ripped up in his home."

A murmur of agreement from those nearest him.

"And if the Mothman is connected to Will's death, don't we owe it to our friend to see the damn thing doesn't hurt anyone again?"

"What are you suggesting?" Painter finished his wing and sucked the bone clean. He wiped his sticky fingers on his jeans.

Shawn spread his hands. "Maybe it's time we got organized and went into the TNT together. That's how they did it before the bridge went down. They piled into cars and went out there with shotguns."

"And didn't find a damn thing." Tucker shook his head. "I'm old enough to remember sixty-six when the woods were full of flashlights and guns. I was one of the idiots roaming around in the dark. We were damn lucky no one got killed by accident."

Shawn grit his teeth. No matter how hard he tried, he was unable to quell the heat in the glare he leveled on Tucker. The bartender didn't seem to notice. Glancing to the side, he addressed the group at large.

"Will's dead. I don't know if the Mothman was involved, but going out there on some fool's mission armed with guns isn't going to do anyone any good. Especially Will."

Murmurs of agreement, louder this time. Unseen below the bar, Shawn clenched his hand into a fist. He longed to draw the knife and put an end to Tucker's righteous tirade. The guy droned on, talking about leaving matters in the hands of the sheriff's department. A lot of responsible drivel that made Shawn's gut twist. His mouth curled downward, the nails of his right hand digging into his palm.

Someone nudged him in the ribs. He jerked his head to the side to find Mitch watching him. The heavyset man's gaze was direct. "We don't need an army," he said in a low voice so that only Shawn and Painter heard. "It only takes one good shot to kill the thing and there are three of us."

Shawn grinned.

Not exactly what he'd planned, but he'd run with what he had.

* * * *

Quentin popped the top on a beer and eased into a rocker on the hotel porch. Earlier, he'd grabbed dinner at the café, but the place was too crowded tonight. He'd felt out of his element with so many locals gathered to remember one of their own. His waitress had told him about Will Hanley's murder. Afterward, he'd found a copy of the *Point Pleasant Herald* in the lobby and read the account firsthand. The details left him uneasy.

Sadly, people were killed every day even in small rural communities, but he couldn't help feeling Cornstalk's curse was connected. He'd overheard a few patrons in the café muttering the same thing. People talked in hushed whispers about mutated creatures in the TNT, red water seepage, and Mothman sightings.

A blight hung over the town.

Lightning framed the buildings across the street, the air ripe with ozone. The night felt alien, something that existed on the fringe of colliding worlds. Every now and then a rumble of thunder shattered the stillness. Main Street was empty, not a single car trolling its length or a lone pedestrian haunting the sidewalks. Quentin imagined everyone tucked inside, safe behind glass storefronts ablaze with light.

"May I join you?"

He jerked at the intrusion of a lightly accented voice. A glance over his shoulder revealed Lach Evening regarding him expectantly. He shrugged. "Why not?"

Evening settled into a rocker, his dark eyes trained on the street. Two blocks down, a man appeared at the door of the dry cleaner and flipped a hanging sign to Closed. A few seconds later the lights went out. "I am curious if you ever discovered anything about your ancestor, Jonathan Marsh."

Quentin shook his head. "You told me I wouldn't find his grave in Pioneer Cemetery." He studied Evening openly. "And, incidentally, I never mentioned his last name or mine. Interesting how you just seemed to know it."

Evening was unfazed. "I make it a habit to know certain things."

"Sounds to me like you know more about Jonathan than I do."

"Perhaps." Evening tapped a bubble-topped finger against his lips. "He lived during the days of Chief Cornstalk." A calculating sideways glance. "Tell me, Mr. Marsh, do you believe in curses?"

A harsh bark of laughter escaped Quentin. "Curses." He lifted his right hand. "What do you think this is? I used to be a concert pianist, now I sell advertising." Bitterness burbled awake in his gut and rooted like a rancid seed. "If you know something about Jonathan, spit it out." Mention of the injury soured his mood. He downed the last of his beer and thought about getting another.

"Alcohol does not help." Evening seemed to read his thoughts.

"I know. I tried that route before." It had only taken getting rip-roaring drunk once to make him realize he wasn't the type to drown his misery in booze. "I'm here because of my sister." Might as well get the whole thing said. Leaning forward, he braced his knees apart and cupped the empty can between his palms. "She thinks my family is cursed."

"It is."

Quentin balked. "That's a bold statement."

"I wish it were otherwise. You might say I am a historian, Mr. Marsh. I know a bit about your family, including the man you came to learn about."

"Jonathan?"

"Yes."

"What about this?" Quentin dug the amulet from his pocket. In the pewter veil of twilight, the blue stone appeared darker than normal. "Do you know about this, too?"

Evening's mouth tightened as his gaze settled on the trinket. "It belonged to him."

"To Jonathan?"

"Sutton kept it upon his death."

The name caught Quentin off guard. "Who?"

"Jonathan's brother." A sudden gust of wind scattered the hair on Evening's forehead. "Sutton is responsible for unleashing Cornstalk's curse."

Neither Penelope nor Madam Olga had mentioned Jonathan had a brother. "If you know so much about this, why not say so? Why these bits and pieces?"

"It is not easily explained."

Quentin's irritation ratcheted higher. Across the street, lightning silhouetted the rooftops of the dry cleaner and a bookstore. A gust of wind drove a stray piece of paper down the sidewalk. Electricity danced down Quentin's arm, fanning over his scarred hand and tingling the length of his fingers. "Start by using words."

Evening's mouth thinned in amusement. "I suggest you talk to Caden Flynn."

"Flynn?" Quentin drew back. "What's he have to do with this?"

"Nothing now, but by tomorrow everything will be clear."

More riddles.

Evening stood. "If you will excuse me, I have other matters to attend."

Quentin would have blocked his path but saw little sense in the childish bullying. Evening had said all he was going to say. At least now Quentin had a new name to focus on. He didn't recall seeing Sutton referenced in the archival records, but after a while the lists had blurred together.

With the threat of a storm brewing on the horizon, he turned back to the hotel. Someone in the bar was sure to know Sarah, and right now, he wanted to find out where she lived.

Chapter 7

Sarah stood rooted to the floor staring out the kitchen window. Flashes of lightning illuminated a heavy blanket of clouds; the treetops in her rear yard tossed about by a strong wind. Every now and then thunder rumbled in menace, jarring her nerves. Why was it so hard to outgrow her ridiculous fear of storms?

Nibbling on a fingernail, she paced to the table. The top was covered by several books she'd taken from the public library. Quentin's interest in Cornstalk's curse had prompted her to reacquaint herself with the details leading up to his death. On a whim, she'd also checked out a book on witchcraft. Leafing through the tome made her uneasy, but her mind kept tracking back to the strange symbols on the wooden case belonging to Shawn. The cyphers could be nothing more than idle scratching, but she was curious enough to try to establish their meaning, especially in light of the letter she'd discovered. There was a slim possibility the Jonathan mentioned in that short missive could be Quentin's ancestor.

A knock at the front door made her jump.

The clock above the sink indicated it was after nine. Tomorrow was a workday, making it unusual for anyone to call on her so late. Slightly uneasy, she moved to the front window and flicked the curtain aside. In the glow from the porch light she spied a maroon Monte Carlo parked in her driveway.

"Quentin?" Sarah tugged the door open. "What are you doing here?"

His mouth curled in a lopsided grin. He raised a bottle of wine. "I come bearing gifts."

"You didn't answer my question."

Lightning flickered, wrenching an involuntary gasp from her lips. Hastily, she motioned him inside. "Come in."

He stepped through the doorway with a glance for her tiny living room.

Her face grew warm as she recalled he came from an affluent family. Someone who'd attended Juilliard and played concert halls probably found her trailer rustic. Biting her lip, she took in the simple decorations—a tufted sofa and rocking chair, her grandmother's pitcher and bowl, a brass table lamp with a beaded shade her mother had loved. Many of the furnishings were antiques, cherished pieces she couldn't bear to part with. Did he see them as simple and backward?

"Nice place."

"Thank you." She wished she knew if he was sincere. "Is it raining yet?"

He shook his head. "Just a lot of thunder, lightning, and wind. There's been a lot of that lately."

She'd noticed it too. People in town discussed the weather over coffee or when they stopped to pick up the mail at the post office. Only yesterday, Sarah had overheard Mrs. Quiggly prattling about the strange weather at the library. The old woman said it was an omen of bad things to come.

"Sorry I showed up unannounced, but I didn't have your phone number." Quentin dragged fingers through his tousled hair, taming it in place. The wind had left him disheveled with high color on his cheeks. "I found the name of an ancestor I wanted to run by you. And I thought you could use a glass of wine after what happened with the Mothman."

"I have to work tomorrow." A stupid thing to say.

"I won't stay long."

"No…it's fine." She motioned him to the kitchen. "I was doing some research anyway."

He walked to the table and gave a once-over to the array of books. "More stuff on Cornstalk?"

"Witchcraft too."

His gaze flashed to her face. "Should I ask why?"

"Let me get some glasses for the wine and I'll explain."

Five minutes later, seated at the table together, Sarah told him about the odd wooden case she'd discovered among Shawn's possessions and the etchings on top.

"Do you remember what they looked like?" Quentin asked.

"Not really. Mostly runes or hieroglyphs. I do remember a spider. That seemed to be the prominent marking." Thoughtfully, she sipped her wine. "I hoped if I saw something similar in the book it might jar my memory."

Quentin pulled the tome toward him. "What was in the case?"

"I don't know. It was locked, but it gave me a creepy feeling." A bolt of lightning flared beyond the window and she tensed involuntarily. "Kind of like all this bizarre weather."

"We're safe in here." Quentin seemed to hone in on her unease. "Maybe it's just heat lightning."

Flashes from a storm too far away to affect them. She knew different and guessed he did too. The streaks were too vivid, the thunder too loud. "Mrs. Quiggly calls it a witch storm."

He shot her a sideways glance. "A what?"

"Witch storm. She said it's an omen of bad tidings." A shiver skittered down her spine. Wetting her lips, she rolled the stem of the wine glass between her fingers. "After encountering the Mothman I'm starting to believe her. Everywhere I go, people are on edge. Like they're waiting for something horrible to happen."

"Maybe it already has." Quentin flipped through the book. "You heard about Will Hanley?"

She nodded, morose. "He was a good man." Her voice cracked when she thought of how he'd died. "His wife passed away a few years ago. She was my teacher in grade school. When I think of Will and what happened to him—" She pressed a hand to her lips. "I heard rumors the Mothman was involved."

Quentin's mouth thinned. "Not to make light, but isn't the creature at the root of everything?"

"Cornstalk's curse is at the root of everything."

"Yeah." Exhaling, he slumped in his chair. "Everything goes back to that, doesn't it?" He took a long swallow of wine and set the glass down. A domed lamp suspended from the ceiling cast shadows over his face, changing the color of his eyes from whiskey to bark. "You remember the man who showed up at the TNT when we were there? The one with blond hair?"

"Lach Evening?" Sarah fidgeted. In the living room, her grandmother's mantel clock chimed the quarter hour.

"He seems to know a lot about my family. He told me Jonathan had a brother named Sutton. I think he's the one I need to research."

"A brother?" Shock seeped into her voice. Fiddling with her necklace, she began to pace.

Quentin eyed her critically. "Sarah, what's wrong? Do you know who Sutton is?"

"No." She never heard the name before. Never came across it in any record she could recall. "It's just...Lach Evening is different. He knows things."

"What do you mean?"

She knotted her fingers. She didn't fully understand who or what Evening was, only that he was connected to Indrid Cold. If she believed the stories Eve and Katie had told her about the being in the igloo, then she had to accept Evening was as alien as Cold. There was no sense trying to convince Quentin of something so inexplicable. Believing in the Mothman was one thing. Accepting that otherworldly beings existed in a cross reality was entirely different.

Folding her arms, she gripped her elbows and turned to face him. "Lach is a little bit like your Madam Olga. He has knowledge of past and future events." Comparing Evening to the psychic seemed a good way to explain his abilities. "If he said Sutton is your ancestor, then it's probably true."

"Great." Quentin finished his wine and stood. "But there's no record of Sutton or Jonathan—"

"Unless Jonathan is the same Jonathan mentioned in the letter I found." Sarah moved closer and gripped the back of the nearest chair. "That would have put him at Fort Randolph around the same time Cornstalk was there. And from the letter, we know he was killed by Indians."

Quentin seemed to consider that. "Before or after Cornstalk was murdered?"

The wind battered a tree limb against the window. Sarah jumped then instantly flushed at her jittery nerves. To cover, she picked up the book and hugged it to her chest. "There has to be a way to find out."

"Evening is the way to find out." Quentin shook his head. He paced a short distance away. "Although, according to him, I'm supposed to talk to Caden Flynn."

"Caden?" The name tumbled from her lips with a distinctive note of worry. Eve didn't need to have her husband dragged into something that didn't concern him. This was Quentin's issue to resolve, not Caden's. She exhaled a defeated breath. "I wish Lach would have explained and left Caden out of it. He and Eve have only been married a little over a month. My friends have enough to worry about, and now with Will Hanley's death…" She raised her head to meet his gaze. "Are you going to talk to Caden?"

He spread his hands. "What other choice do I have?"

She nodded. "You're right. Maybe I'll go with you if that's okay."

"Sure." He stepped closer and gazed down, grasping her arms. "I'm sorry I dragged you into this."

"It's okay. I think I was already involved without knowing it." She thought of the wooden case with the odd markings, of the letter touting Jonathan's death. The author of that message had lost her fiancé to a brutal attack, and was left to face a bleak future alone. Just imagining the woman's grief made Sarah's heart constrict.

For the first time she grew conscious of how close Quentin was standing, of the care and concern in his eyes as he gazed down at her. Heat warmed her face and she stepped away to set the book on the table. "What time were you planning on seeing Caden?"

"I guess it depends on his schedule, but if you'd like to go along, I can wait until you're off work."

"That sounds great."

Quentin hovered at her back, his presence filling the room in a manner she hadn't noted before. She moved slightly and her arm brushed his, a tempest of electricity flaring between them. She turned to face him, her mouth suddenly dry. "I should call it a night. I've to get up for work tomorrow morning."

He nodded, still looking down on her, his gaze too intent to be mistaken for casual. Without speaking, he slipped a finger under her chin, then tipped her head up and kissed her softly. When he stepped back, the hint of a smile flitted over his lips. "I think I can end the night with that memory." His smile faded within seconds as his gaze shifted over her shoulder. "Looks like you found your spider."

"What?" Sarah was still digesting the kiss.

Quentin pointed and she turned. On the table, the book had fallen open, splayed on its spine to a random page. Sarah's eyes skimmed the text, landing on the symbol of a spider. A perfect match for the crude etching on the wooden case. "That's it."

Leaning closer, Quentin swept his finger down the page. His mouth tightened. "Nice symbol. It signifies treachery and death."

* * * *

Caden examined the file on his desk then scrubbed his eyes. Thursday morning, four days after Will Hanley had been killed and the case was going nowhere. Ryan had left earlier to track down several members of Hanley's church in the hopes of unearthing buried information—someone who remembered Will mentioning anyone who might hold a grudge against him, issues with his farm, or anything else that might throw up a red flag. In the meantime, Caden slogged through old phone records and mail, contacting vendors who'd had business contracts with Will, while looking for any unusual numbers on the list of calls. So far all he'd managed to learn was that Will had been highly respected in the community. No one had anything but praise for the deceased farmer.

"Sergeant Flynn?"

Caden glanced up to find Lach Evening standing in front of his desk. He hadn't heard the man enter but that didn't necessarily mean anything where Evening was concerned. Joy, their resident clerk, had vanished, off delivering mail, which explained why Caden was alone in the room. With Ryan and Rosling both working the Hanley case from the field, it had left him juggling paperwork for a change.

Caden tossed a pencil on the file folder and sat back in his chair. "Lach, what are you doing here?"

"I need to speak with you."

Caden waved to a chair. "Have a seat."

"Privately."

"The room's empty."

Lach didn't move. "This will take some time."

"Meaning?" Caden arched a brow, then sighed when he received no answer. Pushing back his chair, he stood and motioned Lach to follow. "This way." A turn took them down a short hallway to a room with a small table and chairs. It served for holding, questioning suspects, and even the occasional conference when needed. Caden sat down then indicated a chair across from him. "I'm kind of tied up in a murder case right now."

"I am aware of that. But there is something darker in Point Pleasant than a killer."

There were times Evening could be as obtuse as his father. Knowing it wouldn't do any good to rush the man, he waited for Evening to get to the point.

"Do you believe in curses, Caden?"

The rare use of his first name sharpened his attention. Evening seldom called him anything other than "Sergeant" or "Sergeant Flynn." "I'm going to take a wild stab and guess you're referring to Cornstalk's curse." Exhaling, he leaned forward and braced an arm on the table. "I don't have time for moldy folklore. Will Hanley's killer is still out there, and—"

"Did you get a match on the fingerprints?"

The interruption stopped him cold. Drawing back slightly, he shook his head. "No match in the system, but it just means the killer isn't on record."

"Of course not. He doesn't exist. Not in this century."

Irritation twisted Caden's mouth. "What are you talking about? I don't have time for games."

"Neither do I." Evening leaned forward and motioned him closer. "That brand on your wrist—the marks from the Mothman—may I see them?"

Suspicious, Caden narrowed his eyes. "Why?"

"It is easier if I show you rather than trying to explain."

Still uncertain where he was headed, Caden unbuttoned his sleeve and extended his arm. The lines wrapped around his forearm were black. If he didn't know better, he might have mistaken the gashes for a tattoo. His mouth tightened at the sight.

"They don't normally look like that." Not a question.

"No." It had been several days since the color mutated. In the past he'd always been conscious of the marks, a slight pressure on his skin as if a hand gripped him. Often they tingled or warmed with heat. Sometimes when the Mothman was close they even burned. Now there was nothing to suggest a connection. "It's like something has been severed."

"Your link to the creature."

He'd guessed as much himself. "Because I shot it?"

"Perhaps. Or perhaps something happened earlier." Gripping Caden by the wrist, Evening splayed his bulb-topped fingers over the marks. The wide tips fused to Caden's skin, each fleshy pad locking in place with the power of a suction cup. Instinctively, Caden tried to jerk free.

Evening held fast, his eyes jet-black stones beneath the fluorescent glare of overhead lights. "This is what I came to show you."

As his voice faded, the room twirled away in a kaleidoscope of dizzying motion. The floor heaved upright then contracted, hurling Caden into empty space. Light was devoured by darkness, darkness consumed by light. His sense of direction and time bled into a weightless void. Seconds later, order restored, he found himself standing in a sparsely furnished room with roughhewn walls.

A slender girl sat with her back turned. Seated at a small desk, she gazed through an open window overlooking a vista of green grass and rolling hills. Dressed in an old-fashioned gown with a full skirt, she couldn't have been more than eighteen. Strands of blue ribbon adorned her light brown hair, which was wound into loose ringlets and curls. A piece of parchment rested on the desk in front of her. As Caden watched, the girl dipped a feather quill into an ink well, then began to write.

I thought the weeks would become easier, but I find each day harder to bear, Mama. I often wake thinking Jonathan will be waiting for me in the next room, only to realize the foolishness of my desires. I have tried to talk to Sutton about everything that has happened but he is remote. He's closed himself off since his brother's death, and now with the passing of his poor infant...

His dear wife, Lenore, tends to the daughter that survived, but I feel the death of his son has robbed his heart of gladness. The birth of twins is difficult at best, but already there are those who whisper the baby's death was the result of Chief Cornstalk's curse. Did I tell you Sutton killed the Shawnee? Given that atrocity, I can't help wondering if the rumors are true.

Mr. Obadiah Preech returned to the fort with Jonathan's mutilated body. I thank our dear Lord that I was not present to witness his arrival, but I have heard the tales. How he came upon Jonathan in the woods, a savage bent over my beloved, ready to scalp him. Mr. Preech shot the Indian, but the redskin was only wounded and escaped, fleeing into the woods. There are strange things among the trees, Mama. Unusual lights in the nighttime sky and sounds that make a brave man's blood run cold. I pray the savage met his own untimely end.

As for Jonathan, my beloved's soul had already departed for the next world by the time Mr. Preech found him. I was not present when that good man returned to the fort and told his tale—I learned of Jonathan's demise later that evening—but Sutton was with the crowd that greeted him. I shudder to imagine the scene, for I have no doubt that Mr. Preech's tale filled Sutton with fury. Is it any wonder he incited the soldiers to turn on Cornstalk? I am told Mr. Preech prodded him toward it, but that gentleman was surely filled with rage after witnessing my beloved's brutal demise. The sin of the savages is beyond my comprehension. We are under a treaty that calls for peace, yet they have taken Jonathan from me. How can I forgive such wickedness? I should feel remorse for Cornstalk and the others, but my heart is too heavy, laden with grief for Jonathan.

I am told a group of soldiers stormed the guardhouse, slaying the Shawnee chief, his son, and the other native who was with them. Jonathan's friend, Private Charles Younger, told me he saw a corporal shoot Cornstalk's son in the head, but that Sutton killed the chief with a knife. Charles said the blade was coal black, dark as the night sky. How very odd is that?

Alton was incensed by the violence but it was too late for him to do anything. I am sickened to confirm there was celebrating after Cornstalk's death. I wish I could report a higher level of conduct among the men sworn to protect us, but you must understand the threat under which we've lived. For months, we have heard rumors of Indians massing in number. I'm afraid Jonathan's death was equivalent to the bursting of a dam.

Charles later told me Chief Cornstalk cursed the land as he lay dying. He placed a hex on the people and on Sutton's descendants. Perhaps that is why Sutton's wife delivered prematurely only a month later, and why one of her twins died. It grieves my heart to think of that poor innocent baby. Already Sutton is talking about returning to Philadelphia with his family. I do not think he will stay here, especially now that Jonathan is gone.

I would be grateful for your visit, Mama. Charlotte and Alton have been most kind to me, but I cannot impose upon my dear sister and her husband forever. I am undone since losing my beloved. Even this rugged colony of Virginia, with its towering mountains and majestic trees, leaves me feeling empty.

Mama, despite all I have said, I beg you not to worry about me and Charlotte. We are well protected by the soldiers of Fort Randolph. Charlotte's brave husband, Alton, is a highly capable and respected Captain, and all of the settlers are well guarded. Without Jonathan, I suffer bouts of homesickness, but I feel I must stay. For my beloved and the life we would have led together.

Sometimes, I am taken aback by the strangeness of this new land.

The other day I strolled by the river and saw a most unusual thing. I was a good distance away, so I question my vision, but it appeared to be a man with wings crouched upon the bank. I encountered Mr. Preech shortly thereafter. When I told him about what I saw, he grew very pale and said I must never speak of it again. He was so stricken by my tale, I continued to prod him until he confessed that he too had seen the winged man in the past. He said it was a fiend with glowing red eyes, an abomination conceived of the devil—forgive me, Mama—and that it had claimed the soul of his wife.

I shudder to imagine such a thing. Can demons walk in flesh upon the land? Am I marked too, as Mr. Preech's late wife, for having seen the creature? Oh, Mama, come quickly. Despite all the beauty of this place, I fear there is evil here.

Your faithful daughter,
Etta Sherman

Caden jerked, wrenched from the scene. He blinked the interrogation room into focus, the sights and sounds of a bygone era fading into memory. For a moment, he was certain he'd been dreaming. Somewhere down the hall a phone rang and a door banged shut. The smell of burnt coffee and vinyl floor wax assailed his nose, grounding him in the twentieth century. Lach Evening regarded him steadily.

Releasing Caden's wrist, he sat back in his chair. "Quentin Marsh is descended from Jonathan and Sutton, the men referenced in this vision."

Caden dragged a hand over his face. Vision, hell. He felt like he'd been on a carnival ride. He was used to Evening working an occasional trick, but getting tossed through time topped the Richter scale for nerve-wracking. He latched onto the table to make sure it was real. "Don't do that again."

"What?"

"Toss me through time."

"My apologies." Evening didn't sound the least bit remorseful. "Now you understand why I needed to speak with you in private."

Caden grunted. There was a certain sadistic logic in the observation. He tried to wrap his mind around what he'd seen. "Where does Etta Sherman fit in?"

"As you have no doubt already surmised, she is Sarah's ancestor." Evening seemed disappointed Caden hadn't picked up on the obvious.

He might have reached the conclusion if he could piece his mind together. "So, Jonathan and Etta were engaged?" And the descendant of the man who'd killed Cornstalk had surfaced in Point Pleasant. Nothing was ever commonplace in a town beset by interdimensional travel, cryptids, and curses. But what were the odds of Quentin turning up now? Coincidentally, around the same time Will was killed? Two murders—one centuries ago, one in the present. Gut instinct told him he'd overlooked a connection.

Caden scowled openly. "How do you know all this?"

Lach smoothed the fabric of one crisp black sleeve. "Because I was there. You forget how old I am."

As ancient as the Mothman, or close to it. "Are you telling me you were at Fort Randolph?"

"Precisely. I knew Jonathan, Sutton, and Etta personally. It is why I can vouch for the letter you saw."

Resting an elbow on the table, Caden pressed two fingertips to his temple. He should be focused on Hanley, not caught up in ancient distractions. Yet, somehow the two were joined or Evening wouldn't be sitting across from him, showing him these things.

"Jonathan was not killed by a Shawnee," Lach said into the silence.

Caden wet his lips. "Obadiah Preech found the body."

"Preech killed him." A flat statement with no room for doubt.

Caden shifted in his chair. According to Shawn, his ancestor was a hero. Someone who'd fought in Lord Dunmore's War then stood fast at Fort Randolph when the settlers were in need. But Shawn had never mentioned anything about Willa Preech or how she'd died.

Evening seemed to read his thoughts. "Three months prior to Jonathan's death, Willa Preech was drawing water by the river when she spied the creature. It gave her a horrible fright. Two days later, she came down with a fever and passed in the middle of the night. Obadiah became convinced the creature was at fault. I tried to tell him his wife's sickness was not supernatural in origin, but he refused to listen. Within time his grief transitioned to hatred, and he vowed to kill the cryptid."

Caden cupped the brand on his forearm. If Obadiah's wife had succumbed to fever, it was likely she'd babbled about the creature in her delirium. No wonder Preech had set off to kill it.

"He failed."

"Precisely." In a seemingly absent gesture, Evening rubbed his thumb against his fingertips. "I believe the creature's net of fear was too great for him to withstand. Obadiah returned to the fort shamed by his failure. He believed the creature was a demon summoned by the Indians through sorcery, and that a knife stained with the blood of Cornstalk—leader of his People—would banish the demon back to hell."

Caden frowned, trying to follow. "But Sutton killed Cornstalk."

Lach nodded. "Obadiah turned to dark magic in his efforts to destroy the Mothman. I believe Jonathan came upon him in the woods when he was performing a ritual. Obadiah killed him in order to silence him. When he returned to the fort with Jonathan's body, he concocted a false story, placing the blame on the Shawnee. After that, it was easy to incite the soldiers, particularly Sutton, against Cornstalk." Evening paused briefly, allowing Caden to absorb the information, before continuing. "In a final cowardly act, he goaded Sutton into killing Cornstalk. The Marsh family has carried the Indian's curse ever since."

Caden's head pounded. If anyone else had spun the outlandish tale he would have passed the ramblings off as drivel, but Lach Evening didn't do gibberish. Standing, he flattened his palms on the table. "I'm still trying to grasp why you're telling me this."

Lach studied him openly. "Events have been set in motion. Sarah Sherman is here, Shawn Preech is here. Quentin Marsh is here. All descendants of the original players. Do you think the Mothman is oblivious to that? The creature hates Obadiah with the same zeal Obadiah harbored."

"Obadiah is dead."

"Was." Lach's gaze narrowed in a concentrated stare. "You will not find matches for your fingerprints, Sergeant."

A surge of incredulity made Caden draw back. "Are you trying to tell me Obadiah Preech killed Will Hanley? The ghost of an eighteenth-century warlock?" Raising his hand to deflect the absurd suggestion, he shook his head. "Look, I've seen a lot of strange stuff go down around here, but I'm drawing the line on this. Even if I believed you—which I don't—there's no motive."

"Yet you found one?" Evening's mouth thinned and his gaze narrowed. "Robbery?"

"No." Caden sensed where he was headed.

"A crime of passion? Perhaps anger?"

"It doesn't look that way."

"A personal vendetta or a business deal turned sour?"

"We're working those angles."

Evening pushed his chair back and stood. "I have booked a room at your wife's hotel, Sergeant. You know where to find me should you wish to discuss anything further."

"Why would I do that?"

"I told you once before something would be required of you when past and present join." Evening's gaze dropped to the marks on Caden's forearm. He nodded slightly, indicting the gashes. "That time has been set in motion. I have only to look at your arm to see the dissolution of all that came before."

More riddles. This time, rather than chasing UFOs, Evening wanted him to believe in witchcraft and spirits.

Deciding he wasn't going to get anywhere, Caden crossed the room and opened the door. "I've got to get back to work." Unusual for him to end the conversation before Evening, but he was tired of the alien calling the shots.

Without a word, Evening stepped into the hallway.

"Why are you here anyway?" Caden said to his back.

Evening stopped but did not turn. "To be certain you do what is required."

"Which is?"

This time Evening did turn. "Kill the Mothman."

Chapter 8

Treachery and death.

Knowing the meaning of the spider etching on the wooden case Sarah had found tucked among Shawn's belongings made her apprehensive. Why would anyone carve such a vile symbol on a trinket box? As much as the she wanted to dismiss the matter, she couldn't help wondering what the case contained.

It was time to talk to Suzanne.

She hadn't seen her friend in several days. During the week, she usually stopped by Suzanne's coffee shop to grab a cup of decaf on the way to work. The last few mornings, she'd found someone else covering for Suzanne. Today, the girl behind the counter told her Suzanne wasn't feeling well.

The news left Sarah feeling badly for not having checked in with her sooner, especially given her impending divorce. Finagling her hours to leave the courthouse early on Thursday afternoon, Sarah drove to Suzanne's new home. Her friend's car was in the driveway, the blinds drawn on the windows. The house had a strange shuttered feel to it, an impression compounded by an overcast sky. Overhead, the sun played hide and seek with angry layers of clouds, the ever-present charge of electricity clinging to the air.

Sarah picked up three newspapers lying in the driveway and headed up the sidewalk. Pressing her finger to the doorbell, she glanced about. Two flowerboxes below the front windows had a slightly neglected look as though they hadn't been tended for a while.

When the doorbell brought no answer, she opened the screen and tried knocking.

"Suzanne, it's Sarah. Are you home?"

The wind whipped through the grass and a cloud passed over the sun. A muted shuffling rose from somewhere behind the door. "Suzanne?" She knocked again. To her left, the dangling flutes of a chime tinkled a shivery note.

Goose bumps broke out on her arm. Worried, she pounded again. This time the blind to her right flicked to the side briefly before dropping back in place. A moment later the interior door opened a crack.

"I'm not feeling well, Sarah." Suzanne hovered behind the door, hidden in shadows. The interior of the house looked dark, the air stuffy as though it had been closed up for days.

Sticky air struck Sarah in the face. She inched to the side, hoping for a glimpse of Suzanne.

"That's what Tina at your shop said. I wanted to drop by and see how you're doing…if you need anything." She'd also wanted to ask about the box, but now that she was here, her concern shifted to Suzanne. Her friend was normally outspoken and vivacious, not someone to tuck herself away in a dark house even if she wasn't feeling well. Suzanne was more likely to be visible, hoping to garner sympathy.

"No, I'm fine." Suzanne's voice was rough around the edges, as if she hadn't spoken in a while. Either that or she'd been crying.

"You don't sound fine." Sarah splayed a hand against the door. "Can I come in?"

Suzanne's hesitation was nearly tangible. Finally, she sighed and stepped backward. Her movements were stiff as she shuffled to the couch. Whatever her ailment, she clearly wasn't well.

Sarah shut the door behind her. "You look like you need a doctor."

Dressed in pajamas, her blond hair a tangled cloud around her head, Suzanne curled into the corner of the sofa. Tucked in a hunched position, legs drawn up beside her, she had the look of a frightened animal.

Something was seriously out of whack.

Sarah moved to the blind. "Why's it so dark in here?"

"Don't!" Suzanne flung out an arm but the movement came too late.

Sarah tugged on the cheap plastic, guiding it open. Diffused light streamed into the room, cutting a path to the couch. In the sudden wash of illumination, Suzanne's face was mottled with bruises. One eye had swollen nearly shut, feathered at the edges with purple. An ugly blotch of yellow and black fanned outward from a cut on her cheek.

Sarah's stomach rolled over. "My God! What happened to you?"

Suzanne flinched, one hand jerking to her face. Her mouth quivered and her eyes filled with tears. Hugging her arms to her chest, she ducked her head.

Sarah was at her side in an instant, sinking onto the sofa, brushing the messy platinum mane from her shoulder. She wanted to shriek, demand who was responsible for the brutality, but her friend's huddled body language was a strong indication of fragility. Sarah spoke softly, her grip one of support rather than command. "Tell me what happened."

Suzanne swallowed audibly and wiped a tear from her cheek. Two of the nails on her left hand were broken and ragged. "I can't."

"It was Shawn, wasn't it?" She'd never thought him capable of violence but no one else had reason to treat Suzanne so horribly. Just the mention of his name made her bite her tongue in anger.

Sniffling, Suzanne grabbed a Kleenex from a box on the coffee table. Several used tissues were balled up and scattered on the floor, something Sarah hadn't noticed upon entering.

Soothingly, she rubbed Suzanne's shoulder. "Oh, honey, I'm so sorry. When did this happen?" Her friend hadn't admitted Shawn was responsible, but she hadn't denied it either.

Suzanne kneaded the tissue between her fingers. "Sunday. He...he showed up in the driveway." Her voice caught and cracked. "I think he'd been drinking."

A big surprise there.

Sarah forced the sarcasm silent. Scorn wouldn't help. "You have to report him. You have to tell Ryan Flynn."

"No!" Suzanne shook her head vehemently, her eyes widening in a look of pure terror. In high school, she'd had a thing for Ryan. Later, Sarah suspected she'd kept that attraction tucked away, a temptation she'd harbored throughout her marriage. But the crush had always been one-sided. Ryan would help her because it was his job to help.

"I don't want anyone to know, especially Ryan." Fire had made Suzanne's voice crack, but now the fight was gone. Tears rolling down her battered cheek, she slumped against the cushions. "Shawn said it would be worse... the next time...if I told anyone what he did."

Sarah fought rising fury. "Don't you realize he said that to make you afraid? He's counting on you not to tell anyone. You have to stand up for yourself."

"You don't understand how it is."

"No. I guess I don't, but seeing you like this..." Wrapping an arm around Suzanne's shoulders, she hugged her close. "How long has this been going on?"

"It was just once." Suzanne swiped a palm over her face, mopping up tears. Sarah handed her a clean tissue.

"Thanks." Struggling for composure, Suzanne patted her face, then lightly blew her nose. "When he showed up at the house, I told him to get lost." Her face contorted as she looked inward, dredging up the memory. Fresh tears flooded her eyes. "He chased me inside, and…" She shook her head. "It was awful. I never knew he could be that way."

He'd shown a bad side once before. "He pushed you when you were pregnant."

"That was different. He was drunk, and it was the only time he'd ever raised a hand against me." Sniffling, she dabbed her face. "He was hung over Sunday morning but he was sober. He knew exactly what he was doing, and," her voice broke, "I think he enjoyed it."

Sarah's stomach clenched. "If you won't talk to Ryan, talk to one of the other deputies. Or go to the Point Pleasant police."

Suzanne looked miserable, torn between wanting to go and fearful of what would happen if she did. "We don't live in the town limits."

"Then you need to see Ryan."

"Please, don't push me. I just need to think."

"Okay." She knew when to back off. Continued prodding would only make Suzanne more resistant to the idea. Her friend was a strong woman, one who was used to calling the shots. The role of victim had turned her world upside down.

"Why don't I hang around and make you dinner? We can watch a movie or something. You need to get your mind off what happened."

The hint of a smile curved Suzanne's lips. She lowered her eyes almost shyly. "Thanks. I'd like that. I haven't talked to anyone in days."

"Good. I'll tell you what…" Sarah stood. Having a task filled her with renewed purpose. "You just stay here and relax. I'll go bang around in the kitchen. I left work early and don't have any plans for tonight. We can do a girls' thing."

"You're a good friend, Sarah." Suzanne rested her head against the rear of the sofa. "I don't have many left these days."

Sarah bit her tongue, unwilling to point out that Suzanne's sometimes snooty personality was at fault. Even Eve, who was friendly with Suzanne, was often put off by how she came across. Many people considered the former Miss Point Pleasant stuck-up and condescending, but Sarah had noticed a change in her when she'd become pregnant then lost her baby. "Do you want me to switch on the TV?"

"Not now." Suzanne folded her hands over her stomach. "I just want to close my eyes and forget about everything for a while."

"You do that." Sarah walked back to the blind and tugged it down halfway. "If you fall asleep, I'll wake you when dinner's ready."

Later that evening, after a dinner of baked chicken and rice with a green salad, Sarah was reminded of the box. She hated to bring up Shawn, but seeing how he'd treated Suzanne made her more determined to know what the object contained.

She popped a movie into the VHS player for Suzanne while she cleaned up the kitchen, then puttered around doing a few other chores. Suzanne told her not to bother, but she watered the plants outside, straightened up the living room, and brought in the mail. There was several days' accumulation, a sign Suzanne hadn't been out of the house since her violent encounter with Shawn. She thought about making some tea, but Suzanne had her open a bottle of cabernet instead. With the TV muted to low, they sipped their drinks on the sofa.

"This has been nice." Suzanne had taken the time to freshen up and comb her hair, but the bruises on her face were still starkly evident. "I appreciate everything you did to get my mind off Shawn. I can't believe I actually wanted to know more about his family line." She sipped delicately at her wine, then gently fingered a cut on the corner of her mouth. "Did you ever have any luck digging into his background? Was Obadiah really at Fort Randolph?"

The perfect opportunity to ask about the wooden case. Sarah doubted Suzanne wanted details, so she kept her explanation brief. "Looks like that part was true, but I didn't discover much. I ended up giving the carton of documents back to him." Lowering her eyes, she swirled the wine in her glass. "Do you remember a wooden case with a spider marking on top? It was in the box you gave me."

Suzanne frowned. "It was? I always thought that thing was creepy."

"So, you know what I'm talking about?" Apparently, she wasn't the only one who found the box unnerving.

"Yeah. His dad tried to give it to Shawn a few days before we got married, but his mom freaked out. She said it was evil and called it devil magic."

A chill scampered down Sarah's spine. "Devil magic?"

"I know. Spooky, right? Gertrude claimed to have second sight. I blew off a lot of what she said, but I was glad when she took the box back. I didn't want it in the house."

Sarah didn't blame her. Especially after hearing it labeled "devil magic."

Suzanne stretched her legs. "After Shawn's dad died, I guess it got mixed in with the stuff he inherited. He never went through most of those cartons, thinking they were just old photos and books He and his dad didn't get along, so he wasn't eager for any reminders."

Sarah wondered if Job Preech had ever hit his wife. She remembered Gertrude as a stern, pious woman, and couldn't imagine her being pushed around. "I don't know if there was a key, but the box was locked."

"Oh, sure." Suzanne bobbed her head. "That was part of the riddle."

"Riddle?"

"If there was a key, it was lost ages ago. The lid had some kind of secret release mechanism but no one ever figured out how to work it."

"And no one was curious about what was inside?"

Suzanne shrugged. "Shawn didn't care. He liked the idea of being descended from one of the original settlers in Fort Randolph but didn't care beans about his family. Especially not his dad."

She'd never realized how bitter Shawn was beneath his boasting. Small wonder that rancor had given way to violence. "Do you know anything about the markings on the lid? The spider symbol?"

Suzanne eyed her openly. "You're really curious about this, aren't you?"

A flush of warmth rushed to Sarah's cheeks. "Sorry. I guess it's because of the genealogy angle." She hated lying but knew she'd been pushing too hard.

Suzanne accepted the explanation. "I only know what Gertrude told me. She was convinced the thing was evil. Part of me always wanted to know what was inside, but the other part was too spooked by what she told me. Job kept the thing locked out of sight, otherwise I'm sure she would have thrown it away. She definitely didn't want Shawn having it."

And now he did.

The idea that someone in Shawn's ancestral line practiced witchcraft seemed too farfetched to believe. As much as she disliked Shawn, she hoped he'd shoved the thing back in the attic where it belonged.

She finished her wine and set the glass aside.

Leaning forward, Suzanne retrieved the half-full bottle from the coffee table. "Want some more?"

"No thanks. I should probably head out soon. I have a few things I need to do before work tomorrow." Uncomfortable leaving Suzanne alone, she hesitated. "I'm not sure I like the idea of you here by yourself. What if Shawn comes back?"

Suzanne winced. A flicker of fear crossed her face, but she hid it quickly by sipping her wine. "I'll be careful. I won't answer the door."

A drunken Shawn Preech wasn't going to let a door stop him. "You can't hide out here forever."

"I know. I just don't want anyone to see me until these bruises heal." She fanned a hand near her face, her eyes brightening with a sheen of moisture. "It's humiliating."

Sarah considered prodding her again to report Shawn but feared too much pressure would make Suzanne bolt in the opposite direction. During dinner, she'd hinted she was considering contacting the sheriff's department. In the meantime, it wasn't out of the question for him to come back.

"Shawn's been doing a lot of drinking. I think he's getting worse and worse. If he winds up drunk again, there's no telling what he might do." Sarah gnawed on her bottom lip as she studied her friend.

Suzanne was proud and vain. She'd never take a room at the hotel even if Eve let her stay without charge. She'd be too embarrassed to let anyone in town see her, not to mention staying at the hotel would put her near Shawn, a regular at the River. Logic aside, Sarah couldn't bring herself to leave Suzanne on her own. "My trailer's small, but you could stay with me for a while. We'd make it work. I could sleep on the sofa."

"You won't do anything of the sort." Sitting forward, Suzanne set her wine glass on the coffee table. Snatching up a tissue, she pressed her lips together in a visible effort not to cry. "I can't deny I'm scared, but you're one of the only friends I have. If Shawn did go on a bender and wanted to track me down, your place would be the first he'd look. I won't put you in the middle of that." Tearing up, she dabbed at her eyes. "I'll be all right." A weak smile curved her lips. "I'll stay here and keep the doors locked. If I hear him outside, I'll call the sheriff's office."

"That's not good enough." Pushing from the couch, Sarah paced across the floor to the window. Suzanne's driveway was hidden from the porch and a hedge line on the side made it easy for someone to creep up unseen. If something happened to Suzanne she'd never forgive herself. She was tempted to call Ryan Flynn on her own but knew it wouldn't do any good. A report of abuse had to be made by the victim. If only there was somewhere Suzanne could stay for a few days until she came to her senses.

Once she wasn't feeling so vulnerable, she'd probably be itching to nail Shawn's butt to the wall. Labeling him as an abuser would give her more power in the divorce. With time, Sarah was sure she could convince Suzanne to follow through on the report but for now she had to make sure Suzanne was safe: Shawn's drinking, coupled with the thought of the spider marking, made her uneasy. Who knew what the jerk was capable of doing if he got thoroughly trashed?

"Stop worrying," Suzanne said to her back. "I'll be healed up in a few more days. In the meantime, I'm just going to have to buck it up. Unless you want me to go to the TNT, there's nowhere I can hide from Shawn."

"The TNT?" Sarah turned, an off the wall idea springing to life in her mind. "I should have thought of that myself."

Suzanne shook her head. "What?"

"I know just where you can hide out for a while. It's the last place Shawn would ever look for you."

"Where?"

Sarah smiled. "How do you feel about UFOs?"

* * * *

"Sure you're up for this?" Shawn grinned, looking between Mitch and Painter, measuring each with a quick glance. Wednesday night with beer fueling their bravado, they'd been up for anything. Now, Friday morning, a gray sky feeding the nesting shadows of the TNT, they were subdued. It all came down to saving face, though Mitch appeared to have more balls than Painter.

The red-haired man was skittish as a colt, constantly glancing over his shoulder at the slightest sound. He'd probably bail before the whole thing played out, but that was okay. Shawn only needed one victim and Mitch's bulk would make him slow.

They'd each brought guns, hunting rifles for distance. He wasn't crazy about having them armed, but he'd played along and lugged a thirty-gauge from home. You couldn't go Mothman hunting without a gun of some sort. If the idiots only knew the real reason they were there.

A lick of adrenalin made him giddy, and he had to fight to keep from laughing.

Mitch shielded his brow with the flat of his hand and took an eagle-eyed look around. "Pretty dense woods in this spot. What makes you think we're going to find the creature here?"

"Don't know." Shawn tugged on the brim of his bright orange ball cap, seating it more comfortably on his head. Mitch and Painter each wore one too, making them easy to spot. After they split up, Shawn planned on ditching his. "Had to start somewhere, and this is where that tourist couple saw the thing last summer. Remember?"

A couple staying at the Parrish Hotel had stumbled over the Mothman while exploring, the woman managing to snap a blurry image of the thing. Eve Parrish had the photo hanging in the lobby of her hotel, something for tourists to gawk over. Shawn thought it looked like a gray blob, but everyone else babbled about it like it was gospel. He'd overheard several awestruck debates about where a wing started and whether this or that curve was part of an arm or a leg.

"We should probably split up. Meet back here in an hour or so."

"I don't know." Painter shifted, scratching the stubble on his cheek. "This is starting to feel like a waste of time. I could be doing something else on a day off."

Mitch guffawed. "Like what? Chasing Judy Freiz? That girl isn't going to look twice at your skinny ass."

"Stuff it, Mitch."

"Hey come on." Shawn held up his hands, wanting to usher proceedings along. "I thought we were here to take down the bird, not each other." He adjusted the rifle strap over his shoulder. "We deliver the Mothman, you guys can have the pick of any girl you want. They're gonna be all over us."

"You already had the best-looking girl in town and lost her." Painter let an edge of disgust creep into his voice. "I don't get how you could cheat when you had someone like Suzanne waiting at home. Hell, she was Miss Point Pleasant before you were married."

Shawn clenched his jaw, struggling to keep anger from his face. His Adam's apple bobbed as he ground words out between his teeth. "Looks aren't everything."

"Don't get testy." Mitch picked up on his aggravation. "It's already sweltering out here." He wiped a meaty hand across his brow. "Let's get going so we can wrap this up by noon. I want to get back for a cold beer."

Shawn nodded. He struck off in one direction while Painter and Mitch headed in another.

Damn. He hadn't wanted them together. He could take either down easily, but in tandem they presented a problem. Hopefully, they'd split up.

He waited until he was certain they were a good distance away, then circled back to the cars—his Dodge, Mitch's Ford truck, and Painter's beat-up wagon. Shawn ditched his hat and the rifle in the Charger, then dug under the passenger's seat for the knife.

A prickle of anticipation traveled up his fingers when he grasped the handle. Against his palm, the wood was rough and warm, a perfect fit that made his breath quicken. Gummy air kept his T-shirt plastered to his skin and a fat bead of sweat oozed down his neck. Licking his lips, he leaned against the car door. He'd do everything right this time, the way he should have done with Hanley. A butchered body in the TNT would immediately scream "Mothman," and that would bring hordes of hunters to track the monster down. When they flushed it out, he would be there to confront it.

And unlike centuries ago, this time he would end the creature's miserable life.

Slipping the knife through his belt, Shawn jogged into the TNT.

* * * *

Quentin knew if he stuck to the weedy path jigsawing through the woods, he'd reach the igloo eventually. Trampled briars and crushed grass defined where other curiosity-seekers had stepped before. According to Sarah, the old World War II bunker attracted everyone from spiritualists and UFO fanatics to kids up for a dare. After encountering the Mothman on his last visit to the TNT, he hadn't been eager to return, but a phone call to Pen earlier that morning made him reconsider. He'd caught her in a depressed mood, pregnancy hormones and his lack of progress leaving her sniffling into the phone. He'd tried to assure her she was getting worked up about nothing. That Madam Olga's warning had been a typical carnival trick, but she'd rattled off a string of calamities and deaths in their family tree, all related to twins. Quentin hated to hear her cry, and his protests had sounded hollow even to him. It was hard to refute fact while staring at the fat scars road-mapped across his hand.

His call to Pen had been all the incentive he needed, especially with Sarah at work and time on his hands. Stopping by the local hardware store, he picked up a can of yellow spray paint, then pointed his Monte Carlo in the direction of the TNT. The trail had been easy to find, the entrance marked by the graffiti-stained post with Beware the Mothman scrawled in the center. He grabbed a flashlight from his glovebox, then wound his way down the overgrown path, pausing every so often to mark a tree with a short line of yellow paint.

Trampling through the woods was outside his usual comfort zone and he wanted a clearly defined exit should he need it in a hurry. Knowing the Mothman could reappear at any moment added fuel to slumbering anxiety.

Eventually, he found the igloo. The domed shell was recessed into a hillside, blanketed with a crown of foliage and trees. He had to pick his way through a tangle of brambles to reach the entrance. Rusting metal doors gaped open on either side, yawning to reveal a heavy web of shadow within. A single gash of diffused light slanted across the dirt floor but otherwise the bunker was dark.

Quentin set the paint can by a pile of rocks. Flicking on his flashlight, he stepped inside.

The place smelled of mold, damp leaves, and wet stone. It was cooler in the dome, but not remarkably so. Beer cans and cigarette butts littered the ground, along with a few dented ammo containers. Someone had dragged a broken crate inside and had tried to use it for kindling, judging by the charred remains. A whisper of soot lingered in the air.

He played the beam of the flashlight off the walls, picking out veins of dirt and patches of lichen. Pen would probably hone in on a supernatural vibe standing in his place, but he felt nothing. The air was slightly moist and clung to his skin displacing the heat outside, but otherwise the igloo was barren.

"Stupid legend." He raised a hand and scrubbed the back of his neck. For Pen's sake, as long as he was there, he might as well follow through on the fool's errand. He should have asked Sarah more questions. Maybe there was a ceremony he had to perform, ritualistic words to mutter.

"I'm looking for Jonathan or Sutton Marsh." His voice was overly loud, cast back with a slight echo. It dawned on him he could no longer hear the breeze rustling through the trees outside. The drone of insects had vanished, taking with it the trill of birdsong. Had that heavy maw of silence hung there since he'd entered? "Hello?"

Nothing.

He stepped closer to the wall and brushed his hand over the rough stone. A bolt of cold shot up his arm. Quentin wrenched backward. "What the hell?"

The stone was old, recessed into the earth. Of course it would be cold. Wetting his lips, he rubbed the pad of his thumb over his fingertips. A faint residue clung to his skin. In the beam of the flashlight, it looked faintly blue, almost phosphorous. Squinting, he moved closer to the wall, studying the buildup on the moldy stone. Just dirt and grime—until he touched the sediment and it flecked off in his hand with that same blue tint. Quentin raised his fingers to his nose but the stuff was odorless.

Something moved behind him. He glanced over his shoulder but the interior of the igloo was empty. Probably just a displacement in the air.

It had grown noticeably colder, the gray slant of light across the ground dimmer.

Quentin hesitated. "Hello," he called again.

There was no echo this time. Coalescing shadows swallowed his voice and crushed the word silent. Turning slowly, he kept his back to the wall. Cold radiated from the stone, rolling over him in a cloak of chill air. Something filmy brushed against his cheek and he batted at it as if swiping away a cobweb. A rustling erupted from the corner. Pivoting, he swung the flashlight in that direction.

"Who's there?"

All around him the walls began to glow with scattered flecks of blue. The same luminescent color bled from his pocket. Quentin dug into his jeans and extracted the amulet. The stone pulsed with light, the veins of black deepening to thin slivers of ink. A wash of blue spread from his hand and fanned across the floor. He no longer needed the flashlight to see. The sharp bite of cold against his palm almost made him drop the amulet.

Ask, a masculine voice instructed, the word heard only in his head.

He gaped at the darkness. Something unseen moved in the shadows. It made his skin crawl, his gut clench up. "Who are you?" His mouth was dry.

No reply.

His fingers tightened around the amulet. Sarah told him the thing only answered in the positive or negative. She said it was an alien—or at least, that's what some people believed. He groped for a name, trying to remember everything she'd told him.

"Are you Indrid Cold?"

Yes.

A dozen thoughts spider-walked through his head. He could be hallucinating, the glowing sediment on the walls tainted with some kind of chemical. It was no secret the TNT was on a government Superfund site. Pollutants and toxins had leeched into the soil. Who was to say those same impurities didn't contaminate the walls of the igloo, affecting him subliminally? Cold could be a figment of his imagination, dredged from his subconscious.

But what of the amulet? The damn thing glowed, reacting to that otherworldly light with an eerie pulse of its own.

"My sister..." He wet his lips, deciding to accept Cold's oracle-like abilities at face value. At least for now. "My sister thinks my family is cursed. Is that true?"

Yes.

No hesitation. Not exactly the answer he wanted. Shifting, he squinted, hoping for a glimpse of the thing in the corner. Shadow lay upon denser shadow, untouched by the blue light.

"Did Cornstalk curse my ancestor?"

Yes.

The word of a disembodied alien to match the word of a carnival fortune-teller. He'd scoffed at Pen, but he couldn't counter the reality of an alien voice inside his head. Lach Evening said the amulet had belonged to Jonathan, and that his brother, Sutton, was responsible for unleashing Cornstalk's curse. Quentin could think of only one reason for the Shawnee chief to curse the man. After what Sarah had told him about how the Indian had died, he saw no way around the grim truth.

"Did Sutton kill Cornstalk?"

Yes.

His gut plummeted. Dragging a hand over his face, he blew out an impatient huff. No one wanted to delve into their family tree and discover a murderer. "Why twins?" All the catastrophes and untimely deaths Penelope had unearthed related solely to twins in the Marsh line. There had to be a reason.

Heavy silence resonated through the igloo. Quentin swore softly. Yes or no answers only. Taking a moment to refocus, he concentrated on what he already knew. He'd come to Point Pleasant to learn about Jonathan Marsh, but Sutton seemed to be the one responsible for the curse.

Something clicked in his head. "Were Jonathan and Sutton twins?"

Yes.

Both were at Fort Randolph around the time Cornstalk was murdered, but Sutton was the one who'd released the curse. "Was Jonathan there when Cornstalk was killed?"

No.

The blue light faltered, dimming slightly. A sliver of warmth crept into the air as the slash of sun angled over the ground brightened in intensity. The shadows flinched away as if stung by the blossoming light. Quentin sensed Cold withdrawing.

"Wait!" He took a hasty step forward. "I'm not through. I have more questions." A shitload of questions, but the protest did no good. As quickly as Cold's presence appeared in the igloo, the aura vanished. The change was immediate. In the span of a single breath, the sound of the surrounding woods intruded into the dome, and the ethereal blue light radiating from the walls faded completely.

Quentin swore softly. Striding from the igloo, he halted outside the doors and examined the amulet. The stone had returned to its natural opaque state, making him wonder if he had imagined the glow. The snap of a twig drew his head up sharply. A rustling noise grew in the distance as if someone—or something—cut a path through the trees. Jamming the amulet into his pocket, he jogged toward the sound.

Whoever, or whatever, it was moved away from him, threading deeper into the trees. Ducking beneath a branch, he veered from the path to follow. A few minutes later, he stopped to listen, the noise shifting course to a different direction. The Mothman was winged, but would the creature also prowl on foot?

Wiping sweat from his lip, Quentin changed direction, maintaining pace with the crunch of underbrush in the distance. He hadn't gone far when he realized he'd left the can of spray paint behind. One elm or spruce looked almost identical to another, and he hadn't counted the turns he'd taken. Stupid mistake.

He wasn't lost so much as disoriented. All he had to do was get his bearings, refocus, and track his steps back to the igloo. He should be able to see signs of a path. Bent ferns, trampled grass, something along those lines. An outdoorsman he wasn't.

Up ahead, a flash of fluorescent orange flitted through the trees.

A hunter. Not only was he lost, he'd been chasing a damn hunter. The best thing he could do was turn around. He didn't know the hunting laws, or if he was in an off-limits area, but the last thing he needed was to be mistaken for game—or worse—the Mothman.

Hesitating, he thought about calling out, but the hunter would probably think him some stupid tourist who didn't know his way around a stand of trees. Now that he was closer, he could see the man was heavyset with a mop of brown curls sticking from beneath an orange cap. Walking in a half-crouch, he held a rifle clutched at the ready in both hands, his expression edgy, a little scared.

Mothman hunting?

Deciding a little ridicule was better than being lost, Quentin was about to call out when an inhuman shriek sent every bird within a hundred yards bursting from the treetops. The hunter yelped, jerking his gun to his shoulder. He pivoted to sight down the barrel and Quentin instinctively ducked for cover.

Somewhere in the distance, a man's terrified voice exploded over the screech of crows and blackbirds: "Mitch! Painter! Help me kill the fucking thing!"

Chapter 9

Shawn was decent at stalking. If his old man had taught him anything, it was how to move quietly through the woods and zero in on prey. His dad knew how to put game on the table, how to skin it, too. He'd always carried a big buck knife with him for the job, but never the knife Shawn clutched in his hand.

Licking his lips, he hunkered down and waited. It took a while, but Mitch and Painter eventually split up. He'd already flagged Mitch as the slower prey. The guy's bulk would make him harder to take down, but his flab would rob him of dexterity. Painter was edgy, greased-hog slick. The more skittish of the two, he was also unpredictable. Best to play it safe and go after Mitch. Shawn couldn't afford to screw up again.

The spirit inhabiting him was restless, its need for revenge growing greater each day. His ancestor's urgency ate at Shawn, hollowing him from the inside out like an empty husk. Hunger was a constant pang. No matter how much he scarfed down, his stomach grumbled in protest. Even his thoughts had become muddled, less and less his own as Obadiah cluttered his head.

Willa. Dear, lovely Willa. Your face haunts me even now.

Shawn shifted the knife to his left hand to rummage a peanut butter cup from his pocket. He peeled off the wrapper and stuffed the candy in his mouth. The orange covering fluttered to the ground, becoming trapped among a clump of weeds. Crushing it under his foot, he followed the path Mitch had taken.

When he'd killed Hanley, he'd been excited by the prospect, now he wanted the task done and over. Mentally, he calculated how many more cuts of the knife it would take to bring down Mitch than it had the farmer.

Slash. Do not plunge the blade.

Yeah, yeah, he knew the score. Only the Mothman had multiple claws on each hand, and he had a single-bladed knife. No one would buy the creature as the killer. He saw that now, as clearly as he saw he'd lost control over his vengeful ancestor. Obadiah was too consumed by hatred to spot the flaws in his plan, but the screw-ups didn't matter. Once Shawn did as the spirit required, he'd be free of the thing, and the power of the knife would be his. When he killed the Mothman, he'd be walking on fame. Real fame, not the petty shit he earned from dirt track racing. He'd kick the local circuit goodbye and move on to better things, a man of wealth and power.

All because of the blade.

A flash of orange through the trees made him pause and suck on his bottom lip. Mitch was close, unaware he was being tracked. He'd have to wait until the guy's back was turned. Even then, if Mitch pivoted at the last minute it was doubtful he'd suspect anything wrong. Buy a man some wings and beer, bond over plans to hack up a bug-eyed creature, and you had a friend for life.

Sidestepping a root jutting from the ground, Shawn inched closer. A fly buzzed near his head and he swatted it away. Within seconds it was back, louder than before.

He stopped abruptly.

Not a fly.

The drone grew in volume, drilling into his skull. Something foreign, something evil.

The creature!

A blood-curdling cry rent the air, launching a flock of birds from the treetops. Shawn's teeth clacked together. Instinctively, he dropped to one knee, clutching the knife to his chest. His breath hitched in his throat, growing ragged.

He'd heard that unholy shriek before, the sound forever embedded in his mind.

Leaves matted on the ground, wet with rain...his hand drenched with the lifeblood of the demon...the piercing scream of something primordial and unholy...an explosion of crushing pain...daylight tumbling into a black abyss...

His head spun, memories that were not memories hurling rapid-fire through his mind. Light plunged into shadow as the sun was blotted from view and the sweep of a wing spurred a cyclone around him. He tucked and rolled, propelled by the buffeting whirlwind. Pressure built in his head until he thought his eyes would pop.

Get up. Fight it! Kill it!

Terror gripped him, the sheer malignancy of the creature pinioning him in place. Overcome, he dropped the knife and babbled a plea for mercy. For one insane moment, he remembered Hanley sounding every bit as pathetic.

Get up. Fight it! Kill it!

Sickle-sharp talons raked through the air awakening the memory of death.

His chest flayed open, blood bubbling from his mouth....

Shawn screamed and rolled to the side. "Mitch! Painter!" Panic ripped the words from his throat. "Help me kill the fucking thing! Get over here!" He bolted in the direction Mitch had gone, the pounding of his feet swallowed by the roar of the creature's wings.

Branches stuck his face and grazed his hands. He tripped over a rock and almost fell. Righting himself, he stumbled forward, barely pausing to gulp a breath. Terror drove him, dark and blood-soaked, robbing him of courage.

"You bastard, Obadiah! You didn't tell me it killed you."

If he could only get away. Hide. Rethink the plan.

Coward.

Shawn burst through a tangle of trees just as a rifle shot exploded in the air. He nearly collided with Mitch, clutching at the big man to keep from falling.

His face the bloodless white of a cadaver, Mitch stood with his mouth gaping open, his rifle raised for another shot.

And just that quickly the incessant droning ceased. The roar of wings retreated in the distance.

Pivoting to look behind him, Shawn sucked air into his lungs.

The nightmarish creature vanished into the sky.

* * * *

Quentin jogged into the open where Shawn stood with the heavyset man just as a lanky redhead burst from the trees. The latecomer waved a rifle above his head.

"It was here! It was here! Did you see the fucking thing?"

"No shit!" Shawn Preech was clearly shaken to the core. "It tried to kill me, you asshole. Where were you?" The words held an edge, but quaked too much to carry a threat. Hands on knees, Shawn gulped air like a fish on dry land.

The redhead barely noticed him, quickly churning up the distance to the heavyset man. He looked close to hyperventilating. "Did you hit it, Mitch?"

"Couldn't." The big guy shook his head. His hands trembled noticeably. "I missed it. Couldn't get past those eyes, like they were boring into my head or something. I'm not too proud to admit I went weak in the knees. It's going to take a hell of a lot to kill that damn bird. Maybe more than we've got."

Shawn straightened up. "You should have shot it, Painter."

The redhead—Quentin guessed he had to be Painter—was starting to calm down. His eyes narrowed. "Why didn't you? Where's your rifle?"

Shawn recoiled, lapping a tongue over his lips. "Jammed on me early. I took it back to the car."

Mitch rounded on him incredulously. "You were out here unarmed?"

"I dropped my knife." Shawn looked away, zeroing in on Quentin for the first time. "What the hell are you doing here?"

Quentin wondered the same thing. How had he gotten caught up in something that was probably better avoided? Shoving his hands in his pockets, he stepped closer. "I was hiking. I heard you yell."

"Did you see the Mothman?" Mitch asked. "Did you hear it scream?"

The unholy sound had made every nerve in his body stand on end. "I heard the birds. Saw them burst from the trees." An inner voice warned him not to mention the creature. He'd seen it wing away when Mitch triggered his rifle, but he didn't want to be a collaborating witness on whatever tales these three decided to spread. He glanced at Shawn. "Are you all right?"

A grunt and a curt nod served as his answer. Shawn tugged his shirt down. "Never better, but you've all seen what a menace this thing is. Even you." He hooked a thumb in Quentin's direction.

"Quentin Marsh."

"Yeah, I remember you from the River. Tourist at the hotel, right?"

Quentin returned his nod.

"Might be time to bring in Pete Weston's men." Painter was jittery. He didn't seem able to stand still. Pacing back and forth, he glanced over his shoulder repeatedly as if expecting the Mothman to swoop into their midst. "I'm all for admitting I'm outclassed and letting guys like Caden and Ryan Flynn handle this."

"Me too." Color had returned to Mitch's face, but of the three he appeared the most shaken.

Quentin couldn't blame him. Mitch had stared headlong into the creature's eyes; an unnerving encounter Quentin had experienced firsthand. He expected Shawn to be more traumatized, but the dirt track racer looked angrier, less terrified with every passing second. He and the others had obviously come to the TNT with the sole intent of hunting the Mothman.

That Preech ditched his gun had made him the most vulnerable, probably why the creature singled him out.

"So, we go back and report it." Shawn wiped his palms on his jeans, glancing at each in turn. "You too." He pointed to Quentin. "Even if you didn't see the thing, you know something happened. The more voices we have shaking up Mason County, the more likely Pete Weston is to get off his butt and do something. He isn't going to like the idea of tourists turning into Mothman snacks. If you add your voice to what we say, it's gotta help."

Quentin hedged.

Mitch and Painter looked at him expectantly, Painter bobbing his head on a skinny neck. Both were clearly in agreement with Preech's reasoning. He needed to talk to Caden Flynn anyway. Maybe he could be the voice of sanity in what was likely to become an embellished tale.

"Yeah, okay. But I got turned around in here when I heard you yelling. I'm going to need help getting back to the road."

"Mitch and Painter can show you." Shawn was already turning away. "I gotta go back for my knife. I'll meet all of you at the sheriff's office."

"Yeah, okay." Mitch clapped Painter on the back.

As Shawn disappeared into the woods, Quentin looked between his two guides, wondering why neither found it odd Preech had been hunting the cryptid armed only with a knife.

* * * *

Shawn backtracked at a brisk jog, his mind working overtime. He needed to get the knife before anyone found it. Not that anyone else would be able to call on its power. That ability came from Obadiah, the warlock inhabiting his body. The same black magician who'd met his death in the area that would become the TNT.

He ground his teeth.

All those thoughts...images in his head...he should have realized the truth before. Obadiah had been killed by the Mothman, a brutal attack that ended with his body ripped to shreds. No wonder he wanted the thing dead. His need for vengeance had nothing to do with his wife.

It has everything to do with Willa!

Clenching his jaw, Shawn willed the internal voice silent. That was something he hadn't been able to do before. Learning the truth had given him a meager amount of leverage. Obadiah remained coiled in his mind, feeding on his strength, filling him with insatiable hunger.

"Don't worry, old man. I still intend to kill the thing, but this time we do it my way."

With Mitch, Painter, and the tourist backing him up, Pete Weston would be forced to flush the thing out. If it took every law officer in the state of West Virginia, Shawn would make sure the cryptid couldn't hide. The time of reckoning had come.

For Obadiah. For the Mothman. For Shawn Preech.

Threading between pockets of trees, he slowed and glanced from side-to-side. He'd dropped the knife somewhere near here. He'd told the others he'd meet them at Weston's office, but there was no way he was leaving without the weapon.

He kicked apart a cluster of weeds to peer closer. Bending, he rummaged through the grass, rifling aside small stones and twigs. He turned in a circle, flattening toadstools and thistles as he widened the arc. It took several minutes of searching but eventually his fingers butted against a hard wooden handle.

An exhale of relief whistled through his teeth.

He didn't understand what gave the blade power, but the rush he got from holding the knife was a better high than any drug could give. Closing his eyes, he tried to place his failure in context.

He'd never seen the Mothman up close before, but the next time he would know what to expect. No cowering, no running. He would face the demon as a man, the one destined to slay it. Weston and the Flynn brothers might flush it from the trees, even riddle it with bullets, but he would hold the satisfaction of plunging the dark metal blade into the creature's heart. The knife had already drunk its share of blood in the past.

He sensed that now. Felt a feather touch of memories awaken.

As the malignancy of the weapon surged through him, the whispers of those other deaths flirted at the edge of his consciousness—Marsh and Cornstalk, one dead by his hand, the other because of him. And the killing that had been the most astonishing to discover, buried deep in his ancestor's subconscious—the slaying of the Mothman's offspring.

* * * *

Gripping a ceramic coffee mug by the rim, Caden set it in front of Shawn.

The younger man nodded his gratitude, his knee bouncing up and down like a yo-yo bolstered by speed. Hollow-cheeked and red-eyed, he perched on the chair beside Caden's desk. His antsy fidgeting suggested he was ready to bolt from the room at any moment.

"Then what happened?" Resuming his seat, Caden spared a glance for the report he'd been writing before returning his attention to Shawn. At the back of the room, Ryan interviewed Mitch Kennit and Sid Painter at a table littered with papers and used Styrofoam cups. They'd already polished off a full pot of coffee and half of another. Shawn and his friends had been three shades past rattled when they burst into the office, jabbering about a Mothman attack. Only Quentin Marsh, who spoke to Wayne Rosling at Rosling's desk, appeared subdued. He hadn't committed to seeing the cryptid, only to being in the area.

"Why do you keep asking what happened?" Shawn drummed a frenzied beat against his thigh. *Rap-rap-rap-rap.* "Why aren't you out there, hunting that winged freak down?"

"We have several deputies in the vicinity." Available patrols had been rerouted to the TNT yet again. The continued surveillance without results was starting to mimic a Boy Who Cried Wolf parable, but public safety couldn't be ignored. Shawn, Mitch, and Painter would blab news of the attack from one end of Point Pleasant to the other. If Pete Weston didn't flush the creature from the woods, there were enough residents eager to arm themselves and protect their town. It had happened before.

Whatever was at fault for spurring the Mothman into bouts of terrorizing, the creature was no longer content to lie low. Shawn Preech was proof of that. "Why would you go out there in the first place?"

"Huh?" Shawn's mouth fell open. "You're not seriously asking why we'd want to off the Mothman?"

"You've lived here all your life, Shawn. The creature's been part of that. Why go after it now?"

Shawn stared blankly. Caden could almost see the wheels spinning in his head as he scrambled for an answer. It didn't take long to find one. "Man, that fucking thing tried to kill me just now. It chased after Clark Richards when he was biking the other day—told me he thought he'd have a heart attack—and it damn near scared the bejesus out of old lady Quiggly. You seriously got to ask why now?" He shook his head vehemently. "Cornstalk cursed us with that damn bird. It's time we get rid of it for good."

"So, you, and Mitch, and Painter decided to do that?"

"Yeah, why not?" Shawn slurped coffee, then dragged a hand across his mouth. "Hey, you wouldn't have anything to eat around here? It's getting on toward lunch and I'm starving." More knee-bouncing as if he'd ingested a barrel of caffeine.

"We shouldn't be too much longer." Caden picked up the report and studied it again. "You said your rifle jammed shortly after the three of you split up, and you carried it back to the car."

"Yeah."

"What were you shooting at when it jammed?"

"Uh…" A blank look that lasted for all of ten seconds as Shawn scrambled for an answer. "I thought I saw something in the trees. I took aim, but it turned out to be nothing."

In the background, Painter's voice lurched higher as he relayed some particular point in his story. Neither Mitch nor Painter had been friends with Shawn, yet the three had teamed up on a whim. Earlier, Shawn had told him they'd made the plan over beers and wings in the River Café. He couldn't imagine Shawn being that persuasive, but once plans were made few men would back out for pride.

"You no longer had your rifle with you." Caden waited while Shawn let the statement sink in. "How were you going to hunt the Mothman without a weapon?"

"Thought I'd team up with Mitch or Painter." Shawn scratched his cheek. His fingernails were ragged and dirty. "Told you I had a knife."

"What kind of knife?"

"Hunting knife. Big one." He slurped more coffee. "It's in the car."

"Go get it."

"Huh?"

Caden leaned back in his chair. Across the room, Quentin Marsh stood, then headed toward the coffee pot. "Get the knife. I want to see it."

"What the hell for? What good will that do?"

"It'll back up your story."

"I got Mitch and Painter to back up my story. I even got the tourist over there." He jabbed a finger in Marsh's direction. "I don't need more back up than that."

"If I say you do, you do. Especially if you want to get out of here in time for lunch." Caden was being hardnosed but didn't care. Something about the encounter felt off. When it came down to it, something about Shawn felt off.

Heaving a disgusted sigh, Preech shoved from the chair and stomped toward the door. A muttered string of profanities trailed behind him.

"Make sure you come back or I'll toss your report in the trash."

The door slammed.

Caden rubbed his eyes. It was going to be a hell of a long day. They still didn't have a solid lead on Hanley's death, a situation that had the city council and residents in general putting pressure on Weston. Once word spread about the Mothman, concern would give way to panic. People were already whispering the cryptid had caused Will's murder. Fear and paranoia had a way of morphing into mass hysteria.

"Just so you know…" Marsh appeared beside Caden's desk, his voice low. "I didn't tell them about the other encounter with the Mothman. I haven't said a word to anyone."

Caden nodded. Before he could comment, Shawn returned and stomped across the room to his desk. He dropped the knife in the center of Caden's paperwork.

"There." Preech jutted his chin. "Satisfied?"

Caden picked up the weapon, noting the swage at the tip. There was no visible notch, but the blade was the right size and style for the weapon used in Will Hanley's murder. He prodded the tip lightly and felt the pad of his thumb catch on a small nick. The defect might not be visible, but would it be enough for Redmond to flag in an autopsy report? As Caden had told Weston, half of Mason County carried hunting knives. Imperfections in a blade were common after repeated use.

"That's a hell of a knife." The etching of a spider decorated the handle a few inches from the base. Apparently hand-carved, the grooves in the image had blackened over time. Caden eyed Shawn directly. "You use this for hunting?"

"Sometimes." Shawn dropped in the chair. The heel of his right foot beat a rapid tempo against the floor. "My dad did."

Caden had never seen Shawn's father with the knife and suspected it was a lie. "It looks old."

Shawn shrugged. "Like I said, it was my dad's. I don't know where he got it." He swiveled to retrieve his coffee, then downed a healthy gulp.

Caden nodded to the etching on the handle. "Kind of a weird mark for a hunting knife."

"I've seen that symbol before." Wandering closer, Quentin Marsh peered over his shoulder.

Shawn shot him an annoyed glance. "Look, it's just some kind of family thing." He plunked the coffee mug on Caden's desk with enough force to splatter liquid over the edge. "I got you the knife like you asked. I gave you my report like a concerned citizen. It's up to you and Pete Weston to get that damn bird before it kills somebody. I'm freaking starving and want to get lunch. And you can bet I'm gonna make sure everyone in town knows what happened today."

"Yeah." Caden was tempted to hold him for attitude, but knew it would never fly. He shoved a written report under Shawn's nose. "Sign this and get the hell out of here."

Shawn scribbled his signature, then stood and grabbed his knife. He was halfway to the door when Caden's words stopped him.

"Be careful about how much trouble you stir up, Shawn. It could come back and bite you in the ass."

The door slammed for the second time when Preech left. Swearing softly, Caden gathered his paperwork and stood. At the back of the room, Mitch and Painter were still engrossed with Ryan. He noted Quentin waiting nearby and approached.

"Marsh. I've been meaning to talk to you."

"Same here."

"Huh?" The revelation caught Caden off guard.

"Lach Evening suggested it." Quentin waited a second for the name to register. "You do know him, right?"

"Yeah." Interesting how Lach managed to pull strings. "Actually, he shared some information recently I think you and Sarah would find interesting. That's probably what he was referring to."

Quentin didn't question why Lach didn't tell him directly, or why Sarah was involved. Maybe he already had an inkling the man in black stingily doled out information the way a mystery writer meted out clues.

"Sarah and Eve are good friends," Caden said. "Why don't you and Sarah drop by for dinner tomorrow night? How's six-thirty? Sarah knows where we live."

Quentin hedged.

"It will be easier to talk," Caden said. "What I have to share can't be said in ten minutes."

"Okay. I'll get in touch with Sarah." Quentin was about to turn away when Caden stopped him.

"One more thing...you said you recognized the spider symbol on Shawn's knife."

"Yeah." Quentin's mouth tightened. "Sarah and I found it in a book about witchcraft. It means treachery and death."

* * * *

Fifteen minutes later the office was nearly empty. A single clerk worked in the background, pattering away on an IBM Selectric. Ryan had finished with Painter and Mitch, then headed out to grab lunch. Rosling ended his shift for the day, hinting he was going to drive by the TNT on the way home. Caden took a moment to phone Eve and share the impromptu dinner invitation he'd extended to Marsh. She was surprised, but looked forward to seeing Sarah. Adding Quentin as a quasi-date for her friend only made her more intrigued.

Reviewing the Mothman report he'd taken, Caden replayed his conversation with Shawn. There was something off about the dirt track racer, a jitteriness that grew more pronounced each time Caden saw him. Shawn's dad had been an avid hunter, but that interest had never found a foothold in his son. So why had Shawn taken to skulking around the TNT, hunting the worst possible creature he could encounter? Even if he'd suddenly developed a taste for the sport, why arm himself with an antique knife? Caden doubted Shawn's father had ever used the blade for gutting deer, so why lie?

Caden leaned back in his chair, mulling over the thoughts.

A typical buck knife fit the bill for the weapon used in Will Hanley's murder, but most weren't owned by a man who'd suddenly taken to fidgety actions. Whose bloodshot eyes and hollowed-out appearance hinted of drug use. With a divorce hanging over his head, Shawn might have decided booze wasn't enough to get through the day. A man under the influence of narcotics could easily crack, driven to committing a violent crime without even realizing what he did. Hanley had known his killer, and Hanley knew Shawn.

Caden's gaze shifted to the coffee cup on the corner of his desk, a gift much too convenient to overlook. The mug had Shawn's fingerprints all over it. He'd never have a better opportunity to dig deeper where Shawn was concerned. Retrieving the cup by the rim, Caden dropped it in an evidence bag. Shawn had drained the thing dry.

He carried it down the hall to the crime lab where he found Roy Baxter shuffling through several weeks of paperwork.

"Hey, Roy."

The shorter man stopped mid-shuffle to peer at Caden over a pair of tortoiseshell glasses. He heaved a harried sigh. "If Pete sent you for an update, I'm on it, but it's going to take time. Do you know how many case samples we have on that damn bird?"

Word of the latest Mothman scare had obviously spread through channels. Since the first sighting in sixty-six, Roy had cataloged every minor scrap of evidence related to the cryptid. Foliage, broken twigs, bits of trash— anything found at the sighting locations had been collected, cataloged, and analyzed for residue. Given Shawn and the others were sure to broadcast their encounter, Pete was taking the latest uproar seriously.

"Sorry you got the paper trail." Caden leaned against the counter. "I need something run through the lab." He set the cup in front of the other man. "You'll find my fingerprints on the rim, Shawn Preech's on the handle and body."

Only half listening, Roy continued to flip through papers. "So, what do you need me for?"

"Shawn works on the docks. They fingerprint a lot of those guys for security. I want you to check to see if the two sets match."

"That's it?" Roy looked up sharply, a scowl digging at the corners of his mouth. "Pete's preparing for Mothman Armageddon and you want me to match prints on a dock worker who moonlights racing cars?"

"That's not all I want you to do." Caden waited until he was certain he had Roy's undivided attention. "When you're through, I want you to match Shawn's fingerprints against the latents from the Hanley murder."

* * * *

Sarah was on a phone call when Quentin appeared in the records division. She signaled she'd be with him in a moment, then finished with the caller.

"Hi." The smile came of its own accord as she stepped to the counter. They'd spent so much time together lately—research, dinner, lunches, even his unexpected visit last night—that she would miss him when he finally left town. "I didn't expect to see you today."

"I hope you didn't mind that I dropped by last night."

"Not at all." She hadn't minded the kiss either. It had been on her mind most of the day. "Did you walk from the hotel?"

"The sheriff's office."

Somewhere in the background a phone rang but she left it for her coworkers to snag. "What were you doing there?"

"Filing a report." He told her about his early morning experience in the TNT. "I'll tell you about what happened in the igloo later," he said when he was through. "The important thing is that I saw the Mothman again."

Sarah shot a glance over her shoulder. No one seemed to be paying them any attention. Patty had retrieved the phone call, and Carol was pounding out a form on her typewriter. Leaning closer, Sarah lowered her voice. "Did you tell Caden everything that happened?"

Quentin shook his head. "I didn't tell him I saw the creature. I didn't want to back up Preech's claim." He shrugged as if unable to explain his actions. "I said I heard yelling and came on the scene after the fact. Caden wants us to have dinner with him and Eve tomorrow night. I think he knows more than he's letting on."

Of course, he did. Somehow, some way, Caden was connected to the Mothman. She'd held suspicions about Eve's husband for a long time, but Eve had always been quick to turn her curiosity aside. "I can do that. But I'm worried about what happened. Did the Mothman go after you again?"

"Not even close. It was focused on Preech." Pausing, Quentin scrubbed his hand over his face. The scars across the back of his fingers stood out like angry welts. "Here's the thing, Sarah—Preech had an old knife. The thing looked ancient. I saw it when he showed it to Caden."

Shawn Preech with a knife. A lot of guys carried them when hunting or hiking in the TNT, but after what Shawn had done to Suzanne, she didn't like the thought of him with a weapon. Quentin didn't know about her friend or where she was hiding, so she focused on the knife instead.

"A lot of guys carry them in the TNT."

"Yeah." His voice was flat. "That might be, but this one was different. It had a spider carved on the handle."

* * * **

When Sarah's workday ended, she stopped by the hotel, knowing Katie would be working that evening. Her friend had been instrumental in helping Suzanne out of her bind, even if Suzanne and Katie didn't have good history between them.

It was hard for Sarah to focus on the whirlwind of thoughts battering her mind. She'd never been so grateful for the workday to end. Word had already spread through town about the latest Mothman sighting—people were referring to it as an attack. The thought of Shawn with a knife embellished with a spider made her sick to her stomach. On top of that, the wind had kicked up again, the sky alternating between cloudy and storm-black. The paltry smidgen of sunlight they'd enjoyed was quickly devoured, the last hour bringing nothing but thunder and lightning mixed with a few drops of rain. The constant threat of a storm had her on edge.

"Hi." Stepping into the lobby, Sarah was glad to find it empty of guests. Behind the registration counter, Katie worked at adding tags to several skeleton-style keys strewn over the counter. The antique hardware was yet another whimsical element of the lodging's old-fashioned charm. "How is everything?"

Katie glanced up from deftly coding a tag. "If you're referring to the hotel, it's quiet, but I don't think it's going to stay that way."

"Oh?" Concern drew Sarah's brows into a frown. She approached the counter and set her purse on top, careful not to make a shambles of Katie's work. "What's wrong?"

"Shawn Preech showed up at the café about an hour ago."

Alarm kicked in, matched by a prickly swell of anger. "He doesn't know about Suzanne, does he?"

Katie shook her head. Her blond hair was pulled back in a ponytail, a casual style that made her seem younger than her twenty-eight years. The girlish youthfulness vanished when her mouth tightened in a hard line. "Any man who hits a woman isn't going to get so much as an acknowledgement from me, let alone information about his ex." Although Katie spoke quietly, her words carried a harsh edge. The hostility probably came from watching her mother suffer at the hands of more than one abusive ex-boyfriend.

She pushed a handful of keys aside, the metal scraping across the smooth wood of the check-in counter. "I know Suzanne and I weren't friendly in the past—if anything she was cruel to me—but I do think she's trying to change. Any buried resentment I might have had I'm happy to direct at Shawn. What a bastard."

"I know." Sarah leaned against the counter. She'd been hesitant to check in with Suzanne today, but knew Katie would have gotten an update from Jerome.

Jerome Kelly was as backward and awkward as Suzanne was gorgeous. Point Pleasant's local conspiracy theorist, he held a radical fascination with UFOs and the Mothman. Most people tended to overlook him. Few took him seriously. Katie had befriended him over the fall, and he'd quickly glommed onto her. Since then, she and Ryan had been doing their best to include him in their circle of friends in an attempt to make him less of an outcast. In the process, Jerome had developed a puppy-dog crush on Katie. There was little he wouldn't do for her, exactly why Sarah had asked her to intercede with him on Suzanne's behalf.

Jerome's house was tucked in a remote location on the outskirts of the TNT. The last place Shawn Preech would ever think to look for his estranged wife was with a loser—in Shawn's mind anyway—like Jerome.

"Did Jerome say how Suzanne settled in?" Sarah had a hard time picturing the two in Jerome's small rancher but at least the setup was only temporary. In a few days, Suzanne would come to her senses and file charges against Shawn for assault. Or at least, that was the outcome Sarah envisioned.

Katie picked up several loose key tags and deposited them in a metal storage box. "If I know Jerome, he's tripping over himself, treating Suzanne like a queen. I hope she appreciates what he's doing. Jerome might not be the most popular person on the planet, but he's loyal to a fault. He won't say anything about her situation to anyone."

"I know." Thanks to Jerome's graciousness in providing Suzanne a place to stay, Sarah could dispense with worry over Shawn's whereabouts. Part of her wanted to march into the café and give the jerk a piece of her mind, but she'd promised Suzanne to keep her mouth shut.

"How are things going with Quentin?" Katie abruptly changed the subject, her smile flavored with a hint of teasing.

"I'm not sure what you mean." Sarah didn't plan on being baited into the Oujia board prediction. "He's a nice guy and I'm helping him with some genealogy research." There had been that kiss in her kitchen, an interlude she wouldn't mind experiencing again, but sharing the thoughts would only bring greater prodding. In some ways, she deserved it. She'd done the same to Katie when her friend had been coy about her relationship with Ryan. "Quentin and I are supposed to be having dinner with Eve and Caden on Saturday night."

Katie raised a brow. "That sounds interesting."

"It'll be nice to see Eve." She tried not to make more out of it than it was. "Caden told Quentin he has some information to share. I think it has to do with Quentin's interest in his family tree."

"Still no luck there?"

"It's slow going."

The sound of footsteps drew her attention to the hallway. A couple she didn't recognize walked from the direction of the café, the woman clutching the man's arm, her face crinkled in worry.

"But what if it's true? What if we can't leave town tomorrow?" The woman's voice carried to the front desk as they drew closer. "Cora is expecting us no later than ten."

"Hi, Mr. and Mrs. Nettles." Katie smiled at the couple who looked to be somewhere in their late forties. "Is there anything I can help you with?"

"Oh." Mrs. Nettles paused, her hand fluttering to her throat. Her expression shifted between relief and concern. "I hope so. Have you heard about it, too?"

Katie exchanged a glance with Sarah before looking back to the couple. "About what?"

"The Mothman. That horrible creature…it attacked people this afternoon. The man in the café said it tried to kill them."

No doubt Shawn Preech was the man in the café.

"We get a lot of those rumors around here." Katie's casual reply indicated she hoped to defuse the situation. The Mothman was good for bringing tourists to the hotel, but for those passing through the legend could backfire. "I wouldn't put too much stock in it."

"But that man was empathic about what happened." Mrs. Nettles wasn't ready to dismiss her fear. "He said the sheriff's office would be setting up roadblocks around the TNT area, and we're planning on leaving that way. Our niece is getting married tomorrow and my sister is expecting us early."

Katie's mouth tightened as if she fought a slow burn of anger that Shawn would pretend to be an authority on the workings of the sheriff's department. "If that man in the café was named Shawn, he's blowing hot air. My fiancé is a sergeant with the Mason County Sheriff's Department and I haven't heard anything about roadblocks."

"Oh, could you check with him, please?" An expression of eager hope crossed Mrs. Nettles' face. Stepping away from her husband, she latched onto the registration counter. "It would mean a lot to know we won't have a problem. Otherwise, I think we should leave tonight."

"Clara, leave the lady alone." Mr. Nettles spoke for the first time. "If she said we won't have a problem, we won't have a problem. We'll leave in the morning as planned. I'm not fighting Friday night traffic based on a rumor. Besides, it looks like it's going to storm any minute."

"It's looked that way since we got here." Mrs. Nettles bit her lip.

Sarah felt sorry for the woman, who appeared on the verge of tears. Shawn must have put on quite a performance.

"It's all right." Katie reached for the phone. "If it will help, I'll make a quick call."

"Katie, I'm going to step into the café. I'll talk to you later." Sarah waved to her friend. She hadn't seen Quentin since he showed up at the courthouse and hoped to catch him in the café. Factor in morbid curiosity that made her want to hear Shawn's account of his Mothman encounter firsthand, and she hurried down the hallway. Too bad the creature hadn't done a real number on him. After what the creep had done to Suzanne he deserved to suffer pain and fear firsthand. She was going to have a hard time keeping her mouth shut when she saw him.

Slipping inside the café, Sarah found Shawn holding center court at the bar. A crowd had gathered around him, several people nursing beers as they swapped tales about the TNT and Mothman sightings. Even those seated at nearby tables appeared to be listening, unconcerned that Shawn's voice carried over their dinner conversations.

"If Pete Weston knows what's good, he'll have his entire force scouring the TNT. I'm telling you that thing's got to be flushed out." Shawn took a swig of beer, then set his glass on the bar. With his back pressed to the counter, he shoved a handful of fries in his mouth. "From now on, I'm not going anywhere without a rifle."

A chorus of agreement rose around him. Two men seated close to the doorway debated the best weapon for protecting their families. "Pistol won't do no good," the first man was saying. "You need a long gun for distance. Shoot the thing before it gets close enough to use its claws. I heard some teens saw it over near Gallipolis the other day, and..."

The man's words faded as Sarah moved closer to where Shawn sat. Did he have the knife on him now? The one with the weird spider mark on the handle? She stepped closer, watching as he polished off the remains of a hamburger.

Shock coursed through her.

Shawn looked like a man suffering from terminal illness. His clothes hung on his thin frame and his eyes were sunken, excessively bright as though fired with fever. She almost didn't recognize him. He'd never been overly concerned with appearance, but his clothing had been clean, his hair neatly combed. Even when he'd gone on a drinking binge, he washed up and shaved. Now he looked like a derelict. Someone who should be sleeping off a narcotic high in a gutter. Was it possible he'd started experimenting with drugs?

He caught her staring. "You got a problem?"

She clamped down on her tongue. Yes, she had a problem. He'd beaten the shit out of his estranged wife. If anyone was a monster, it was Shawn-stinking-Preech, not the Mothman. "I was surprised to hear you were in here." Sarah struggled to keep venom from her voice. "I heard you haven't been to work all week." She'd glommed onto that bit of scuttlebutt at Doreen Sue's hair salon when she'd swung by for can of hairspray on her lunch hour.

"Been sick." Shawn snagged a slice of pizza from a plate on the bar, folded it in half and chomped off the end. It dripped cheese and sausage onto his fingers. Licking at the goo, he reached for his beer. Another three slices waited on the plate. How much could one person eat, especially someone who'd grown stick thin?

"Yeah. A sick bastard." There were so many people talking around her, she doubted he'd hear.

His ears were as sharp as his appetite. "What'd you say, bitch?" Red-faced, Shawn swiveled around on the barstool.

Conversation stopped immediately as if someone dropped a shroud over the room.

"Hey! You don't talk like that in here, or I'll kick your butt onto the street." Behind the bar, Tucker stalked from his place to confront Shawn. A meaty finger broached the distance between them. "Apologize or get the hell out."

"She called me a bastard."

"Probably had reason to."

"Just like I got reason to stay." Shawn shoved to his feet. Gripping the edge of the bar, he leaned forward until his face was only inches from

Tucker's. "You best remember who's keeping all these people in here, buying booze and food. They wanna hear about the Mothman and what that damn creature almost did to me, Mitch, and Painter. You toss me out, I can tell the same tales on the street. You won't be ringing up sales on your cash register then."

Tucker's mouth twisted in disgust. "You're an ass, Shawn."

"But he's right about everything he said." Mitch Kennit muscled his way from a corner. His face was red, thick fingers wrapped around a can of Budweiser. "All I want to know is what we're going to do about that damn creature. The thing's a menace. It tried to kill us."

"Got that right," someone echoed.

Other voices chimed in. "...terrorized our town long enough...poor Will Hanley...probably at fault...got kids to worry about..."

"Mr. Kennit, perhaps I am mistaken, but I believe you were not in the immediate vicinity when the creature attacked Mr. Preech." A man's voice cut through the hubbub of conversation, drawing Mitch and Shawn around like marionettes on a string.

Recognizing the unusual accent, Sarah turned as Lach Evening approached from the doorway. Once infatuated by his looks and enigmatic personality, all she felt now was a keen sense of relief. Lach was not someone to be trifled with. If anyone could put Shawn Preech in his place, it was Point Pleasant's mysterious visitor.

The crowd parted before him as if recognizing the oddity of a man wearing a black suit on a hot July day. Add in his white-blond hair and coal-black eyes and Lach invited stares.

Mitch grunted, no longer sure of himself. "Who are you?"

Ignoring him, Lach nodded politely to Sarah. "It is good to see you again, Miss Sherman."

A streak of warmth shot through her. Her infatuation may have waned, but his attention still brought a flush to her cheeks. "And you."

"Hey, I remember you." Shoving past Mitch, Shawn angled his beer bottle to point at Lach. "You're one of those weird Men in Black who showed up last fall when we had all that UFO shit going on. You—" His gaze dropped to Lach's hands, which were folded in front of him. Spitting out a croak, he jerked violently backward. His face drained of color.

"Holy shit." Shaking his head, Shawn backed away. Panic flitted through his eyes.

Sarah stood close enough to catch his shocked whisper.

"Can't be. Not freaking possible." Stumbling to the bar, Shawn bobbled his beer onto the top. "Tucker, give me my bill. I'm settling up and getting out of here."

"Only too glad to comply." Tucker flipped through a few slips and located his tab.

Shawn's fingers trembled as he tossed a handful of bills onto the counter.

"Hey, Shawn, where are you headed?" Mitch seemed upset to be losing his partner in conspiracy.

"Outside." Shawn didn't bother to raise his head. "Gotta get away. Gotta think." Head down, he stalked to the door and blundered onto the street.

Sarah stared after him, unable to comprehend his sudden change in attitude. Conversation resumed, mostly murmurs about the Mothman. When she glanced back to speak with Lach Evening, she discovered the Man in Black had vanished as silently as he'd appeared.

* * * *

Shawn stalked into the kitchen, wrenched open the refrigerator, and stood staring at the empty shelves. Why hadn't he stopped at the store and grabbed some lunchmeat and bread? He'd downed a mound of food at the River, but renewed hunger gnawed at his gut. If he hadn't been so freaked over Evening, he would have had enough sense to buy groceries.

Left to foraging, he poked around in the cupboard until he found a can of Chef Boyardee ravioli. Processed cheese and doughy carbs had never looked so good. Salivating, he rummaged up a manual can opener and impatiently cranked off the top. No sense heating the stuff up. Pacing to the window, he forked the cold pasta into his mouth.

What the hell was he going to do about Evening?

It cannot be him. It is not possible.

"No shit, but you saw his hands."

He chewed mechanically. Dropped a glob of sauce onto his shirt, then swabbed it clean. He sucked the residue off his fingers, worrying the problem through his head. A clock above the stove ticktocked methodically as shadows seeped into the room. No need for light. He'd learned to see in the dark, thanks to Obadiah.

His ancestor stirred restlessly.

Evening looked different, his hair loose about his face rather than drawn back in a pigtail queue, his clothing tailored to modern styles. Changes aside, there was no disguising his features, his unusual accent, or those peculiar hands. The man who'd confronted him in the café was the same person who'd frequented Fort Randolph as a tradesman.

Rowan Wynter. He would be long dead.

"Like you."

I live as a spirit. He walks as a man.

Flesh and blood. A week ago, Shawn would have dismissed the idea as crazy, but that was before his life had taken a nosedive off a supernatural cliff. Anything was possible in his fucked-up world.

The alternative was that Evening resembled Wynter—right down to his freakazoid fingers. Maybe it was some kind of birth defect that materialized every so many generations and Evening was descended from the man who'd tried to save Cornstalk. Wynter had taken a blow to the head for his trouble.

A blow that should have killed him.

"You didn't hit him hard enough."

He liked lording it over his ancestor, pointing out where the mighty Obadiah had failed. Wynter hadn't died. In the scuffle of men fighting to drag Cornstalk from the barracks, no one had been able to say who hit him. Not even Wynter himself.

I repeat. It cannot be him.

Shawn plopped the empty ravioli can in the sink. When it came right down to it, Evening didn't matter one way or another. The course had been set in motion, Point Pleasant one step closer to mass hysteria every day. All he had to do was keep fanning the flames. When the TNT was flooded with hunters scenting cryptid blood, he would finally kill the thing that haunted his dreams for centuries.

When the Mothman was dead, Shawn Preech would start to live.

Chapter 10

Caden hung up the phone then crossed to the coffee pot to refresh his mug. The caffeine would keep him functioning on what was beginning to look like a long night. Hesitating near the kitchen door, he listened to the voices drifting from the screened-in porch. Saturday night had arrived sooner than anticipated, Quentin and Sarah dropping by for dinner as planned. To keep things casual, he'd tossed a few steaks on the grill while Eve whipped up a brown mushroom gravy. Baked potatoes and a large green salad rounded out the meal. Afterward, the four of them had congregated on the porch for strawberry pie and coffee.

Eve seemed to enjoy having her friend over, and the conversation kept to the light side. Quentin talked about his time at Juilliard and his family, sharing his reasons for visiting Point Pleasant. Caden couldn't delay relaying the information Evening had shown him much longer, yet sensed he would be setting something unstoppable in motion.

Ryan, working late shift, had called to give him an update on the Mothman. Taking the latest threat seriously, Pete had flooded the TNT with every available man. In another hour, it would be dark. Pete would pull back the patrols, but send a few cars to traverse county roads. Maintaining a visible presence would hopefully keep fear to a minimum. At least, that was the plan.

Caden set his coffee down on the counter. Frowning, he pushed back his sleeve. The marks on his forearm remained ink-black as if diseased. What would happen the next time he encountered the Mothman? Had that brand been his protection, a barrier that kept him from experiencing the fear the creature evoked in others?

"Caden?" Eve's voice drifted from the porch. "Are you coming back? Who was on the phone?"

He picked up his coffee then pushed through the door. "That was Ryan, checking in with an update."

"Nothing bad, I hope." Eve made room for him as he sat down on a cushioned glider beside her. Twilight hadn't quite settled outside, but Eve had lit several squat candles. A large citronella bowl occupied the center of a glass-topped wicker table. The porch was screened, but an occasional mosquito still drilled through to the interior. Most evenings Caden enjoyed the tranquil setting, candlelight enchanting the quiet times he spent with Eve.

Tonight, he was edgy. His mouth tightened at a faint flicker of lightning. The air was dry, smelling more of the hydrangeas that bloomed off the porch than looming rain.

"Still looking for the Mothman," Caden answered Eve's question.

Seated on a chair beside Sarah, Quentin shifted. "The elephant in the room. I enjoyed dinner and the conversation, but don't you think it's time to address the reason we're here?"

"Quentin." Sarah appeared taken aback.

"It's okay." Always the peacemaker, Eve smiled. "Caden and I just aren't used to people being open-minded where the Mothman is concerned."

"I don't have a choice." Quentin motioned with his right hand. In the flickering wash of shadows and candlelight, the scars on his skin were starkly visible. "I've met Indrid Cold."

Caden flinched. He should have known if Cold had returned.

Sarah regarded Quentin wide-eyed. "You went back to the igloo?"

"Yesterday. That's when I ran across Shawn and the others in the woods."

"But Cold's a myth. At least I thought—" Sarah appeared at a loss, looking from Quentin to Eve and back again. "Even with Katie and Ryan, and all that happened last fall, I never really believed…" Sitting forward, she bit her lip. "You actually got *answers*? Why didn't you tell me?"

"I had to convince myself I didn't dream the whole thing."

Caden rubbed the back of his neck. He hadn't missed Eve's sharp glance at the mention of Cold. Both had thought Lach's father gone for good. "Eve and I have both had encounters with Cold."

"So, I'm not crazy." A hint of sarcasm marked Quentin's tone. "What about the inside of the igloo? Did it glow blue when you were there?"

"Blue?" Caden shook his head.

Quentin dug something from his pocket and set it on the coffee table. In the glow of the candles, the blue stone tended toward cobalt threaded with black.

Eve's eyes widened. "Sarah, it's just like your necklace."

"I know." Sarah touched the pendant at her throat.

"That was glowing, too." Quentin pointed to the amulet. "Same color as the walls. Almost as if one activated the other."

Thunder rumbled in the distance.

Leaning forward, Caden picked up the amulet. He rubbed his thumb over the stone. "You don't know where this came from?"

"Only that it's been in my family for generations."

"Same as mine." Sarah glanced over her shoulder as a flicker of lightning backlit a cluster of clouds.

Heat lightning.

Caden blew out a breath. "According to folklore, the TNT is crisscrossed by ley lines. Some people believe the igloo is located on a thin spot, an area where the walls between dimensions are weak. That allows entities from other worlds to cross into ours. Cold is one of those beings."

"You mean an alien?" Quentin chuckled softly. "Look, something freaky happened in that igloo. I'm still not entirely sure what it was, but I won't rule out supernatural. By the same token, I might have suffered a chemically induced hypnosis. I could have hallucinated the whole thing."

"But it didn't feel that way." Caden's gaze remained fixed on the amulet. It wasn't a question so much as a statement.

"No. And I keep going back to that." Quentin pointed to the stone in Caden's hand. "What are the odds Sarah and I would have similar pieces, and they'd both be family heirlooms?"

"I think they were promise stones." The pieces were falling into place in Caden's mind. Jonathan Marsh and Etta Sherman had been engaged. It made sense they would exchange some token of affection.

"You mean like they were given in pledge of marriage?" Eve asked.

Caden nodded. "Before we go there," his attention returned to Quentin, "you said this was passed down in your family."

"Yes. From one set of twins to another."

"But according to your sister, twins in your family are cursed," Sarah protested.

"So it seems." Leaning back in his chair, Quentin hooked an ankle over his knee. It was hard to read his gaze. "I came to Point Pleasant trying to learn something about Jonathan Marsh. Lach Evening told me I should concentrate on Sutton Marsh instead."

"Sutton?" Caden set the amulet on the coffee table. He hadn't realized Evening had been talking to Quentin, too. The alien was a never-ending source of frustration. Why not explain everything outright?

Earlier, Sarah had told them about Lach's appearance in the River Café and how Shawn reacted to him. For someone who usually kept a low profile, Evening had been doing a lot of meddling.

"Sutton and Jonathan were twin brothers," Quentin said into the silence. "I got that much from Cold." He shook his head, a tight smile quirking his lips. "And he confirmed my family is cursed, something I'm sure Pen's going to love hearing."

"But that doesn't make sense." Leaning forward, Sarah gripped his wrist. "Why would your family be cursed?"

"Because Sutton murdered Chief Cornstalk."

Disbelief washed over Sarah's face. "I've never come across Sutton's name in any of the research I've done. How can you be so sure?"

Quentin spread his hands. "I'm not. I'm just repeating what I learned from Evening and Cold."

"I think I can build on that." Caden glanced at Eve, who gave him a slight nod. He'd already gone over everything Evening had shown him with her. It was time the others knew, too. He'd protect Evening's identity as much as he could. The less people who knew he was a centuries-old intergalactic traveler, the better. "Lach was able to share some information with me, but you're going to have to take it on faith that it's authentic."

Quentin narrowed his gaze. "What does that mean?"

"Just that Lach has methods of gaining information outside of traditional channels. I'm unable to share what they are, but I believe they're valid. And I agree Sutton was responsible for Cornstalk's death. He must have left Fort Randolph not long after the murder, and that's why there's no record of him. I think he was prodded into killing Cornstalk by Obadiah Preech."

"But Obadiah was supposed to be some kind of hero." Sarah no sooner voiced the objection than her mouth twisted in distaste. "At least, according to Shawn."

"I don't think Obadiah was anything of the sort."

"Lach told you that," Quentin guessed.

"Yes. We already know from history that a soldier was killed outside the fort on the day Cornstalk was murdered, supposedly by the Shawnee. That's what incited the uprising. What if that person was Jonathan Marsh?"

Silence settled over the group as they digested the theory.

Beyond the screened porch fireflies winked to life, creating lazy patterns in the heavy air. The atmosphere was close, weighted with pent-up energy. Night would fall soon, another day in which Mothman sightings overshadowed Will Hanley's murder.

Caden clenched his jaw. Gut instinct told him that Hanley's death and Cornstalk's murder were tied together in some morbid mesh of parallel realities.

"A desolate hour when a tear in time renders past and present as one." Lach Evening had said those words to him when predicting the Mothman's death.

"If Jonathan was the soldier killed outside the fort, then how was Obadiah involved?" Sarah broke the silence, her eyes overly bright in the semidarkness. She looked a bit like Etta Sherman with the same petite build and soft curve to her face.

Caden wondered if Quentin resembled Jonathan. "He found the body and brought it back to the fort. The story he told the soldiers was that he'd arrived too late to save Jonathan."

Quentin narrowed his eyes. "Story?"

"Exactly. Obadiah killed Jonathan."

Sarah blinked rapidly. "But that doesn't make sense."

"It does if Jonathan stumbled over Obadiah when he was doing something forbidden—like practicing black magic."

Sarah choked on a short laugh. "You're suggesting Shawn Preech's ancestor was engaged in witchcraft?"

"It might sound crazy, but—"

"No. Maybe not." Sitting straighter, she tucked a strand of hair behind her ear. "The more I learn about the past, I realize everything I thought I knew is open for interpretation. I let Shawn's bragging about Obadiah color my opinion of him. But I still don't understand how you were able to learn all this."

Unwilling to comment, Caden fell silent.

Quentin picked up the slack. "As far as I'm concerned, it sounds as plausible as anything Madam Olga told my sister. If I drove all this way to track down the origins of a curse based on the opinion of a psychic, I might as well buy the rest of the story."

"Which is?" Sarah asked.

"Sutton believes what Obadiah tells him…that his brother was killed by an Indian. He probably goes nuts—rage, grief. In that state of mind, it would be easy for Obadiah to prod him into killing Cornstalk."

"There's just one problem with that." Sarah nibbled on a fingernail. "Why would Obadiah want Cornstalk killed?" She flinched at the sound of thunder.

"Who knows?" Quentin spread his hands wide. "Maybe Preech had nothing to do with it. Maybe Sutton didn't need any prodding. Either way it ends up with Cornstalk dead and my family cursed."

"Don't forget the town of Point Pleasant," Eve added.

"Hold on." Caden pinched the bridge of his nose. Lach had left him a puzzle—probably because the alien wasn't permitted to intervene directly—but he'd provided enough pieces for Caden to sort through the rubble. Quickly, he told them about Willa Preech and Obadiah's reasoning for wanting the Mothman killed.

"Why didn't he just kill Cornstalk himself?" Sarah asked when he was through.

Quentin's mouth twisted. "Because he was a coward. If he believed the Indians had summoned the Mothman, then he probably believed they'd curse him for spilling the blood of their chief."

"What a monster." Sarah shook her head. "First, he murders Jonathan, then he convinces Sutton to kill Cornstalk."

"Hold on." Caden raised a hand. "There's more you need to know. Jonathan was betrothed to Etta Sherman when he died."

"Sherman?" Sarah blinked rapidly. "Do you mean—?"

"Yes. Your ancestor and Quentin's were engaged to be married. I think the blue stones from your pendant and Quentin's amulet were a pledge between them. Sutton must have kept the amulet after Jonathan died. My guess is that Jonathan probably found the stones somewhere in the area that's now the TNT. If you believe the UFO stories, then it's entirely possible they came from another world."

Sarah's lips parted, her gaze darting to Quentin. "George Washington reported strange lights in the sky when he surveyed the area." Her fingers tightened around her pendant. "I'm not sure I believe in UFOs, but the idea fits in theory. And I do know that my ancestor, Etta, never married. The Sherman name continued through three of her brothers."

Quentin eyed the amulet on the coffee table. "Say I buy all this..." He rubbed his jaw. "It clarifies my family history and the curse, but it doesn't explain how to break it. It doesn't do Pen any good."

"Maybe understanding is enough," Eve suggested. "If you believe in superstition, sometimes perception is enough to have mastery over a spell."

"I think it goes deeper than that." Caden shifted his attention to Quentin. "Not long after Cornstalk's death, Sutton's wife gave birth to twins. One of the babies was stillborn."

"The curse in action." Quentin gave a grunt of disgust. "And the first of the twins in my family to be cursed." He dragged a hand through his hair. "I can't let that happen to my sister."

"We won't. We just need to fit the pieces together. You told me you and Sarah found a book with a spider symbol."

"Yeah. The symbol represents treachery and death."

"Why were you researching it in the first place?"

"He wasn't. I was." Sarah tucked her legs to the side as she leaned forward. "I saw the symbol on a wooden case. It was mixed in with a bunch of papers Suzanne had given me to research Shawn's family ancestry." Biting her lip, she shrugged. "I can't explain it, but I got a creepy feeling looking at the case. It was locked, though I'm not sure I would have opened it anyway. I was curious about the symbol, so I picked up some books from the library to research what it meant."

"Same symbol that was on the handle of the knife Shawn had." Quentin shot Caden an unwavering stare. "I'm not a hunter, but that seemed an unusual knife to be carrying."

"Suzanne told me it belonged to Shawn's father," Sarah said.

"Probably as old as your amulet"—Caden nodded to Quentin—"and Sarah's pendant."

"What would make you say that?" Quentin asked.

"You saw the blade."

"Yeah. It was black."

"A knife with a black blade was used to kill Cornstalk."

Sarah shook her head. "How can you possibly know that?"

When Caden didn't reply, the answer became obvious.

"Lach Evening?" Quentin guessed.

Caden nodded. "I think the knife belonged to Obadiah. You have to remember when Cornstalk and the others were killed, it was probably pandemonium. We know a group of soldiers rushed the guardhouse."

"So, whether Obadiah gave Sutton his knife, or Sutton took it from him, it was the weapon that killed Cornstalk." Quentin blew out a breath. "Neat package." He stood and paced a short distance away, pausing at the rear door opening to the yard.

Darkness had settled over the grounds, a few stars visible through the cloud cover. The silhouette of Eve's gardening shed jutted in the distance, a cluster of trees further away where the grass sloped to a small stream.

Caden's coffee was cold. He thought about getting more, but the caffeine had started to sour his stomach. "How do you break a curse?" he asked no one.

Quentin turned from the door. "You destroy the item responsible for initiating it in the first place."

"You mean the knife?" Sarah asked.

"Yeah, but I don't think Shawn's going to surrender it willingly." Grimacing, he stuffed his hands in his pockets. "That aside, I think we've overlooked something crucial."

Caden frowned. "Such as?"

"The Mothman. He's part of it."

"How do you know that?" He was used to being the expert where the Mothman was concerned. Instinct told him the cryptid had to be at the heart of what happened in the past, but he hadn't anticipated someone else realizing that, too. "The creature went after you in the TNT when you were with Sarah."

"It didn't attack me." Quentin walked back to the group and resumed his seat. He flexed his scarred right hand as if working stiffness from his fingers. "It's almost like it was trying to communicate with me."

"How?"

"Mostly images...woods and blood. Something screaming."

Sarah shifted. She obviously hadn't heard this before. "You mean someone?"

"No." Quentin shook his head. "No human could make the sound I heard. It was like something dying. Something not human."

Caden slumped in his chair. It was too late to track Evening down at the hotel, but he had every intention of cornering the alien tomorrow. Between what he'd learned from Evening, and what Quentin had learned from Cold, he had a fairly concise idea of what occurred the day Cornstalk was killed. But there were questions that remained unanswered.

Namely, how did the Mothman factor into Cornstalk's death?

Something had changed in the creature. It was no longer content to be reclusive but had taken to prowling the area as if searching for something. Or someone. Volatile and unpredictable, it was bent on wreaking destruction. Desolation had been replaced by rage, misery by wrath. In the past, it had driven others away through fear. Now, that same bombardment of fear had taken on deadly edges, a weapon that was no longer defensive in nature, but used for attack.

Caden studied Quentin. "You weren't afraid when you encountered the Mothman?"

"Afraid?" Quentin's brows drew together.

"I'm not questioning your courage, just your response. The Mothman uses fear as a defensive weapon. Anyone who encounters the thing is immediately bombarded by a wave of terror. Like a psychic onslaught."

"I can vouch for that." Sarah shifted in her chair. "I was never so frightened in my life. I was certain I was going to die."

Caden glanced back to Quentin. "What about you?"

"No. Sorry." Quentin shook his head. "I was freaked out by the whole thing, but…" Pausing, he frowned. "I just remember being caught up in the images. Not terrified. More like surprised…trying to make sense of it all."

Thoughtful, Caden tugged a thumb and forefinger over his bottom lip. At first glance, he'd feared the Mothman was moving to attack Quentin when he'd come upon them in the TNT, but what if the creature had sensed the amulet in his pocket? The stone could very well be from the cryptid's home planet. It may have been reacting, reaching out.

And Caden had shot the thing.

Wearily, he shook his head. "Let's keep all of this to ourselves. I'll try to talk to Lach again tomorrow."

"I think the creature was trying to show me something," Quentin said. "I need to go back to the TNT and find out what it is."

"Forget it." Caden shook his head. "The whole area is going to be overrun with patrols. We're keeping people out, not letting them in."

"Is that Sergeant Flynn talking?" Quentin's voice held challenge, boldness that was mirrored in his gaze.

"I can make it an order if that's what you mean."

"Okay, you two. Enough." Eve stood, shutting down their verbal sparring. "It's getting late, and I don't know about the rest of you, but my head's spinning."

"But what about Shawn?" Clutching the arms of her chair, Sarah looked between them.

"What about him?" Eve asked.

"He's got to be involved somehow, and…and he has that knife. Maybe the blade is cursed, too. What if he's dangerous?"

"I think we have enough to worry about without including Shawn," Quentin said.

"But you don't know what he's capable of."

Caden frowned. Sarah's body posture and tone indicated her concern came from more than grasping at straws. "Sarah."

She swiveled her head around, pupils wide, reflecting candlelight.

"Is there something you're not telling us?"

She sucked on her bottom lip. A handful of seconds slid by before she shook her head. "It's just…haven't you noticed how belligerent Shawn is lately? He's always angry."

"Not to mention eating." Eve rolled her eyes. "He's been racking up large tabs at the River. Tucker said it's like he's eating for three people."

"Exactly!" Sarah immediately glommed onto the observation. "But look how much weight he's lost. It's not natural for a person to lose that much weight that quick."

"Unless they're doing drugs." Quentin pointed out the obvious.

Sarah folded backward into the chair. Her gaze dropped to her hands. "I just think that someone should keep an eye on Shawn. Make sure he's not doing anything he shouldn't be." She snuck a glance at Caden.

Sarah Sherman was probably the last person he'd expect to finger Shawn as trouble. She didn't make a habit of spreading gossip or of broadcasting unflattering opinions. In this case, her intuition aligned perfectly with his. He fought down a grin over the irony. "He's on my radar."

"Good enough for me." Quentin stood. "Thanks for dinner to both of you." He nodded to Caden and Eve, then extended his hand to Caden. "I appreciate it if you'd keep me up to date on anything else you might learn."

Caden shook his hand. "Same here." He wasn't convinced Quentin would stay out of the TNT, but at least they were on the same page when it came to getting to the bottom of the curse. For Quentin, it was about freeing his family from the consequences and helping his sister. For Caden, it came back to the same reason it always did.

The Mothman.

Chapter 11

Sarah drew her arms close to her chest, shielding herself from the nighttime air. It wasn't cold by any means but the heavy cloud cover, coupled with several low rumbles of thunder, drew goose bumps down her arms. "Do you think all this strange weather has to do with Cornstalk's curse?" she asked Quentin as they walked up the sidewalk to her trailer.

"I thought everything in Point Pleasant was connected to Cornstalk's curse." Quentin draped an arm over her shoulders. His smile was a white flash in the darkness.

They'd been spending so much time together she wasn't sure what she'd do to occupy herself when he left. The last week had been a whirlwind of puzzles and clues she'd enjoyed exploring. Mostly because he'd been part of that. "Can I ask you something?" They stopped in front of the steps leading to her small porch.

Quentin turned her to face him. In the darkness most of his face lay in shadow, but the glint of his eyes was bright. "What do you want to know?"

She wet her lips, daring to ask what had lingered in the back of her mind since he'd told her about Juilliard. "Do you...do you ever still play the piano?"

A bitter huff of laughter escaped him. "What kind of question is that?"

She reached for his hand, twining her fingers around his, the scars thick beneath her fingertips. "It's just that I'd like to hear you play sometime."

"There's not exactly a piano around."

"I know." She chided herself for speaking what was in her heart. "I just don't want you to give up on your gift."

"The gift is gone. Playing, I can still do. Not nearly as well as I should. For an artist that means avoiding reality." Smiling faintly, he brushed her cheek. "I have some old recordings I can send you."

Her heart lurched. "Do you ever listen to them?"

"Too painful."

Depression pushed a lump against her throat. "It's so unfair. You had nothing to do with Cornstalk's death."

"Curses aren't based on fairness." He slid his hand to her throat, his palm warm against her neck. "I'm talked out about Cornstalk, but I feel bad for Jonathan and Etta. They had their future stolen."

She gazed up into his eyes, her heart pounding faster. What were the odds their ancestors had been romantically involved? She'd allowed herself to become infatuated with him, but could no longer tell if that attraction stemmed from her own feelings or the tragic history of Etta Sherman. Raising her free hand, she wrapped her fingers around her necklace. "Do you think we were fated to meet?"

"I don't know if it was fate." Quentin leaned closer, his breath warm against her skin. "But I'm glad it happened all the same." Lowering his head, he kissed her lightly.

Sarah closed her eyes, her legs trembling. He would be leaving soon and she'd end up with a broken heart. "Do you want to come inside?"

For answer, he deepened his kiss.

* * * *

As predicted, Caden couldn't sleep. A repeat of everything they'd covered during the night played an endless loop through his head. Over the years, he'd developed the habit of shutting his thoughts down when needed. Working different cases made the practice essential. But tonight, nothing he did let him throw the switch.

Heaving a breath, he sat up in bed and swung his legs over the side. Eve slept soundly beside him, curled close for comfort. Bending, he brushed the hair from her face and kissed her lightly. "Can't sleep. I'm going to head into the department."

She murmured something, but didn't come fully awake.

Ten minutes later, dressed in jeans and a T-shirt, he scrawled a note and left it on the nightstand. His watch read 12:36 a.m. when he backed out of the driveway. Traffic was minimal given the early morning hour and he made it to the sheriff's office in record time. He parked behind the building, noting the patrol car he normally used was missing. For that matter, there wasn't a single Mason County car in the lot. An unusual number of personal cars took up the space.

Inside, Caden found three clerks manning phones, with Chris Gardner the only deputy on shift. The clerks kept busy relaying information over dispatch while Gardner looked like he'd downed a pot of coffee.

"Hey, I thought your shift ended two hours ago." Caden approached Gardner's desk, noting a large map of the TNT spread on the surface. The paper had been marked up with red circles, hours and minutes noted to the side of each. "What's going on?"

Gardner blew out a frazzled breath. "The Mothman, what else? I'm surprised you didn't get a call."

"What do you mean?"

"A couple of guys got it cornered in the TNT. At least that's the last word I had. We've got patrols everywhere and Pete is setting up roadblocks. He wants me to try to leech more men from Jackson County. The whole place is going to hell in a hand basket."

Alarm shot through Caden. He couldn't believe Ryan hadn't called, knowing his connection to the Mothman. Maybe his brother had decided it was best he stay out of it. Who the hell knew what Pete was doing out there with that many patrols.

"Shit." Caden strode for the door. "If my brother's out there, tell him I'm on my way." He rounded the hall to the exit and nearly plowed over Roy Baxter in the process.

"Caden." Roy backpedaled two steps then stopped. "You're just the person I need."

"Not now, Roy, I'm on my way to the TNT."

"But those fingerprints you wanted." Roy waved a folder in his face.

Even focused on the Mothman, Caden quelled his urge to fly out the door. "What is it?"

"You were right. They had Shawn Preech's fingerprints on file at the dock."

"And?"

"They don't match."

He'd suspected as much after his discussion with Evening. "Roy, Preech's fingerprints were all over that cup."

"I'm telling you, they don't match his employment records."

"Is that all?" His expression must have conveyed he expected more.

Roy's gaze was stark, like he'd stumbled over something incomprehensible. He wet his lips. "The fingerprints didn't tally up with Shawn's, but they were a perfect match for the latents we lifted from Hanley's place. Those fingerprints belong to Will's killer."

Caden's heart thudded to his throat. He stepped closer. "Are you sure?"

"Positive." Roy handed him the file.

He flipped it open and scanned the contents. He should have known whatever hints Lach tossed his way would prove solid in the end. Between the prints, the knife, and Shawn's erratic behavior there was more than enough to have him brought in for questioning.

Caden shoved the folder back at Roy. "Hang onto this and don't say anything to anyone about the findings."

Lips pursed to the side, Roy clutched the folder. "What are you going to do?"

"Have Shawn brought in for questioning. Right now I'm headed for the TNT, and until I can get to Preech, I don't want anything tipping him off."

"You think he's a flight risk?"

"Hell." Caden shook his head. "At this point, I don't even know *who* he is."

* * * *

The two main arteries into the TNT—Potters Creek Road and Fairgrounds Road—were both blocked by patrol cars when Caden arrived. Flickering strobes of red light swiveled through the darkness, defining the chaotic scene. Flares sputtered on the road and traffic cones wrapped with bands of reflective tape kept vehicles at bay. After a quick update from Deputy Morris, Caden headed for the hub of activity six miles into the derelict munitions site.

He parked behind several patrol cars then jogged to the front of the string where he found Pete Weston and Wayne Rosling conferring over a map similar to the one Gardner had used. Weston hunched over the hood of his vehicle, one broad palm pinning the map in place. Behind him, Rosling angled a flashlight over his shoulder.

"...last report places it here." Caden caught the tail end of Weston's words as he approached. Across the road, three patrol cars lined the grass, flashing lights painting Weston's face a garish shade of red. "Caden, what are you doing here? Did Ryan call you?"

"No." When he caught up with his brother, he'd have a few choice words for the oversight. "I couldn't sleep so I went into the station. Gardner brought me up to speed." Jamming his hands in his pockets, Caden stepped closer to the map. Lightning sputtered overhead. "What's the latest?"

"Two sightings within the last fifteen minutes. Here and here." Pete tapped the map indicating one of the area's thirty-four ponds, followed by a location harboring the shell of a crumbling building. "I've got three patrols out there. Ryan's heading up one."

Rosling lowered his flashlight. "The thing's toying with us."

"I heard it was cornered," Caden said.

Weston shook his head. "No dice. We thought we had it at the old north power plant, but the thing...hell." Sweating abruptly, Weston yanked a handkerchief from his pocket and mopped it over his face. "Nearly forty years in law enforcement and I've never backed down like that. All that thing had to do was turn those demon eyes on me and I froze."

"We all froze." Rosling's expression said he wasn't proud of his actions either. "I went from being stalker to prey in a matter of seconds. I used to think the whole thing was some kind of hoax, but now that I've seen it..." He shook his head.

"It uses fear as a weapon." Caden wasn't sure if he was relieved or apprehensive to learn the creature had escaped. If Weston and the others were going to track the Mothman, they needed to know what they were up against. "It feeds on emotion. The more terrified the victim, the more it's able to broadcast that terror back."

Pete's skepticism showed on his face. "How would you know that?"

Caden hedged. He couldn't afford to let his fellow law enforcement officers blunder around in the woods. The creature's aggression appeared to be mounting, and shooting the thing would only serve to make it angrier. People no longer questioned if the Mothman existed. There were enough recent eye witnesses for over a dozen reports. Even Pete and Rosling had seen the thing firsthand. If he told them the truth, they might actually believe him.

"I've got..." He swallowed, trying to explain without sounding like he had a screw loose. "A sort of connection to the thing."

"Huh?" Rosling's mouth gaped. His radio crackled, but he ignored it.

"These marks." Caden raised his arm to reveal the three gashes angled over his skin. "You've seen them before."

"Sure." Pete frowned. "You've had them ever since the Silver Bridge went down."

"Exactly. The Mothman made them." He didn't give the statement long to sink in. "I've encountered the creature before. More than once."

Pete leaned back, shooting a long look from under his brows. The air was heavy and charged, lightning now a steady flicker on the horizon. "You never said anything about this before." His tone carried criticism, a match for the reprimand in his gaze.

"Yeah, well..." Caden flashed a hard smile. "It's not like I expected anyone to believe me."

Rosling's radio squawked again. Raising the microphone to his lips, he walked away, talking in a low voice.

"Here's the thing, Pete." Caden forced the sheriff's attention back to him. "If the creature's turned aggressive, this could get ugly. The more guys you've got tramping around in the woods, the more chance for injury."

"So you think you're going to stroll up and have a chat with it?" Pete gave a disgusted snort and kicked a stone clear. "Damn, Caden, we've been chasing this phantom for how long and now I'm supposed to buy you know more about it than any of us? It could rip you to shreds."

"Not likely. It's had that chance multiple times." Even if he got Weston to pull everyone back, then what? The standing order for the creature was shoot to kill. How was he going to reconcile hunting the thing down with the promise he'd made Indrid Cold?

Before he could say anything further, Rosling returned at a fast clip. "Pete, that was Ryan. He and Oates just saw the thing. He said—" His voice was cut off by a rapid report of gunfire. Three sharp cracks echoed through the darkness not more than several hundred yards distant, judging by the sound.

"Ryan." Tearing the flashlight from Rosling's hand, Caden bolted for the woods.

"Caden!" Pete's voice boomed behind him. "Sergeant Flynn, get back here. You're not even armed."

No, but his brother was. And Ryan wouldn't shoot unless his life was in danger.

* * * *

Shawn shoved another handful of potato chips in his mouth and paced the length of Suzanne's driveway. Her car was gone and the house was dark, not that he'd expected to see any lights at 1:20 a.m. He normally wouldn't bother with her, but he was bored and edgy. He'd been looking forward to a tumble in the sack, willing partner or not. All the better if she wasn't willing. The bitch could use another lesson. They were still married on paper, even if she planned to divorce him.

Cursing, he leaned against the trunk of his Charger. Suzanne must have hooked up with one of her friends. Probably crying her eyes out about how he'd smacked her around. All he needed was for one of her slutty pals to convince her to go whining to the sheriff.

Digging into the bag of Lays, he fished for crumbs. Even as he licked the salty residue off his fingers, his stomach rumbled. It was getting harder to eat enough, and sleep had become elusive no matter how much he tossed and turned. If he didn't show up at work tomorrow he was probably going to be out of a job, but so what? Why work when he could take what he needed? He should have robbed Hanley instead of trying to make the old man's killing look like the Mothman had been involved.

Shawn wadded the used chip bag into a ball and shot it into Suzanne's yard. She was probably with Sarah Sherman. The two had always been chummy, but they'd gotten closer ever since Suzanne gave Sarah those moldy family papers to look through. As if she could have discovered shit about Obadiah anyway.

He fished a cigarette from the pack in his T-shirt, then cupped his hands to strike a match. Exhaling a long stream of smoke, he tilted his head back to study the sky. A few stars gleamed overhead, the moon a thin sliver behind a thread-thin net of clouds. Lightning danced to the west, a rapid flicker he barely registered, it had grown so common.

No thunder, no wind. He could almost believe that breakneck flash was heat lightning if not for the restlessness gnawing at his gut.

The storm was growing nearer.

His storm.

In the meantime, he had every intention of showing Suzanne who was in charge. And if that meant visiting Sarah Sherman and convincing her of the dangers in meddling, he wouldn't say no to a round of extra fun.

* * * *

Quentin rolled over, conscious of the flicker of lightning through the blinds. Almost one-thirty in the morning and he couldn't sleep. The story Caden Flynn had spun earlier that evening rattled through his head with the clatter of a freight train. He'd always known his family was cursed even when he'd mentally attempted to deny it, but hearing the reason behind that blight sickened him. Nobody wanted to be the descendant of a murderer, especially one who had taken the life of a prominent and peaceful leader. Ladle in his frustration over not knowing how to break the curse, and Sarah's innocent question about playing the piano, and he'd opened the door for several mental demons to romp through his head.

Rubbing his scarred hand, he massaged the points between the knuckles. Why did Sarah have to go and ask about his playing, resurrecting all he was missing? His position as vice president in his family's business was something he should be grateful for, even proud of. He'd accomplished a lot in the last two years. And if his hand was the worst of Cornstalk's curse, he'd gotten off lucky compared to some of the other tragedies in his family.

A rumble of thunder drew his attention to the windows. The storm felt nearer this time, the air oppressive, dancing with charged ions. Probably part of why he couldn't sleep. Or maybe he was worried about Sarah, alone in her trailer with the storm squatting on the horizon. He should have stayed and camped out on her couch. Kissing her had been one of the only pleasures of the night. He hadn't dated anyone since the injury, but she had his mind going in directions he hadn't contemplated for a while. When he was finished in Point Pleasant he wouldn't mind coming back and seeing her again. Knowing that their ancestors had been engaged made him feel a connection to her as well as the town. He'd been attracted to her before, but now there was a tie he hadn't expected.

When lightning forked behind the blinds, illuminating the inside of the room in a bright flash, Quentin sat up in bed.

Maybe Sarah was sleeping instead of pacing and worrying herself sick. If the storm broke with the pent-up fury that had been feeding it for days, it would turn into a deluge.

He scrubbed a hand over his face and swung his feet to the floor. There was no sense in calling her. If she was asleep, he'd only wake her up. Since he couldn't sleep, he might as well go for a drive. Standing, he reached for his jeans, then pulled them on and walked to the window. He opened the blinds wide, and stood staring down on the street.

A tingle against his leg made him reach into his pocket and withdraw the amulet. A hiss of air passed between his lips at the soft blue light radiating from the stone. The only other time it glowed like that was when he'd conversed with Indrid Cold—an alien and dimension traveler if he was to believe local folklore.

Quentin's gaze tracked back to the street.

Lach Evening walked from the porch and headed for a black Cadillac parked beneath the window.

* * * *

"Ryan!" Caden's pulse throbbed in his temple as he raced through the night-blackened woods. The beam of his flashlight bobbed erratically. He knew the TNT, had hiked the area countless times, yet in his panicked state the trees tangled together in a bewildering labyrinth. To his left, a gaping dark patch told him he'd come dangerously close to blundering into a pond. He needed to keep a clear head, not go hurtling into a muck of water and bulrushes. "Ryan," he called again.

"Over here." Ryan's voice came from somewhere up ahead and to the right, his tone uneven, bordering on tremulous.

Caden burst through a clump of trees in time to see him struggle up from the ground. Ryan groaned, his left arm hanging at an awkward angle. The sleeve of his uniform dangled in tatters, his arm wet and glistening with blood.

"Shit." Cornstalk's curse at work. He sprinted to Ryan's side, then quickly gripped him under the good arm. One look at his brother's face had him worrying Ryan might black out. "What happened?"

"It was here." Ryan's skin was pale, his lips drawn in a tight line.

"The Mothman?"

Ryan nodded. "I don't think it recognized me." He'd been subject to the creature's scrutiny once before, but spared the mental bombardment it meted out. Judging by the pallor of his skin, he hadn't been as fortunate this time. "Oates saw it first and shot at it."

Caden glanced around for the deputy. "Where is he? Where's Oates?"

Ryan shook his head. "Shit, Caden. It…"

"What?"

"It dragged him into the woods." Exhaling audibly, he webbed his free hand over his face. "We were both frozen. I never felt fear like that."

"I know. Take it easy." He lowered his voice, speaking calmly. "How bad are you hurt?"

"My arm's ripped up. Once I got past the fear, I tried to get Oates away from it. Hell, I should have shot it."

"Damn right. Why didn't you?" Anger made his voice hard. He was ticked, alarmed at the same time. Infuriated that Ryan hadn't done a better job of protecting himself, and panicked at how quickly the Mothman's aggression spiked out of control. From this point forward the thing would be hunted relentlessly. "I'll get you back to Pete. You need a ride to the hospital, probably stitches." As he talked, he steered Ryan in the direction of the road. "I'll go after Oates."

"And do what?" Ryan looked him up and down. "You don't have a gun."

"Give me yours."

Ryan handed over his rifle. "Use it if you have to. Don't try to reason with the thing."

Caden overlooked the comment. "You should have told me what was going down." Using the flashlight, he guided Ryan through the woods as swiftly as his brother's injury would allow. Once he knew Ryan was safe, he'd search for Oates. He needed to find the missing deputy before the night got any uglier.

Angling a glance to the sky, he caught a flash of lightning. The witch weather, as he'd heard people call it, had been brewing for the last week. Sooner or later the storm had to boil over. He prayed it would hold off another day. At least until he found Oates.

"Don't be stupid, Caden. Don't take chances with it." As the choke hold of terror lessened, Ryan's voice grew firm with warning.

"Drop it."

"Can't do that. It's changed. I don't know what it was before, or what kind of connection it had with you, but it's bloodthirsty now. If I'd realized that sooner, I would have shot it."

"Caden. Ryan." A man called from somewhere ahead of them.

"That's Rosling," Caden said.

"I can make it from here." Ryan pulled away from him, wincing at the jar to his wounded arm. "Find Oates and come back in one piece."

Caden nodded. Without another word, he faded into the trees.

* * * *

Suzanne's car wasn't there.

Shawn sat staring through the Charger's windshield, his thumbs beating out a clumsy rhythm on the steering wheel. Obadiah's knife rested on the seat beside him. He hadn't intended to cut Suzanne—well, maybe just a small slice where no one would see it. Something to remind her to keep her mouth shut and not blab to her friends about what had happened. He'd rolled the entire thing through his head on the drive here, imagining how it would play out. She'd sob and plead, probably even beg him to take her back, but the whole scheme was shot to hell now.

No car. No Suzanne. He scowled and scratched his crotch.

What a waste to leave without having a little fun. Sarah was a self-righteous backbiter, like most of the women in Point Pleasant. Just because she worked at the courthouse, she thought she was a notch above other people. It wouldn't hurt to take her down a peg, especially after she'd dissed him at the River Café.

His hand strayed to the knife and he fingered the blade.

Obadiah was set on offing the Mothman, but there was no reason Shawn couldn't have a little fun on the side. Sarah probably knew exactly where he'd find Suzanne. His ex must have gone into seclusion somewhere, worried he'd come back and mess her up again.

A goatish smile twisted his lips.

The bitch had no idea just how angry he could get.

* * * *

It didn't take Caden long to backtrack to where he'd found Ryan. From there it was a matter of following the signs of a struggle deeper into the woods. The beam of his flashlight picked out broken reeds and twigs. Overturned stones. Approximately three hundred feet in, he stumbled over Oates' revolver.

Tucking the weapon into his waistband, he angled his flashlight through the trees. "Oates? Come on, man, where are you?"

Several yards farther he found the deputy's rifle. A short distance away, Oates' body lay crumpled at the base of a tree. Belly down, he lay with one arm flung in front as if he'd been reaching for something. The back of his shirt was a shredded mess, blood-soaked skin visible among the ragged tatters of fabric.

"Shit! Oates." Caden dropped to his knees beside the deputy. He pressed his fingertips to the man's jugular vein. A faint pulse beat in response. Locating the walkie-talkie on Oates' belt, he ripped it free. "Pete. It's Caden. Come back."

Static burst from the speaker and was cut off by Pete's angry voice. "Caden, where the hell are you?"

"Get the location from Ryan, then head another three hundred feet north. And call for an ambulance. I found Oates."

He shut down the mic, then took a closer look at Oates' back. A few of the wounds looked deep, but most weren't as bad as he'd feared. The deputy was probably suffering from shock as much as the trauma of the attack. Before he could move to render any type of first aid, a screech ripped through the air behind him.

Caden spun, rising to a half crouch.

The Mothman stood ten feet away, wings stretched open to either side.

Caden's mouth went dry as a flicker of fear coursed through him. He stood slowly, rifle trained on the creature. After what it had done to Ryan and Oates, he was no longer certain of the ground he stood. If he had any sense at all, he'd pull the trigger and end the thing's miserable life. But he doubted a bullet would do any good. He'd already shot it twice through the wing without impacting it. The creature's death wouldn't be easily accomplished, if it could die at all.

"It's what you've wanted, isn't it?" He spat the words with venom. He'd protected the cryptid only to have it turn on one of his own. "You don't belong in this world, and if death is the only thing that will take you from it…" Caden tightened his finger around the trigger.

Something alien probed his mind, gouging with the sharpened end of a knife. It speared his thoughts, flaying the edges until he grimaced in pain. Fear bubbled up in the back of his throat, an emotion he'd never felt in the presence of the Mothman. Lightning illuminated the creature from behind, revealing prominent ridges of veins in its wings. Each jagged artery pulsed blue and black, reminding him of the stones in Sarah's pendant, Quentin's amulet. Behind the piercing glow of the creature's eyes, something took shape.

Caden clenched his jaw. "I promise you death."

The breath left his lungs in a rush as he beheld the creature's face.

* * * *

Shawn slipped the knife through his belt then eased out of his car. He closed the door soundlessly, waiting for the latch to catch before moving into the yard. Sarah's trailer sat on a square patch of ground, tucked behind a bend in the road where it was shielded from traffic. Flowerbeds sprawled beneath the front windows, offset with a plump shrub on each end. Wind whipped through the branches of a large maple on the side yard, heralding a prolonged rumble of thunder. The sound prickled along his nerves, warning the storm grew closer. As he bolted for the rear of the trailer, fat drops of rain splattered the ground and a blue-white tongue of lighting warped night into day.

The storm couldn't have come at a better time. It crashed over him with a pulse of electrically charged air, feeding the malevolent energy that mushroomed inside him. Seconds later, the heavens exploded in a deluge. Within moments he was soaked through, his hair plastered to his face, rivulets of warm water dripping from his chin. The wind crashed through the treetops, whispering of Obadiah's death on a rain-soaked night.

The shade of his ancestor stirred.

Shawn licked moisture from his lips. Tasted the tang of wet and sulfur. He crept from the lawn onto a small deck that abutted the rear door. The trailer was dark, three square windows reflecting the frenzied dance of lightning. He caught a glimpse of his face in the nearest pane, startled by the stark white shell frozen in that moment in time. Too much of his ancestor in there. Sometimes he got confused about who he was, especially when images from Obadiah's life invaded his mind.

Treachery and Death.

The spider symbol on the knife murmured to him, promising immeasurable power when Obadiah was gone. It fed the restlessness in his gut, made him hunger to be inside where he could flaunt his dominance. Women were weak. Sarah would be no different. Rain drummed against his back and neck.

Gripping the door knob, he twisted it to the side.

Locked.

Quickly, he moved to the closest window and worked his fingers beneath the edge in an attempt to pry it open. It didn't budge. The bitch had sealed the place up like a drum. No matter. There was more than one way to get inside. Drawing the knife from his belt, Shawn wedged the tip against the joint in the door and concentrated on weakening the lock.

* * * *

A loud crash of thunder pulled Sarah from a deep sleep. Jerking upright in bed, it took her a moment to realize where she was. A flash of lightning whitewashed the room, illuminating the bulk of her dresser and the stark outline of her nightstand. Within seconds, she became conscious of the hammering drum of rain against the roof.

She pulled the sheets to her throat. The storm had finally broken. It flung her back in time to the night when she was ten years old, alone and terrified in the TNT, the mangled shell of her parents' automobile behind her. She'd been sleeping in the back seat and awoke to the same bellow of rain and thunder, the car screeching to a jarring halt. A part of her remembered crying out to her parents, another part only that the night had been cold, black, and forbidding. When she'd climbed from the car, she'd wandered for an hour before finding help. A lonely, desolate hour filled with night terrors that still had the power to choke her in the light of day.

Those same fears tumbled down on her now. Pushing from the bed, she fought to still the frantic thump of her heart. It was just a storm. Another summer storm that had brewed too long on the horizon.

Thunder cracked again, and she sucked down a breath. Wind and rain combined in a violent racket that had her automatically reaching for the light on the nightstand. The switch turned over with a hollow click but the room remained dark, draped in shadows.

No electric.

Sarah's pulse kicked up a notch. Storms frequently knocked out the power. Most of Point Pleasant was probably dark. Repeating the mantra, she locked her fingers on the pendant around her throat. She normally wouldn't have worn her mother's necklace to bed, but something had prompted her to keep it close. Thoughts of her parents and her grandparents filled her head, all the people she'd loved taken too soon. A wave of sadness washed through her, fed by a blue backwash of lightning. The flash lit her bedroom end to end.

Run from the thunder,
Run from the rain,
Lightning can't hurt you,
The wind is in vain.

Breathing through her mouth to calm herself, she snatched a silken robe from the bedside chair and slipped it on over her nightgown. The robe was nearly as short as her nightie, brushing mid-thigh, leaving her legs bare. Goose bumps pimpled her flesh.

It's only a storm. It can't hurt you.

Wide awake, she moved down the hallway. She was halfway to the back door when she heard something jiggle the handle.

Sarah's heart lurched to her throat. For a moment she stood frozen, unable to move as the sound repeated over and again, a soft click and rattle warning that someone was trying to get inside. Her immediate impulse was to race for the door and secure it from entry, but it was already locked. Terrified, she crept to the closest window and risked a peek outside.

A dark form hovered on the rear deck, head bent over her doorknob. Fear formed a vice around her neck as she recognized Shawn Preech's limp blond hair and lank frame. Anger boomeranged through her, quickly quelled beneath a potent rush of alarm as she recalled his viciousness with Suzanne. If he was here, trying to break in, then he had to think she knew something about his wife's whereabouts.

Panicked, Sarah stumbled into the living room and grabbed the phone. Thank God there was a dial tone. Frenetically, she pushed out the number for the sheriff's office, then clutched the receiver close with both hands.

A woman answered on the third ring: "Mason County Sheriff's office."

"Please." Her voice was a scratchy whisper. She dared not speak any louder. "This is Sarah Sherman from 11 Farling Road. Shawn Preech is trying to break into my trailer. Please send someone right away."

"Ma'am, hello? Can you repeat your address?"

The joggling at the back door grew louder as if Shawn had somehow sensed her cry for help. Sarah was still clutching the phone, looking frantically over her shoulder when the door burst open and Shawn lurched inside. A blaze of lightning illuminated the sharp end of a knife.

Sarah screamed and bolted for the front door.

* * * *

Rain.

After a freaking week of witch weather, the storm had finally broken. Quentin flipped his windshield wipers to high and pressed on the gas as he rounded a bend in the road. Sarah would think he was crazy, arriving at her trailer after one in the morning, but a growing sense of dread propelled him to drive faster.

The hell with the thunder. The hell with the rain.

The storm was just one more element to convince him that something pivotal had taken place that night. His sister was normally the one given to intuition and dark omens, but with each passing second his sense of foreboding grew stronger. He prayed it was merely restlessness, but as second slipped into second, he grew more and more convinced Sarah was in danger.

Lightning exploded overhead when he rounded the final bend in the road and found himself in front of her trailer. A blue Dodge Charger was stationed in the driveway, a car he'd noticed in town his first night at the Parrish Hotel. It hadn't taken him long to pick up on scuttlebutt that it belonged to Shawn Preech. You couldn't be a semi-celebrity in a small town without everyone knowing what kind of vehicle you drove.

Quentin slammed the Monte Carlo into park, then bolted into the rain. The front door of Sarah's trailer hung unlatched, yawing open. Quentin scrambled onto the porch then into the trailer.

"Sarah?"

He hit the light switch, but the interior remained dark, shrouded in shadows. Within seconds his eyes had adjusted enough to pick out an overturned chair. A table beside the couch lay on its side, the phone on the floor. Quentin stooped to pick up the receiver, the drone of a dial tone spitting in his ear. A rhythmic *tap-tap-tap* drew him down the hall, where he found the rear door repeatedly striking the frame with each bellowing gust of wind.

"Sarah?" Gut lodged in his throat, Quentin dashed down the hall to her bedroom. The sheets were balled on the bed but there was no sign of the woman he'd come to care for. Swearing violently, he pivoted and swung back to the hallway.

She was out there—somewhere in the night—and Shawn Preech was with her.

Quentin raced for the door.

* * * *

Sarah had seen his face.

Oh, God, he was crazy.

The moment Shawn had burst through the rear door, she fled through the front. Lightning ripped the sky from one end to the other, freezing her momentarily in place. Paralyzed for three agonizing seconds, she heard him pounding down the porch steps behind her. Heart in her throat, she ran for the road. The long stretch of curving asphalt was barren of traffic, a dark ribbon that cut into deeper night. Small stones scattered on the shoulder bit into her bare feet. Exposed, and at a disadvantage on the hard surface, she veered back onto the grass, looping toward the rear of her property. Fifty feet ahead, the yard abutted a farmer's field. If she could vault the fence and make it to the farmer's house, she stood a chance of escaping Shawn. He wouldn't chase her there. He couldn't be that crazy.

Sarah slipped in the grass, stumbling to one knee. Wind blew her robe back from her nightgown, the chill bite of rain slashing into her skin. The storm blinded her, a deluge unlike any she'd seen since the night of her parents' accident.

"You can't get away from me, you stupid bitch." Shawn's voice cracked through the roar of the storm.

Throwing a hasty glance over her shoulder, she fought the urge to scream. There was no one to help and she'd only be alerting him to where she was in the darkness. All she could do was run.

Run from the thunder,
Run from the rain,
Lightning can't hurt you,
The wind is in vain.

Lightning turned the landscape from charcoal to bone-white ash. In that second of stark illumination, Shawn's form loomed several yards behind her, a hulking silhouette, clutching a knife.

"Stay away from me!" Desperate, she grasped the necklace and scrambled to her feet.

He was deranged; psychotic. What had happened to him, twisting him into a monster she no longer recognized? It was like living a nightmare. Fear wrenched a sob from her throat. She no longer heard the thunder, barely felt the cold chill of wet grass against her feet. All that mattered was the line of split rail fence in the distance, each flash of lightning bringing it that much closer.

Just as she flung out a hand to grip the top rail, Shawn seized her from behind.

Screaming, Sarah swung around and struck out as hard as she could. "Let me go!"

Her fist connected solidly with flesh and she heard him grunt. She fought wildly, flailing in his grip. In the chaos and confusion, she saw him reach for the knife.

"No, Shawn. No!"

He backhanded her, a blow that sent her sprawling at his feet. A knot of pain exploded in her cheek.

"Tell me where you've hidden Suzanne."

Terrified, palms pressed to the wet, muddy earth, Sarah looked up at him. Lightning streaked overhead, and in that garish flash, his features were clearly defined.

The man who looked down on her, hatred and malice twisting his face, was someone other than Shawn Preech.

The necklace looped around her throat exploded in a flare of blue flame.

* * * *

Quentin dashed around the side of the house, setting a blistering path for the rear yard. He hadn't seen Sarah on the road, but knew she had to be out here somewhere. Shawn's car was in her driveway which meant the dirt track driver was out there, too.

"Sarah!" He pitched his voice above the roar of the storm. As he gained the backyard, lightning illuminated his surroundings in a violent flash of white. In the distance, Sarah lay sprawled at the base of a fence. Shawn loomed over her, a knife clutched in his hand.

"Preech!" he bellowed.

The amulet in his pocket blazed to life, brighter than the lightning overhead.

* * * *

Shawn recoiled from the blue light. The glow overtook him, flaring upward from the necklace around Sarah's throat. Almost immediately, a second source shot from behind, blinding him as he turned. Snarling a curse, he backpedaled, his sneakers slipping on the wet grass. He bumped up against a weathered fence and raised an arm to shield his eyes. A man raced across the yard, long hair plastered to his face and neck by rain.

Quentin Marsh.

The tourist clenched something in his fist. Blue light flowed from between his clenched fingers. It coiled onto the ground like fog, and like fog it seeped across the grass, fanning outward in a surreal landscape of cobalt and aquamarine.

Run.

Obadiah's voice echoed in Shawn's head.

He hesitated, transfixed by the smoky blue light. His surroundings disappeared until there was only the cobalt glow, inching closer, whispering of a long-forgotten past. Of death and a life he had stolen—a man named Jonathan Marsh, and a woman who had wept inconsolably at the news of his passing.

The two sources of light joined and erupted in a violent conflagration. The blaze shot skyward, feeding the frenzied lashes of lightning. Bolt after fiery bolt lit up the night sky in a spectacle of blue-crested flame.

Demon fire.

A siren rose in the distance, wailing through the tumult of wind and rain, the devil yowl of thunder. How had he lost control so quickly?

Go!

This time Shawn needed no further prompting. Gripping the fence, he vaulted over the top and crashed to the other side. His palms and knees struck dirt, and then he propelled himself forward, running across the open field as if his life depended on it. In many ways, it did.

He'd done something crazy tonight. Committed a criminal act and stupidly allowed himself to be identified. He could no longer parade around town or scout out his usual haunts. He'd have to wait for everything to blow over before showing his face again. Of course, once he killed the

Mothman he'd be a hero and none of tonight—or even what he'd done to Suzanne—would matter.

Swearing beneath his breath, Shawn ran until the fence fell away behind him and the dance of blue smoke no longer enchanted lightning from the sky. The bulk of a barn loomed ahead of him offering shelter from the rain and a place to crash for the night. But as much as he wanted to escape the storm, the cops would certainly look there. Better to keep running until he could hotwire a car.

He needed to reach the TNT and finalize what he'd set out to do.

No more delays.

The Mothman would die before the sun set on another day.

Chapter 12

"Caden, where the hell are you?" Pete Weston's voice boomed through the trees, followed by the bobbing beam of a flashlight.

Only a handful of minutes had passed yet it seemed an eternity that Caden stood rooted to the spot, spellbound by the revelation of the creature's face. When he looked again, that unexpected glimpse had been swallowed by the red of the Mothman's eyes. Without a sound, the creature faded into the trees, shuffling away on foot rather than taking to the air. Its gait was slow and awkward when land-bound, but the trees provided camouflage the sky could not.

Thunder crashed overhead. Seconds later, the pent-up storm finally broke. "Over here, Pete."

A few more minutes and the sheriff found him, Rosling jogging close behind.

"Oates needs help." Caden indicated the fallen deputy, rivulets of rain already dripping from his hair. "Did you call for an ambulance?"

"On the way." Pete's face clouded as a streak of lightning revealed the extent of Oates' injuries.

Without a word, Rosling hurried to the wounded man and squatted beside him. "Oates." Carefully, he rested a hand on deputy's shoulder.

"He hasn't come to since I found him. The sooner we get him help, the better." Caden shifted his attention to Pete. "How's Ryan?"

"Waiting at the patrol car for the ambulance." It was hard to gauge Pete's expression through the rain, but an unmistakable edge of frustration roughened his voice. "I've pulled everyone back. We're floundering around out here in the dark, perfect targets for that monster to pick us off one by one. I've got no intention of losing any more men." He stared at Caden directly. "Have you seen it?"

"No," he lied easily. Five minutes ago, he would have replied differently. "You made the right call, Pete. There are too many pitfalls in these woods and too many places for the creature to hide. Now with the storm…" He frowned up at the sky. It had taken all week for the thing to break, and it looked like it was going to be a bad one. "It'll be easier hunting in daylight."

Maybe by then he'd have a plan. At least now he had a goal.

But to see it to conclusion he needed help from the one person who continued to disappear—Lach Evening.

* * * *

"Sarah." Wrapping his arms around her, Quentin helped Sarah up from the ground. The moment he touched her, the blue glow radiating from his amulet and her pendant died. Shivering against him, she clung to the front of his shirt and buried her face against his chest. They were both soaked through. She trembled so violently he feared she might be going into shock.

"He had a knife," she gasped.

His gut twisted. He'd seen the knife up close and didn't want to think about the kind of damage it could inflict. "Are you hurt?"

She shook her head.

Quentin gazed over the field. Despite a jagged flash of lightning, he could no longer see Shawn. "He's gone now." Behind them, a revolving red light cut a swath through the darkness, announcing the arrival of a patrol car. The siren reached a crescendo and died. "Come on. You're soaked. Let's get inside."

She didn't argue, but clutched her drenched robe close as he led her back toward the trailer. An hour later, she slept peacefully curled up beside him. She'd given her report to the police, taken a hot shower, then changed into shorts and a top. While she did that, Quentin stripped in the laundry room and tossed his clothes in the dryer. It was too late to drive back to the hotel and he had no intention of leaving her alone. Instead, he lay fully clothed on the bed and held her in his arms until she'd fallen asleep.

As groggy as he was, rest eluded him. He'd come close to losing Sarah tonight, an ugly reality that made his gut clench. They'd only just met, but there was something intrinsic at play in their connection. Madam Olga and Pen would tell him it had to do with past lives, but he didn't believe he was Jonathan Marsh reincarnated any more than Sarah was Etta Sherman. He wasn't in love, not by a long shot, but he was attracted to the fragile woman beside him, and wanted to explore that attraction in greater depth. Maybe it was fate at play, bringing him and Sarah together centuries after their ancestors had been denied a chance at happiness. Or maybe it had to do with the odd blue light that had danced as wildly as the storm tonight.

He and Sarah had talked about it briefly after the officer responding to the call had left, but neither had been thinking clearly, still operating on adrenalin and nerves.

Something supernatural had happened at that fence as if the light from the amulet and pendant were in themselves a part of the storm. He'd seen Shawn recoil from the blue glow. If Deputy Gardner hadn't arrived when he did, Quentin was positive the mysterious light would have prevented Shawn from harming Sarah. It was almost as if Jonathan and Etta had banded together to protect their descendants...paving the way for Quentin and Sarah to have a future they'd been denied.

* * * *

Caden lost track of time, but not long after returning to the sheriff's station, word came through of the incident at Sarah's trailer. Gardner reported that Shawn had fled on foot, abandoning his car at Sarah's home. For Caden, the episode was one more nugget of proof that Preech had crossed the edge. Locating the report Roy had processed on Shawn's fingerprints, he grabbed the file and headed for Pete's office. The door stood open, Pete visible behind his desk where he sat hunched forward, elbows resting on top. The sheriff looked as haggard as Caden felt.

"Got a minute, Pete?"

Weston raised a cup of coffee to his lips and waved him inside. The caffeine would keep him going through the night, a trick Caden often employed. It was already nearing three o'clock in the morning, with no end of activity in sight. He wondered how Eve was doing and if she slept through the storm, which was proving to be one of the worst Point Pleasant had seen in years.

"You've heard about Shawn Preech?" Caden dropped into a chair in front of Pete's desk.

"Yeah." Setting his coffee down, Pete parted with a weary exhale. "Already released a BOLO on him. Seems like the whole county has gone crazy."

"You know he's armed?"

"With a knife."

"A knife with a four-inch blade and a trailing point." The same type of knife that had killed Will Hanley.

As if reaching the same conclusion, Pete frowned. "What are you saying?"

"Take a look at this." Caden slid the file across the desk. "I had Roy lift Shawn's fingerprints off a coffee mug he used when he was in here." He waited a beat for Weston to digest the report. "They're a match, Pete."

"What the hell?" Disbelief washed over the older man's face. "Are you saying Shawn killed Hanley? *Shawn Preech?*"

"I know it sounds crazy, but look at his behavior lately. Something's going on with him, and tonight proves it. He didn't go to Sarah's place for a chat."

Report clutched in one hand, Pete scanned it swiftly. "Wait a minute. This says the prints don't match those on file for Shawn."

"Yeah, I know." That was the kicker, sure to come back and bite them in the butt. In the hands of the right attorney, that anomaly could result in accusations of deliberate framing and evidence tampering. "I don't understand it, but those were Shawn's prints on the mug and those"—Caden pointed to the papers in Pete's hand—"are the prints we lifted from the Hanley scene. It casts enough suspicion to bring him in for questioning."

Pete tossed the report on the desk. "If we can find him."

"He's on foot. He's not going far."

"Shit, I've known that guy since he was a kid." Pete shook his head in bewilderment. "I won't deny he turned out to be jerk, but I never thought he'd be capable of murder."

"We need to find out."

Pete reached for his phone. "I'll update the BOLO. If I were you, I'd go home and get some sleep. You're going to need it if we manage to pick him up."

"Right after I get an update on Ryan and Oates."

Caden intended to drive to the hospital to check on his brother, but five minutes later as he straightened up his desk, Ryan called him.

"I ended up with stiches and a small pharmacy of pain meds," Ryan told him over the phone. "They're sending me home."

Caden breathed easier. "Need a ride?"

"Sure. Give me about fifteen minutes to do the release paperwork. You can pick me up in the ER." Ryan's voice was groggy, threaded with the tautness of residual pain.

"How's Oates?"

"He's going to be okay, but he'll be here a few days. They've got him sedated right now. One of the guys called his wife and she's here with him."

Not a pleasant scene, Caden was sure. "Does she know what happened?"

"You mean that the Mothman attacked him?" Ryan hesitated briefly. "We had to tell the doctors what went down. Word has a way of getting around."

Caden swore softly, knowing renewed panic was sure to follow. Pete had drawn everyone out of the woods for the night, but tomorrow they'd be back in force. Not only to search for the creature, but to block vigilante hunters from getting hurt in the process. Now, more than ever, it was imperative he reach Evening.

* * * *

Sarah woke to the smell of bacon and coffee. Gray light bled into her bedroom, seeping from beneath the curtains drawn at the windows. Rain beat against the glass pane and the roof, reawakening memories of the previous night. She looked around for Quentin, but found the room empty. Grabbing her robe, she headed for the bathroom.

The mirror was far from kind, reflecting circles under her eyes and the ugly discoloration of a bruise splayed over her left cheek. Had Shawn really gone after her with a knife?

Shivering, she splashed water on her face and ran a comb through her rumpled hair. Ten minutes later, wearing a pair of soft lounge pants and a T-shirt, she wandered down the hall to the kitchen. Quentin stood at the stove, flipping bacon in a pan.

"Good morning."

"Good morning." He spied her immediately and grinned. "I hope you don't mind I rooted through your refrigerator and took over your kitchen. I thought you might like a hot breakfast."

"That sounds great. And the coffee smells divine." She pulled a mug from the cupboard and helped herself to a cup. Her movements were stiff, slower than usual, her energy off from last night. "What can I do to help?"

"Nothing. Sit at the table." He pointed with a spatula. "I've got batter ready for French toast."

"What a nice surprise." Sarah slid into a chair at the breakfast table, and glanced out the adjacent window. The rear of her property was washed in hues of pewter and gray, rain coming down in sheets. For once she was thankful for the weather. The storm made it difficult to see the split-rail at the perimeter of her yard. She could still feel Shawn's crushing grip as he'd yanked her back from scrambling over the fence.

Shuffling the thoughts aside, she looked back to Quentin. "You're pretty handy in the kitchen."

"Comes from being a bachelor." He didn't seem to notice anything was wrong. "There are a few things I can throw together." Using tongs, he dipped a piece of bread in a bowl of creamy batter then flopped it on a griddle. "How are you feeling this morning?"

"Stiff. Sore." She took a sip of coffee. "Still trying to make sense of what happened last night."

"Me, too." Quentin adjusted the flame under the griddle. "Why would Shawn come after you like that?"

Sarah hesitated. She'd promised Suzanne she wouldn't tell anyone how Shawn had battered her, but that was before his newly acquired taste for violence escalated. He'd actually had a knife with him. A horrible knife with a black blade. Would he have used it, or had he just brandished it to frighten her?

"He wanted me to tell him where his wife is."

Quentin cast a glance over his shoulder as he worked at transferring bacon from the pan to a plate. "Suzanne, right?"

"Yes. They're getting divorced, but Shawn did something horrible to her." Haltingly, Sarah told him what she knew about Suzanne and how she'd arranged for her to stay with Jerome. "I'm so glad he hasn't found out where she is. After what happened last night, I'm really worried about her."

"You need to tell her to contact Caden."

Biting her lip, she wrapped her hands around her coffee mug. "I tried to convince her."

"It's beyond that now. Preech has gone off the deep end. He came after you with a knife and could do the same to her." Quentin plated two pieces of French toast with two slices of bacon, then set the breakfast in front of her. "You need to tell her what happened to you. By protecting her, you've placed yourself in danger. Jerome, too."

"She's my friend."

"I realize that, but if she knew what happened last night, she'd probably call Caden willingly. If she's as much of a friend as you say she is, she isn't going to want to place you in jeopardy."

Sarah glanced down at her plate. She'd been hungry before, but her appetite fled as she thought of everything that had gone wrong in the last week. Cornstalk's curse in play. Had Quentin's arrival in Point Pleasant truly triggered a nefarious ancient power into seeking revenge?

She fingered the pendant at her throat as the storm raged outside.

Something, or someone had protected her last night. The bonfire of blue light seemed surreal in retrospect, but she'd witnessed that otherworldly spectacle as surely as Quentin had.

"I'll talk to Suzanne." She fiddled with her fork, sliding it over her napkin as the memory of the light jogged awake another. "You're right that she needs to know about Shawn and what happened. There's something else, too." Her gaze sought his and she waited until he sat beside her. He must have read the anxiety in her expression because he leaned forward and took her hand.

"Tell me."

"Last night...when Shawn stood over me...I saw..." The memory burst in her mind as startling and ugly as it had been last night. "Quentin, it was like someone else was there."

His brows drew together. "What do you mean?"

"I looked up into his face and it was like someone else was standing over me." Tightening her fingers around his, she prayed she didn't sound delusional. "He didn't look like Shawn at all. I saw someone else. Almost as if..." She swallowed hard, slightly nauseous as the idea settled in her gut. Something had protected her last night, possibly Jonathan Marsh or Etta Sherman, maybe both. If she believed in their presence, then she had to believe in the presence of evil too. "I think Shawn is possessed by Obadiah Preech."

* * * *

Caden grabbed a few hours' sleep, enough to function the next morning when he rolled out of bed. A quick shower and a change of clothes later, he felt halfway human. Afterward, he downed a bowl of cereal while standing at the kitchen sink. He explained the events of the night to Eve between bites of cornflakes. Her eyes grew wider with each moment that passed.

"You're sure Ryan's okay?" she asked when he was through. Seated at the kitchen table, she poked a spoon through her breakfast of fruit and yogurt. Normally they would have eaten on the screened porch, but the morning downpour made the air humid and uninviting.

"He was out of it when I dropped him off last night. Doped up on meds and sore." Caden had helped his brother into the house and gotten him settled before turning in. "He'll probably sleep most of the day."

"What a horrifying experience." Eve set her spoon down and fingered her napkin, her brow creased in concern. "I can't imagine what poor Mary must be going through."

Mary was Oates' wife, someone Eve had gotten to know through department functions—picnics and the annual Christmas party. Like most sectors, the men and women of the Mason County Sheriff's office were a tight-knit group. There was bound to be an update on Oates by the time Caden made it into town. Someone had probably been checking throughout the night.

"I'll let you know if I hear anything." Caden scraped the last soggy flake from his bowl, then set it in the sink. "I'm going to go to the hotel and talk to Lach."

"Do you want me to come with you? I should be there, in case—"

"I just need to ask him a few questions, Eve. There's no need to get involved." She'd taken a shine to Lach, but he'd never fully trusted his alien friend. He might have to rely on Evening for answers, but his skepticism remained intact through each encounter.

Eve bit her lip. "I can't sit here and do nothing, knowing everything that happened last night."

He hadn't told her about Shawn's fingerprints matching those on the knife used to kill Will Hanley, or about what he'd seen in the TNT. The Mothman's face haunted him, a disturbing memory he had to force from his head. Instinctively, he rubbed the brand on his forearm. The marks remained the same bitter black as they had all week.

"Call Sarah. She probably needs a friendly voice this morning."

"You're right." She nodded reluctantly.

"Of course I am." He stepped to her side and kissed her on the head. "And it wouldn't hurt to check in with Ryan and my mom later today. You'll probably find Katie over there." He'd breathe easier knowing she'd be occupied. Gut instinct told him a storm was about to break over Point Pleasant. One that had nothing to do with the inhospitable weather outside.

When that happened, he wanted those he cared about as far away from the danger as possible.

* * * *

Lach Evening was gone.

Caden arrived at the hotel to find Eve's part-time employee, Sharon, manning the front desk. When he inquired about Evening, the girl told him she'd found Lach's key and the money he owed in an envelope on the counter that morning.

"He must have left sometime overnight." Sharon chewed around a wad of pink bubblegum, as she waved a room key for evidence. "I already checked out his room and it doesn't look like he even used the place. You know what I mean? Spotless."

Did someone like Lach even sleep? The thought made Caden realize how little he knew about the alien he'd grown so dependent on for answers and advice.

"Do you know if anyone happened to see him leave?"

Sharon shook her head, sending a ponytail of glossy hair wagging behind her. "Weird thing though…he wrote a single word on the envelope."

Caden's pulse quickened. Of course Lach would leave a message. "What word?"

Sharon's face scrunched up in a puzzled expression. "Cold."

It was all Caden needed to hear. He bolted for the door.

* * * *

Shawn's clothing was soaked through. His T-shirt stuck to his body, plastered in place by the steady downpour, and his jeans were waterlogged. He'd only managed two hours of sleep tucked in some kid's tree fort he'd stumbled across before dawn. Fear of discovery had kept him moving. He might be able to talk his way out of what happened at Sarah's trailer—say he was drunk and didn't know what he was doing—but his gut told him the clock had wound down to zero hour.

Obadiah propelled him toward the TNT. At times his ancestor ranted incessantly, garbled words that bled into Shawn's brain like white noise. It was growing harder to separate himself from the spirit as his thoughts merged with those of Obadiah and his ancestor chained them together.

Starving, his body so hollow it felt like a strong wind would carry him away, Shawn kept to any cover available. Unable to find a car he could hotwire, he was reduced to creeping through backyards and racing across mud-splattered fields. As miserable as it was, the weather helped shield him from prying eyes, conjuring fog that hung in tattered patches above the rain-soaked ground. Eventually, he wandered far enough from town to parallel the road for an easier path. Few cars passed, but those that did sent him diving for cover. He feared the next vehicle to round the bend would have a light-bar mounted on top.

Sooner or later he'd have to flag a ride, but he wasn't ready to risk the danger. First he needed to concoct a plausible story why he was so far from town, drenched-through, without transportation. Mechanical problems? An empty gas tank? Both had possibilities. Except he was headed *away* from town not toward it. In the end, he'd probably plaster a phony smile on his face and hope someone would stop.

He was still working through the dilemma when the vibration of tires on wet asphalt arose behind him. Immediately, Shawn ducked into the tree line that had paralleled his path for the last half mile. From his crouched position sheltered by a group of pines, he watched a large black vehicle roll from the fog. The Cadillac advanced slowly, the crunch of its tires over scattered stones almost as loud as the hiss of rain. Square headlights pierced the mist, flaying aside the fog. There was no mistake the driver searched for someone.

Gripping the trunk of the nearest tree with both hands, Shawn stooped lower in his hiding place. Water dripped from the end of his nose. More trickled down his back. The pines protected him from the worst of the downpour, but as soon as the car was gone he'd be back on the road trudging through the muck. How much better to be dry and warm? To have transportation that would take him where he wanted to go?

His hand strayed to the knife struck through his belt. He fingered the handle, tracing the rough outline of the spider carving.

Ten feet past his hiding place, the Cadillac came to a stop.

Shawn rose slightly, sniffing the air. There was something ominous about the way the car sat unmoving, the driver invisible through slanting sheets of rain. A second later, the passenger's door swung open.

Shawn's heart thudded. How could anyone know he was there? It wasn't possible someone from the road could see him among the cluster of trees, yet the car sat unmoving, the open door a clear invitation.

The loud rumbling of his gut decided matters for him. He needed food, a place to hole up and sleep for a few hours. After that, he'd take care of business in the TNT and he'd be in the clear. The knife would give him the power he needed and he'd be a hero to everyone in Point Pleasant for killing the Mothman. If he had to off the driver of the vehicle for being a nosy bastard, it wouldn't be the first time he'd killed.

Biting down on the inside of his cheek, Shawn slipped the knife under his T-shirt and sprinted for the Cadillac.

* * * *

Quentin took Sarah to the hotel. He needed a shower and a change of clothes, and didn't want to leave her alone at her trailer in the event Preech returned. Shawn's Dodge Charger had been towed earlier that morning, but there was still the chance he'd come back for the car. Sarah put up a fuss until Quentin pointed out she'd been concerned enough about Suzanne's welfare to have her stay with Jerome and this was no different. Reluctantly, she agreed.

It was late morning by the time they arrived, Point Pleasant waking from a sleepy after-church Sunday. Quentin ushered Sarah into the lobby of the hotel, finding it deserted. He expected to see Eve or Katie but Sarah told him neither usually worked on Sunday.

"Sharon's probably around somewhere. I don't mind hanging out here while you shower and change clothes."

"Ok. I won't be long." Quentin gave her a quick kiss, then bounded up the steps. True to his word, he was back in the lobby in a record fifteen minutes, changed into fresh jeans and a light pullover shirt.

"That was fast." Sarah smiled up at him from her seat on the window bench. She'd been staring out the window, watching the rain. Every now and then a soft grumble of thunder added to the downpour but it was nothing like last night.

"Told you I wouldn't be long." Quentin glanced around the lobby. "Where's Sharon?"

"Taking an early lunch break in the café."

"I didn't think it was open on Sundays." Quentin hadn't realized it had gotten so late.

"It's not, but she eats her lunch in there."

He crossed the lobby and joined her on the window seat. "Isn't she worried about the front desk being unmanned?" Small-town business in action when you trusted your clientele to find you. Every now and then the reality of Point Pleasant's close knit community still caught him by surprise.

Sarah shook her head. "Turns out you're the hotel's only guest at present."

"What about Evening?"

"According to Sharon he left sometime during night."

After one-thirty to be precise. Quentin recalled spying Lach from the window in the early morning as he'd walked to his car. "I was hoping to talk to him about what happened last night." Especially in light of Sarah's revelation that Shawn's face had changed when he attacked her. Could Preech really be possessed by the spirit of his dead ancestor? After all the other strangeness they'd experienced, it wasn't out of the realm of possibility.

Sarah wrapped her fingers around her blue stone pendant. "The storm?" she guessed.

"That too."

"I'm not afraid of them anymore, you know."

Her admission surprised him. Shifting on the seat to regard her directly, he forked a knee onto the cushion between them. Somewhere off in the distance lightning flickered behind the clouds. "Because of Jonathan and Etta?"

"Partially." She wet her lips. "I can't explain it, but it's as if all of my fear came down to that single moment when I faced Shawn. I told you he looked different—that I think he's Obadiah. *That's* the storm I've been running from. Obadiah shattered my family centuries ago. Cornstalk's curse made that reality so much worse. I lost my parents and my grandparents and let myself be controlled by fear, but I don't have to be afraid anymore." Her gaze shifted to the window and the steady beat of rain outside. "I don't think Cornstalk's curse is broken, but I do think whatever blight Obadiah brought to my family was washed away in last night's storm."

A cleansing.

He wasn't one for symbolic thinking but recognized the logic of what she said. For her, the storm had been purifying. She'd been swept up in a gale of supernatural proportions and rather than being torn apart—as the storm that killed her parents had once ripped apart her family—she'd survived, emerging stronger for the experience.

Hooking his arm around her shoulder, he pulled her close and kissed her.

She smiled under his lips.

"Did Sharon say where Evening went?" he murmured.

"No." Drawing back, Sarah laid her palm on the side of his face. "But I think I know. He wrote Cold on the envelope."

Stunned, Quentin stared down at her. "The igloo?"

She nodded. "But don't think you're going alone."

* * * *

Shawn ducked his head to look inside the open car door. The man in the driver's seat sat faced forward, but there was no mistaking the distinctive profile of Lach Evening. Shawn hesitated only briefly, the spirit of Obadiah warning of danger. Somehow Evening had been at Fort Randolph when Cornstalk was killed. Shawn didn't understand the wherefores and whys any more than he understood how his ancestor lived in his body. All he knew was that the dry supple leather of the car was too inviting after a night of slogging through rain and mud. He slid into the seat and latched the door. Without a word, Lach eased the car onto the road and continued ahead.

Shawn fidgeted, sweeping a hand through his drenched hair. Evening didn't seem to mind that he dripped over the seats, or that his jeans were filthy, splattered with grime. The car looked like it had just rolled off the assembly line, the massive dash trimmed out in wood grain, the Cadillac emblem gleaming in the center of the steering wheel like a newly minted coin. Shawn was a muscle car fanatic, but experienced a twinge of envy as he took in all the buttons and knobs on the dash and doors. More than a few looked custom, setting off dollar signs in his head. The vehicle exuded a new-car smell that overrode the reek of wet denim and rain. The seat was like sinking into a cushion of air. Damn, if the car didn't cost a fortune. He might be able to unload it somewhere for quick cash and get something less noticeable.

"Hey, uh…thanks for the ride." Shifting sideways, Shawn unobtrusively slid the knife from beneath his shirt and concealed it in the space between the seat and the door. He kept his right arm twisted behind him, a position that would give him leverage when he lashed out with the blade.

"Uh…I really appreciate you coming along when you did. My car broke down a while back." The lie was plausible, but sweat broke out on his forehead when it rolled from his tongue. He gave a short laugh, which came out in a burst of jittery energy. "I've been hoofing it in that crappy weather. Sorry I'm dripping all over your car. Must be brand new, huh?" He cursed himself for jumpy chatter, but something about Evening unnerved him. It would be a hell of a lot easier if the guy talked, even acknowledged him for crap's sake, but he kept his gaze straight ahead and didn't say a word. The silence ate at Shawn.

He chewed on his thumbnail. "Where are you headed?"

More silence. The only sound in the car was the repetitive snick of the wipers against the windshield. Shawn's uneasiness spilled over into anger. "Hey, you deaf or something?" His fingers tightened around the knife.

"I would not do that, Mr. Preech."

"Not do what?"

Without turning his gaze from the windshield, Evening extended his right hand between them. Blue flame sprang from his open palm.

Shawn recoiled. "What the hell?" It was the same insidious glow that had surrounded Sarah and Marsh last night.

"It is our life-force. One that my people are able to manipulate for protection or defense." Evening studied him, his eyes like polished onyx. "It would not be wise to provoke me."

Shawn folded back into the seat, his grip slackening on the knife. Obadiah was strangely quiet, leaving him to fend on his own. "What do you mean, 'your people'?"

Evening returned his gaze to the road, his hand to the steering wheel. The flame died. "It does not matter."

Shawn wiped sweat from his forehead. He searched for the rush he always got from the knife, but the power was silent. A fat slug of fear crawled through his gut for the first time since he'd come into possession of the weapon. "Where are you taking me?"

"To the TNT."

"Why there?"

Evening's lips curled in a tight smile. "The spirit of Obadiah Preech lives inside of you and still you ask?"

Shawn swallowed hard. Whatever Evening was, he was far from an ordinary guy in a black suit driving a fancy car. Not bothering to conceal the action, Shawn slid the knife through his belt. The weapon would do him no good against Evening. "How do you know about Obadiah?"

Evening palmed the wheel, rounding a bend in the road. The car banked smoothly and silently. "Because I was there when Cornstalk was murdered."

It was true. Shawn didn't understand how, but everything Obadiah had insinuated about the man beside him was true. His breath quickened in fear as a dozen thoughts tumbled through his head. Was Evening a spirit in the flesh? The reincarnated soul of a soldier who had witnessed the murder? No, that wasn't impossible. Yet, Obadiah had struck a man who'd resembled Evening. More than resembled him.

Rowan Wynter.

His ancestor stirred awake in a mushroom cloud of hate. Oh, how he'd despised Wynter. Too righteous, too perfect. A man who'd almost foiled his plans of killing Cornstalk. The bastard had tried to interfere, but Obadiah had bested him with a blow to the back of his head.

That wouldn't work this time. They were no match for Evening.

His name is Wynter.

Whatever Obadiah called him, Shawn wasn't stupid enough to fight him.

Shawn turned his gaze out the side window. He grew quiet, increasingly uneasy around Evening. The man—if he truly was a man—was someone beyond his comprehension. If it weren't for his need to reach the TNT, he'd abandon the car.

Finally, as the Cadillac drew closer to the old World War II munitions site, Shawn found his voice. "Why are you helping me?"

"I am not helping you, Mr. Preech. My intervention is given on behalf of the Mothman. Now I suggest you get down on the floor as there will be a roadblock ahead."

"What?" Panic shot through Shawn. Instinctively, he reached for the door handle. "Let me out."

A sudden click announced he was locked inside.

"What the hell are you doing?" Shawn pulled on the latch with both hands but it wouldn't budge. Frantic, he ran his fingers along the buttons and knobs on the side panel. Nothing. Twisting, he fumbled for the lock but the metal stem had retracted into the door too deeply for him to grasp. "Evening, let me the hell out."

The man in black said nothing, merely gazed ahead. Shawn swiveled, his heart jackhammering out his terror. Through the windshield, he spied the light bar of a Mason County cruiser. The vehicle blocked the entrance to the TNT.

Of course. They were searching for the Mothman, exactly as he'd intended. Only now that plan left him vulnerable to seizure.

Desperate, he wrenched the knife from his belt. "You're going to get me arrested."

"You are running out of time, Mr. Preech. Get down on the floor."

The patrol car loomed closer. Evening was an idiot. The Cadillac was huge, but even crouched on the floor Shawn would be visible. If the man thought huddling under the dash was going to keep Shawn safe from arrest, he was insane. Any yet, what other option did he have?

Kill Wynter. Take control of the moving carriage.

Fat chance of that. Obadiah might not know what a car was, but he had to know any attempt to wrest control of the vehicle from Evening would end in disaster.

As if reading his thoughts, Evening extended his right hand. Blue light bloomed in his palm. Out of options, Shawn crouched under the dash, the knife clutched tightly. He would not go down easy.

Evening fanned his fingers from left to right in a slow, elegant wave. The motion reminded Shawn of a magician performing a trick. And like a feat of magic, the motion conjured a glowing turquoise net. He recoiled sharply as it settled over him, remembering the same eerie blue glow from last night. But this time there was no element of danger, only a muffling of sound and vision.

Less than a minute later the car rolled to a stop. The hum of the electric window rolled into the door panel as a deputy approached the car.

Evening rummaged up a pleasant smile. "Good morning, Deputy. How may I help you?"

* * * *

Caden didn't bother stopping at the sheriff's office but headed straight for the TNT. The constant rain would make the hunt for the Mothman every bit as miserable as last night, but at least the search parties wouldn't be fumbling in the dark. A few had now been diverted to look for Shawn, a search warrant underway. Caden was convinced there had to be something in his house to tie him to Hanley's murder. As for the TNT, the less people in the Mothman's orbit, the better.

He slowed as he neared a barrier at the entrance of Potters Creek Road. Deputy Morris flagged him down, then crunched a cigarette beneath his foot. He sprinted for Caden's Capri.

Caden lowered the window. "How's it going?"

"Quiet." Morris was decked out in rain gear, a weather resistant poncho slung over his shirt. The smell of smoke clung to his uniform.

"Anyone come by lately?"

"Like I said, quiet." Bending lower, Morris rested an arm on the open window. "We're good so far, but Pete's worried about fallout when word spreads the Mothman attacked your brother and Oates."

"Yeah." Caden didn't want to examine the possibilities too closely. "Could be enough to keep people away. The Mothman never attacked anyone before." That wasn't entirely true, but it was what people believed. Last summer, the creature had killed Roger Layton, the man responsible for Caden's sister's death, but only after Layton had abducted Eve. The official report said Layton had drowned, his body found in a pond in the TNT.

Speculation the Mothman had become violent would give all but the most reckless pause. It was one thing to traipse through the woods with a gun, another to slog through sheets of rain knowing the thing you hunted had a better advantage at hunting you.

Morris flecked a bit of tobacco from his tongue. "My old man said it went after him back in the sixties."

Morris' father was one of several old-timers who liked to embellish tales. Odds were he'd never even seen the creature, but Caden didn't feel like debating. He changed the subject, more concerned with how Lach was going to maneuver through a roadblock. "I'm looking for a black Cadillac. Fleetwood model with Pennsylvania tags. Have you seen it out here?"

Morris whistled softly and shook his head. "Traffic's been dead. A car like that would stand out."

No doubt about it, so how exactly did the alien plan on reaching the igloo? Potters Creek Road was the most direct route, but Evening could have entered the TNT by way of Fairgrounds Road or Conway. He hadn't bothered checking with the men manning those roadblocks, but the end result was the same. If the Cadillac rolled through, it would have been turned away.

"All right. Radio if you see it. And pull that roadblock aside." He motioned to the wooden barriers blocking the entrance. "I'm headed that way."

"Sure, Sergeant."

Seconds later, Caden waved an acknowledgement to Morris as he drove past. Trees immediately closed in on either side, broken here and there by a narrow path forking into the woods. The steady drum of rain against the windshield and roof was magnified by an unnatural quiet. Too quiet, he realized. As if every other sound had been sucked into a vacuum.

A bright tongue of lightning zigzagged across the sky.

Caden counted the seconds, waiting for a crack of thunder but it never came. His radio was silent, void of the routine chatter from the deputies who scoured the grounds. Driving slowly, he flicked on his fog lights. The mist was thicker here, hovering in dense patches above the ground, billowing like smoke between the trees. The absence of patrols disturbed him. Had they moved to another location, miles ahead?

As he neared the cutoff that led to Cold's igloo, a bulky silhouette materialized from the fog. Caden swore softly, recognizing the Cadillac emblem on the trunk. Rain beaded on the glossy black paint as if the vehicle had been freshly waxed only hours before.

"Not. Freaking. Possible." He pulled off the road behind the Fleetwood and shifted the Capri into park. How the hell had Evening gotten past Morris—or any of the other deputies, for that matter?

Clenching his jaw, he watched as Lach stepped from the car. In addition to his black suit, Evening wore an equally dark fedora to shield himself from the rain. Irritated without understanding why, Caden thrust open the door and stalked forward.

"How did you get past Morris?" he demanded.

"Do you mean the deputy positioned at the roadblock?" Even with the rain hammering around them, Evening's accent was clear. While Caden felt like he needed to shout to be heard, the Man in Black spoke in a neutral tone.

"Yes." Caden thrust an arm behind him, pointing from the direction he'd come. "Morris."

For answer, Evening extended his hand. A sphere of blue light sprang from his palm, driving back the rain. "Have you forgotten my skill with flicker phenomena?"

Caden gaped. This was a trick he hadn't seen before. Evening had used flicker phenomena to hypnotize and regress Katie Lynch's ex-boyfriend. In the process, he'd nearly fried Lyle's brain, turning him into a killer with Caden as his target.

"What did you do to Morris?"

Evening curled his fingers inward, squelching the light. "Nothing but suggest he let me pass then conveniently forget my existence."

Instant hypnosis.

Morris hadn't seemed hurt, mentally or physically. Scowling, Caden stuffed his hands in his pockets. Had Evening ever used that trick on him without his knowledge?

The rain dripped down his neck, sluicing under his dark green windbreaker. Tugging the hood up, he attempted to keep the worst of the weather at bay. By contrast, Evening seemed untroubled by the storm. Rain dripped from his hat, and the edges of blond hair clinging to his face and neck were damp, but he stood as if the sun beat upon him rather than the rain.

"I see you received my message, Sergeant."

"You mean 'Cold.'" He should have known Evening would want him to find the clue. "Why are we here? And why are we standing in the rain?"

"Because it has started."

"What has?"

"Obadiah Preech is out there somewhere."

Caden shook his head. "What are you talking about?"

Evening pointed a slender finger in the direction of the igloo. "Perhaps we should speak outside of the rain."

Caden didn't need further prompting. He jogged back to his vehicle long enough to stuff a flashlight in his jacket, then trailed Evening into the woods.

* * * *

Quentin lowered his window as the deputy approached. He should have realized there'd be a roadblock preventing him and Sarah from entering the TNT.

"That's Rod Morris," Sarah said at his side. "I know him from seeing him at the courthouse."

"Sorry, folks. You're going to have to turn around." Morris leaned down to peer in the car as he made the announcement.

"Hi, Rod." Sarah offered a friendly smile. "We were looking for Caden Flynn. He told us to meet him at one of the old igloos."

Morris' brows drew together, conveying his skepticism. "Sarah." He nodded a greeting, but the frown remained firmly in place. "Caden was through here not more than ten minutes ago. He didn't say anything to me."

"But it's really important we hook up with him." Sarah pressed the issue.

"Sorry. The whole area is off limits to townsfolk right now. Orders from Sheriff Weston."

"Maybe you could radio Caden," Quentin suggested. It was worth a shot. "Let me talk to him."

Morris scrutinized him suspiciously. "Who are you?"

"Quentin Marsh." Quentin extended his hand. "I've been staying at the Parrish Hotel for the last week."

Ignoring the hand, Morris stepped back from the car. "Sorry, folks. Like I said before, you need to move along." He waved his hand, indicating they should turn around or continue down the main thoroughfare.

Expelling a breath, Quentin raised the window and backed the car onto the road. Changing directions, he headed for town.

"Where are we going?" Sarah sounded worried.

"Back to the hotel."

"But Caden could be in trouble."

"I know that, but we can't get past a roadblock."

"So what are we going to do?"

Quentin flecked his gaze skyward to the roiling clouds massing overhead. "Hope he survives the storm."

* * * *

Shaking the rain from his jacket, Caden lowered the hood of his windbreaker. He switched on his flashlight to scatter the darkness clinging to the walls of the igloo. At least it was dry inside, shelter from the downpour.

"You do not need that." Standing a short distance away, Evening nodded to the flashlight.

"Maybe you can see fine in here, but I need more light."

Evening extended his hand, conjuring the same glow he'd summoned earlier. Flecks of luminescent blue immediately sprang to life on the walls of the bunker.

Stunned, Caden turned in a circle, mesmerized by the dazzling pulse of cobalt and aquamarine. "What is this?"

Evening extinguished the flame dancing on his palm. The light radiating from the walls remained steady. "A way for you to see. I trust it is satisfactory."

Caden switched off the flashlight. Evening had a strange way of making a point. "Why are we here?"

Lach folded his hands in front of him. "Because you have something to tell me." In the eerie blue glow, it was impossible to distinguish his pupils from the black of his eyes. He'd never looked more alien than he did now.

Caden shifted, dried leaves and stones crunching under his feet. He raked a hand through his damp hair. "The Mothman attacked my brother and a deputy last night. Ryan's going to be okay, but Oates was seriously injured. The creature's never been violent before."

"Creature." Evening's gaze was penetrating. "Is that how you see it?"

"How else should I see it?"

"I believe you already hold the answer to that, Sergeant Flynn." Evening removed his hat, his long fingers appearing like spider legs in the ghostly illumination. Somewhat absently, he examined the brim. "How did you see it last night?"

Caden shot him a sharp glance. "What do you mean?"

"Is that not why you sought me today? To ask about what you had seen?"

It was only part of a lengthy string of questions too entangled for Caden to dissect. He went to the heart of the matter. "I saw its face."

Evening seemed to consider that. Lowering the hat, he gripped it loosely by the brim, right hand wrapped around his left wrist. Against the black felt of the fedora, the tips of his abnormally shaped fingers looked flat. "Few have seen what you did."

Curious, Caden stepped closer. "Have you ever seen its face?"

"Not in its present state."

Caden digested that. A rumble of thunder took him back to last night when he'd stared up into the creature's eyes. He'd experienced the same crushing terror others felt when trapped by those malignant red circles. But as quickly as the fear came, it had evaporated, the crimson glow of the creature's eyes fading with it.

Caden's mouth went dry. "I...I saw the way it looked when it first came to this planet." *All those thousand yesteryears ago.* "It resembled a man. As you do." Caden's gaze flashed to Evening's face. The Mothman's features had not been as refined as Lach's, the brow much higher and nose broader, but he'd looked as human as anyone Caden might encounter on the street. The clarity of that realization made him dig down in his gut. He dredged up the question he'd shied from asking. "Did it…did he have a name?"

"You would not be able to pronounce it."

"Tell me anyway."

Evening said something that sounded like gibberish to Caden. "The closest approximation in your language is Drayandor."

Drayandor.

Once you put a name to something, you can no longer think of it as a thing. Caden wet his lips. It was dangerous to imagine the creature as a man. He forced the thought from his head, concentrating on what he knew.

There had been others like the Mothman, who'd come to Earth when the creature did, all left behind by Indrid Cold. Standing in the igloo that had been a channel of communication with Lach's father, Caden was reminded of what Lach once told him. Earth's atmosphere had warped the appearance and minds of the aliens, altering them into misshapen beings that became the subject of human nightmares. Only later did Cold's people discover a way to prevent that. By then, it was too late for the Mothman and that initial group of alien visitors.

Last night, the creature had allowed him to see what others could not. With that single glimpse of its face, he'd understood the motive that compelled it to survive when all it truly craved was death. It was old. Tired. Unable to return to its own planet, but the last of those who'd lived with the mutation caused by time on Earth. Before death, it would have vengeance.

"It wants Obadiah Preech."

Evening nodded. In the blue glow pulsing from the walls his hair was threaded with silver. "Preech killed its…offspring, if you will." He seemed to recognize Caden's difficulty in thinking of the creature as anything remotely human. "Preech believed the Mothman was responsible for his wife's death and enacted his own brand of retribution. He believed there to be one creature, but there were two."

Two.

On edge, Caden paced to the opposite side of the dome. Biting down on his lip, he tapped the top of the flashlight against his palm. "It's been alone since then. All those centuries ago when its…offspring"—he stumbled over the word—"was killed."

"Murdered." Evening's accent was clipped. "Now you understand why nothing will stop it from going after Obadiah. It has waited centuries for justice."

"And you expect me to believe that Shawn Preech is possessed by the spirit of his dead ancestor?" Caden pivoted to face the alien.

"The storm I predicted." Evening spread his hands to indicate the steady rain hammering down on the igloo. "Do you think Shawn Preech would have murdered a man in cold blood if he were not controlled by a demon?"

"Will Hanley." Caden's gut twisted. "Shawn's as much a victim in this as Hanley was."

"Do not feel too remorseful for him, Sergeant. The curse that brought about these circumstances is the result of a knife that has been in Mr. Preech's family for generations. Obadiah waited and selected Shawn because the young man welcomed the corrupting stain of darkness. Shawn Preech would not have been able to carry out a deed as ugly as murder were he not already capable of it in his heart."

"He went after Sarah Sherman last night."

Evening settled his fedora on his head. "I am aware of that. She was protected."

"Protected?"

"The same blue light that illuminates this igloo kept her from harm. It comes from the stones she and Quentin Marsh carry."

"You said it was a life-force."

"From the people of my planet. Just as the flame you saw in my hand is an extension of my own life-force. When we pass from this life to another, we leave a portion of ourselves behind. Like a shell. Imagine a reptile shedding its skin or a butterfly abandoning a cocoon."

"The stones." Understanding clicked in Caden's head. "Jonathan Marsh found them, and gave one to Etta Sherman as a promise token. Later, they must have been set in silver to create jewelry. Something that would become an heirloom in each family."

"Yes."

"They were left by others like the Mothman. Others of your kind who died centuries before Cornstalk lived."

Evening nodded. If there'd been energy in those stones, energy of any kind, it would have bound Jonathan and Etta together in an afterlife and protected Sarah when needed. Through everything that had happened— Cornstalk's death and curse, the tangled lines of the Marsh, Sherman, and Preech families, everything came back to one source—Indrid Cold, the alien responsible for bringing the Mothman and others from his planet to Earth.

"Your father is responsible for this mess."

"He never intended for any of this to happen."

"It doesn't matter. It's why you're here. Why you've been here all along." Pacing off a circle, Caden pressed his fingertips to his temple. "I should have realized it before. Your father fucked up and you came to Earth to do damage control. Cold is responsible for the Mothman, for opening the ley lines in the TNT, for UFOs and dimension travelers." The enormity of what Cold had done left him stunned. He spun to face Evening, his thoughts tumbling over one another in rapid succession. "He led your people here eons ago, and in the process, opened a door that should have remained shut."

Evening stiffened, a hint of tension evident in the tightening of his jaw. "My father made a mistake. A horrible mistake. Our planet was dying. He attempted to find a suitable terrain for our people. You would have done the same."

"He didn't consider the consequences." Caden lurched forward. "For your people or mine. Damn it, Lach. All of this...everything that's happened—Obadiah, Cornstalk, Shawn, Hanley. All of it can be traced back to that single mistake." His gut contracted. Were it not for Cold, the Mothman wouldn't exist. Point Pleasant's stability had been altered by the legend of the creature, shaped by the curse of Cornstalk. Through centuries and decades, each event could be traced back to the damage Cold had done.

Even the Silver Bridge.

Caden sucked air through his nose. So many had perished, claimed by the frigid waters of the Ohio River or crushed beneath deadly debris. His own sister. It wasn't enough Cold had fried the mind of Parker Kline and saddled Caden with the guilt, he was responsible for every tragedy enacted from Cornstalk's curse, if only indirectly. When it came down to it, his own failure had caused the Shawnee's death.

Evening moved in front of him, his gaze level.

"What would you have me do, Caden?"

The rare use of his first name forced Caden to focus. Whatever Cold's faults, they were ancient history. He might not always see eye-to-eye with Evening, or even trust the alien implicitly, but Lach had done what he could—in his roundabout way—to help. Caden would be in worse straits without the nuggets of information Evening provided.

"Tell me what I'm facing." A gust of wind blew through the igloo, hurling a handful of leaves to the corner. How many times had he stood in this same bunker, chasing the supernatural? It was no different now, except he directed his questions to Evening rather than Cold. "If Obadiah has really taken possession of Shawn, how will I defeat him?"

Evening's dark eyes glittered in the light pulsing from the walls. "As you would any man. Despite the spirit that inhabits him, Shawn Preech is still flesh and blood. Obadiah must have a heart that pumps. Lungs that breathe. He cannot exist in this world otherwise."

Caden nodded. He didn't want to think what would happen when he arrested Shawn. He still had the anomaly of fingerprints found at Hanley's house to deal with. First and foremost, he had to find Shawn before Obadiah goaded him into harming someone else.

"All right." His brain was on overload, pumped full of information that was useless to anyone but him. Strolling into Pete Weston's office and announcing their killer was the ghost of an eighteenth-century settler wasn't an option. "Whatever happens, stay out of my way, Lach. You might find it entertaining to bullshit the patrols out here, but we've got to find the Mothman before Shawn does."

Caden stalked toward the door.

"You're too late for that," Evening said behind him.

Anger made him turn. "What do you mean?"

"I brought Mr. Preech here, and deposited him in the TNT."

"What?" Sudden heat shot up the back of Caden's neck. How could Evening remain so calm, almost as if he'd planned the whole thing down to this millisecond in time? Hell, he probably had.

Caden stalked closer. "Why would you do that?" He didn't bother asking how Evening had found Shawn when half of Mason County was looking for him. Some questions weren't worth the effort, especially when the answer was bound to be vague.

"Preech is not the only one who craves vengeance, Sergeant." Evening spoke sharply, his accent more noticeable than before. Somewhere, a switch had flipped, his cool demeanor replaced by a sliver of hostility. "I brought him here to end the battle begun centuries ago. He must confront the Mothman."

"Hell, whatever." At last he didn't have to worry about Shawn doing something crazy in town. "Tell me where he's headed. You've got to know."

Evening regarded him steadily but said nothing.

Caden swore. "Look, your father's partially responsible for this mess. Help me out."

Nothing.

Damn if the man hadn't turned to stone. He might as well have been for the lack of emotion on his face. Caden was about to call him on it when the flecks of blue light clinging to the walls pulsed brighter. The glow intensified, creeping into the farthest corners until no hint of shadow remained. Caden tensed, uncertain what the change signified. Even Lach appeared surprised, glancing behind him, a look of wonder on his face.

Go.

Indrid Cold's voice echoed in Caden's head. The accent resembled Lach's but carried a deeper inflection. Caden hadn't heard that intonation since promising to safeguard the Mothman. Is that why Cold came now after all this time, because the creature's life was in danger?

Light bled from the wall and crept across the ground in a rickety finger of blue. It lengthened and grew, stretching in a thin line beyond the door. Caden strode to the opening, watching as the string of light disappeared between the trees, swallowed by fog.

A path to lead him to the Mothman.

Cold was pointing the way.

He was halfway through the door when Lach's voice stopped him. "The creature killed Obadiah once before, Sergeant Flynn."

For killing its offspring. Caden paused as the ugly reality washed over him. What would he do if someone killed his child? No wonder a storm had descended on Point Pleasant. A clash of cataclysmic proportions had been resurrected from the ash of yesteryear.

And he was caught in the center.

Caden slipped from the igloo into the mist.

* * * *

For the first time in days Shawn's mind was astonishingly clear. Even the constant hunger that gnawed at his gut had grown quiet. The musky scent of the woods invigorated him, reminding him of something primal in a time long past. He'd hunted here, scouted for danger, and killed savages among these ancient trees. He'd butchered the creature that had taken Willa from him here, thinking it the only one of its kind.

But there'd been another, a monster that claimed his life in a bloodbath. Just as Cornstalk had uttered a curse with his dying breath, Obadiah had vowed to return and seek retribution.

Shawn's grip tightened on the handle of the knife. The creature was out there, lurking in the shadows. Watching.

Let it come. He welcomed the chance to face it. This time he would not fail, but would send the demon to the abyss of Hell from which it had been sprung.

A steady thrum grew behind his eyes. A low-level vibration that overrode the rapid tapping of rain pattering against the leaves overhead. Tilting his head back, Shawn turned in a circle, searching the sky. Dense layers of fog made it impossible to see more than a few feet. Wet dribbled against his face and sluiced down his neck.

"Where are you?"

The drone grew louder, a familiar sound that made him grind his teeth. After all this time, centuries of waiting in a nether realm of darkness, retribution would be his. "Come, you demon. Come face me."

Releasing an ear-splitting shriek, the Mothman plunged from the sky.

* * * *

Caden had been following the shimmering thread of blue for approximately half a mile when an inhuman screech ruptured the air. Wrenching his gun from his holster, he bolted for the sound, fully aware he raced to a destination Lach had predicted months ago.

The culmination of a desolate hour.

* * * *

Shawn tucked and rolled, buffeted by a gust of wind from the creature's massive wings. He fought to get his feet under him, but slipped on the wet ground and crashed to one knee. A clawed hand sent him pinwheeling into a tree. The drone in his head exploded like a rocket, then plummeted into the white noise of rain. Blood oozed over his lips, dribbling from a fresh laceration on his cheek.

Scrambling to his feet, he pressed his back against the tree. Like a phantom, the creature had struck and fled. He sensed it hidden in the fog, but the haze was too dense for him to see properly. Heart pounding, he tightened his grip around the knife. His lungs expanded with the effort to breathe. He knew the creature's tricks, had faced it before. With effort, he forced his terror silent.

"Come for me, demon." Obadiah's voice poured from his mouth, the sound strange to his ears. He remembered butchering the thing's offspring, hacking at it until he was covered in a cobalt blue substance that could only be blood. It had shrieked and thrashed, powerful even in its death throes. He'd suffered greatly, the creature's claws gouging strips of flesh from his chest and arms. But in the end, he'd triumphed, driving the knife cursed by Cornstalk's blood through a single crimson eye. The creature's wail had made him fear Hell itself had risen from the bowels of the Earth.

Then the other had come, summoned by its cries—the thing that was out there watching from the fog. How foolish to think there'd only been one.

Weakened from his fight, Obadiah had been no match for the stronger, larger demon. Shawn shuddered as he witnessed the brutal death of his ancestor unfold in his head. The Mothman had been ruthless, ripping his adversary limb from limb. When the creature was done, blood and organs littered the ground like offal.

Choking on the images, Shawn breathed heavily through his mouth. He couldn't die like that.

Fear is the demon's weapon.

Yes. He couldn't give in. Wouldn't remember. Wouldn't end up the same way Obadiah had.

We are one. We fight it together.

He licked his lips nervously. "Stop hiding." His voice cracked. Would the knife really give him the power he needed? Before he could so much as draw a breath, the thing burst from the fog. Shawn caught a glimpse of wings and red eyes before the creature was upon him. He thrust wildly, but was battered aside like so much dung. Wings pummeled him, blotting the light from his head, battering with a force to shatter bones. Something snapped in his shoulder and he screamed. He crumpled to his knees, the knife tumbling from his fingers.

No!

He couldn't lose it now. Frantically, he scrambled forward, pushing on his belly to reach the weapon. His fingers closed on the handle just as the sharp bite of claws burrowed into his back.

Shawn bellowed in pain. His screams cut off abruptly when he was wrenched into the air. Blood bubbled into his throat, the hot metallic tang of copper flooding his mouth. Choking on the foul taste, he flailed out blindly with the knife. The blade blundered into alien flesh, met resistance, then tore free. With a hiss, the creature dropped him.

Now. Attack it now.

Obadiah forced him to his feet. The blade should have been lethal. It was tainted with Cornstalk's blood. One strike should have killed the Mothman. It's what he'd believed all along.

"You lied to me. You said the knife would kill it."

Panicked, Shawn backpedaled. His head spun and the ground lurched beneath him with a sickening jolt. He pressed up against a tree, feeling the rough scrape of bark against his lacerated back. Plastered in place by blood, his shirt stuck to his skin. He tried to draw a breath, but each ragged gasp for air brought fresh agony.

Kill it! Kill it!

Obadiah was insane.

Shawn tilted his head and stared up into the creature's baleful red eyes. It loomed over him, wings arched high above its back. Up close, the variations of color in its flesh stood out sharply—mottled gray leeching into charcoal and ash. Flecks of cobalt blue stippled the creature's left shoulder below the wing.

Blood.

He'd succeeded in wounding it.

"You can be hurt." His tongue struggled to form words. His right arm dangled at his side, fingers wrapped around the knife, but he barely had the strength to lift the weapon. One feeble strike was all he'd managed. How pitiful. It sucked being the weaker opponent. Like Hanley and Suzanne. Like Obadiah.

With a roar wrenched from his gut, Shawn hefted the knife above his head and charged. His bellow of rage became a scream of agony when the Mothman ripped his arm from his body.

* * * *

Caden burst onto the scene in time to see Shawn drop at the creature's feet. It took him a second to process what he was looking at—Shawn on his back, legs curled to his chest, his left hand clamped over a gaping hole where his right arm should have been. Ragged bone jutted from the grisly cavity, a glut of blood painting the rain-sodden ground scarlet. Ten feet away, the shorn appendage lay among a snarl of brambles, Obadiah's knife clutched in the upturned hand.

Caden's gut churned. Dropping into a firing stance, he unloaded six bullets into the Mothman's back.

With a hiss of rage the creature whirled, one wing sweeping in a deadly arc toward Caden. He dove to the side, tucking and rolling as he hit the ground. A gust of wind kept him pinioned in place as leaves and twigs rained down from the tree overhead. On his stomach, Caden dug into his pocket for more ammo. As the creature hobbled away, he flipped open the cylinder and expended the used shells.

Shawn's screams had died to moans. Caden propelled himself through the fog, quickly dropping to one knee beside the injured man.

"Shawn." The bitter reek of blood struck his nostrils. Extending a hand, he touched the younger man's cheek. Shawn was nearly incoherent, fresh blood on his lips and chin testifying to internal injuries in addition to the maiming.

"Make…him leave," he moaned.

Shrugging from his jacket, Caden glanced nervously to the trees. The Mothman was still there, hidden somewhere in the fog.

"Obadiah," Shawn insisted.

Caden wadded the jacket into a ball and pressed down hard on the amputation site.

Shawn screamed.

"I'm sorry. I've got to try to stop the bleeding." Hooking an arm behind Shawn, Caden tried to raise his shoulders. Beneath the garish smear of blood, Shawn's lips were turning blue.

One-handed, Caden dug his walkie-talkie from his pocket and radioed for help. He had no idea where the patrols were, but raised Morris and gave his location. "We'll get you an ambulance, Shawn. Hang on and you'll pull through this." The lie sounded hollow even to him.

Something rustled in the trees.

Had he injured the Mothman? Had the bullets done any good?

His arm was soaked with blood where he gripped Shawn behind the back. More of the dying man's blood saturated his jeans. As the rain beat the grass around him, he sensed Shawn's life slipping away.

Caden clenched his jaw. The man had butchered Will Hanley yet he couldn't help feeling a flicker of remorse.

A faint smile curved Shawn's lips. "He'll die with me." His eyes popped wide. Arching his back, he jerked violently upward, contorting his spine like a fish tossed onto dry land. A loud hiss of breath escaped his lips then his gaze froze in place, locked on something far above.

Caden swore. Easing Shawn's body to the ground, he swallowed bile. His hands were stained with blood, but already the rain washed the telltale evidence of Shawn's death away. Locating his gun, Caden tucked the revolver into his waistband. It would do little against the creature. Six shots had proven that.

He forced himself to walk the distance to Shawn's bloody arm. The spider symbol was plainly evident on the handle of the knife. With a grimace of disgust, Caden bent and tugged the weapon from the upturned fingers. Touching the thing filled him with revulsion. The cursed weapon was responsible for so many deaths—Jonathan Marsh, Cornstalk, the Mothman's offspring.

He slipped the knife through his belt, then switched off his radio. Leaving Shawn's mangled body behind him, he ran into the woods, reckless, welcoming the exertion. Putting as much distance between him and Shawn's corpse as possible.

How ironic that in the past, he had always been the one to seek the Mothman, but now the creature would seek him. He sensed it, somewhere behind and above, following at a distance. It took him fifteen minutes of running to realize the rain had stopped, that lightning no longer arced above his head. Already the mist thinned, tattered gray phantoms scattered by the wind.

The storm was over. The clash of Obadiah and the Mothman had ended the only way it could.

Caden burst into a small clearing and stopped. The area would serve for his needs, far enough away from the igloos and Shawn's body that no one should find him. Winded, he doubled over and planted his hands on his knees. There was no drone or incessant humming to announce the Mothman's presence. One moment the creature wasn't there, and the next it stood in front of him.

He straightened slowly, his attention drawn by the bright beads of cobalt dripping from the back of its wings. Six bullets hadn't killed it, but he'd wounded it. Pain slammed into him, projected emotion to convey the agony it suffered.

He staggered under the deluge. It was sheer lunacy to face a creature that could inflict pain with a mere flicker of thought. "So that's it?" He spat the words and tried to straighten. "You're going to kill me like you killed Shawn?" Gulping for air, he groped for his gun. Barrel down, he held it from his body like an offering, then dropped it on the ground. Acknowledgement the creature was in control.

Slowly the pain abated, slithering away on a parting serpent kiss of fire.

Unnerved, Caden dragged the back of a hand across his mouth. His gaze dropped to the brand on his forearm. Still black, the marks were now riddled with cracks, a few sections showing skin underneath like a scab peeling away. He rubbed his hand over the lines, sensing when the Mothman tracked the movement.

For several seconds there was no emotion from the creature, then a barrage of exhaustion hit him in force.

Old. Tired.

Caden stared up into the glowing red eyes suspended above him.

I will not see it for what it is. What it was.

A creature he could kill, but a thing that possessed spirit and soul….

He pulled the knife from his belt. The weapon would kill the creature not because it was tainted with Cornstalk's blood but because the Mothman had chosen it as the weapon of its death. It would die by the same blade that had murdered its offspring. Ash clogged his throat, turned his grip slick with sweat.

It was a sentient, intelligent being.

It had a name.

Drayandor.

The droplets of blue trickling from its back were larger now, thick globules that stained the grass with alien blood. The creature folded its wings, drawing them close to cocoon its body. It stumbled backward, the light dimming in its eyes. In that instant when it touched his mind, he understood that it was already dying. Left alone, it would crawl into one of its hiding places. It might even recover, bullets alone not enough to end its life.

But it had chosen him to do what it could not.

Firmly clutching the knife, Caden lurched forward and plunged the blade into the Mothman's chest.

The weapon shattered into a dozen pieces.

* * * *

Quentin drummed his fingers on his leg. When he left the TNT, he'd intended to take Sarah back to the hotel, but somehow they'd ended up at Eve's. It worked out well as Eve had been relieved to see them. She'd been calling Sarah's trailer all morning and was just getting ready to drive there when they pulled up in front of the house.

After inviting them inside, she and Sarah had caught up on the events of last night and this morning. A half hour later, Ryan wandered over, helped by Katie. In no time, the group was congregated in Eve's living room, discussing the events of the last few days.

Quentin had tuned out the conversation when he suddenly realized the unusual dexterity with which he manipulated his fingers. Breath whistled between his teeth when his gaze dropped to his hand.

"Quentin, what's wrong?" Seated beside him, Sarah twisted to face him.

Stunned, it took him several seconds to lift his hand and turn it toward her. "No scars."

Her mouth parted in shock. "My God. How is that possible?"

"The Marsh family curse." Eve was the one to piece it together. Seated near the entrance to the dining room, she leaned forward on her chair. "Something must have happened to break the curse."

"The knife?" Ryan guessed.

Earlier, Quentin and the others had brought him and Katie up to date on everything that had transpired. Odd how easily Quentin fit into their group. "Shawn had the knife. At least, he did last night," he reminded them.

"That knife is tied to Obadiah and to Cornstalk." Eve's attention was diverted by the sound of car pulling into the driveway. Relief washed over her face. "Oh, thank God! Caden must be back."

She was halfway to the door when her husband strode inside. Quentin took one look at him and knew something terrible had happened. He wore a clean uniform, not a speck of dirt to account for the storm that had raged all morning but his gray eyes were haunted, dark as gunmetal.

"Caden?" Eve's brows drew together. "Where are your clothes?"

"I changed at the station." He closed the door behind him. "Between the rain and the TNT, I got a bit...muddy."

"I'm just glad you're home. I was worried." Sliding a hand onto his chest, Eve gave him a light kiss. "Come in and join us. Ryan's here. He's doing better."

"Hey, brother." Caden nodded in greeting, then collapsed into a loveseat under the front window. "Good to see you functioning again."

Ryan snorted. "I never stopped." A pause to refocus. "I heard you went after Preech."

"More or less. I was looking for Evening and bumped into Shawn along the way."

"You mean he's in custody?" Eve eased onto the cushions beside him.

"No." Caden's expression was bleak. "He's, um...dead."

Stunned silence settled over the room.

Quentin tried to rummage up a shred of remorse for Shawn but couldn't conjure anything beyond relief. "How?"

"The Mothman killed him. Leave it at that."

There was an edge to Caden's voice, but whether it was bitter or haunted, Quentin couldn't say. From what he'd been led to believe, the Mothman had never killed anyone. Until last night, it had never been truly aggressive.

"Something happened to the knife."

"Destroyed." Caden seemed to recognize it wasn't a question. "How did you know?"

Raising his arm, Quentin turned the back of his hand to the sergeant. It would take time to digest that the scars were truly gone and to rekindle the fleet dexterity of his fingers. He was out of practice, but that wouldn't stop him from embracing his passion for music. "Should I take it this means Cornstalk's curse is broken?"

Caden didn't appear overly surprised by the sight. "So it would seem. At the least the curse on the Marsh family."

"What about the town?" Katie asked.

Ryan took her hand. "Was there ever really a curse?"

"Something drove Shawn to act the way he did." Eve shook her head. "I don't know if it was Obadiah or Cornstalk, but I pray whatever it was never touches anyone again."

"It was Obadiah's spirit that controlled him, Eve. That spirit is gone. There are no other descendants in the Preech line. Even if it were possible without the knife, Obadiah can't return."

"So it's over?" Sarah's eyes were wide, her expression hopeful.

Caden nodded. "Over."

Quentin found the hollow echo of his words difficult to believe.

* * * *

Three days later when Quentin checked out of the Parrish Hotel, Sarah was waiting for him in the lobby. He tossed his luggage in his car then walked with her to the riverfront. The water was still high and muddy from the storm, but the sun shone brightly for the first time since he'd arrived in town. The pillars where the Silver Bridge had once stood jutted from the water in the distance, a stark reminder of all the rural town had suffered.

The Marsh curse was broken. He wondered if Cornstalk had also forgiven the town.

"Will you call me?" Sarah walked at his side. Head bowed, her auburn curls glinted like a copper penny in the morning light.

"And write." He wished she lived closer. The concert circuit would keep him busy once he returned, and it might be months before he could visit again. He fished in his pocket for the amulet his grandfather had given him. Drawing to a halt, he gripped her shoulders and turned her to face him. "This was a pledge from Jonathan to Etta." He opened his hand to display the blue stone.

Sarah touched the pendant at her throat. "And this from Etta to Jonathan."

Quentin nodded. "So now they are our pledge to stay in touch." His lips stretched in a grin. "After everything we've been through in the past week, you really don't think I'm going to let you vanish from my life, do you?"

"I hoped not." Her smile matched his. "If need be, I suppose I can become a crazed fan and stalk you down at one of your concerts."

"You've never even heard me play."

"Which is the first thing you're going to correct when we get back together." Gripping his shirt, she tugged him down for a kiss. He sensed it was the first of many to come in the years ahead.

* * * *

It took Caden a week before he rummaged up the courage to return to Indrid Cold's igloo. Barren and dark, the bunker betrayed no hint that it had once been a gateway to another world. Even the TNT felt different, as if a shroud had been lifted. The woodlands seemed brighter, busier with insect life and the constant trill of birds. Leaving the igloo behind, he struck deeper into the woods, retracing the path that led to the clearing where he'd killed the Mothman.

He didn't know what he expected to find. The creature's body had sunk into the ground shortly after it breathed its last, flesh dissolving into the soil as though pulled under by quicksand. The eyes had been swallowed last, the glow of red visible for several seconds even after dirt swallowed them.

Without a body, the legend of the Mothman would continue to haunt Point Pleasant. The public had been told a bear killed Shawn. That he had fled to the TNT after it was discovered he was Will Hanley's killer. Already people had forgotten why there was a need for patrols at the TNT, deciding Mitch and Painter must have seen a bear as well. Most went back to scoffing at the idea of a winged cryptid that haunted the ammunitions site, too preoccupied to learn Shawn had been a murderer. But others would gather and whisper, keeping the tales of a red-eyed creature alive.

Pausing in the center of the clearing, Caden glanced down at his forearm. The brands that he'd carried for the last sixteen years were gone, not a trace to indicate they'd ever marred his skin. Like the Marsh family curse, the bond he'd had with the creature had shattered.

"I wondered if you would return here."

Caden turned at the sound of the familiar voice with its light accent.

Evening stepped from the trees on his right. He wore black jeans and a black T-shirt.

A grin stretched Caden's lips. "You look different, Lach." He'd never thought to see the usually impeccable alien dressed so casually.

Lach spread his hands, glancing down at his clothing. "When in Rome."

Caden's grin held. "Were you there?"

The alien's smile made his amusement clear. "A discussion for another time." He stepped to Caden's side, silent as he gazed out over the surrounding woodlands. After a moment, he seemed to reach a conclusion. "This has been difficult for you."

Caden fought back bitter laughter. A string of sarcastic rebuttals danced across his tongue but he resisted the impulse to lash out. "Far more than for you."

"That is where you are wrong, Sergeant. It has been extremely difficult for me."

Caden was sure skepticism showed on his face. "Because you had to return to a town you'd rather avoid?"

"Because the Mothman—Drayandor—was my brother."

"What?" Shock rocketed through Caden. He took a faltering step backward, the staggering reality hitting with the force of a physical blow. It wasn't possible. Couldn't be possible. Yet Lach's reply to a question he'd asked earlier suddenly made sense.

"Have you ever seen its face?"

"Not in its present state."

But Evening had seen it before. As the creature was before it had been changed by Earth's atmosphere. How stupid that he hadn't made the connection.

"Why do you think my father has returned year after year?" Lach queried. "Why he has remained a force in the igloo, and why I have long held an interest in Point Pleasant?"

Caden shook his head. He felt cheated, used. "I should have realized sooner." The Mothman, Cold, Evening—all three hailed from the same planet. Evening had lived every bit as long as the creature. He'd even been at Fort Randolph when Cornstalk was killed. How did you exist century after century, decade after decade, knowing your brother had become a mutation? A monster?

"You brought Shawn here. To the TNT. Knowing full well he had come to kill…" Caden swallowed, forcing words that even now left him blindsided. "Your brother. You let me track the Mothman, knowing I had no choice but to kill it."

"As Drayandor chose." Evening folded his hands in front of his waist. "There was little of the brother I knew left in the creature he had become. He died easily."

Anger shot through Caden. "You weren't there."

"Do you think my guilt is any less? My father's?" Evening pulled a smooth blue stone from the pocket of his jeans. He dropped it into Caden's hand. "Had the Mothman passed violently, the stone would not be smooth."

Caden scowled. A series of fine black lines riddled the surface of the object, but the stone was as smooth as polished amber. "I plunged a knife into its chest. How is that not violent?" The harsh bitterness of his voice surprised him.

Lach's expression remained neutral. If he felt pain at the loss he'd suffered, he hid it well. "He was ready to die. With Obadiah gone, he had no reason to continue."

"And what about you?" Caden's gaze narrowed. He wasn't sure if he felt anger or gratitude for knowing the truth in the end. "Now that the creature is gone, what reason do you have for remaining in Point Pleasant?"

"None, actually." Lach held out his hand. "I merely came to say goodbye."

Caught off guard, Caden stared. A part of him remained bitter over the way he'd been used, another part understood he couldn't expect a member of an alien race to react as he did. He supposed he should feel grateful Evening had taken the time to share the stone with him. Lach didn't owe him anything, yet wanted to assure him he shouldn't harbor guilt. "Where will you go?" Caden shook his hand.

The hint of a thin smile flirted at the corners of Lach's mouth. "Who can say? There is always somewhere plagued by rumors of UFOs or supernatural creatures. More than enough cities and small towns to keep me occupied."

Caden nodded. With the Mothman gone and Cold retreating back to his home planet, he envisioned Lach doing just that—going from town to town to investigate claims of paranormal activity. Of the three aliens who had left Lanulos for Earth, Lach was the only one who had adapted. "Think you'll ever be back this way again?"

Evening shrugged. "If I am, I shall look you up, Sergeant. But I have a feeling you will be more than content to live a life that does not include dimension travelers and extraterrestrial visitors." He turned away then hesitated, glancing over his shoulder. "For the record, you have been a good friend, Caden Flynn."

In case you missed it, keep reading for an excerpt from the first Point
Pleasant novel:

A THOUSAND YESTERYEARS

Behind a legend lies the truth...

As a child, Eve Parrish lost her father and her best friend, Maggie Flynn,
in a tragic bridge collapse. Fifteen years later, she returns to Point Pleasant
to settle her deceased aunt's estate. Though much has changed about the
once thriving river community, the ghost of tragedy still weighs heavily
on the town, as do rumors and sightings of the Mothman, a local legend.
When Eve uncovers startling information about her aunt's death, that
legend is in danger of becoming all too real . . .

Caden Flynn is one of the few lucky survivors of the bridge collapse but
blames himself for coercing his younger sister out that night. He's carried
that guilt for fifteen years, unaware of darker currents haunting the town.
It isn't long before Eve's arrival unravels an old secret—one that places
her and Caden in the crosshairs of a deadly killer . . .

A Lyrical e-book on sale now.

Learn more about Mae at
http://www.kensingtonbooks.com/author.aspx/29541

Prologue

December 15, 1967
Point Pleasant, West Virginia

"Do you think Caden Flynn will go?" Eve Parrish kept pace with her friend, Sarah, as a brisk December wind pushed them down Main Street toward the Crowne Theatre. Eager for a glimpse of the movie poster that had everyone in the tiny river town of Point Pleasant, West Virginia, talking, she barely felt the sting on her cheeks. Her mother would box her ears if she knew what Eve was up to, but all the boys at school said the poster hung in the window, plain as day for anyone to see. That had to mean she could sneak a peek. She was twelve now, practically a teenager.

Her parents had called *The Graduate* racy, and Mrs. Quiggly, who sold brown eggs and fresh milk from her farm outside town, said the poster was shameless. She wanted to bring a petition against the theater and make them take the "vile thing" down.

"Silly busybody," Aunt Rosie had chided behind her back. Never one to get hung up on proper behavior, Aunt Rosie did artsy things like taking photographs and hosting moonlight picnics for friends. She even had a dark room in her home and occasionally sold shots to the local paper who proudly displayed them with the byline *Photo courtesy of Rosalind Parrish.*

"I heard Caden tell Wyatt Fisher they should take their girlfriends to see it," Sarah said, interrupting her thoughts.

Eve gasped. It was bad enough the boys might see a movie as shocking as *The Graduate,* but more appalling that girls would go, too.

"Maybe they'll chicken out." She had a hopeless crush on Caden, an awkward situation given he was eighteen and the brother of her friend,

Maggie. Although careful not to make a fool of herself whenever Caden was around, she usually ended up tongue-tied.

Sarah shrugged and tugged the collar of her coat higher against the wind. Several cars drove by in the pre-holiday rush, the glow of headlights holding the night at bay. Sunset was still a half hour away, plenty of time for Eve and Sarah to reach the theater and ogle the poster. The movie didn't open until next week, but the buzz it generated had already swept through their school.

"I wish Maggie was with us," Eve said with a touch of melancholy.

Sarah rubbed her reddening nose. "Me, too."

The walk to the Crowne was only a few blocks from the Parrish Hotel, owned by Eve's parents and Aunt Rosie. Despite the short distance, it was cold enough to make her wish she'd brought a scarf. At least she'd have something titillating to share with Maggie once she saw the poster. Maybe her gushing about how improper the advertisement looked would make her friend smile.

"Do you think she really saw the Mothman?" Sarah's voice was barely audible. Nervously, she glanced over her shoulder as if fearing the giant birdlike humanoid would sweep from the sky. "Was she near the TNT?"

Eve shook her head.

A remote area of dense woods and small ponds, the TNT had once been used to store ammunition during World War II. Eve's father had taken her there on a few occasions, allowing her to explore the abandoned weapons "igloos." But ever since the Mothman was first spied in the region, she hadn't been back. Her father said bad things happened there, and Mrs. Quiggly insisted the place was a haven for UFOs.

"She was visiting Nana and followed Mischief into the Witch Wood."

A fat orange tabby, Mischief belonged to Maggie's grandmother, an elderly woman who everyone called Nana. She lived in a sprawling house snuggled up to a thicket of woods at the farthest end of town. Eve and Maggie had dubbed the thicket the "Witch Wood" after discovering a sycamore tree that resembled an old woman with legs.

"But it's too cold to go into the Witch Wood now," Sarah protested.

Eve nodded. She, Maggie, and Sara occasionally played there, but usually in the spring and summer when the trees were green with leaves, making it easy to catch caterpillars and grasshoppers.

"Maggie was afraid Mischief would get lost."

Sarah made a *pffing* sound. "As if! He's always getting into trouble and always finds his way home. I wish she hadn't followed him."

"Me, too." Eve bit her bottom lip, worrying it between her teeth. She'd visited her friend for a brief time yesterday, finding Maggie huddled beneath the blankets in her bedroom. She hadn't been to school for three days. "She's afraid to go outside."

They had almost reached the theater. Farther down the street, traffic was lined up at the red light that led to the Silver Bridge. Her father would be home soon, returning from Gallipolis, a neighboring city nestled on the Ohio side of the river. He'd headed there earlier in the afternoon to meet a friend, and like everyone else, would need to cross the Silver Bridge.

"I heard the Mothman's eyes are red," Sarah said.

"Maggie thought so. She told me when she couldn't find Mischief, she got an odd feeling, like something bad had happened. Her skin broke out in goose bumps."

Sarah's eyes widened. She rubbed her nose again. "My mom says people get a weird sensation when they see the Mothman. I've heard her talking about it to my dad when she thinks I'm not around."

"My parents do the same thing." How strange to be focused on something scary when everything around them reflected the festive mood of the coming Christmas holiday. The streetlights on Main were decorated with cheerful ribbons, wreaths, and pinecones, and a lighted Christmas tree brightened the display window of G. C. Murphy, the local five-and-dime. At the store entrance, a man in a Santa Claus suit called out holiday greetings and beckoned shoppers inside. A sense of excitement and seasonal cheer hung in the air.

"Maggie was scared." Eve wet her lips, remembering what her friend had told her. "She thought she heard a noise. Like scraping, or someone digging."

"What did she do?"

"She crept closer, but stayed hidden behind the trees. At least, she thought she was."

There was no mistaking Sarah's nervousness as she squeezed her mittened hands together. "But she wasn't?"

Eve shook her head, only then realizing how frightened she was for her friend. A lot of people thought the Mothman was trying to warn the town about something terrible, like a looming disaster, and that's why it kept reappearing. But Maggie said the creature was awful. A hideous monster with hateful eyes that bored into her soul. Those who'd seen it said its eyes were so ghastly, they couldn't recall any other feature of its face. Rumored to be at least seven feet tall, it had large wings that allowed it to fly vertically like a helicopter. Most said it was gray in color, and the Mothman's terrifying eyes glowed scarlet even in the daylight.

"She got close and peered through the trees," Eve explained. They stopped in front of the theater, but the poster they'd come to see no longer felt important. Someone blew a horn as the light for the Silver Bridge turned green, but traffic remained at a standstill. "That's when she saw it, crouched on the ground."

"What was it doing?" Sarah's eyes filled with fear.

"Maggie didn't know. It was hunkered down with its wings draped around it like a cape. Then it turned and saw her, and she screamed."

Sarah looked like she wanted to do the same.

A chorus of horns blared from the stalled traffic, causing Eve to knit her brows. "Why do you think all the cars are backed up like that?"

Sarah appeared too focused on the story to pay attention to the vehicles bottled up at the entrance to the Silver Bridge. "Did she run? Did it chase her?"

"Of course she ran. Wouldn't you?"

"I would have screamed my head off."

"Me, too." Her heart kicked into a prickly rhythm. Was it because of her fear for Maggie, or the cold sensation that crept over her as she stared at the unmoving traffic two blocks away? Instinctively, she headed for the backup, Sarah keeping pace beside her. "Maggie heard it chasing her, but she managed to get away and run to Nana's home. She didn't tell anyone about it until two days later. She pretended to be sick so she wouldn't have to go to school."

"But Dr. Pullman couldn't find anything wrong with her." Sarah's observation was half question, half statement.

"Nope. And that's when she had to tell the truth."

"How awful." Sarah soaked in the story as they continued walking, seemingly unconcerned they hadn't stopped to gawk at the poster for *The Graduate* as planned. The sidewalk was busy with Christmas shoppers heading in and out of G. C. Murphy and the local bank.

Any other time, Eve would have delighted in the festive mood, but something didn't feel right. Was she the only one who sensed the ominous undercurrent in the air? And why were there so many birds flitting around overhead, as if they couldn't find a place to rest?

"What happened to Mischief?" Sarah asked.

"He came back later. I heard he was fine."

"He's such a bad cat." Sarah shook her head. "I feel just awful for Maggie. Do you think anyone believes she saw the Mothman?"

"Her parents didn't. They tried to convince her she saw a large bird or something."

"What about Ryan and Caden?"

Ryan was Maggie's other brother. Only a year older than the three of them, they often hung out with him and his friends. Fun and kind of goofy, he was unlike Caden, who Eve thought as dreamy and mysterious as an ancient knight.

"She said Ryan believes her, but Caden thinks she's overreacting."

"Well, he is eighteen." Sarah shrugged. "He's one of them. An adult."

How could she have a crush on an adult? "My mom was talking to Mrs. Flynn earlier, and she said Caden was going to try to get Maggie to go Christmas shopping tonight. You know how she's wanted to visit that new department store in Gallipolis? He thought that might get her out of the house."

"I hope it worked."

"Me, too." Eve's stomach did a queasy flip-flop. Did she really hope so? It would mean Caden and Maggie would be on the Silver Bridge. "It's getting near dinner time. If it worked, they're probably headed back right now." *Like my dad.* "Do you notice all the birds?"

Sarah eyed the sky. "Yeah. Weird, isn't it?"

More horns from the stalled traffic.

"Something's wrong." She started walking faster, bypassing the Santa who waved shoppers into the five-and-dime with a hearty "ho-ho-ho." As the doors opened and closed, the cheerful notes of "Jingle Bells" carried onto the street, spurring her into a jog.

"Eve, wait." Sarah hurried to catch up. "What's wrong with you?"

"The traffic." Goose bumps broke out on the back of her neck. "Look." She'd never seen it stacked up like this before. Friday nights were always busy, especially around rush hour, but even with the addition of Christmas shoppers, there were far too many cars.

The pungent tang of exhaust snarled with the rumble of idling motors as they neared the entrance for the bridge. From her vantage point on the sidewalk, she spied the tall rocker towers erected against the sky. The sun had yet to set, the fiery ball ebbing toward the horizon, painting the silver framework with splashes of tangerine and copper.

"The light's green," Sarah said at her side. "Why aren't they moving?"

Eve glanced at the traffic signal just as it cycled to yellow, then red. Not a single car had inched forward. "The light must be out on the Ohio side. Everything's backed up."

"So people are going to be stuck on the bridge."

Like her father. Like Maggie and Caden.

It shouldn't have bothered her, but an unsettled feeling gnawed at the pit of her stomach. The Silver Bridge defined Point Pleasant, much like the Parrish Hotel. Eve had been on the bridge once when the rocker towers swayed slightly, but her dad had told her they were designed to be flexible, and she shouldn't be afraid. The towers moved with suspension chains to help reduce strain on the bridge piers. She didn't understand the construction, but knew the people of Point Pleasant were inordinately proud of their beloved Silver Bridge.

Sarah shook her head, apparently deciding they'd seen all there was of interest. "Hey, we missed the poster for *The Graduate*. Let's go back."

Eve nodded, trying to mask her uneasiness. "Okay. If my dad's on the bridge, he's going to be stuck in traffic anyway."

She started to turn from the sight when a deafening boom split the air like thunder. A woman's shrill scream knifed deeply into her bones. Within seconds, the terrified shriek was echoed by a dozen more voices raised in horror. Those stalled in traffic poured from their vehicles. On the ramp for the Silver Bridge, reverse lights flashed as cars tried to back away from the traffic signal amid a mad chorus of blaring horns.

"Oh!" Sarah shrieked. "Oh, no. No, no, no!"

Her friend lurched forward, rushing toward the bridge, and Eve jerked in her wake as if pulled by an invisible string. A sob built in her chest. It wasn't happening, couldn't be happening! But even before her gaze fell on the rocker towers looming above the Silver Bridge, she understood the horrified screams, the frenzied bleat of car horns, the chaotic cries of starlings wheeling overhead.

As if trapped in a slow motion bubble, the solid framework twisted sickeningly above a bridge crippled with stalled traffic. Christmas shoppers, truckers, workers returning at the end of the day, even visitors crossing from state to state. How many lives were clustered in that frozen string of cars? Her father. Her friend. Caden.

"Daddy." The name was a pitiful squeak, pushed past the lump in her throat. She lurched another step, vaguely conscious of people swarming past her. They came from cars and stores, from traffic that had stopped haphazardly on Main Street. Screams and voices that made no sense. Birds shrieked above her. Somewhere in the background "Jingle Bells" still played through the open doors of the five-and-dime. Even the suited Santa raced past, waving and hollering for people to get off the entrance ramp.

A scream built in her lungs. Someone yelled for police, someone else for an ambulance. Three steps ahead of her, a woman huddled on the street, hugging a small child to her chest. From the look of the open car door behind her, she had been on the ramp but managed to scramble free, abandoning a brown station wagon. Both the woman and the child were sobbing.

No more than thirty seconds had passed, Eve was sure. Why couldn't she scream? Why couldn't she look away from the twisting rocker towers? In the span of a single heartbeat, they collapsed, the entire bridge folding like a mammoth deck of cards. A heap of metal, steel, and headlights plummeted into the Ohio River.

Eve stumbled to her knees, the scream in her chest ripped lose in a mournful wail.

In little more than sixty seconds, the Silver Bridge was gone, claiming the lives of those she loved.

Chapter 1

June, 1982
Point Pleasant, West Virginia

Eve Parrish stared through the windshield of her Toyota Corolla at the two-story house her aunt had bequeathed to her in her will. A house she remembered fondly from childhood, it had been in her family for four generations, just like the old hotel in downtown Point Pleasant.

Tightening her grip on the steering wheel of the parked car, she vowed to worry about the hotel later. *One problem at a time.*

At twenty-seven, it was staggering to find herself the sole owner of her family's homestead *and* the Parrish Hotel. She'd inherited the latter after her father died, and Eve's mother had signed her ownership of the property over to Aunt Rosie. Not long afterward, her mother had uprooted them, determined to put the tragedy of the Silver Bridge in the past. It had always been Aunt Rosie who came to visit Eve and her mom in Pennsylvania.

But Aunt Rosie was gone.

Why couldn't she have told them about the cancer? Eve would have done something, anything to help. Insisted she get treatment.

"She didn't want treatment," Adam Barnett, Rosie's lawyer, had explained as he'd passed her the keys for the hotel and the house earlier that day. "She went quickly, which is how she wanted it."

Eve swiped a tear from her cheek. Aunt Rosie had planned to marry in the summer of '68, but the Silver Bridge altered those plans. Shaken by the tragedy, Eve's aunt had called off her engagement to Roger Layton and never married. Was that why she'd allowed herself to go so quickly once diagnosed with breast cancer? Did she think no one loved her?

A spasm of guilt twisted Eve's stomach. Her small apartment was only six hours away in Harrisburg, but her mom had drilled a steady dislike of Point Pleasant into her head from the time they moved away. It was the place where her father had met his end in the icy waters of the Ohio River only weeks before Christmas and a hotspot for bizarre Mothman and UFO sightings. Was it any wonder her mother had insisted on burying the town in their past?

Right or wrong, Eve hadn't returned in fifteen years. She barely recognized the sparse streets now, so changed from the thriving river community she remembered. She'd been glad to see the Crowne Theater still in operation, but saddened to know G. C. Murphy's had closed its doors. How she, Maggie, and Sarah had loved their soda fountain.

Taking a deep breath, she popped the door on the Corolla and stepped onto the street. Aunt Rosie's house—the same house in which her father and his sister had grown up—was located several miles from downtown Point Pleasant. Every bit as imposing as she remembered, the large two story was offset by a covered porch and a towering chestnut tree in the front yard. Her father had once hung a tire from the lowest branch at Aunt Rosie's behest so Eve and her friends would have a swing when they visited.

Reluctantly, Eve glanced to the house next door. Not quite as large, the cheerful colonial looked in far better condition than the imposing structure Eve had inherited. The paint appeared fresh, the shrubs neatly trimmed. Colorful blooms had already sprouted in the flowerbeds, and a pot of pansies welcomed guests to the front porch.

She'd spent countless afternoons playing in Maggie's home. Countless Friday night sleepovers when they'd stayed up late eating Mrs. Flynn's peanut butter cookies and giggling about boys. She'd never told her friend about the crush she'd had on Caden, but Maggie had known. Best friends always did. Unlike his sister, Caden had survived that fatal night on the Silver Bridge.

With an inhale of determination, Eve hooked her purse onto her shoulder. She would leave her overnight bag and suitcase in the car for the time being. She'd packed light, hoping to finalize plans for the house and hotel within two weeks. Hopefully, Adam Barnett could recommend a real estate company capable of handling residential and commercial sales.

He'd warned her about the break-in. "Nothing taken, it appears. Just vandalism. It happens sometimes when a house sits empty. Probably teenagers looking for a thrill. I had all of the damaged items removed and disposed of as you requested."

The key turned easily in the lock. According to Mr. Barnett, the vandals had gained entrance through the screened porch in the rear, and then busted the kitchen door. Both doors would require reinforcing. With any luck, the rest of the damage would be minimal.

As she stepped inside, a swarm of memories assaulted her. The house smelled stale, closed up for too long, but a trace of Aunt Rosie's signature scent lingered beneath the mustiness. A light bouquet that whispered of spring flowers and clover. On the heels of having visited her aunt's grave at the cemetery, the fragrance brought tears to Eve's eyes. Hugging her arms close to her chest, she blinked them away.

Mr. Barnett had made sure all of the utilities were working, but it was stuffy in the house. She'd have to set the ceiling fans to circulate the air. At least no one had covered Aunt Rosie's pretty furniture with those dreadful white sheets people used when closing an estate.

Her aunt had kept most of the furniture Eve remembered from childhood. The gold and crystal lamps on the end tables were new, but the heavy-footed couch and easy chairs upholstered in crimson brocade were as she remembered, if faded from time. Black walnut tables and thick butternut drapes covered with climbing grapevines accentuated the décor. Surprisingly, there was little damage to the room.

Tracing her fingers along a chair rail, she headed for the dining room. Whoever bought the old monstrosity would have to crave a home with character. It certainly had that. From its wide windowsills to arched openings and massive moldings, it echoed the detailing of a different time.

In the kitchen, she found the door leading to the screened porch reinforced with plywood to prevent further break-ins. The upstairs fared worse. The room her talented aunt had employed as a dark room had been completely ransacked. Mr. Barnett had been hesitant to volunteer the information but said there were chemical spills, and many of her aunt's beloved photos had been found torn and littered on the floor. Looking at the damage, Eve felt a slow burn of anger that someone would destroy her aunt's work. They had no right! As if in mockery of the act, the vandals had used black spray paint to leave a large squiggle on the wall like a brand. Stupid, stupid kids.

Two of the bedrooms had barely been touched, but the last—her aunt's room—had suffered nearly as badly as the dark room. The contents had been dumped from the dresser and closet. At least Mr. Barnett had seen to it that her aunt's lovely clothing had been piled on the bed for her to sort through and replace. Someone had obviously overturned the bureau—the mirror was shattered—and the bedspread had been ripped off and thrown on the floor. This time when the tears welled, she couldn't stop them. It wasn't fair. Her aunt had been taken prematurely at forty-nine by an ugly disease, and this is how her memory was honored? Lifting a soft terry robe from the bed, she inhaled her aunt's scent and pressed the fabric to her cheek.

"I'm sorry, Aunt Rosie. I'm sorry I wasn't there for you when you needed me."

Eve jerked reflexively when a sharp pounding interrupted her thoughts. Given the vandalism she'd witnessed, her heart lurched frightfully, sending a flutter through her stomach. It took a few seconds before she placed the sound as someone banging on the front door. Mr. Barnett had indicated someone from the sheriff's office would likely stop by to talk to her about the damage. She hadn't expected them so soon, but was eager to learn the details of the report. Tucking a stray strand of hair behind her ears, she hurried down the steps, then yanked open the door.

"Why hello there." The petite woman standing on her front porch offered a friendly smile.

"I…" Eve mentally stumbled, her mind doing cartwheels. Something about the woman was familiar. The appearance was off—there was gray in the woman's hair that hadn't been there before, and her eyes looked watery, not bright like Eve remembered—but the inflection of her voice was the same. She swallowed hard. "Mrs. Flynn?"

"I saw your car. Maggie said you were coming."

"Excuse me?"

Her dead friend's mother smiled indulgently and patted her hand. "It's all right. I realize things are different now." Turning, she roamed to the edge of the covered porch and rested her hands lightly on the railing as she gazed over the front yard. "Maggie has waited a long time for you, Eve."

Flummoxed by her unexpected arrival and the strange comments, Eve trailed after her. "Mrs. Flynn? I…don't understand what you mean." Surely, her best friend's mother wasn't discussing Maggie as if she were still alive. Perhaps the woman was ill. Her odd behavior made the whole scenario seem like a dream.

A car passed in front of the house, sending a flutter of leaves into the yard on a puff of air. The breeze smelled of honeysuckle and exhaust, and a clingy kiss of sunlight warmed Eve's face. She couldn't be dreaming.

"Did you know they didn't find her body until June of '68?"

Eve bit her lip, uncertain how to respond. When her mother had uprooted them the spring after the bridge collapse, the bodies of three victims were still missing. She'd later learned that Maggie's remains had been located during the summer, but there was no talk of returning for the funeral. Her mother wouldn't hear of it.

"I'm so sorry." At least her father's body had been discovered in the debris pile on the Ohio side of the river, allowing him the dignity of a proper burial. Not Maggie. For nearly six months, her remains had been battered and misshapen by the cold currents of the river. If the knowledge ripped at Eve's heart, how much more the heart of her friend's mother?

"Would you...would you like to come inside?"

"No thank you, dear." Mrs. Flynn turned to face her. "I just wanted to welcome you back. Maggie asked me to."

Oh, God. The woman was certifiably crazy.

She might have contemplated the thought further but for the arrival of a police car in front of Aunt Rosie's house. Mrs. Flynn shook her head at the sight, then quietly left the porch without so much as a goodbye. She was halfway across the yard when the man in the car stepped onto the street.

"Mom," he called.

Mom?

Eve felt her eyebrows launch into her bangs as she watched the man dart around the rear of his car to greet Mrs. Flynn on the grass. They exchanged a few soft words before the woman continued her path back to her home and the man jogged toward the porch. As he hustled up the steps, Eve got the shock of her life.

"Ryan?"

"Hey, you remembered." Maggie's brother grinned and extended his hand.

When she slid her fingers into his, he yanked her close, hugging her tightly. In no time, she found herself laughing breathlessly.

"It's so good to see you, Ryan." She hugged him back, delighted by the warmth his unexpected presence brought. "Mr. Barnett never said you worked for the sheriff's department."

"Yep. A sergeant." He tapped the badge pinned to his neatly pressed uniform, then held her at arm's length, his smile igniting a sparkle in his blue eyes.

It was hard to believe the skinny thirteen-year-old she remembered had matured into such a tall, broad-shouldered man. His black hair, no longer curly but wavy, lay tousled over his brow, his grin as infectious as always.

"God, it's good to see you after all these years." Ryan seemed reluctant to release her. "I ran into Adam Barnett at the bank, and he told me he'd given you the keys. I can't believe you're really here."

"I can't either." She hugged him again, then laughed. "You got so tall."

"And you got so..." He paused and wiggled his eyebrows, molding his hands in the shape of an hourglass. "Curvy."

She swatted his arm. "You always were a trouble-maker. Do you want to come in for a while? The house is a wreck, but—"

"Actually, that's why I'm here. I wanted to go over the vandalism report with you." He sobered abruptly and stepped away. "And I'm sorry about my mother. I hope she didn't say anything to upset you."

"No, I..." How did she explain the odd conversation? She'd only been in Point Pleasant a short while. The last thing she wanted to do was offend a childhood friend by pointing out that his mother was off her rocker.

Ryan shook his head, clearly conscious of what may have been said. "Sometimes she gets confused and gets caught up in the past."

Eve let the remark slide without comment. "I was just going to get my bags out of my car." She steered the conversation elsewhere. "Maybe you could give me a hand?"

"Sure."

Together, they trudged to her Corolla. Ryan grabbed her suitcase and overnight bag while Eve snatched a jacket from the back seat along with a few boxed goods she'd brought for the trip. Later, she'd hit the grocery store and stock up on perishable items. At least the refrigerator was in working order.

In the house, Ryan carried her luggage upstairs while she detoured to the kitchen with her small parcel of crackers, instant rice, and peanut butter. She wished she had something to offer him, but the best she could manage was peanut butter and crackers. Mentally, she bumped the grocery store higher on her to-do list.

"I put everything in the spare bedroom for you," Ryan announced, entering the kitchen. "I guess you saw Rosie's room is a mess."

Eve added her box of instant rice to the nearest cupboard, nudging aside several cans of Campbell's soup left behind by Aunt Rosie. A vivid memory flashed through her mind as she recalled her aunt feeding her tomato soup and a grilled cheese for lunch on a brisk autumn day.

"Her dark room, too." Eve shut the cupboard and turned, bracing her back against the counter. "The vandals hit the upstairs hard. Do you have any idea who would have done such a thing?"

"Afraid not." Ryan motioned her toward the dining room. "Let's sit down."

At the dining room table, he withdrew a folded sheaf of papers from his breast pocket. "I thought you should have a copy of the vandalism report."

Eve eyed the papers he handed her. It was standard stuff—date, time, damage done. "Who reported it?"

"No one. I still live next door with my mom. It's um...complicated." He cleared his throat awkwardly. "After Rosie died, I kept an eye on the place. Several days after her death, I was walking around the house when I noticed the door on the screened porch had been busted. I guess the vandals chose it because it was hidden from the street. Easy entry."

"Did they take anything?"

"Not that I could tell, but Rosie isn't here to answer that question. I should have said it before, Eve, but you have my sympathies." He covered her hand with his where it rested on the table.

She managed a wan smile and nodded a thank you. It was good to see him again, a familiar face that made the shock of returning to her childhood home less traumatic. Even if he was grown, no longer the thirteen-year-old boy she remembered, he was still the brother of her one-time best friend.

"So you think it was just kids out for some fun?" She winced, unable to comprehend how anyone could view destroying the home of the recently deceased as entertaining.

He hesitated. "It looks that way."

"Is there something you're not telling me?"

"Nothing of importance." He patted her hand again and stood, then paced a short distance away. "What are you going to do with the place?"

The million-dollar question. "Sell it, of course." It hurt to say, as if she was turning her back on Aunt Rosie and all her aunt held dear. "Vandalism aside, the home needs work to make it desirable. I'm no expert, but it looks like it could use a new roof and several of the rooms should be repainted. If I want to put it on the market, I'm going to have to fix it up first." It was a sobering thought. "I don't suppose you could recommend someone?"

He surprised her with a quick answer. "Do you remember Caden?"

"Your brother?" Her heart lurched again. How could she forget her childhood crush?

"He has a contracting business. Home remodeling, repairs. That sort of thing."

"It sounds ideal." For some reason she hadn't considered encountering him when she'd returned to Point Pleasant. "Do you have a phone number for him? I'd like to talk to him about taking on the repairs."

"How about if I have him stop by tomorrow? Will that work?"

"Perfect." She was planning on addressing the hotel tomorrow, something that would probably take most of the day. "Do you think he can stop early? Around nine? I was planning on visiting the hotel later."

"It shouldn't be a problem." He shot her a sideways glance as if measuring her reaction. "The hotel is still the center of town."

"I thought as much." Eve glanced at her hands, thinking back to the years when her parents and Aunt Rosie had made the hotel the focus of their lives. It had been her family's defining legacy long before she was born. Her great-grandfather Clarence had paid for its construction in 1922, then quickly turned the establishment into a thriving operation, bolstered in part by Point Pleasant's blossoming river trade. It hadn't taken her more than a few hours in town to realize those days were nothing more than a memory. "I noticed things are different."

A shadow crossed Ryan's face. "A lot's changed since you left."

"The Silver Bridge affected everything."

He nodded, shoulders slumping as he stuffed his hands in his pockets. "It wasn't just the catastrophe. Bruce Mechanical closed up shop shortly afterward. That dried up half the employment in town. Point Pleasant isn't the thriving river community it used to be."

How sad. Eve had fond memories of watching riverboats and tugs traverse the waters of the Ohio and Kanawha Rivers, ushering barges loaded with coal from Ohio to West Virginia and vice-versa. When Bruce Mechanical launched a new boat, the event was guaranteed to draw a crowd. She, Maggie, and Sarah had eagerly raced to the docks as the newly built ships slid sideways into the water, tilting so far she feared they would capsize before righting themselves.

Ryan returned to his seat at the table, then reclined comfortably, crossing an ankle over his knee. "Main Street is pretty much a ghost town these days. I'm sure you noticed."

She nodded. "They moved the Silver Bridge."

"We call it the Silver Memorial Bridge now, but you're right." A frown flitted across his mouth. "The new bridge diverts the flow of traffic out of town, bypassing Main. As much as we appreciate the Silver Memorial Bridge, it's partially responsible for sapping Point Pleasant's lifeblood."

"What about the hotel?" She had to know.

"It holds its own." Ryan gave a one-shouldered shrug. "It may not pull the traffic it did in its heyday, but according to Rosie, it was solvent. I'm sure you've seen the books."

"Enough of them." The hotel was a juggernaut she needed to tackle.

"So you really want to sell it?" Ryan asked.

She glanced at her hands. The Parrish Hotel was as much a part of Point Pleasant as the historic Silver Bridge. Her family had invested decades in its growth. The idea of fluffing it off for financial gain was nothing short of sacrilege.

"I'm still undecided." It wasn't an entire lie. Part of her resisted the idea of unloading an institution that had been her family's legacy. "Right now I'm using two weeks of my vacation time from Labor and Industry. I do clerical work, not the most exciting thing, but it's a Commonwealth job, and the benefits are good. I don't know the first thing about overseeing a hotel."

"That's what a manager is for."

"I'm not sure I want to go that route." The thought of entrusting so much to someone she didn't know left her uneasy.

"You've got a lot on you," Ryan conceded. "Half of the businesses on Main Street were forced to close."

"But the hotel survived."

"Along with the Crowne Theater. At least for now. Your aunt saw to the hotel's prosperity. The Parrish name still has enough clout to draw visitors from neighboring states."

She nodded and laced her hands on her lap. "I'll look into it tomorrow." Wrapping her head around the house was enough for the day. Suddenly, she didn't want to think about the past or the pressing matters looming over her head. She simply wanted to bask in the warmth of seeing an old friend. "Thanks for bringing the vandalism report. I never would have pegged you as a cop. You always got into so much trouble as a kid."

He laughed. "Odd how things turn out. What about you? Did you marry?"

"No."

"I didn't either. No luck yet, or just not ready to settle down. I can't figure out which."

"That doesn't surprise me." He'd always been a free spirit, much like Rosie, playful and prone to trouble. "What about Caden?" She hoped the query appeared as nothing more than the innocent probing of an old friend trying to catch up on the present. Her heart gave a little flutter when she thought of him. Amazing her long-buried attraction was still there.

"Caden's single, too." Ryan shook his head. "He'll probably end up an old man living alone unless he moves past his guilt."

"What do you mean?"

Ryan waved a hand as if brushing away the thought. "He hasn't forgiven himself for taking Maggie shopping that night. Most of us have moved on. Caden hasn't."

She thought of herself, her mother. Their world had come to a crashing halt that cold December night when her father's car fell into the Ohio River. And yet somehow they'd rummaged up the strength to continue. It had taken uprooting, leaving the shadow of the disaster behind in Point Pleasant, but somehow her mother had managed to put the pieces together for herself and her twelve-year-old daughter. Eventually, her mother had remarried, and Eve found herself with a stepfather. As much as she loved the man, part of her understood Caden's refusal to relinquish the past.

"What about your parents?" She couldn't help venturing the question given the odd discussion she'd had with Mrs. Flynn. Should she tell Ryan what his mother had said about Maggie…talking about her as if she were still alive?

He shrugged, and she sensed his reluctance. "My father passed away a few years ago."

"I'm so sorry." She had fond memories of Mr. Flynn.

"It was his lungs. All those years spent working in a coal mine finally caught up with him."

"What about your mother?"

"She's accepted his death, but Maggie's…" Again a shrug that said far more than words. "A part of her died when that bridge went down."

Eve bit her lip. She could understand Mrs. Flynn's pain.

"Most of the time she's okay," Ryan continued. "But other times, she retreats into the past and insists Maggie is still alive. She talks about her as if they share discussions. It's the reason I still live at home…to take care of her. She can be a handful when she's in the past."

Eve wasn't sure what to say. So much tragedy had happened when the Silver Bridge collapsed. The town had suffered, but more than that, the populace had crumpled under the blow of individual losses. Fifteen years later, splinters of that residual pain reached far and wide.

"I'm sorry." There were no words for the loss or the choking reach of its tentacles.

"We do the best we can." As if deciding he'd had enough gloom, Ryan stood. "It's good to have you back, Eve, even if only for a short while. I'll tell Caden to drop by tomorrow morning."

She walked him to the door, thankful to have encountered a familiar face. It had been a stroke of luck to learn Caden was a contractor. It would save her the trouble of looking for someone to do the repairs and speed the sale of the house that much more quickly.

"What about Sarah?" she asked as he stepped onto the front porch. Eve stayed inside on the threshold, a breeze scuttling past her like an uninvited guest. "Does she still live in town?"

He nodded. "She works in the records division at the courthouse. We had a bad situation there several years back. I'm not sure if Rosie told you about the bomb blast."

She had. A suicidal ex-convict had forced his way inside with a shotgun and a homemade explosive device. Despite attempts at negotiation, the bomber had leveled the entire first floor, killing three and injuring six others. After hearing about it, Eve had called her aunt to make sure she was safe.

"Another tragedy in a town plagued by them," Aunt Rosie had said. "Fools around here are saying it's the curse of Cornstalk come to blight us again."

"I saw it on the news when it happened," Eve told Ryan. At the time, she'd wondered if it was in some way connected to the Mothman. She didn't believe in the curse of Cornstalk, an Indian chief who'd been murdered in the days preceding the American Revolution. Local legend said he'd cursed the town with his dying breath. You couldn't grow up in Point Pleasant without having the shadow of that legend leech into every event that took place.

"Sarah wasn't hurt, was she?" Cold fear gripped her stomach as she thought of her childhood friend.

"No, she wasn't working then, but we lost a lot of good people. Strange how things keep happening in this town." He raised a hand in farewell. "Stay in touch, Eve. Don't leave without saying goodbye."

She stayed at the door, closing it only after he'd driven off in his police cruiser. The emptiness of the house settled over her with a marked hush, and she wondered how Aunt Rosie had managed living there on her own for so many years. Then again, like the hotel, the house was part of Parrish history.

* * * *

A loud bang woke her from a sound sleep.

Eve sat bolt upright in bed, panic spiking through her chest. The unfamiliar surroundings made her inhale sharply until she remembered where she was. Wind rattled the rafters, sending creaks and groans through the old house. After a trip to the grocery store and a phone call to her mother, she'd spent the remainder of the day sorting through the mess the vandals had left. She'd concentrated on Aunt Rosie's bedroom, wanting to clean up the violation as if the destruction had been a personal affront to her aunt. Dinner had been a can of soup heated on the stove, after which she'd taken a shower and collapsed into bed. Whether it was the emotional toll of returning home after fifteen years or the long hours she'd spent cleaning and disinfecting to erase every last trace of the vandals, she'd fallen asleep easily.

A glance at the bedside clock told her it was after two in the morning. Another bang reverberated through the upstairs hallway.

Easing from bed, she slipped on her robe and padded to the bedroom door. Hesitating, she wrapped her fingers around the doorknob, straining to hear. Her heart pumped a frenzied beat as she debated switching on a light. Part of her wanted to call the police. She feared the vandals may have returned, but knew she'd looked foolish if the noise turned out to be something trivial. Maybe a stray animal had found its way inside through the broken kitchen door.

Bang. Bang. Bang.

The noise came again, steady and in sync, like someone pounding on a wall.

Not an animal.

Whatever the cause, it originated in Aunt Rosie's room. Deciding she had no choice but to investigate, Eve eased open the door and crept down the darkened hall to her aunt's bedroom. As she neared, the sound stopped, then started again. The frantic flutter of her heart had her gulping down fear as she peered into the room. By then, her eyesight had grown accustomed to the dark, allowing her to pick out shapes easily. A full moon splashed pale light through the rear window, sketching elaborate shadows on the ceiling and floor. One separated from the rest, moved, then fell back into place.

Bang. Bang.

Relieved, Eve released a pent-up breath. Just a loose shutter caught in the wind. She crossed to the window and opened it wide, a light breeze beading goose bumps down her arm. Feeling for the shutter, she pushed it in place, uncertain if the effort would secure it temporarily. It would have to do for the night. Tomorrow, she'd add it to the list of items she intended to broach with Caden. At least whoever had vandalized the house hadn't returned for a second round.

As she closed the window and stepped back from the curtains, her gaze was drawn by movement in the rear yard where her aunt's property ceded to a tree line. If not for the bright wash of moonlight, she might have missed it entirely. A shadow broke from the others, then flowed into the trees. A shadow that had been standing, watching the house. One that had likely seen her in the window.

Eve swallowed hard.

A shadow shaped like a man.

Meet the Author

Mae Clair opened a Pandora's Box of characters when she was a child and never looked back. A member of Thriller Writer's International, she loves creating character-driven fiction in settings that vary from contemporary to mythical.

Wherever her pen takes her, she flavors her stories with mystery, suspense, and a hint of romance. Married to her high school sweetheart, she lives in Pennsylvania and is passionate about cryptozoology, old photographs, a good Maine lobster tail, and cats.

Discover more about Mae on her website and blog at MaeClair.net.

Afterword

It's hard to believe that after two years of research and writing, this series has come to a close. I'm truly grateful to everyone who has taken the time to read the books and, most especially, for leaving reviews on Amazon. Reviews are paramount in helping a writer achieve success and all are greatly appreciated.

Because the series is a mix of history, folklore and fiction, I've been asked by multiple readers to share how much is research and how much I created. Sadly, the Silver Bridge catastrophe is historic fact, as is the downturn in economics for Point Pleasant after Bruce Mechanical (the fictitious name I used in the series) closed up shop.

The town did experience a UFO Flap in 1966-67 and Men in Black, driving shiny black Cadillacs—most looking like they'd come straight off the showroom floor—descended on the streets. Plain panel vans (which I used in *A Cold Tomorrow*) were also spotted on rural roads with technicians working on lines, possibly to tap into phone discussions. Many who had seen and reported UFO activity were warned silent.

Indrid Cold is probably as deeply ingrained in Point Pleasant folklore as the Mothman. He is also known as "the grinning man" and was first reported by resident Woodrow Derenberger who encountered him in November of 1966. Cold supposedly hailed from the planet Lanulous and was in contact with Derenberger multiple times. Googling Indrid Cold will return a host of information as well as an interview with Derenberger who later wrote a book about his encounters. I gave Cold my own spin by making him the "oracle" in the igloo my characters visit. I also connected him to the Mothman and Lach Evening through my own twist with fiction. Evening has no basis in folklore and is my own creation.

As for the igloo and the oracle, I picked that up on a visit to Point Pleasant when speaking to one of the local residents. He told me "if you go into the igloo and ask a question, you might get an answer." That was all the prompting I needed to embellish the thought with an alien being.

The information I supplied on the TNT is accurate and historical. It was once a Government Superfund Site and George Washington did survey the area prior to the start of the Revolutionary War. There are suggestions he saw more than a few things he couldn't explain.

Numerous beliefs can be found about the TNT—from ley lines to thin spots and an Indian Burial Grounds—at one point or another I heard (or read) them all.

In writing this series, I made two trips to Point Pleasant, read any historical information I could find, and sat through numerous documentaries and videos on the Mothman. I owe a debt of gratitude to the late author, John Keel, for his bestseller *The Mothman Prophecies*. It inspired me to dig deeper into the legends of Point Pleasant by reviewing eye witness accounts, scouring through newspaper articles and tracking down books on the area. In leaving Point Pleasant behind, I feel like I am leaving a place I have come to know well.

The information contained on Chief Cornstalk is true, although there is nothing other than folklore to support his curse on the town of Point Pleasant. He was a great leader who met an unfortunate fate while trying to serve the common good. You can find a wealth of information about him online, and by visiting Fort Randolph and Tu-Endie-Wei State Park in Point Pleasant. While there, I also suggest a visit to the Point Pleasant River Museum and Learning Center.

I hope you have enjoyed this series, and I thank you for journeying with me… and the Mothman.

Mae Clair
February 2017